THE RŌNIN'S MISTRESS

ALSO BY LAURA JOH ROWLAND

The Cloud Pavilion

The Fire Kimono

The Snow Empress

Red Chrysanthemum

The Assassin's Touch

The Perfumed Sleeve

The Dragon King's Palace

The Pillow Book of Lady Wisteria

Black Lotus

The Samurai's Wife

The Concubine's Tattoo

The Way of the Traitor

Bundori

Shinjū

THE RŌNIN'S MISTRESS

Laura Joh Rowland

ST. MARTIN'S MINOTAUR
NEW YORK

THE RŌNIN'S MISTRESS. Copyright © 2011 by Laura Joh Rowland. All rights reserved. Printed in the United States of America. For information, address St. Martin's Press, 175 Fifth Avenue, New York, N.Y. 10010.

www.minotaurbooks.com

The Library of Congress has cataloged the hardcover edition as follows:

Rowland, Laura Joh.
    The Rōnin's mistress : a novel / Laura Joh
Rowland.—1st ed.
        p.   cm.
    ISBN 978-0-312-65852-6
    1. Sano, Ichiro (Fictitious character)—Fiction.
2. Japan—History—Genroku period, 1688–1704—
Fiction.   3. Samurai—Fiction.   4. Domestic
fiction.   I. Title.
    PS3568.O934R66 2011
    813'.54—dc22

                                        2011018771

ISBN 978-1-250-01523-5 (trade paperback)

D 10 9 8 7 6 5 4 3 2

To my husband, Marty.
After thirty years of marriage, you've earned
another dedication.

Historical Note

I AM FASCINATED by the true story of the forty-seven rōnin, which is one of the most famous, beloved tales in Japanese history. A difficulty in understanding it is that although there are many sources of information on it, few historical details have been established beyond doubt. Much information about the forty-seven rōnin's vendetta is based on speculation by historians during the course of more than three hundred years. The many fictionalized accounts further obscure the truth. Details that appear in books, plays, and movies have been repeated so often that they pass for facts even when they are not indeed facts. Setting the record straight is probably impossible, and I won't try. Here I will lay out the facts that are known and explain what in this novel is a product of my imagination.

In 1701, Lord Asano of Harima Province was the host for visiting envoys from the Emperor's court. Kira Yoshinaka, the master of ceremonies at Edo Castle, was responsible for instructing Lord Asano in the necessary etiquette. On April 21, 1701, Lord Asano drew his sword on Kira, mentioned that he had a grievance against him, attacked him, and wounded him. The only witness to the attack was Kajikawa Yosobei, a keeper of the castle. Drawing a sword inside Edo Castle was a capital offense, and Lord Asano was forced to commit ritual suicide that same day. His retainers became rōnin, masterless samurai. The house of Asano was dissolved. Kira claimed that Lord Asano had attacked him for no reason. Kira wasn't punished for his part in the fiasco, and the government ruled that no action should be taken against him. On February 1, 1703, after some secret conspiring, forty-seven of the *rōnin* sought revenge on Kira, whom they blamed for Lord Asano's death. They invaded Kira's house, fought the guards, killed Kira by decapitating him, then carried his severed head to Sengaku Temple and laid it at Lord Asano's grave. There they awaited orders. A big controversy developed: What should be done with the forty-seven *rōnin,* who had fulfilled their duty to their master by avenging his death but broken the law? A supreme court was created to decide.

Those are the bare bones of the story. Intriguing questions remain. Why did Lord Asano attack Kira? If there was a quarrel, what was it about? Why did the forty-seven *rōnin* wait almost two years to avenge Lord Asano? What orders were they expecting?

Many writers have posed answers to these questions. *The Rōnin's Mistress* offers my answers. In presenting my version of the events that led up to and came after the vendetta, I have followed the real timeline and based characters on actual historical figures. Oishi was Lord Asano's chief retainer and the leader of the forty-seven *rōnin.* He did have a wife and a mistress, as well as a son named Chikara, who was one of the forty-seven. Lord Asano's wife went to live in a convent after he died. The shogun and Chamberlain Yanagisawa are based on the real men. (I have left out some historical figures from the forty-seven *rōnin* tale, in order to keep this book from growing too long and unwieldy. I have also altered minor details.) One of the supreme court judges was a magistrate, but he wasn't Magistrate Ueda, who is my creation. My creations also include the personalities, actions, and words attributed to the "real" characters. I invented everyone else, including Sano, Reiko, Hirata, and their families.

Although I believe that some dark, dirty secrets must have motivated Lord Asano's attack on Kira, and the forty-seven *rōnin's* vendetta, there is no historical evidence for the scenario that I have presented or for my ending to the trial. (No one knows exactly what happened during the time between the forty-seven *rōnin's* arrest and the supreme court's verdict, or what was said in the courtroom on the day the verdict was rendered.) This book is fiction. I ask readers to keep in mind that most of the things in it—and in the previous books in my series—never happened.

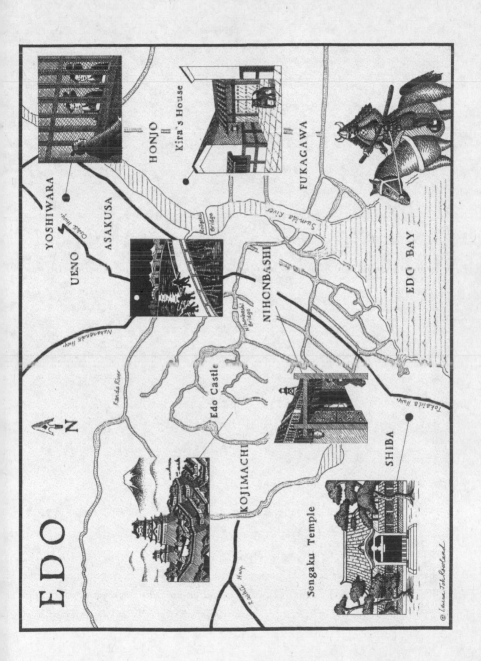

EDO

N

Kanda River

Nakasendo Hwy.

Oshu Hwy.

YOSHIWARA

UENO

ASAKUSA

HONJO

Kira's House

Ryogoku Bridge

Sumida River

FUKAGAWA

EDO BAY

Nihonbashi Bridge

NIHONBASHI

Edo Castle

KOJIMACHI

Kofu Hwy.

Tokaido Hwy.

SHIBA

Sengaku Temple

© Laura Hartland

Edo, Month 12, Genroku Year 15

(Tokyo, February 1703)

Prologue

SNOW SIFTED FROM the night sky over Edo. The wind howled, whipping the snow into torn veils, piling drifts against the shuttered buildings. Flakes gleamed in white halos around lamps at the gates at every intersection. Time was suspended, the city frozen in a dream of winter.

A band of forty-seven samurai marched through the deserted streets east of the Sumida River. They wore heavy padded cloaks and trousers, their faces shaded by wicker hats and muffled in scarves. Their boots crunched in the snow as they leaned into the wind. Each wore two swords at his waist. Some carried bows and slings of arrows over their shoulders; others clutched spears in gloved hands. The men at the end of the procession lumbered under the weight of ladders, coiled ropes, and huge wooden mallets. They did not speak.

There was no need for discussion. Their plans were set, understood by all. The time for doubts, fear, and turning back had passed. Their feet marched in lockstep. The wind blew stinging flakes into eyes hard with determination.

They halted in a road where high earthen walls protected estates inside, gazing up at the mansion where their destiny waited. Two stories tall, surrounded by barracks, it had curved tile roofs that spread like snow-covered wings. All was dark and tranquil, the sleeping residents oblivious to danger.

The leader of the forty-seven samurai was a lean, agile man with fierce eyes and strong, slanted brows visible above the scarf that covered the lower half of his face. He nodded to his comrades. Twenty-three men stole around the corner. The leader stayed with the others. As they advanced toward the front gate, a watchdog lunged out from beneath its roof. He uttered a single bark before two samurai tied his legs and fastened a muzzle over his snout. He whimpered and writhed helplessly. Other samurai positioned ladders against the walls. Up they climbed. Some let themselves down on ropes on the inside. Archers leaped onto the roofs. The leader and his remaining men gathered by the gate and waited.

Three deep, hollow beats struck on a war drum told them that their comrades were in position at the rear of the mansion. Two samurai took up the wooden mallets and pounded the gate. Planks shattered.

Inside the mansion's barracks, the guards slumbered. The pounding awakened them. They leaped out of their beds, crying, "We're under attack!"

Grabbing their swords, they ran outside, barefoot and half dressed, into the blizzard. Through the broken gate charged the invaders, swords drawn, spears aimed. The guards tried to defend themselves, but the invaders cut them down. Swords sliced open throats and bellies; spears pierced naked chests. Blood splashed the snow. The guards scattered, turned, and fled toward the mansion, crying for help.

More guards poured out of the barracks. The archers on the roofs fired arrows at them. The samurai who'd breached the back gate came rushing to join their band. They intercepted the guards trying to escape. The battle was a tumult of ringing blades, colliding fighters, falling bodies, and whirling snow. Soon most of the guards lay dead or wounded.

Accompanied by a few men, the leader of the forty-seven ran to the mansion. They brandished their swords in the entryway, but no one stopped them. The leader took down a lantern that hung on the wall, carrying it as he and his men moved along the dark corridors. All was quiet until they penetrated deeper into the mansion, when they heard sobbing. The lantern illuminated a room filled with women and children, huddled together in fright.

"Where is he?" the leader demanded.

The women hid their faces and cried. The samurai continued searching. They came to a bedchamber whose size and elegant furnishings were fit for the lord of the mansion. A futon was spread on the floor, the quilt flung back. The leader touched the bed.

"It's still warm," he said.

His gaze went to a large scroll hanging on the wall. He yanked aside the scroll. Behind it was a door, which he opened. Cold air and snowflakes blew in from a courtyard. Bare footprints in the snow led to a shed. The samurai rushed to the shed and flung the door open. The leader shone the lantern inside.

On the floor, amid firewood and coal, sat an old man. His knees were drawn up to his chin, his arms folded across his chest. He wore a cotton night robe and cap. He shivered, his teeth chattering, his breath puffs of vapor. His lined face was white; his eyes shone with terror.

"Who are you?" asked one of the samurai, the youngest, a sturdy boy.

The old man lashed out with a dagger he'd been hiding. The boy grabbed his wrist and wrenched the dagger from his grasp. He cried out in weak, pained protest. The leader pulled off the man's cap and held the lantern near his head. A white scar gleamed on his bald crown.

"It's him," the leader said. "Bring him outside."

The samurai threw the old man on his back in the snow. They pinned his arms and legs while he screamed. The leader stood over the captive. He removed the scarf that hid his face, then held up the lantern so that the old man could see him. Below his fierce eyes, his nose was long with flared nostrils, his mouth thick but firm. He wasn't young, and his features wore the stamp of suffering.

"You know who we are. You know why we're here." He chanted the words as if he'd rehearsed them. "Now you'll pay for the evil you've done."

The old man tried to turn his head away, but the boy grabbed it and held it immobile. He moaned and rolled his eyes, seeking help that didn't come. He struggled to escape, in vain. The leader drew his sword, grasped it in both hands, and raised it high over his head. The old man's lips formed words of silent protest or prayer.

The blade came slashing down. It cleaved the old man's throat. All the samurai leaped backward to avoid the blood spurting from the cut that severed his head from his body. An involuntary convulsion splayed his limbs. His face froze in an expression of blank-eyed, open-mouthed horror.

The boy put a whistle to his lips and blew. The shrill, piercing sound signaled that the old man was dead and the forty-seven samurai had accomplished their mission.

Soon would come their reckoning with fate.

1

THE BLIZZARD ENDED by morning. The sky cleared to a pale blue as dawn glided over the hills east of Edo, leaving the city serene under a mantle of fresh, sparkling snow. Cranes flew over the rise where Edo Castle perched. The great fortress wore white frosting atop its walls and guard towers. In the innermost precinct of the castle stood the palace. Dark cypress beams gridded the white plaster walls of the low, interconnected buildings; gold dragons crowned the peaks of its tile roofs. In the garden, boulders and shrubs were smooth white mounds. Ice glazed a pond surrounded by trees whose bare branches spread lacy black patterns against the brightening sky. The snow on the lawn and gravel paths was pristine, undisturbed by footprints. The garden appeared deserted, but appearances were deceiving.

Under a large pine tree, in a shelter formed by its spreading boughs, three samurai crouched. Sano Ichirō, the shogun's *sōsakan-sama*—Most Honorable Investigator of Events, Situations, and People—huddled with his two top detectives, Marume and Fukida. Although they'd covered the ground with a quilt and they wore hats, gloves, fleece-lined boots, and layers of thick, padded clothing, they were shivering. They'd been here all night, and their shelter was cold enough that they could see their breath. Sano flexed his numb fingers and toes in an attempt to ward off frostbite, as he and his men watched the palace through gaps between the bristly, resin-scented pine sprigs.

"Pretty, isn't it?" said Fukida, the slight, serious detective.

"I would think it a lot prettier if I were sitting in a hot bath." The big, muscular Marume was usually jovial but was cross now, after an uncomfortable night.

Sano didn't join the conversation. He was too cold and too downcast after a long run of trouble. Although he usually put on a cheerful appearance for the sake of morale, that had gotten harder as the months passed.

Footsteps crunched the snow. Sano put his finger to his lips, then pointed outside. A man slouched into view. He wore a straw snow cape and a wicker hat. Furtive, he looked around. No one was watching that he could see. Sano had given the patrol guards the night off.

"It's him," Fukida said. "At last."

Their quarry sidled up to the palace, climbed the stairs to the veranda, and stopped by the door. He lifted his cape, exposing stout legs, the loincloth wrapped around his waist and crotch, and voluminous white buttocks. He squatted and defecated.

This was the person who'd been sneaking around and fouling the palace late at night or early in the morning.

Sano, Marume, and Fukida leaped out from under the pine boughs. Marume yelled, "Hah! Got you!"

The man looked up, startled. He was a pimple-faced youth. Terrified by the sight of three samurai charging toward him, he jumped up to run, but he slipped in the snow and fell on the dung he'd just dropped. Marume and Fukida caught him. They held him while he struggled and began to cry.

"You're under arrest," Fukida said.

"Phew, you stink!" Marume said.

Sano asked the captive, "What's your name?"

"Hitoshi," the man mumbled between sobs.

"Who are you?" Sano said.

"I'm an underservant in the castle." Underservants did the most menial, dirtiest jobs—mopping floors, cleaning privies.

"Why have you been defecating on the palace?" Sano said.

"My boss is always picking on me. Once he made me lick a chamber pot clean." Hitoshi turned sullen. "I just wanted to get him in trouble."

"Well, you succeeded," Marume said. The supervisor of servants, who was responsible for keeping the castle clean, had been reprimanded by the shogun, the military dictator who lived in the palace and ruled Japan. The shogun had ordered Sano to personally catch the culprit. "Now you're in even bigger trouble."

What Hitoshi had done wasn't just unsanitary. It was a grave criminal offense.

"Come along," Fukida said. He and Marume hauled Hitoshi down the steps.

Hitoshi resisted, dragging his feet. "Where are you taking me?"

"To the shogun," Sano said.

As Hitoshi protested, pleaded, and wept, the detectives hustled him along. Fukida said, "Another job well done."

"Indeed." Sano heard the rancor in his own voice. This was a far cry from solving important murder cases, as he'd once done. It was also a huge fall from the post he'd once held—chamberlain of Japan, second-in-command to the shogun. But Sano couldn't complain. After the catastrophe almost two years ago, he knew he should be thankful that his head was still on his body.

Marume said quietly, "Sometimes in this life you just have to take what you can get."

IN THE AUDIENCE chamber inside Edo Castle, Shogun Tokugawa Tsunayoshi sat on the dais, enfolded in quilts up to the weak chin of his mild, aristocratic face. He wore a thick scarf under the cylindrical black cap of his rank. Smoking charcoal braziers surrounded him and three old men from the Council of Elders—Japan's chief governing body—who knelt on the upper of two levels of floor below the dais. The sliding walls were open to the veranda, where Sano stood with Marume and Fukida. Hitoshi knelt at their feet, sobbing. The shogun had forbidden Sano to bring the disgusting captive inside the chamber. Hence, Sano and his detectives were out in the cold, as if they were pariahs—which, in fact, they were.

"So this is the man who has been defiling my castle?" The shogun hadn't even bothered to greet Sano. He squinted at Hitoshi.

"Yes, Your Excellency." Sano knew the shogun didn't owe him any thanks for his work or for fourteen years of loyal, unstinting service. That was Bushido, the Way of the Warrior, the samurai code of honor. But the snub rankled nonetheless. "We caught him in the act."

The shogun said to Hitoshi, "What have you to say for yourself?"

"I'm sorry!" Hitoshi was hysterical with fright. "Please have mercy!"

The shogun flapped his hand. "I hereby sentence you to execution." The elders nodded in approval. The shogun spoke in Sano's general direction: "Get him out of my sight."

Marume and Fukida raised the blubbering Hitoshi to his feet and dragged him away. Sano frowned.

At last the shogun deigned to acknowledge Sano's presence. "What's the matter?"

"The death penalty seems excessive," Sano said.

Two years ago the shogun would have quailed in the face of criticism from Sano, his trusted advisor; he would have doubted the wisdom of his decision. But now he said peevishly, "That man insulted me. He deserves to die."

"Any act against His Excellency is tantamount to treason," said one of the elders, Kato Kinhide. He had a wide, flat face with leathery skin, like a mask with narrow slits cut for the eyes and mouth. "Under Tokugawa law, treason is punishable by death."

Another elder, named Ihara Eigoro, said, "Not in all cases. Some people are the lucky exceptions." Short and hunched, he resembled an ape. He looked pointedly at Sano.

Sano tried not to bristle at this mean-spirited reference to the incident that had precipitated his downfall. He faced the two elders, his political opponents. "There was no treason in the case you're referring to." He'd never betrayed the shogun; he'd not committed the horrendous act for which he'd been blamed.

"Oh?" Ihara said. "I heard otherwise."

The third elder spoke up. "You've been listening to the wrong people." He was Ohgami Kaoru, Sano's lone ally on the council. Quiet and thoughtful, he seemed young despite his eighty years and white hair.

The shogun frowned in vexation. "You're always saying things that don't make sense." Not known for intelligence, he never grasped the

10

veiled allusions, the undercurrents of a discussion. Entire conversations took place over his head. But lately, Sano noticed, the shogun perceived that they were taking place even if he didn't comprehend them. "I don't like it. Say what you mean."

"I'll be glad to explain what everyone's talking about, Your Excellency," Chamberlain Yanagisawa Yoshiyasu said as he strode into the room, accompanied by his son, Yoritomo. Mirror images, the two had the same tall, strong, slender physique, the same dark, liquid eyes, lustrous black hair, and striking, masculine beauty. Sano didn't react outwardly to them, but inside he seethed with anger and hatred.

He and Yanagisawa had been rivals since he'd first joined the regime fourteen years ago. Yanagisawa had then been chamberlain. Events had led to Yanagisawa's being exiled and Sano's becoming chamberlain. But Yanagisawa had staged a miraculous comeback. The shogun had then decreed that Yanagisawa and Sano would share the position of second-in-command and run the government as co-chamberlains. Sano would have accepted that, but Yanagisawa couldn't. With a brilliant, stunning act of cruelty, Yanagisawa had engineered Sano's fall.

"Good morning to you, too, Honorable Chamberlain," Sano said. "To what do we owe the honor of your company?" But he knew. Yanagisawa had a sixth sense that warned him whenever Sano was with the shogun. He always managed to put in an appearance.

Yanagisawa ignored the greeting. "Sano-*san* and the Council of Elders are discussing the terrible crime that he committed against you two years ago, when he investigated a case of kidnapping. Five women were kidnapped and raped. One was your wife. She suffered terribly because Sano-*san* didn't solve the case soon enough to prevent her from becoming a victim."

"Now she's too sick and too afraid to leave her bedchamber," Yoritomo said. He always tagged after his father, whom he adored.

Under other circumstances the shogun might have forgotten the whole affair. Two years was too long for his capricious nature to sustain a grudge, and he cared nothing for his wife. Their marriage was a matter of political convenience, and he preferred men to women. But Yanagisawa and Yoritomo were always reminding him. Now he glared at Sano.

"How could you do such a terrible thing to me?" the shogun demanded. Never mind that his wife was the one who'd suffered; he took everything personally. "After all I've done for you. Without me, you would be a, ahh, nobody!"

Sano had been a *rōnin*——a masterless samurai——until he'd entered the Tokugawa regime as a detective inspector in the police department. During his first murder case he'd caught the shogun's attention. The shogun had created a new position just for Sano——Most Honorable Investigator of Events, Situations, and People. Ever since then he'd accused Sano of ingratitude and overlooked the fact that Sano had more than earned his good fortune, often paying for it with his own blood.

Nettled, Sano defended himself yet again. "With all due respect, your wife's kidnapping wasn't a part of the set of crimes. Chamberlain Yanagisawa engineered her kidnapping and rape."

"Rubbish," Kato scoffed.

Ihara seconded him; they were both Yanagisawa's cronies. "You've no proof."

Sano had tried and failed to turn up any evidence against Yanagisawa, who'd thoroughly covered his tracks.

"Sano-*san*'s accusation is a pitiful attempt to shift the blame, Your Excellency," Yanagisawa said. "It's his word against mine. And you've already decided whom to believe."

He mounted the dais and knelt in the position of honor at the shogun's right. He gave Sano a smug smile, enjoying his own privileged status and Sano's ignominious position outside in the cold. Yoritomo sat close to the shogun, on his left. He gleamed maliciously at Sano.

An eerie shiver rippled down Sano's spine. The resemblance between Yoritomo and Yanagisawa grew stronger every year, while the son aged and the father never seemed to change. And they shared a history as well as their looks.

In his youth, Yanagisawa had been a mere son of a vassal of a minor lord. Then he'd enchanted the shogun with his beauty, charm, and sexual skills. The shogun came to rely on his counsel and turned over the administration to Yanagisawa.

Yoritomo was the product of an affair between Yanagisawa and a court lady-in-waiting, a distant cousin of the shogun's. Yoritomo too had enchanted the shogun with his beauty, charm, and sexual skills. Now he occupied his father's former position as the shogun's favorite lover. The shogun relied more and more on his advice. Yanagisawa and Yoritomo had a hold over the shogun that no one could break.

Sano thought of his own son, Masahiro, who was eleven years old. He could never make Masahiro into such a political pawn. He loved Masahiro too much.

"You're right," Yoritomo said to Ihara. "Sano-*san* has been bad for the Tokugawa clan, and he's lucky to be alive."

He hated Sano as much as his father did. When Yanagisawa had been exiled, Yoritomo had stayed in Edo with the shogun. Sano had befriended the youth, who was vulnerable to his father's enemies. Then Yanagisawa had secretly returned, and Yoritomo had helped him stage his comeback. Yanagisawa had attacked Sano from behind the scenes until Sano had lured Yanagisawa out of hiding. Sano had used Yoritomo for bait, in a cruel trick that Yoritomo couldn't forgive, even though Sano had apologized. It didn't matter to Yoritomo that he'd conspired against Sano and deserved retaliation. Yoritomo was now Sano's bitter enemy.

"Yes, I, ahh, should have put you to death for what you did to me, Sano-*san*." The shogun looked puzzled. "Why didn't I?"

Everybody spoke at once. Sano said, "Because you know in your heart that I'm innocent," while Yanagisawa said, "Because you're too kind, Your Excellency." "Because Sano-*san* manipulated you," Yoritomo said. Ohgami said, "Because you need his services."

There was truth to all these reasons why Sano had been demoted to his former position instead of being forced to commit ritual suicide, the samurai alternative to execution. The shogun wasn't entirely cowed by Yanagisawa and Yoritomo, and he probably suspected they'd set Sano up. He did have some compassion under his selfishness. Some fast talking by Sano had convinced the shogun not to give him the death penalty. And the shogun had always needed Sano to save the regime from various troubles.

Furthermore, Sano still had friends among important Tokugawa officials and powerful *daimyo*, feudal lords who ruled the provinces. They'd pressured the shogun to keep him alive. And Yanagisawa had many enemies, who supported Sano as their best hope of checking his rise to absolute power. But no one could say any of this openly. The shogun didn't know about the struggle over control of the regime. Yanagisawa and his rivals didn't want their lord to find out. A conspiracy of silence reigned.

But that didn't prevent Yanagisawa and Yoritomo from doing everything they could to denigrate Sano in front of the shogun. Yanagisawa said, "Even though Sano-*san* deserves a harsher punishment, at least he's back where he belongs."

Sano gritted his teeth. The demotion was an extreme loss of face, a crushing blow to his samurai honor. Although he knew he must persevere for the sake of his family, his retainers, and everyone else whose fortune depended on him, in his darkest hours he thought death would have been better than this constant humiliation.

"Being chamberlain was too big a job for Sano-*san*," Yoritomo chimed in. "Catching louts who defile the palace is more his size."

Ihara and Kato nodded their agreement. Ohgami said, "That's ridiculous, considering that Sano-*san* did a commendable job running the government in the past." He aimed a pointed glance at Yanagisawa. "Better than some people."

The corrupt Yanagisawa had embezzled from the treasury, had bribed and threatened officials and *daimyo* into swearing loyalty to him, and had usurped power from the shogun. The honest men in the regime didn't like the return to that state of affairs. Less did they like the fact that the current strife between Sano and Yanagisawa wasn't just another episode in a long-running feud. Yanagisawa was more dangerous than ever. Yanagisawa had demonstrated his willingness to shed blood to win power. If provoked, he could start a war that Japan couldn't survive.

Ohgami was too afraid to speak openly against Yanagisawa. The other elders ignored Ohgami. The shogun frowned, irate because the conversation was going over his head again.

"Well, I hope you have, ahh, learned your lesson, Sano-*san*." The shogun waved his hand. "You're dismissed. Oh, and shut the door before you go. I'm cold."

"Yes, Your Excellency." Sano had no right to object; the shogun could treat him however he chose. A samurai must serve his lord without complaint, regardless of the lord's behavior or character faults. That was the

14

Way of the Warrior. But Sano's endurance was stretched to its limits. He turned to leave before he did something he would regret.

"Wait," Yanagisawa said, enjoying Sano's humiliation, wanting to prolong it. He asked the assembly, "Haven't we any other jobs for Sano-*san*?"

"I hear there's been a rash of shoplifting in the Nihonbashi merchant quarter." Yoritomo smiled spitefully at Sano. "Maybe he should investigate that."

"That's a good idea," the shogun said.

Indignation rose in Sano. That he should be relegated to chasing petty thieves! "Fine," he said. "I'll investigate the shoplifting." Duty was duty, and delivering petty criminals to justice was serving his personal code of honor, even though on a small scale. "Then I'll go after the real criminals." He cut a hostile glance at Yanagisawa and Yoritomo.

They were planning nothing less than to take over the country. Yoritomo had Tokugawa blood, which made him eligible to inherit the regime when the shogun died. He was far down the list for the succession, but Yanagisawa was determined to make Yoritomo the new shogun someday. He meant to rule Japan through Yoritomo for as long as they both lived.

That was nothing new. But Yanagisawa's chances of success increased every day. The shogun was getting older and frailer. Someone had to stop Yanagisawa soon.

Yanagisawa narrowed his eyes at Sano, then smiled a slow, tantalizing smile. "You're in no position to make threats. Not as long as your family is on this earth."

That was the threat that held Sano at bay—the harm that his enemy could do to his beloved wife and children. There was no place they could hide from Yanagisawa. His reach was long, his spies everywhere. Sano began to fear that he would never recover from the blow Yanagisawa had dealt him, that he would only fall further. But he resisted the defeat that tried to creep under his skin. He must regain his status and honor, and he must satisfy his burning need for revenge on Yanagisawa.

But how? And when? At age forty-five, he felt in danger of running out of time.

A palace guard entered the chamber. "Please excuse me, Your Excellency, but I have a messenger here, with news that can't wait."

"Bring him in," the shogun said, smiling with a childlike delight in surprises.

Sano lingered on the veranda. Even though most affairs of state were no longer his business, he was curious about the news.

The guard ushered in the messenger. He was a boy, about twelve years old, dressed in a faded coat. He was panting and shaking. Snow clung to the hems of his trousers. He fell to his knees before the dais and bowed. His face was flushed, his eyes round, dark pools of fright.

"Speak," the shogun commanded.

The messenger gulped, then said in a thin, trembling voice, "The honorable Kira Yoshinaka has been murdered!"

Shock stabbed Sano. A murmur of consternation rippled through the assembly. The shogun gasped. "My master of ceremonies? Ahh, what a blow to me this is!"

Master of ceremonies was a very important post. The court had elaborate rituals for banquets, audiences with the shogun, religious observance, and countless other occasions. That had made Kira indispensable. He'd been in charge of overseeing all details of the rituals. He'd coached the participants and rehearsed them. He'd been the only person who knew every minute, arcane rule of etiquette.

"How do you know Kira has been murdered?" Yanagisawa asked the messenger.

Kato said, "When was this?"

Ihara said, "Where?"

The messenger struggled to compose himself. "Last night. At Kira-san's estate. I'm a kitchen boy there." A sob caught in his throat. "I saw."

Because his relationship with Kira had been strictly professional, Sano didn't feel any grief over Kira's death, but without Kira, Edo Castle could dissolve into chaos. Aside from the duties he'd performed for some forty years, Kira was a *hatamoto*—a hereditary Tokugawa vassal—from a high-ranking family, as well as a distant relation of the Tokugawa clan. His murder was bound to cause a sensation.

"How did it happen?" the shogun asked fearfully.

Tears spilled down the messenger's cheeks. "His head was cut off."

Exclamations of horror arose. "Who did it?" Yanagisawa seemed personally disturbed. Kira had been one of his cronies, Sano recalled.

"A gang of samurai," the messenger said. "They invaded Kira-*san's* estate."

Fresh shock reverberated through Sano and the assembly. This was a crime of astonishing violence, even for a city in which violent death was common. "Who were they?" Yoritomo asked. "Why did they do such a thing?"

"I don't know," the messenger said, shamefaced. "I was too afraid to look while it was happening. I hid, and I didn't come out until it was over and they were gone."

Sano's heart began to pound as hope rose in him. He looked to the shogun.

The shogun was a picture of woe and confusion, his wish to take strong action vying with his tendency to let others handle problems for him. Meeting Sano's gaze with relief, the shogun pointed at Sano.

"You shall investigate Kira's murder." In the shock of the moment he'd forgotten he was angry with Sano, only recalling that Sano was his expert on solving crimes. "You shall capture the killers and, ahh, get to the bottom of this."

Elated, Sano didn't mind that he was freezing cold. He saw the murder case as his chance to win back the ground he'd lost. It was a thin straw to clutch at, he knew; but it was better than nothing. "Gladly, Your Excellency."

Yanagisawa's and Yoritomo's faces registered dismay. "Not so fast," Yanagisawa said. "Your Excellency, we've established that Sano-*san* is unfit for any work more complicated than catching shoplifters. You should assign someone else to investigate Kira's murder."

"Do you mean yourself?" The shogun wore his most gullible, eager-to-please expression.

Yanagisawa gave Sano a quick, nasty smile, as if he'd snatched a bowl of rice away from a starving beggar and was glad. "Why, yes, if that's all right with Your Excellency."

The shogun's features altered into a resentful pout. "No, it is not all right!" He sometimes chafed at the control Yanagisawa and Yoritomo exerted over him. They looked appalled that he was rebelling now. He withdrew his hand from Yoritomo's grasp. "I want Sano-*san* to investigate." He cast an ominous gaze around the assembly. "Does anyone else object?"

Kato and Ihara looked at the floor, remembering that the shogun had the power of life and death over them and they had better not cross him. Ohgami gave Sano a covert smile.

"What are you waiting for, Sano-*san*? Go!" the shogun said.

"Yes, Your Excellency." Sano decamped before the shogun could change his mind.

2

SANO'S CHIEF RETAINER Hirata awakened when a heavy weight landed on his chest. He choked on a snore, opened his eyes, and saw the laughing face of his eight-year-old daughter Taeko, who crouched atop him. Another weight thudded against the bed. It was her brother Tatsuo, aged five. Hirata's wife Midori rolled over beside him, clasping her pregnant belly.

"How many times do I have to tell you not to jump on us in bed?" she scolded the children. "You'll squash the baby." She groaned. "It's not due until next month, but it almost feels like I'm going to have it today."

"Come here." Hirata pulled the children under the quilt, between him and Midori.

"Can I go see Masahiro?" Taeko asked.

Masahiro was Sano's eleven-year-old son. He and his younger sister, Akiko, were favorite playmates of Hirata's children.

"No," Midori said. "You're in their quarters so often that Sano-*san* and Lady Reiko are probably tired of you." Because they lived in the same estate in the precinct in Edo Castle where the high officials resided, Hirata's and Sano's families spent much time together. "Let them have some time alone."

Taeko turned to Hirata. "Papa? Will you let me go see Masahiro?"

Hirata smiled at her attempt to play her parents off against each other. "Sorry. Your mother's word is the law." He asked, "You like Masahiro, don't you?"

"He's all right," Taeko said with studied nonchalance.

Midori and Hirata exchanged a look that combined amusement and concern. Their daughter had a crush on Masahiro. Although she was so young, children grew up fast in this world of theirs, and they hoped she wouldn't be hurt. A marriage between Taeko and Masahiro was impossible; it could bring political benefits to her family but not to his.

"Masahiro got in a fight with some boys yesterday," Taeko said.

"Why?" Hirata asked.

"They were making fun of us because the shogun demoted our fathers," Taeko said.

Hirata looked at Midori and saw his dismay on her face. When Sano had been chamberlain, Hirata had taken over Sano's former position as chief investigator. When Sano had been demoted, Hirata had, too. Hirata and Midori worried about the effect that his demotion would have on their children. Hirata minded less for himself. He didn't mind giving up his position to Sano, because he knew how lucky he was.

Fourteen years ago, he'd been a lowly police patrol officer who couldn't afford to marry. Then he'd met Sano, who'd made him his chief retainer. He owed his career to Sano. And Sano owed his life to Hirata, who'd stopped an attack on Sano and been wounded so severely that he'd almost died. But Hirata had recovered and gone on to achieve things he'd never dreamed of. He had a wife he adored, two beautiful children, and a third on the way. Life was good.

Still, he feared for Taeko's and Tatsuo's future. The world was cruel to the progeny of disgraced fathers, and his children and Sano's were already feeling the sting.

"Was anybody hurt in the fight?" Midori said anxiously.

"No," Taeko said. "I scared the boys away. I told them that if they didn't stop bothering us, my father would beat them up. I said that my father is the best fighter in Edo."

"You shouldn't brag," Midori said. "It's not polite."

"But it's true," Tatsuo piped up.

Hirata shrugged modestly. He *was* the best, as he'd proven in the many tournaments and duels he'd won. After his injury, he'd been a cripple, in constant pain. Then he'd apprenticed himself to a mystic martial arts master, an itinerant priest named Ozuno. Five years of rigorous training had restored his health, transformed his broken body into muscle, sinew, and bone as strong as steel, and developed his combat skills to the point that he was almost invincible. Secret rituals had conditioned his mind, endowing him with a wisdom far beyond his thirty-six years and a new perspective. The Tokugawa regime was but a dust speck in the cosmos. Political machinations couldn't take away the fruits of his hard work. Nothing could.

At least nothing had yet.

"Excuse me, Honorable Master." A servant knelt at the threshold of the bedchamber. "There's a message from the *sōsakan-sama*. He wants your help with a new case."

Hirata was intrigued and excited. He said to Midori, "Maybe this is what we've been waiting for."

After washing, eating a quick breakfast, and donning his heavy winter clothes, Hirata took his swords down from the rack in the entryway and fastened them at his waist. He hesitated at the door.

The best martial artist in Edo was afraid to go outside.

Resisting his fear, he threw the door open. A rush of cold air that smelled of charcoal smoke greeted him. Servants were shoveling snow off the path through the garden. Hirata breathed deeply, slowing his heartbeat, calming his nerves, heightening his trained senses. He heard guards patrolling the castle, servants rattling buckets, and in the distant city the dogs barking, shopkeepers hawking their wares, and the ripple of the river. He smelled and tasted fish sizzling on grills, noodles cooking in garlic-flavored broth, night-soil in barrows headed for the countryside. Through the flood of sensory details he felt the auras given off by the million people in Edo. Each was distinct, an energy that signaled its owner's health, personality, and emotions. Although there were far too many auras to memorize, Hirata recognized those of people he knew. He projected his senses outward, searching the city.

Midori came to stand beside him. "Is he there?"

"No." Hirata didn't feel the aura he was looking for, that he'd encountered for the first time eighteen months ago.

He'd been at Ueno Temple when he'd felt an aura more powerful than any he'd ever met. It emanated from a man with powers far beyond what Hirata had thought possible for a mere mortal. Struck with awe and terror, Hirata had waited for the man to reveal himself—but he hadn't.

Instead, the man had begun loitering invisibly near him, taunting him. Once only, he'd let Hirata catch a glimpse of him, then slipped away.

Since then, Hirata had been searching for the man he called his stalker, whose name and face he didn't know, whose fighting skills he probably couldn't match, who could follow him anywhere. He lived in fear of an attack that might hurt his family and friends as well as himself. He spent days riding through the city, trying to lure his stalker into the open; but so far his stalker remained hidden and anonymous.

"Maybe he's not coming back," Midori said. She was one of the few people that Hirata had told about his stalker. Sano was another. He'd sworn them all to secrecy. He didn't want anyone else to know he was afraid of a ghost that nobody but himself could detect.

"Yes, he is," Hirata said. "He's hovering in the distance, biding his time."

"For what?" Midori tried, not very hard, to hide her skepticism.

"To fight me," Hirata said.

Many men would like to beat him in combat and replace him as Edo's top martial artist. Many had tried. All had failed. But Hirata realized that even his mystical powers couldn't keep him in his prime forever. Eventually someone would come along who could defeat him. He feared it was the stalker. He sensed that the time for a showdown was near.

"What are your teacher's sayings that you're always quoting?" Midori said. " 'What we fear, we create.' 'His own mind is a warrior's most formidable adversary.' I wonder if your mind is driving you crazy. Maybe this stalker doesn't really exist. Maybe you made him up."

"I did not." Annoyance prickled Hirata.

His wife didn't entirely believe in his mystical powers, even though she'd seen him perform astonishing feats. A practical woman, she thought everything had a rational explanation. But of course Hirata hadn't believed in the supernatural until he'd experienced it himself. He couldn't expect Midori to understand. And he had to admit that there could be truth to what she'd said. Perhaps his mind and his fear had built the stalker into a bigger, stronger person than the man really was. But Hirata didn't think so.

"I have to go," he said.

Concern for him crept into Midori's eyes in spite of her doubts that he was in any real danger. "Be careful."

3

GUARDS IN THE towers and enclosed corridors atop the walls of Edo Castle looked down at the main gate, which opened to let out a procession of mounted samurai. Sano rode in the lead, Hirata by his side. Marume and Fukida followed with fifty soldiers from his army. His heart lightened as it always did when he escaped the castle's confines. As he and his men crossed the bridge over the moat, he breathed the eye-watering, cheek-stinging cold and the fresh atmosphere of hope.

They turned on the avenue that separated Edo Castle from the *daimyo* district, where the feudal lords lived in vast, walled compounds. The wooden framework structures of fire-watch towers were sketched against a blue sky pillowed with white clouds. Snow lay shin-deep on the wide avenue. There wasn't much traffic except a squadron of samurai on horseback approaching from the opposite direction. Poles on their backs flew banners that bore the crest of a *daimyo* clan allied with Yanagisawa. They barreled straight toward Sano, their chins tilted up at an insolent angle.

Marume and Fukida galloped forward. "Hey!" Marume said. "Move aside!"

The soldiers kept going. Sano clenched his jaw. While the shogun had backed him, he'd commanded the respect of almost everybody. Since he'd lost favor, no one deferred to him. He should be used to it by now, but it was still hard to take.

Fukida, Marume, and his other troops reached for their swords. Sano said, "Let it go." The satisfaction of teaching the soldiers a lesson wasn't worth the loss of human lives. Early on, Sano's younger, hotheaded retainers had fought many brawls on his behalf. Too many had died. Not only did Sano hate the waste, but he needed all his troops.

His men reluctantly desisted. The soldiers snickered and started to ride through Sano's army.

Hirata blocked them. He'd moved so swiftly that they were startled to find him in their path. "Go around us."

His voice was quiet, but his aura of power stopped the soldiers. Their fright showed as they recognized him. They knew he could kill them before they could strike him once. Nobody dared insult Sano in Hirata's presence. Laughing as if at a joke that wasn't funny, they slunk around Sano's group.

Hirata steered his horse back into position beside Sano. Marume and Fukida nodded approvingly to him, but Sano sensed the tension among the three men as the procession continued down the avenue. The detectives didn't object to Hirata taking his rightful place next to Sano; but when Hirata had been *sōsakan-sama* and Sano had been chamberlain, Marume and Fukida had acted as Sano's chief retainers. They'd enjoyed the status and responsibility, and they disliked being shunted to the background. And although the detectives liked Hirata, he'd changed since learning the mystic martial arts. They feared him, even though he was their comrade.

But today nothing could darken Sano's or his men's spirits for long. One murder investigation fourteen years ago had launched Sano on an extraordinary rise to power. One murder investigation now could be his redemption. His men were excited to be on an important mission, and the city had a festive air. White, sparkling snow covered roofs, streets, and dirt. Women swept their doorsteps, sending flurries of flakes over brightly dressed children pelting one another with snowballs. Pine boughs hung over doors, decorations for the coming New Year. Sano and his men crossed the Ryōgoku Bridge, which arched over barges and fishing boats on the glittering Sumida River. They joked and laughed.

Their humor abruptly ended when they found the first evidence of the murder.

24

The snow in the street between the earthen walls of the estates in Kira's neighborhood was red with bloody footprints and spatters. These originated at the gate of a mansion two stories tall, whose many curved tile roofs rose above surrounding barracks. As Sano and his men dismounted, Fukida said, "Merciful gods."

"I thought we were coming to investigate one murder," Marume said, his usual cheer sobered. "This looks like the scene of a massacre."

Near an empty guardhouse, ladders leaned against the wall. "That must be how the killers got into the mansion." Sano glanced up and down the street. People peered out the gates of other estates. When his gaze met theirs, they withdrew. "Let's go in." He and his men approached the gate. "Be careful. The messenger said that the killers are gone, but we don't know what to expect."

Swords drawn, they lined up on either side of the portals. Hirata gingerly opened the gate. They walked between the barracks, along a path that was covered with more bloodstained snow. Two men lay facedown, dead. Both were samurai, half naked, barefoot. Arrows protruded from their backs. Sano and his men proceeded to the courtyard. Here the blood was so plentiful that it had turned the snow into a crimson slush. Many more bodies were scattered about. Sano's troops exclaimed and muttered. A few retched. Sano frowned at the gashed chests, the bellies oozing entrails, the throats cut. Vacant eyes gazed up at the sky. Sano almost stepped on a severed hand. His stomach lurched, even though he'd seen plenty of carnage in the past. This attack was surely the most brutal, inflicted on men who clearly hadn't been prepared.

"This was no battle," Marume said. "This was a slaughter."

"But where is Kira?" Hirata asked.

They turned to the mansion. It huddled under the weight of the snow on its roof, its façade in shadow, the veranda dark beneath overhanging eaves. Crows and vultures perched on the gables, waiting to feast on the corpses. The house was as quiet as a tomb. Sano and his men followed bloody footprints up the steps and through the door. They didn't bother taking off their shoes as polite custom required. The corridor they entered was awash in melted snow and more blood. They crept past silent, empty rooms.

A man rushed from around a corner. He was small and stooped, and he carried a spear. "Don't come any farther! Get out!" He clumsily thrust his spear at Sano and the other men.

"Hey, be careful with that thing." Marume seized the spear. The old man squealed and cowered.

"We're not going to hurt you," Sano said, and introduced himself. He and his troops sheathed their swords.

The old man gasped, dropped to his knees, and bowed. "*Sōsakan-sama*. A thousand apologies. I thought they'd come back."

"Who are you?" Sano asked.

"Gorobei. I'm Lord Kira's valet." Grief contorted the old man's face. "I was."

"The shogun sent me to investigate Kira-*san*'s murder," Sano said. "May I speak to his chief retainer?"

Gorobei sobbed. "He's dead."

"What about his other officials?"

"They're either dead, too, or wounded."

"Who's in charge?" Sano said.

"Nobody," Gorobei said.

"Who sent the messenger to Edo Castle?"

"I did. I also sent for a doctor to take care of the wounded men. They're in the barracks."

"You've done well," Sano said. "Where are the women and children?" He knew Kira had a large family. "Are they all right?"

"Yes, thank the gods. The gang didn't touch them. They're in the private quarters, with the servants." Gorobei added, "The watchdog was also spared. I found him tied up and muzzled outside."

Tokugawa law forbade killing dogs. The shogun had been told by his spiritual advisors that if he protected dogs, then the gods would grant him an heir. It hadn't worked so far, probably because he had sex with men much more often than women. Sano was amazed by the gang's combination of violence and respect for the law.

"Can you take us to Kira?" Sano said.

Gorobei nodded, choking back tears. He led Sano's party to the bedchamber. More bloody footprints soiled the *tatami* around a bed whose quilt was folded back as if the occupant had just risen. Gorobei lifted a scroll painting that hung on the wall, revealing a door.

26

"My master had this door built, in case of an emergency." He preceded Sano through the door, into a courtyard. This contained a shed whose door was ajar, the interior filled with coal and firewood. A tarp lay on the ground. Sano could see the shape of a body underneath. Blood had soaked through the fabric.

"I didn't want to leave him here," Gorobei said, ashamed and regretful. "But I couldn't move him by myself, and no one else would touch him."

"It's better that you left him until we got here." Sano was glad to have any clues intact.

Fukida and Marume peeled back the tarp. Bony feet with bunions appeared; next came withered, veined calves, and a beige kimono with blood spatters that grew bigger as the tarp drew away. The whole upper garment was dyed red. Kira's arms extended out from his sides, fingers stiff. The corpse ended at the neck. Bone, windpipe, and sinews showed through the blood that had clotted around the severed flesh and congealed into a half-frozen puddle.

The detectives let the tarp drop. Fukida sucked air through his teeth. Marume winced. Gorobei wept. Sano and Hirata gazed in silence, paying their respects to their colleague. Sano endured the spiritual pollution that the dead exude. He brushed aside the irreverent thought that he'd stepped in so much blood that he would have to burn his boots when he got home. Then he asked the obvious question.

"Where is Kira's head?"

"They took it." Gorobei clarified, "The men who killed him."

"Who are they?" Sano said. "Did you get a look at them?"

"No. But I know who they must be. They're former retainers of Lord Asano."

Sano realized he should have known. Hirata and Fukida nodded in comprehension. Marume said, "Lord Asano. So that's what this was about. The incident at Edo Castle—when was it? Two years ago?"

"Twenty-two months, exactly." Sano recited the details of the incident. "Envoys had come from the Emperor's court in Miyako. The host in charge of entertaining them was Lord Asano Naganori, age thirty-four, *daimyo* of Ako Castle in Harima Province. Kira's job as master of ceremonies was to instruct Lord Asano on how to conduct the ritual. An antagonism developed between Lord Asano and Kira."

"Has anyone ever figured out why?" Hirata asked.

"No. That's still a mystery," Sano said. "But one day Lord Asano drew his sword, struck at Kira, and cut his head. Kira survived, but Lord Asano broke the law against drawing a sword inside Edo Castle, which is a capital offense. Lord Asano claimed he and Kira had a personal quarrel, Kira had provoked him, and he had to defend his honor. Kira claimed there was no quarrel and Lord Asano had attacked him for nothing. The shogun believed Kira. He ordered Lord Asano to commit *seppuku*. The house of Asano was dissolved, its wealth and lands confiscated by the government, and all Lord Asano's retainers became *rōnin*."

That was a serious disgrace for a samurai, even when he lost his warrior status through no fault of his own. Sano knew because it had happened to his own father. His father's lord had run afoul of the third Tokugawa shogun, who'd confiscated his lands and turned all his retainers, including the Sano family, out to fend for themselves. Sano's father hadn't recovered from the humiliation until Sano had gotten into the Tokugawa regime and restored the family's honor.

"It appears that these *rōnin* blamed Kira for their lord's death and they've taken revenge," Sano said.

"But didn't the shogun rule that Kira wasn't guilty of anything and therefore shouldn't be punished?" Fukida said. "Didn't he forbid any action against Kira?"

Marume covered the corpse with the tarp. "Yes, but apparently that didn't stop the *rōnin*."

"This shouldn't come as a surprise," Sano said. Loyalty to one's master was the highest principle of Bushido. Avenging the death of his master was a solemn duty that a good samurai could not neglect.

"Except that it happened so long after Lord Asano's death," Hirata said.

"And except that so many *rōnin* were involved and they killed so many people besides Kira," Fukida said. "I've never heard of a vendetta like this."

Vendettas usually involved only two people—the perpetrator and the individual who'd wronged him—although sometimes relatives or friends would join in on either side. The scale and sheer brutality of this revenge astounded Sano. It would surely cause an uproar.

"I don't suppose the *rōnin* bothered to register the vendetta," Hirata said. Vendetta was legal when the perpetrator notified the authorities of his intentions. This notification served as a warning to his target, who was then on his guard and had time to hide.

"You're right," Sano said. "The shogun's orders prohibited a vendetta in this case."

"My master was always afraid it would happen anyway," Gorobei said. "That's why he had so many guards. That's why his bedchamber had a secret exit."

"That just goes to show: If someone's determined to get you, they will," Marume said.

"Well, at least the mystery appears to be solved," Sano said. "We know who killed Kira and why."

He felt a massive letdown. Kira's murder was supposed to be the big case that he could impress the shogun by solving, the pathway to regaining his status and honor, but it had proved to be disappointingly simple, almost over as soon as he'd begun.

"We still have to arrest the *ronin*," Hirata said, then asked Gorobei, "Where did they go?"

"I don't know," the old man said unhappily.

"We'll find them." Sano hoped that he could accomplish some good by finishing the investigation quickly. "Let's get to work."

4

"I HAVE GOOD news and bad news," the matchmaker told Lady Reiko. "Which do you want first?"

The two women sat in the reception room in Sano's mansion, at the *kosatsu*—a table built over a sunken charcoal brazier. Their feet and legs were warm in the space around the fire. A quilt covered the table and their laps. They wore silk kimonos lined with fur. The old matchmaker's was dark gray, Reiko's a plum shade suitable for a matron of thirty-three. A teapot, cups, and a spread of sweet cakes shaped like flowers lay before them on the table.

"Tell me the bad news," Reiko said.

The matchmaker was Lady Wakasa, the mother of Lord Ikeda, who was one of Sano's most powerful allies. She was seventy-nine years old but vigilantly preserved, her hair dyed an unnatural black that matched her teeth, which were also colored black in the fashion of samurai wives. Age had shrunken her to the size of a child and withered her face, but she had the energy of a woman twenty years younger. She liked meddling in other people's business, and when she'd heard that Sano and Reiko were looking for a bride for their son, she'd volunteered to act as the go-between who conveyed proposals to and from families with marriageable daughters.

"The Fukushima clan rejected your proposal," she said.

That clan was another of Sano's allies, with a large domain and much wealth. "Oh," Reiko said, disappointed.

Lady Wakasa jabbed her finger at Reiko. "I told you that you were reaching too high." She was blunt and outspoken to the point of rudeness, a trait common in old women, a privilege of age. "When your husband was chamberlain, they would have leaped at a chance to intermarry with your family, but now—"

"I know." Reiko cut Lady Wakasa off before she could chew over the story of how Sano's troubles had reduced Masahiro's marriage prospects. A curse on Yanagisawa! Reiko was furious at him for jeopardizing her children.

"Here's the good news," Lady Wakasa said. "A representative from the Chugo clan has offered Masahiro the youngest daughter of the main branch of their family."

"We were hoping for something better," Reiko said. The Chugo clan were Tokugawa vassals, but their leader was only a captain in the army. An alliance with them would do little to improve the political standing of the Sano clan. Furthermore, Reiko knew the girl, a dull creature.

"Are you directing me to say you're not interested? We've had sixteen refusals in a year, and this is our first offer. Don't be too quick to turn it down."

"All right," Reiko said reluctantly. "Tell them we're considering their proposal. But keep looking for new prospects. There's still time. Masahiro is only eleven."

Samurai boys didn't officially reach manhood until age fourteen; yet children were often betrothed, and Sano and Reiko needed to safeguard Masahiro's future. If Masahiro was betrothed, he would have another family to protect him while he was young and give him a place in society when he was an adult—if Sano wasn't there to do it. Reiko must find Masahiro a bride quickly, because Sano's situation wasn't getting any better. But she felt as if she was hurrying the end of his childhood. She wanted him to remain her baby for as long as possible.

"Time goes fast," Lady Wakasa warned. "The sooner your son is settled, the better, and your daughter, too. You can bet that Chamberlain Yanagisawa isn't wasting any time getting his sons married. Have you heard the rumor? It seems that Yanagisawa is in marriage negotiations with Tokugawa Ienobu, to arrange a match between his daughter and Yoritomo." She added, "Ienobu is the shogun's nephew."

"I've heard that he's the man most likely to succeed the shogun," Reiko said, disturbed.

"So have I," Lady Wakasa said. "The shogun will die eventually. If Yoritomo marries into Ienobu's family, then Yanagisawa has a chance to control the regime for another term."

And Sano would have to fight Yanagisawa at an even greater disadvantage. "In that case, it's all the more important that we find the best possible match for—"

Reiko stopped because she saw Masahiro standing in the doorway, holding a bamboo scroll container. She didn't like to talk about his marriage prospects in front of him. She didn't want him to hear himself discussed as if he were a commodity for sale, which buyers rejected. But he had a talent for sensing when something important was happening. He would appear on the scene before Reiko knew he was there.

Lady Wakasa understood. "I'd better go." She rose, grimacing as her stiff joints creaked. On her way out she told Reiko, "Remember what I said: Don't wait too long."

Reiko extended her hand to Masahiro and drew him beside her. How tall he was! And how handsome in his white martial arts practice clothes. He didn't look like her or Sano; he was a blend of their best features, her beauty toughened by Sano's strength. Reiko beamed with pride and love. "Have you finished your practice?"

"Yes, Mother." Masahiro asked, "Can't she find a bride for me?"

Reiko sighed. Masahiro knew everything that went on in the household, despite her efforts to shield him. "Not yet."

He looked relieved. "I don't think I'm ready to get married."

"It wouldn't be until you're at least fourteen."

"If I can marry a girl I like, I won't mind." Masahiro sounded hopeful.

Reiko realized with surprise that he was becoming a young man, with a young man's dreams of romance. "I promise I'll do my best to find you a girl you'll love."

Masahiro nodded, reassured. He seemed once more a child, who believed that the three years until his manhood would last forever. But he'd already taken on adult responsibilities. "I have to change my clothes and go to the palace." This winter he'd begun his first job—as a page in Edo Castle, the position in which many boys from good samurai families started. He was inordinately proud of the fact. "The shogun will be wanting me."

His mention of the shogun made Reiko's blood run cold.

The shogun liked sex with young boys. He surrounded himself with male courtesans and actors, and every page, soldier, and servant in Edo Castle was at his disposal. Reiko didn't want Masahiro to become the shogun's concubine, not even to gain influence at court. It was too repulsive and degrading. The shogun's favor could advance Masahiro in the world, but Reiko prayed that Masahiro would never attract the shogun's lust.

Noises outside the chamber interrupted her thoughts. She saw two servants lugging a trunk down the corridor. Her daughter, four-year-old Akiko, skipped after them, hand in hand with a woman in her mid-thirties, who wore a brown silk quilted coat. The woman had a pensive, pretty face, and her hair was arranged in a neat twist at the back of her head. Entering the room with Akiko, she smiled at Reiko and Masahiro.

"Chiyo-*san*!" Reiko rose; she and the woman exchanged bows. "How good to see you."

"Many thanks for your hospitality," Chiyo said.

She was Sano's cousin, the daughter of his maternal uncle, Major Kumazawa from the Tokugawa army. Sano had been estranged from the Kumazawa clan due to a breach between them and his mother that had occurred before his birth. He hadn't known they existed until a crime had brought them together two years ago. That crime had been a kidnapping—the case that had resulted in his fall. Chiyo had been a victim. One of the few good things to come out of the case was a close friendship between Chiyo and Reiko. Although Chiyo had recovered physically from the experience, her husband had divorced her because she'd been violated, and she would have lost her two children to him, had Sano not ordered him to let the children live with her, at the Kumazawa estate, every other month. Still, Chiyo grieved during their absences. Reiko had invited Chiyo to spend those months with her, so that she wouldn't be as lonely. And Reiko was glad of Chiyo's company. Her usual companion, Midori, was pregnant and slept a lot, and Reiko had lost many other friends after Sano's demotion.

Masahiro greeted Chiyo, happy to see her. He and Akiko had adopted

Chiyo into their family. Then he proffered the scroll container to Reiko. "Mother, this just came for you."

Reiko opened the container, which was a roughly cut length of bamboo sealed with crude wooden plugs. She took out a rolled piece of cheap rice paper, unfurled it, and read,

Honorable Lady Reiko,

Please excuse me, a humble stranger, for writing to you. I've heard that you help women in trouble. My name is Okaru. I'm in trouble. Please forgive my poor words—I'm so upset I can hardly think. My man has done something terrible. It's too complicated to explain in a letter, and the scribe is charging me for each line, and I'm running out of money. I'm sorry to impose on you, but I'm new in town, I don't know anybody here, and I have no one else to turn to. Will you please help me? I'm staying at the Dragonfly Inn in Nihonbashi, three blocks from the south end of the bridge. I wait eagerly to hear from you.

Reiko was moved by Okaru's urgent tone. "I haven't received a letter like this in quite a while."

"Didn't you once run a kind of service for helping women in trouble?" Chiyo asked. "Is that what the letter refers to?"

"Yes."

Reiko had once had a reputation for solving problems. She had often assisted Sano with his investigations, and her part in them had been rumored in high-society gossip and in the news broadsheets sold in town. Many people thought her unfeminine, scandalous, and disgraceful, but others—mainly women—had flocked to her in search of help. She'd found jobs and homes for them, paid for doctors to cure their sick children. She'd rescued women from cruel husbands, lovers, and employers. She'd also intervened on behalf of people unjustly accused of crimes. The daughter of Magistrate Ueda, one of two officials who presided over Edo's court of justice, Reiko had used her influence with him to get the innocents acquitted. Helping people made her feel useful, and serving the public also served honor.

"But I don't get many requests for help lately," Reiko said. The whole samurai class knew about Sano's fall from grace, and the news must have filtered down to the commoners. Perhaps Okaru, from out of town, was the only person who thought Reiko had the ability to help anybody anymore. "Only letters from people wanting money."

And she had less of that to give nowadays. His demotion had cost Sano a fortune. His stipend from the government had been reduced, and he'd had to discharge many of his retainers and servants. Too kind to throw them out in the streets, he'd paid other samurai clans to take on the retainers and given the servants money to live on until they found other jobs. He and Reiko were far from poor, but for the first time in her life she was feeling the pinch of tight finances.

"What kind of trouble is this Okaru in?" Masahiro asked.

"Your guess is as good as mine." Reiko headed for the door.

"You're not going to her, are you?" Chiyo said, alarmed.

"I can't ignore such a desperate cry for help," Reiko said.

"But you don't know anything about Okaru," Chiyo said. "Or about this man, except that it sounds as if he's her lover and not her husband."

"I'll know soon," Reiko said.

"I think you shouldn't go."

Reiko was surprised that Chiyo would oppose her. Chiyo had a mild nature; she'd never gone against anything Reiko wanted to do.

"I'm concerned for your safety," Chiyo explained. "Okaru might be someone you'd be better off not knowing."

"If she is, I'll find out when I meet her." Reiko had made up her mind. Not only did she want to help a woman in need, but she had a taste for adventure that had gone unsatisfied too long. She craved an outing to lift her spirits after the bad news from the matchmaker and the grim consequences of Sano's downfall.

"All right," Chiyo conceded with good grace, "but I would like to go with you, if I may." She smiled at Akiko, who was playing with her doll. "I just wish I could stay with her, too." Reiko's children helped to fill the emptiness in her heart left by her own children's absence.

"I would be glad of your company," Reiko said sincerely.

"Maybe there will be an investigation." Masahiro's eyes sparkled with excitement. He loved detective work. He'd done some in the past, and he'd performed well beyond what could be expected of a child. "Can I go, too?"

Reiko hesitated. Masahiro should be at the palace, attending the shogun. If he was absent when the shogun wanted him, the shogun would be displeased, and nobody in their family could afford to displease the shogun. But Reiko badly wanted to keep her son away from the shogun as much as possible.

"Yes," she said. "You can come."

5

OUTSIDE KIRA'S ESTATE, Sano and his men mounted their horses. They followed the bloody footprints in the snow down the street and through the neighborhood until the gang's trail had been obliterated by pedestrians and horses. Sano stopped at a gate at an intersection.

"Did you see a gang of samurai pass by here?" he asked the watchman.

"Yes. They went through, even though I told them it was too early for the gates to open." The neighborhood gates in Edo closed each night, to restrict traffic and confine troublemakers. "I couldn't stop them." The watchman exclaimed, "They had a head stuck on a spear!"

Sano envisioned the gang parading Kira's head around town like a war trophy. It seemed outrageous, barbaric. "Which way did they go?"

The watchman pointed. Sano and his men followed the gang's trail across the Ryōgoku Bridge. They had plenty of witnesses to direct them. Gate sentries, shopkeepers, and other folks had seen the gang. "There were forty-seven of them," said a noodle vendor.

"They didn't even try to hide," Fukida remarked.

Indeed, the forty-seven samurai had made no secret of what they'd done. The Nihonbashi merchant quarter buzzed with the news. People clustered in shops, doorways, and teahouses, glad to pass on information to Sano and anyone else who came along.

"They killed the bastard who caused their master's death," said a teahouse owner. Everyone in the teahouse cheered. "I gave them all free drinks."

Sano wasn't surprised that the gang had aroused the sympathy of the public, which romanticized people who took the law into their own hands. "Did they say where they were going?"

"To Sengaku Temple."

"I might have guessed," Sano said to Hirata as they and their party rode away. "Lord Asano's tomb is at Sengaku Temple. Of course his men would take Kira's head there."

The story of the vendetta spread through town. News-sellers were hawking hastily printed broadsheets: "Read all about the Forty-seven *Rōnin* Revenge!"

"So the crime already has a name," Fukida said.

"It has a nice ring to it," Marume said.

Restaurants had fed the gang; girls at the bathhouses had offered them sexual favors. The city had a carnival atmosphere that seemed a harbinger of more lawlessness. The trail continued through Ginza, the sparsely populated district around the Tokugawa silver mint. Sano and his men turned their horses onto the Daiichi Keihin, the main highway to points south. The highway ran through woods, past walled samurai estates. The gang's footprints showed clearly in the snow and led straight to Sengaku Temple.

Sengaku was a modest temple, a few buildings set apart from the huge Zōjō Temple district to the west and the inns, markets, and brothels that served the religious pilgrims. Sano and his men stopped at the outer gate, a simple square arch topped with a tile roof. They jumped off their horses and looked around.

The sun shone on the snow, which glittered with jeweled lights. Shadows reflected the cold, vivid blue of the sky. Sano saw a few houses in the distance, smoke rising from their chimneys. Crows perched in the leafless trees like sentries; their caws echoed weirdly. An unnatural stillness gripped the landscape. No one moved. Even the horses stood as if their hooves had frozen to the ground. Sano's men listened, their noses red from the cold, their eyes alert. Hirata's gaze swept the scene for danger.

"Just because they didn't hide, that doesn't mean they want to be caught," Sano said. He couldn't help hoping for a challenge that would make the pursuit worthwhile.

He and his men drew their swords. Hirata led the cautious advance through the gate. Beyond it lay an open space, the outer temple precinct. Footprints marked the snow to an inner gate flanked by ornamental pine trees with twisted boughs. The gate was a building with a double-tiered roof; its central doorway led to the inner precinct. From the doorway emerged a priest who wore a hooded cloak over his saffron robe and shaved head. He rushed down the steps to meet Sano and the troops, clearly relieved that the law had arrived.

Clasping his hands, he bowed; then he beckoned. "They're in here."

"What are they doing?" Sano asked as the priest led him and his group to the inner precinct.

"Nothing." The priest sounded perplexed. "They just marched into the temple without a word." He bypassed the worship hall, where a few other priests stood about in confusion. He pointed at a well—a round hole encircled by a carved stone rim. The snow around it was wet and red. "They washed the head there."

They had performed a ritual purification of Kira's head, Sano deduced. His heart began to drum with excitement. The priest led the way through a gate in a stone wall. In a small cemetery, the forty-seven samurai stood crowded amid stone pillars that marked the graves where the ashes of the deceased were buried. Their swords were sheathed, bows and empty slings dangling from their shoulders, spears resting on the ground. Their faded, threadbare clothes were splattered with blood. Grime and whisker stubble shadowed their faces. They gazed at Sano and his party without making a sound, their expressions set in identical hard, stoic lines. They ranged in age from a youth of about sixteen years to old, white-haired men. Some were wounded, with rags wrapped around arms and legs. One fellow had a gory cut across his eye, which was swollen shut and leaking bloody fluid. They all faced Lord Asano's tomb, a pillar elevated on a stone base and enclosed by a fence made of stone posts. In front of the tomb was a stone lantern with a curved lid and a persimmon-shaped ornament on top. Against the lantern's tall base stood the forty-seven *rōnin*'s trophy.

Bled dry and washed clean, the neck smoothly severed, Kira's head looked like a wax prop from a Kabuki play. Sano caught himself thinking how lifelike the details were—the yellowed teeth, the age spots, the gray hairs, the scar on the crown, and the white, wrinkled skin. The mouth hung open; the eyelids drooped. Sano hardly recognized Kira, the prim, stiff-lipped man he'd known.

Sano's party stared in dumbfounded shock.

Hirata broke the silence and addressed the forty-seven *rōnin*. "This is the shogun's *sōsakan-sama*." He indicated Sano. "Which of you is the leader?"

"I am," said the man standing nearest to Lord Asano's tomb. "My name is Oishi Kuranosuke." His voice had the raspy sound of diseased lungs. "I was Lord Asano's chief councilor."

He was in his forties, lean but broad-shouldered. Although his pallor was gray with fatigue, his fierce eyes glittered as if from an inner fire. He reminded Sano of statues of guardian deities in temples. The candlelight on their eyes imbued their carved wooden figures with life.

Oishi gestured at his comrades. "These were Lord Asano's other men." The other forty-six *rōnin* stood as motionless as the grave markers, except for the youngest, who strode to Oishi's side. "This is my son, Chikara."

The two men shared the same long nose, slanted brows, flared nostrils, and thick, firm mouth. But Chikara's face was still soft with youth, his build sturdy. The ferocity in his eyes seemed a deliberate imitation of his father. It flickered on and off, as though he couldn't keep up the act.

"Which of you killed Kira?" Sano asked.

"I did." Oishi spoke quietly. "But we were all in on it together."

He and his comrades radiated savage pride. Although they'd freely publicized their crime, Sano was nonetheless surprised by their candor. "Are you aware that the shogun forbade action against Kira and your vendetta was therefore illegal?"

"We are," Oishi said.

"Then why did you do it?" Sano asked.

"We had to avenge Lord Asano's death. It was our duty."

That was the stock answer Sano had expected, but he heard something in Oishi's voice, a faint dissonance of tone. He sensed that the man's words were true, but perhaps not entirely. "What else?"

"Nothing," Oishi said, adamant.

Sano perceived a wrongness in the air, like a smell. The silence among the *rōnin* was unnerving. They looked eerily alike, even though their ages, shapes, and facial features varied. They seemed part of one monstrous creature, with Oishi clearly the brains.

40

"Why are you standing here?" Sano said. "Why didn't you commit *seppuku*?" Ritual suicide was mandatory for illegal vendettas, which the law considered murder. "Or run away?"

"We're awaiting orders," Oishi said.

Sano frowned in puzzlement. "Orders from whom?" He felt as if he were caught in a nightmare whose events didn't follow ordinary logic. "To do what?"

"We're awaiting orders," Oishi repeated. The other *rōnin* nodded.

"What's going on?" Sano demanded.

"We avenged our master's death. Our mission is accomplished." Oishi's words sounded stiff and formal, recited. Although none of his men spoke, Sano could almost hear cheers shouted from their minds.

"Well, you're all under arrest," Sano said. "You're coming with us."

He braced himself for the *rōnin*'s reaction. He craved a battle even though there had been enough violence for one day. Marume, Fukida, and his other troops stirred, ready for a fight. Hirata alone remained calm. Sano still wanted a chance to be a hero, to regain his lost standing, and although nothing he'd seen of the forty-seven *rōnin* indicated that they would resist arrest, their behavior was so peculiar that he couldn't predict what would happen.

Oishi gave Sano a long, enigmatic look. A moment passed. Salty, metallic blood scented the air. Then Oishi nodded to his comrades. Without protest, the forty-seven *rōnin* let Sano's troops escort them from the temple.

Relief and disappointment trickled through Sano.

"That was a little weird," Fukida said as he and Sano and Marume and Hirata followed their prisoners out.

Marume laughed. "That's the understatement of the year."

"Where are we going to put them?" Hirata asked.

"That's a good question," Sano said. Edo Jail was reserved for commoners. Samurai criminals were usually kept under house arrest, but these didn't have a proper home. They'd lost it after the house of Asano had been dissolved.

"At least the case is closed," Hirata said.

"Maybe not." Sano had a hunch that it wasn't. And he suspected that his hunch was more than just wishful thinking.

6

DRESSED IN PADDED robes and bundled in quilts, Reiko and Chiyo rode through the city in a palanquin carried by four bearers. Mounted guards from Sano's army accompanied them. Masahiro rode with the guards. Reiko looked out the window at him and smiled.

"He's so proud to have his first horse," she said.

"He's already so good at riding," Chiyo said.

Reiko wasn't sure he could control the horse, a brown stallion that seemed far too big. He might be thrown and get hurt. She felt a tender pain in her heart because soon he would be grown up; she couldn't keep him safe at home forever.

After a short, cold journey, her procession arrived at the south end of the Nihonbashi Bridge. Quays and warehouses spread along riverbanks lined with boats. Because the bridge was the starting point for the five major roads leading out of town, the area was crammed with inns and shops. Today Reiko saw few travelers in the snow-covered streets. Along the block to which Okaru's letter had directed Reiko, cheap inns stood side by side, enclosed by bamboo fences. The proprietors looked out their gates in hope of customers. One gate had a tattered paper lantern, which sported a crudely painted dragonfly crest, suspended from its roof. There Reiko's procession stopped. Her chief bodyguard, the homely, serious Lieutenant Tanuma, announced her to the innkeeper.

"This is Lady Reiko, the wife of the shogun's *sōsakan-sama*. She's here to see one of your guests, a woman named Okaru."

The innkeeper had a mouth that was puckered as if he'd just drunk vinegar. "All right, but please be quiet. My other guests arrived late last night, and they're still asleep."

Reiko and Chiyo, Masahiro and Lieutenant Tanuma, followed the innkeeper through a passage to a small garden buried under snow and surrounded by guest rooms in small, shabby wooden buildings. The innkeeper pointed to a room on the right. "She's in there."

Reiko and her companions waded through the snow and mounted the steps to the veranda. She knocked on the door. After a moment it was opened by a tall, broad, mannish-looking woman dressed in a brown-and-black-striped kimono and black trousers. A faint mustache darkened her upper lip. She gazed down at Reiko.

"Who are you?" Her voice was high, feminine, and unfriendly.

Disconcerted, Reiko said, "My name is Reiko. I—"

A little scream came from inside the room. A girlish voice said, "It's Lady Reiko! Let her in, let her in!"

The mannish woman stood aside. Reiko, Chiyo, and Masahiro slipped past her; Lieutenant Tanuma waited on the veranda. The room was barely larger than a closet. Baggage lay stacked against the wall; bedding overflowed from the cabinet. The girl who'd spoken knelt on the floor beside a charcoal brazier, holding a comb. Her long black hair hung damply around her shoulders. She wore a pale pink robe, the sash loose. She'd evidently just bathed. The sweet fragrance of a clean young woman scented the air.

"Honorable Lady Reiko! I prayed and prayed that you would come. I can hardly believe you're here!" The girl gasped. "Oh, I'm sorry, where are my manners?" She dropped her comb and bowed. "A thousand thanks for coming. I'm Okaru."

She was younger than Reiko had expected—perhaps sixteen. Small and slim and lithe, she was also beautiful. She had a heart-shaped face with round cheeks, and large, limpid, innocent eyes. Her skin glowed like pearls. Her teeth were white and perfect, her lips soft and pink as peony petals. Her smile was radiant.

"This is my cousin-in-law Chiyo, and my son Masahiro," Reiko said.

Okaru said breathlessly, "I'm so honored to make your acquaintance!"

Chiyo replied calmly and politely. Reiko couldn't help liking Okaru, the girl was so sweet; but she knew that first impressions could be erroneous. Masahiro stared at Okaru, his eyes wide and mouth open.

"Please allow me to introduce Goza." Okaru's delicate hand gestured toward her companion. "My servant."

Goza squatted on the floor, like a man.

"Please sit down," Okaru said.

Reiko and her companions knelt, crowded together in the small space.

"May I offer you some refreshments?" Okaru lifted the lid of a teapot and said, "Oh, no, the tea is all gone. And I'm afraid we've finished the rice cakes."

"You don't need to give us anything." Reiko remembered that Okaru was short on money. "We've come to help you."

Okaru's beautiful face crumpled. "And I'm so thankful. Because I'm in such terrible trouble! Or rather, Oishi is. I'm so afraid." Tears shone in her limpid eyes.

Chiyo handed Okaru a handkerchief. Reiko could see that Chiyo sympathized with the girl but reserved judgment about her. Okaru wiped her tears, swallowed, and breathed deeply.

"Let's start at the beginning," Reiko said. "Where did you come from?"

"Miyako," Okaru said.

Miyako was the imperial capital, a fifteen-day journey from Edo in good weather, perhaps twice as long in winter. "That's quite far," Reiko said. "And you came by yourself?"

"I had Goza." Okaru smiled at her servant. "She protected me."

"Who is your family?" Reiko couldn't believe they would let a girl so young travel so far with only one female attendant. The highway was dangerous.

"I haven't any family." Sadness filled Okaru's voice.

"What happened to your parents?" Reiko asked.

"They died four years ago, when I was twelve. I've been on my own since then."

Pity filled Reiko. She happened to glance at Masahiro and saw him leaning toward Okaru as if fascinated. "How have you managed to live?"

"I work at a teahouse." Okaru spoke in a small but brave voice. Her cheeks flushed.

Reiko understood that Okaru was one of the many teahouse girls who did more than serve drinks. She was a prostitute, the lowly kind that worked outside the licensed pleasure quarters where prostitution was legal. Reiko marveled that Okaru had retained her beauty and innocence for this long. But Chiyo recoiled from Okaru, as many samurai ladies would. Masahiro frowned in confusion. Although Reiko knew he'd seen teahouse girls soliciting customers, he was too young to understand exactly what they did.

After a brief, awkward silence, Reiko said, "When did you come to Edo?"

"Yesterday." Okaru smiled, thankful that Reiko didn't shun her because of her occupation. "I asked the innkeeper if there was anybody who helps travelers with problems, that I could go to. I was thinking of a convent." Convents and monasteries took in people who were down on their luck. "He mentioned you. He found me a scribe to write my letter."

The innkeeper had been kinder than he looked, Reiko thought. But a man would have to be made of stone to resist Okaru. "What brought you here?"

"Oishi came. I followed him."

"Who is Oishi?"

"Oishi Kuranosuke. My fiancé." Okaru blushed again.

Reiko supposed that teahouse girls liked to refer to their customers as fiancés. Maybe they thought it made them sound respectable; maybe it was wishful thinking. His two names identified Oishi as a samurai, above Okaru's station. Okaru was likely just his mistress. "What has Oishi done?"

"He's killed him." Okaru trembled on the verge of tears again. "I heard the news-sellers shouting it in the streets. They said he cut off his head."

"Cut off whose head?" Reiko said, alarmed yet excited to hear that the problem involved murder.

"I followed him because I love him so much and I wanted to save him." Okaru's voice rose to a wail. "But I'm just a stupid girl. That's why I sent the letter to you." Her hands fluttered like fragile white birds. "Can't you please do something?"

Reiko caught Okaru's hands and held them still. "I won't know what to do until I know the facts. Now tell me: Whom did Oishi kill?"

"I'm sorry, I'm sorry, I'm just so upset." Okaru gulped and sniffled. "It was Kira Yoshinaka."

Reiko recognized the name. "Kira, the shogun's master of ceremonies?"

"I guess. Some important man at Edo Castle."

Reiko was amazed to learn that Kira had been murdered and she had stumbled onto the sequel of a scandalous incident she remembered well. "Is Oishi one of Lord Asano's former retainers?"

"Yes, yes! He came to kill Kira because Kira killed Lord Asano."

She didn't have the facts exactly straight. Reiko said, "But the shogun said Kira wasn't at fault and no action should be taken against him." Now she understood why Oishi was in trouble and Okaru was so worried. "A vendetta would have been illegal."

"That's what Oishi told me," Okaru said. "I begged him not to go. But he didn't care if he was breaking the law."

Many samurai wouldn't. Avenging a master's death was their highest duty, and sacrificing themselves their ultimate act of loyalty. "So Oishi murdered Kira."

"Not just Oishi. He took along forty-six of Lord Asano's other men."

Reiko was stunned. The trouble was even more serious than she'd initially thought. The government might have excused one samurai who'd killed in the name of honor, but forty-seven *rōnin* ganging up on one old man? Reiko couldn't imagine them getting away with it.

"So that's why Oishi and I need your help," Okaru said.

The problem was far beyond Reiko's power to solve. "I'm sorry to say that I can't save Oishi." Reiko watched Okaru's face fall. She hated to disappoint the girl, but it would be crueler to give her false hope. "Oishi and his friends defied the shogun and committed murder. They'll likely be sentenced to death."

Chiyo nodded. Masahiro turned to Reiko in dismay. Reiko was sorry she'd brought him, that he was upset.

"But the innkeeper said your husband is an important man in the government," Okaru said. "Couldn't he protect Oishi, if you ask him to?"

"My husband has to follow the shogun's orders just like everyone else," Reiko said. "There's nothing he can do for Oishi. I'm sorry. My best advice to you is this: Forget about Oishi. Go home. If you need money for traveling, I can give you some."

Okaru conceded without a fight. Indeed, she didn't seem to have a fighting bone in her body. Her shoulders sagged. "I understand," she said, her beautiful face a picture of woe. "I'm sorry for imposing on you. I won't take your money. Thank you for coming."

Her manner showed no resentment, which made Reiko even sorrier that she couldn't help the girl. Then Okaru said, "What I don't understand is how that man Kira could do something wrong, and Oishi will die for trying to set things right. It seems so unfair."

If Okaru knew the facts, maybe she could more easily accept Oishi's fate and Reiko would feel less guilty for letting her down. Reiko explained, "Lord Asano drew a sword on Kira inside Edo Castle. He broke the law. That's why he died. Kira never lifted a finger toward Lord Asano. That's why the shogun forbade a vendetta against Kira and killing him was a crime."

"But Oishi said that was . . . How did he put it?" Okaru frowned in an effort to recall. "The 'official version.' He said it wasn't what really happened. He said . . ." Okaru recited, " 'Nothing about this vendetta is what it seems.' "

Interest and excitement stirred in Reiko. "Are you sure that's what he said?"

"Yes, yes." Nodding, Okaru gazed earnestly at Reiko. "If things are different from what everybody says, then maybe it is unfair that Oishi should have to die. Don't you think?"

"I think there may be extenuating circumstances in this case," Reiko said.

Chiyo looked surprised, Masahiro happier. The servant Goza leaned toward Reiko, suspicious. Okaru's forehead wrinkled in confusion.

"Extenuating circumstances are reasons that the law could be overturned," Reiko explained. "If there are any, Oishi and his friends might be excused for killing Kira."

"And he'll be saved!" Okaru clasped her hands under her chin. Her smile shone through her tears like sunlight reflected in water. "Oh, how wonderful!"

Reiko was alarmed at how quickly Okaru had seized on the slim chance.

"Don't count on it," she warned. "First we have to determine whether there really are any reasons why Oishi shouldn't be sentenced to death. Now, what did he say happened?"

A blank expression replaced Okaru's smile. "He didn't say."

"Did he explain about the vendetta not being what it seems?"

Okaru shook her head. "I asked him what he meant. He wouldn't tell me." She looked anxious. "Does it matter?"

"I'm afraid so," Reiko said. "To save Oishi, we would need to prove that his actions were justified." She was appalled by the violence of his crime; even though she applauded his devotion to the Way of the Warrior, she wasn't sure he deserved to go free. "The government isn't going to excuse him without more information. A vague hint isn't good enough."

"Oh. Then I guess Oishi is doomed. And so am I." Okaru looked forlorn and younger than ever, like a child who'd just discovered that wishes didn't always come true. Her lips quivered. Tears spilled down her cheeks. She was even prettier when she cried.

"Mother, do something!" Masahiro blurted out.

His vehemence surprised Reiko. But she agreed that they couldn't just leave this poor girl alone to fend for herself. "Listen," she said to Okaru. "I'll go to my husband and tell him what you said. I'll see what I can do."

"You will?" Now Okaru wept tears of delight. "Oh, thank you!"

Reiko glanced at Chiyo, who was watching Okaru with a troubled expression. Masahiro beamed. As she rose to depart, Reiko said, "Please don't hope for too much. Oishi's situation is very serious. I can't guarantee that things will turn out the way you want."

7

SANO AND HIRATA decided to imprison the forty-seven *rōnin* in the most secure location available near Sengaku Temple, the three samurai estates along the southern highway. While Sano rode back to Edo Castle to report to the shogun, Hirata divided the *rōnin* into two groups of sixteen men and one of fifteen. He sent troops to escort two groups to their makeshift jails while he and a few soldiers accompanied the other. His sixteen *rōnin* included Oishi the leader and his son Chikara. Hirata and the soldiers rode their horses while the *rōnin* trudged down the highway like obedient cattle.

The estates were private cities carved out of the forest. The barracks that enclosed them had high white plaster walls decorated with black geometric tile patterns. Bushes with spiky, leafless branches grew outside the barracks. Countless other buildings rose from within, their roofs like mountain ranges of snow-covered tile. Along the highway, porters carried litters heaped with charcoal, rice, and other goods in the vast quantities needed to supply the estates. Tokugawa law prohibited all wheeled vehicles except for oxcarts owned by the government; this prevented troop movements and rebellions, at least in theory. The porters stared at Hirata's group of bloodstained *rōnin*. Soldiers from the estates came out to watch the peculiar parade.

Hirata led his group to the estate that belonged to the Hosokawa *daimyo* clan. The Hosokawa was an ancient family that controlled the fief

of Higo Province. Higo was a top rice-producing domain and the Hosokawa clan one of Japan's largest, wealthiest landholders. Their estate was
the grandest in the area, with a gate made of wide, iron-studded planks.
When Hirata and his companions approached it, two sentries stepped out
of an ornate guardhouse.

Hirata introduced himself. "I've got sixteen prisoners. I want you to
keep them under house arrest here."

The sentries looked nonplussed. One said, "That's never been done
before. We'll have to get permission."

"Go ahead." Hirata glanced at the sixteen *rōnin*. They gazed straight
ahead, their faces impassive. None showed any sign of wanting to bolt.
"We'll wait."

A sentry went inside the estate. After a long while he came out with
the *daimyo* himself. Lord Hosokawa was in his sixties, with gray hair tied
in a neat topknot on his shaved crown. He wore robes patterned in neutral colors, instead of the gaudy, fashionable garb that other rich *daimyo*
sported. He had an intelligent, worried face and a reputation for managing his domain with excruciating attention to detail. After he and Hirata
exchanged formal greetings, he said, "You want me to do what?"

Hirata repeated his request. He explained who the *rōnin* were and
what they'd done.

Lord Hosokawa's worried expression deepened. "Why do they have
to be here? Why not at one of the other estates?"

"The other estates are getting prisoners, too," Hirata said. "There
are forty-seven in all."

"I see. But why can't you take them to town and find someplace for
them there?"

"Do you want them wandering around in the open that long?" Hirata
said.

". . . No." Lord Hosokawa gazed at the sixteen *rōnin* as if afraid they
would suddenly go berserk. "But who's responsible for feeding them and
keeping them under control?"

"You are." Hirata knew Lord Hosokawa could afford the expense and
had plenty of guards with nothing better to do.

"Well, I don't like it," Lord Hosokawa said. "There's sure to be a
scandal. I would rather not be dragged into it."

"Don't worry; your honor won't be tarnished by association with them," Hirata said. Under Tokugawa law, guilt by association was a punishable crime. "I'll make it clear to the shogun that you did him a favor by taking in these prisoners."

Lord Hosokawa pursed his mouth. "And if I refuse?"

"I'll make it clear to the shogun that you were derelict in your duty to him," Hirata said.

That was a capital offense. "Oh. Well, in that case . . ." Lord Hosokawa reluctantly moved away from the gate. "If anything bad happens, I will hold your master responsible."

Hirata hoped nothing would go wrong. Lord Hosokawa hadn't yet taken sides in the conflict between Sano and Yanagisawa. He liked the peace that came with neutrality, but if he took offense at Sano, he might change his mind. And Hirata knew that similar scenes were going on at the other estates, where the two other *daimyo* surely wouldn't want to provide a makeshift jail any more than Lord Hosokawa did. Sano couldn't afford to strain their goodwill, either. But if Sano didn't secure the forty-seven *rōnin* at once and they caused problems, that would worsen his position far more.

Lord Hosokawa called his troops to take charge of the prisoners. Hirata glanced at the faces of the men who led the prisoners away. Some regarded the *rōnin* with disgust, others with awe at these men who had followed Bushido to the ultimate degree. Hirata saw a storm brewing, the forty-seven *rōnin* at the center, and spectators already taking sides.

"Behave yourselves," he told the *rōnin*.

"We will," Oishi said, quiet and stern.

Hirata and his troops had mounted their horses to ride back to town, when Hirata felt a strange, tingling sensation. Then came a force that pulsated through the cold air, that boomed in counter-rhythm to his heartbeat. His whole body tensed with recognition and fright. It was the energy aura he'd last encountered two years ago.

His stalker had finally returned.

Hirata resisted two opposing urges—to draw his sword for combat or drop flat on the ground and cover his head. Instead, he called to the troops, "Go ahead." He had to face his stalker alone and not endanger the men. "I'll catch up."

They went. Hirata sat astride his horse and swept his gaze over the scene. He saw the glare of sun on snow and the white plaster wall of the estate across the street. Passersby glanced at him curiously, but none with malevolent intent. The aura seemed to come from everywhere and no-where. It began to fade. Hirata saw a movement to his left—a redness like a splash of blood. He whirled.

It was a strip of red paper stuck on a spiky bush near the Hosokawa gate. Hirata could have sworn that it hadn't been there a moment ago. It fluttered in the wind. Hirata leaped off his horse and snatched the paper. It was clean and neatly cut, not a torn scrap of garbage. Figures written in elegant black calligraphy graced one side. Hirata read,

Sunlight illuminates the darkness inside a black cave.
What you seek has already found you.
Seek no further.

Hirata puzzled over the cryptic message. Was it for him, from his stalker? If so, what did it mean?

Someone came up behind him and tapped his shoulder. Hirata started violently. He turned. The man he saw was a soldier dressed in an iron helmet and a tunic made of iron plates covered with leather and laced to-gether, standard military gear. A scarf muffled the soldier's face up to the nose. His eyes crinkled with amusement.

Hirata drew his breath to speak. In that instant the soldier vanished, then reappeared halfway down the street. He held Hirata's gaze for another instant, then turned and walked away. Hirata hurried after him. A squad-ron of mounted samurai emerged from a gate and blocked Hirata's path. By the time Hirata got around them, the soldier was nowhere in sight.

WHEN SANO, MARUME, and Fukida arrived at Edo Castle, soldiers loitered outside, avidly reading news broadsheets. The broadsheets were illustrated with a crude drawing of the forty-seven *rōnin* on the march, carrying Kira's head on a spear. At the palace, Sano found the very same broadsheet in the shogun's private chambers.

The shogun held a copy above his face while he lay on his back in bed. His robe was open, his naked torso exposed. A physician rubbed spice-scented oil on the shogun's stomach. Chamberlain Yanagisawa, Yoritomo, and two men from the Council of Elders—Sano's friend Ohgami and enemy Ihara—knelt around the shogun, twisting into awkward postures, trying to read the broadsheet. Yoritomo read aloud, "A hundred savage *rōnin* broke into the estate of the shogun's master of ceremonies. They cut off his head and massacred everybody else."

Yanagisawa and the elders listened with concern. The shogun exclaimed, "This is even worse than I feared! Can it be true?"

Yanagisawa noticed Sano standing at the threshold. His eyes narrowed. "Here's the man who should be able to tell us."

"There were forty-seven *rōnin*, not a hundred," Sano said. "They spared the women, children, and servants."

"How nice of them." Sarcasm didn't improve the looks of Elder Ihara's monkey face.

53

Yoritomo started reading a gory description of the murder. The shogun said, "Stop right there, or I'll be sick!" and flung away the broadsheet.

The physician lit a candle and waved the flame inside several bamboo cups, which he placed upside down on the shogun's stomach. This was an ancient Chinese medical treatment that promoted the flow of life energy through the body. The vacuum inside the cups drew blood to the areas underneath. The suction penetrated the tissues and released poisons. The position of the cups told Sano that the shogun was suffering from constipation again. The shogun was always suffering from something, always threatening to die. So far so good, but he had gotten frail. Maybe he would die soon, without a son or designated heir. And then would follow the battle over the succession.

"What are you doing back so soon?" Yanagisawa asked Sano. "Shouldn't you be out chasing the forty-seven *rōnin*?"

"I've already captured them," Sano said.

"Oh." Yanagisawa looked unpleasantly surprised.

Sano described what had happened after he'd tracked the *rōnin* to Sengaku Temple. Everyone was nonplussed.

"That's certainly peculiar," said Elder Ohgami, Sano's quiet, white-haired friend.

"So the forty-seven *rōnin* surrendered. All you had to do was scoop them up," Yanagisawa concluded.

"Nevertheless, the crime is solved," Sano said, controlling his temper. Trust Yanagisawa to minimize his accomplishments. "The forty-seven *rōnin* are under house arrest."

"Is it all over, then?" the shogun said with cautious hope. The cups attached to him looked like the nubs on a caterpillar.

Swiftly, before Sano could say that it was and parlay his success into a pardon for past offenses, Yanagisawa shot down that hope. "No. It's certainly not over."

"Why not?" Anxiety crinkled the shogun's face. The physician slid the bamboo cups around on his pale, droopy stomach, massaging the organs beneath.

"There's still the matter of what to do with the forty-seven *rōnin*," Yanagisawa said.

54

"That's easy. They should be convicted of murder and condemned to death," Ihara declared. "They sought revenge against Kira after His Excellency ruled that Kira wasn't at fault in the incident between him and Lord Asano and he shouldn't be punished. They not only killed a helpless old man in cold blood; they defied His Excellency. It's standard procedure that anyone who does that automatically pays with his life."

"This isn't a standard case," Ohgami pointed out. "The forty-seven *rōnin* followed the Way of the Warrior. They avenged their lord's death. Bushido trumps the law in this case."

"No, it doesn't," Yoritomo hastened to protest. "Their ultimate duty is to the shogun. And they went against his orders."

Sano sensed emotions rising fast among his colleagues. The case had touched a place deep inside them, where their samurai spirit lived. The forty-seven *rōnin*'s vendetta had raised questions about their own worth as samurai, as it had done for Sano.

Exasperation showed on Ohgami's face. "Lord Asano was their hereditary master. They were compelled by honor to avenge him, no matter what."

"Not everyone thinks so," Ihara said. "Some people are already calling the forty-seven *rōnin* heroes, but others think they're criminals."

Sano suspected that those who called the *rōnin* criminals felt guilty about the short shrift that they themselves gave to Bushido. They wanted to punish anyone who made them look neglectful of their own duties. The people who lauded the forty-seven as heroes took a vicarious pride in the deed which they would probably never have the courage to perform themselves. Sano felt torn because he could see both sides of the argument.

On one hand, Bushido was the foundation of his life. His father had raised him to believe that nothing was more important than a samurai's duty to his master. His samurai blood told him that the forty-seven *rōnin* had done right to murder Kira.

On the other hand, he had a duty to his own lord, the shogun. The forty-seven *rōnin* had defied the shogun's orders, and Sano must uphold the law. And they'd killed many innocent people who hadn't deserved to die for whatever Kira had done to Lord Asano—if in fact Kira had done anything to Lord Asano. To complicate matters, Sano had a personal code of honor that often conflicted with Bushido, that compelled him to

seek the truth before he took action, that valued justice above blind obedience. There were too many questions in this case, and he needed answers before he made up his mind about the forty-seven *rōnin*.

The shogun sighed. "Ahh, this is a complicated issue."

"Yes, it is complicated." Yanagisawa refrained from declaring his position. "If you set the forty-seven *rōnin* free, you'll look weak because you let
them get away with disregarding your orders. If you put them to death,
you'll send a message that loyalty doesn't matter, and thousands of other
samurai may decide that they have better things to do than serving you."

Those were good points, but Sano figured that Yanagisawa wanted to
see which way the wind blew hardest before he took a stand. Although
Yanagisawa didn't like rogues who disrupted order, and he would probably like to see the forty-seven *rōnin* dead before sundown, an example
to anyone else who was thinking of misbehaving, he had to consider the
effect that the case would have on his quest for power.

"There will be trouble, mark my words," Yanagisawa said, "and Your
Excellency has Sano-*san* to thank for it."

"You!" the shogun exclaimed, recoiling as if Sano had hit him.

Incredulity struck Sano. "This isn't my fault, Your Excellency," he said,
then turned to Yanagisawa. "What are you talking about?"

"You arrested the forty-seven *rōnin*," Yanagisawa said. "You dumped
them in His Excellency's lap."

"I was following orders to capture Kira's killers," Sano defended
himself.

"I ordered you to, ahh, get to the bottom of things," the shogun retorted. "I didn't say, 'Cause more problems for me.' But that's ahh, exactly
what you've done."

"There you go." Yanagisawa shrugged at Sano. Yoritomo smiled tri-
umphantly.

Trust Yanagisawa to twist things around so that I look bad, Sano thought.
Everyone else looked impressed with Yanagisawa's deft play.

"Since Sano-*san* created this situation, he should be the one to settle
it," Yanagisawa said.

"A good idea," the shogun said. The physician began pulling the cups
off his stomach. Each made a loud, sucking sound as it came up, leaving

a bright red circle on his skin, like a comical rash. "Well, Sano-*san*? Shall we rule that the forty-seven *rōnin* are innocent according to Bushido and pardon them? Or that they're guilty of, ahh, treason and murder, and order them to commit *seppuku*?"

"This needs to be settled quickly," Yanagisawa added.

Sano was aware that peremptory action for the sake of action would be a dire mistake. This was such a sensitive issue that any decision was bound to create discord. It could even ignite a civil war. Yanagisawa wanted to force Sano to decide now. Later he would make sure it turned out to be the wrong choice and that Sano suffered the consequences.

Two could play that game.

Sano said, "Chamberlain Yanagisawa is second-in-command. He's the man who should advise Your Excellency."

"Ahh, you're right." The shogun turned to Yanagisawa. "What do you suggest?"

Yanagisawa couldn't hide his annoyance that Sano had deflected the responsibility onto him. The case of the forty-seven *rōnin* was like a hot coal that would burn whoever held it, and he was quick to toss it to someone else. "I suggest that the Council of Elders should decide."

The elders didn't flinch. They'd been in politics for so long that they recognized a fatal game of catch and they were prepared. Ohgami said, "We should create a special supreme court to rule on the fate of the forty-seven *rōnin*."

"Yes!" The shogun sat up, closed his robe, and clapped his hands, ecstatic. "That's the perfect solution! Who shall be the, ahh, judges?"

The physician packed up his equipment and decamped. A wise move, Sano thought. Everyone else probably wished they could leave, too, lest they end up on the court.

"First, let's decide on how many judges we need," Yanagisawa said, obviously buying time to think how to turn the new situation to his advantage. "I suggest four." He must think he could control that small number of men.

"That's not enough to decide such an important issue. I suggest twenty-five." Sano knew that was too many, but he'd allowed room to negotiate.

"Six," Yanagisawa countered.

Impatience heated up the shogun's temper. "I say fourteen." His rash, arbitrary decision was final.

"The judges should be high, trusted officials in the regime," Yanagisawa said. "I nominate Inspector General Nakae."

"I second the nomination," Ihara said.

In theory, the inspector general was responsible for auditing government operations and making sure they were conducted properly. But Nakae was a crony of Yanagisawa's, which meant he kept a lookout for misbehavior done by everyone except Yanagisawa.

"I nominate Magistrate Ueda," Sano said. Magistrate Ueda was Reiko's father, and not only Sano's ally but an honest man who would do his best to ensure that the court acted fairly.

"Second," Ohgami said.

There followed a heated discussion about who else should be appointed. As Sano and Yanagisawa each vied to stack the supreme court with his own allies, Sano was disturbed to see that the case was becoming more about politics than justice. But he could breathe easier now. With the case in hands other than his, he was safe.

After a while the shogun said, "Why is it so hard to choose fourteen judges? Give me their names now and, ahh, be done!"

Sano quickly recited seven names, including Magistrate Ueda's. Yanagisawa named his seven choices, headed by Inspector General Nakae.

"Inform the judges that they've been appointed to the supreme court," Ohgami told Sano.

The shogun brushed his hands together. "I'm glad that's finished."

"It isn't quite," Yanagisawa said. "The supreme court will need to investigate the case and collect evidence."

Sano realized that Yanagisawa was angling to throw him back into jeopardy. "An investigation isn't necessary. Because we already know that the defendants killed Kira," he said, even though the case wasn't as clear-cut as he would like.

Ohgami backed Sano up. "Why do we need evidence, when the forty-seven *rōnin* have already confessed?"

"This isn't like other murder trials," Yanagisawa explained smoothly.

"What we need is evidence that will justify the supreme court's verdict, so that everyone accepts it and no one starts a war over it."

"What kind of evidence would that be?" the shogun asked, hopeful yet confused.

"Anything that pertains to the forty-seven *rōnin*'s actions or motives, or the events leading up to Kira's death, that hasn't come to light yet," Yanagisawa said.

Sano had to agree that Yanagisawa's point was valid. Neither side in the controversy would be satisfied with a verdict based solely on the results of a judicial debate. If the shogun exercised his right to punish the forty-seven *rōnin,* he had better have solid grounds unless he wanted extreme political strife on his hands. And if the shogun reversed his original decision that prohibited punishing Kira, he had better have a strong rationale unless he wanted to lose face and expose weakness that would practically beg for an attack on his regime.

"I suggest that Sano-*san* be appointed to help the judges investigate," Yanagisawa said.

"Fine," the shogun said, before Sano could forestall him. "Sano-*san,* you are appointed."

Yanagisawa and Yoritomo smiled identical smiles of cruel satisfaction. Sano's heart dropped. Now he would share the responsibility for any bad consequences that arose from the court's decision. His own fate and the forty-seven *rōnin*'s were intertwined.

"One last thing, Your Excellency," Yanagisawa said. "Sano-*san*'s investigations have a tendency to cause trouble. Last time he got your wife raped. Let's give him an extra incentive to do better this time."

Sano saw Yanagisawa getting ready to heap more trouble on him. "There's no need—"

"What kind of extra incentive?" the shogun interrupted.

"If the supreme court doesn't reach a satisfactory verdict, then Sano-*san* should be permanently assigned to a post at some distant location— let's say Kyushu," Yanagisawa said, "while his family remains in Edo as hostages to his good behavior."

"Very well," the shogun said.

9

RIDING HOME IN her palanquin, Reiko brimmed with thoughts about the *rōnin*'s mistress, but her companions seemed disinclined toward conversation. Chiyo sat gazing out the window at the street, where pedestrians clambered over snowbanks to enter shops that sold ceramic jars of pickles, root vegetables, salted fish, and fermented tofu. Masahiro rode his horse alongside the palanquin. He looked straight ahead, his expression somber and pensive.

Reiko waited until their procession turned onto the boulevard that led to Edo Castle, then said, "You're not happy that I agreed to help Okaru."

Chiyo reluctantly assented. "The whole business disturbs me."

Reiko cut to the heart of the problem. "You didn't like Okaru, did you?"

Chiyo hesitated. "She seems very sweet. But her background . . ."

A pang of disappointment chimed in Reiko. She'd thought her friend was more open-minded about people from other social classes. "Okaru can't help that her parents died and left her destitute. She became a teahouse girl because there was no other way to make a living."

"I'm not saying Okaru is a bad person because she's a teahouse girl." Chiyo sounded afraid of losing Reiko's good opinion. "What I mean is that people in her position do whatever they must in order to survive. Sometimes that includes taking advantage of other people."

"I see your point," Reiko had to admit. "But Okaru hasn't asked me for money or a job or a chance to move up in society, the way other people have."

"We've only just met her," Chiyo said. "We don't know her very well."

Reiko also had to admit that she tended to make snap judgments. But she said, "Okaru didn't strike me as being avaricious. All she wants is help for her friend Oishi."

"That brings us to another problem," Chiyo said gently. "We haven't even met Oishi. How can we say whether he deserves help?"

Logic chastened Reiko. "You're right. But we do know he performed the ultimate act of loyalty toward his master. That's a point in his favor."

"We also know that it's an illegal vendetta. That makes him a criminal."

"Not necessarily. Remember, Okaru said he indicated that there's more to the vendetta than meets the eye."

Chiyo was looking more uncomfortable by the moment. "We have only her word for that. And I understand that women in her position are often deceptive."

In order to win customers and earn money, girls like Okaru had to convince the men that they liked them even when they didn't. They could put that sort of skill to other uses. Still, Reiko prided herself on her intuition, even though she knew Chiyo was right to be wary of Okaru. "I didn't think Okaru was lying."

The palanquin neared Edo Castle, and Chiyo leaned forward, as though eager to escape this difficult conversation. "Even if she's not lying, the truth about the vendetta could be something that puts her—and Oishi—in an even worse light."

"Okaru is a teahouse girl and Oishi is a murderer," Reiko said with a touch of irritation. "How could anything be worse?"

"Facts might come out that could cost Oishi his slim chance to get out of his trouble alive," Chiyo said. "They could also implicate Okaru in Kira's murder, in which case she would be punished along with Oishi."

"Maybe so," Reiko said, "but I think the truth is worth finding out."

Chiyo regarded Reiko with doubt leavened by fondness. "I wonder if you want a mystery to solve."

Reiko bristled. She didn't like Chiyo's implication that she was solely motivated by selfish desire. "I do," she confessed. "But I wouldn't even consider getting involved in this if it weren't for wanting to help other people."

"Perhaps you should consider the person who's most important to you. Your husband. What might you be getting him into on Okaru's account?"

For the first time Reiko felt uncomfortable with Chiyo. Their friendship was exposing her faults—impulsiveness, too much taste for adventure, and imposing too much on Sano. Still, Reiko believed she'd done right to take the business of Okaru one step further.

"My husband wouldn't want me to turn my back on Okaru or Oishi," she said. "He's always been committed to discovering the truth and serving justice."

"But in this case?" Troubled, Chiyo shook her head. "It's bigger than just one girl, one man, and one murder. There are bound to be political repercussions, which could make things worse for your husband." She added, "I must say that I have a bad feeling about Okaru."

"Maybe you're right," Reiko conceded. "Maybe I shouldn't bring my husband into this. Maybe I should tell Okaru that I'm sorry, I can't help her after all."

The procession entered the main gate of Edo Castle and wound along the stone-walled passage. Masahiro rode his horse beside the palanquin, put his face in the window, and said to Reiko, "But you said you would help Okaru!" He'd been listening in on the conversation. "You and Father have always told me how important it is to keep promises. You always say that breaking a promise is dishonorable."

Reiko was always irritated yet amused when her clever son threw her own lessons back at her. "This situation is special. It may have been wrong for me to make that promise to Okaru. If so, then breaking it is the only right thing to do."

Chiyo nodded, but Masahiro exclaimed, "No! It would be unfair and mean."

"You shouldn't speak to your mother in that tone of voice," Chiyo said. She and Reiko and their families were so close that they disciplined each other's children with no hard feelings.

Masahiro bowed his head, distraught. "I'm sorry."

Reiko studied him curiously. "Why do you care so much about Okaru?"

"I don't," Masahiro said quickly. "It's just that she's poor and helpless. I feel sorry for her. That's all."

His compassion made Reiko proud of him. He wasn't growing up to be one of the many samurai who thought the lower classes were dirt under their feet. But she sensed that Masahiro had more on his mind besides mere sympathy for Okaru's plight.

"What else?" she asked.

Masahiro fiddled with the reins on his horse. He wouldn't look at Reiko. "When I was kidnapped, some people helped me. They were the two soldiers who let me out of the cage I was locked in. They didn't have to; they could have let me be killed."

Reiko listened in consternation. Masahiro rarely talked about that terrible time a little more than three years ago.

"They helped me even though they were risking their own lives." Masahiro paused. "I think about them sometimes. And I—well, that's why I want to help Okaru."

Reiko was so moved that tears stung her eyes. She said to Chiyo, "How can I refuse to come to Okaru's aid now?"

Chiyo relented with good grace. "Masahiro is right. A promise is a promise."

Still Reiko felt uncomfortable. Chiyo's misgivings about Okaru had rubbed off on her. And there was a new distance between her and Chiyo, a little coolness.

The procession arrived inside Sano's estate. Masahiro and the guards gave their horses over to the stable boys. The late-afternoon sunshine had mellowed to a golden glow that tinted the snow atop the mansion and the pine trees. The sky was a brilliant blue, striped by thin white clouds and crisscrossed by dark tree branches, like a winter quilt. Reiko smiled as she and Chiyo stepped out of their palanquin. On a cold, beautiful winter day like this, home seemed especially inviting.

Akiko ran out of the house to meet them. She hugged Reiko's legs, then Chiyo's.

"Then it's settled," Reiko said. "I'll tell my husband about Okaru and her story. He can decide whether to get involved."

"GET INVOLVED WITH what?" Sano walked toward the mansion.

He smiled at Reiko, who smiled back. Masahiro and Akiko hurried to greet him. "Hello, Father," Masahiro said, while Akiko cried, "Papa, Papa!"

Sano picked up Akiko. He clapped Masahiro on the shoulder and beamed at his son. He loved both his children passionately, but he felt a special pride in Masahiro. Masahiro was not only his firstborn, his only boy, and his heir, who would carry on their clan's bloodline; he was a fine, intelligent, talented, and good-natured child. One of Sano's biggest fears was that something would happen to Masahiro.

Chiyo bowed. "Greetings, Honorable Cousin." She addressed him formally but with affection.

After everyone went into the house, Reiko answered his question: "The forty-seven *rōnin* and their vendetta."

"So you've heard about that," Sano said, setting Akiko on her feet and hanging his swords in the entryway.

"Yes." Reiko helped him remove his hat and cloak.

He could tell that she had something on her mind, but she waited while he said, "I suppose the news is everywhere now. But there's something you apparently haven't heard yet: I'm already involved with the forty-seven *rōnin*."

Surprise halted Reiko in the act of hanging up her cloak. "You are? How?"

"The shogun ordered me to investigate Kira's murder," Sano said.

Eager for news, Reiko said, "Did you? What happened? Come inside. We'll talk there."

Akiko towed Chiyo off to play. Sano, Reiko, and Masahiro went to the private chambers, where they sat around the *kosatsu* and warmed themselves at the fire underneath. Sano explained how he'd tracked down the forty-seven *rōnin* and described the strange confrontation at Lord Asano's grave.

"So they're already under arrest," Reiko said.

"So it's over," Masahiro said. They both seemed disappointed.

"Not quite." Sano watched Reiko's and Masahiro's faces brighten. "There's a controversy about whether the forty-seven *rōnin* are honorable samurai who rightfully avenged their master and should be applauded or criminals who broke the law and should be sentenced to death." Sano explained about the supreme court. "I've just finished notifying the fourteen men who are to serve as judges. One of them is Magistrate Ueda."

"I'm glad," Reiko said. "My father is the one man who can absolutely be trusted to be honest and fair. How did he take the news?"

"With more enthusiasm than the other judges," Sano said. "I ruined their day. But he's intrigued by the legal issues in the case and he's excited about convening the court tomorrow." Although in his sixties, Magistrate Ueda still had a passion for the law.

"Now that there's a supreme court to decide about the forty-seven *rōnin*, doesn't that release you from involvement?" Reiko asked.

"Not exactly." Sano described how he'd been assigned to investigate the case for the supreme court.

"Chamberlain Yanagisawa again! Can't he leave us alone?"

Sano answered with a wry smile and an eloquent silence.

"But that's good!" Masahiro exclaimed. "You can save the forty-seven *rōnin*!"

Sano frowned. He wasn't pleased that his son had taken the *rōnin*'s side so quickly. But then he was partial to them, too, and it was he who'd taught Masahiro the principles of Bushido. "I'm not sure whether they should be saved."

"But you are going to investigate, aren't you?" Masahiro said.

"I don't have much choice," Sano said. "But I'm glad of the opportunity to see that justice is done."

He hesitated to mention the threat that came with his opportunity to regain the shogun's favor. He didn't want to worry Reiko. He wanted to shield Masahiro from adult problems.

"Maybe I can help." Reiko told Sano about the letter she'd received and her visit to Okaru.

"Well, you've been busy." It was Sano's turn to be surprised. "I can always trust you to turn up clues for my investigations, but this time you've done it before the investigation has really started." Drinking his tea, he pondered. "So Oishi's mistress says Oishi claims that the vendetta isn't what it seems."

"I know that's a vague clue," Reiko said apologetically.

"But it confirms my own feelings about the vendetta," Sano said. "The whole business is peculiar."

"Then you'll investigate Okaru's story?" Reiko asked eagerly.

"Yes," Sano said. "At this point I'm thankful for any clues at all."

"I'm glad. I'd like to help that poor girl."

Concern sobered Sano. "What I find out may not be good for her or Oishi. If it isn't, I can't protect them because she's someone you've befriended."

"I know." Yet it was obvious that Reiko couldn't help hoping the investigation would turn out well for Okaru. "Can I at least tell Okaru what's happened to Oishi and let her know you're looking into the matter?"

Sano nodded.

"Isn't there anything else we can do?" Masahiro jiggled his legs under the table.

Sano smiled at his restlessness. His son didn't like to sit idle any more than Reiko did. He'd inherited her impatience, her urge to take action.

"Let's wait and see." Sano glanced at Reiko, remembering times when she had taken part in his investigations, with near-disastrous results.

She must have seen something in his eyes besides misgivings based on past experience, because her brow furrowed. "What is it?"

"Masahiro, go play with your sister and Cousin Chiyo for a while," Sano said.

When he and Reiko were alone, there was no use trying to minimize the bad news. "The shogun decreed that if I don't lead the supreme court to a satisfactory decision, I'll be permanently assigned to a post in Kyushu. You and the children will be kept in Edo, to make sure I don't misbehave." Sano added, "You can guess who was responsible for that."

Reiko was so shocked that she sputtered. "Kyushu! That's the end of the earth!"

Sano couldn't disagree. Kyushu was the island of Japan farthest to the southwest, some two months' journey from Edo.

Reiko clasped her hands to her chest in horror as she absorbed the full implications of the shogun's threat. "We would never see you again!" Her fists clenched; bewilderment mixed with the anger that lit her eyes. "I know Yanagisawa is out to get you, but why did he do this?"

"Because he knows I've been threatened with death and escaped it so many times that the threat hardly fazes me anymore," Sano deduced.

"The shogun has always balked at killing me. Yanagisawa is hoping that this time the punishment will happen. And he knows that being separated from my family would hurt me worse than death."

"It would hurt all of us." Reiko threw her arms around Sano and clung to him. "I can't bear to lose you. Or for the children to lose their father."

Sano stroked her hair. "Don't worry, it won't come to that. Haven't I always managed to get out of trouble before?"

She looked up, still distraught. "But this is different from solving a murder. How can you lead the court to a satisfactory verdict? What would be 'satisfactory'? Condemning or pardoning the forty-seven *rōnin*? What kind of evidence would make either choice the right one?"

"No one knows at this point," Sano admitted. "But I have faith in the power of the truth. My discovering the truth about Kira's murder and the forty-seven *rōnin* will make things turn out right, somehow."

Although clearly doubtful, Reiko nodded, consoled.

Chiyo, Akiko, and Masahiro rejoined them as a maid brought dinner—miso soup with carrots, lotus root, and seaweed; roasted salmon; rice; pickled radish, ginger, and scallions. Sano realized that he was starving; he'd eaten nothing all day except a bowl of noodles from a food-stall. He and Reiko exchanged a glance; they tacitly agreed to keep the shogun's threat to themselves.

"Where will you begin your investigation?" Reiko asked.

"With the man at the center, the leader of the forty-seven *rōnin*," Sano said. "If something about their vendetta isn't what it seems, it may be Oishi himself."

IN THE OFFICE of his secluded compound inside Edo Castle, Chamberlain Yanagisawa sat at his desk. The lantern above his head illuminated a scroll spread before him. On the scroll was a chart he'd drawn, that showed which *daimyo* and top government officials were on his side, which were on Sano's, and which were neutral. Yanagisawa drummed his fingers on the chart. Although Sano had lost many allies, not enough of them had joined Yanagisawa's camp. There were too many men waiting to see how the political landscape shaped up, biding their time before they committed.

Yanagisawa hadn't managed to recruit a new ally in months. He had too narrow a margin, and he might start to slip before he achieved complete dominance.

Yoritomo came into the room. Yanagisawa's spirits lifted; he smiled. His son was the strongest weapon in his arsenal, his hold on the shogun, his best hope of ruling Japan. But Yoritomo was even more than a political pawn to Yanagisawa. His son was his pride and joy, the only person Yanagisawa loved, and who loved him. Yanagisawa had had many lovers, admirers, and sycophants over the years, but none had lasted. None had provided the bond of blood and affinity that he shared with Yoritomo. Now, as Yanagisawa beheld Yoritomo, he experienced a fear like cold fingers gripping his heart.

Love made a man vulnerable. He'd often used that fact against his enemies.

"Is everything all right?" Yanagisawa said offhandedly, trying not to show his concern for his son and the future.

"Yes, Father."

"How is the shogun?"

Yoritomo's smile slipped at the mention of his lord and master. "He's resting. The doctor gave him a potion to help him sleep."

Yanagisawa felt guilty because, unlike himself, Yoritomo got no pleasure from sex with men. And the shogun had been far younger and less repulsive when he and Yanagisawa had been lovers than he was now. Yoritomo never complained, but Yanagisawa knew he had to force himself to perform with the shogun, and Yoritomo wasn't oblivious to the sneers and gossip behind his back. Yoritomo proudly held his head up, but his role of male concubine was wearing on him after nine years. And Yanagisawa hated that he'd put his beloved son in such a position.

Yanagisawa said, "If there were any other way, I would never ask this of you." He didn't remember if he'd ever said it before. He felt a need to say it now.

Yoritomo nodded. They were so close, they could read each other's meanings. "I know, Father. I don't mind. It's my part in your plan to secure our future. I'll do whatever you think is best."

Yanagisawa had explained that unless they could gain control over the Tokugawa regime, their enemies would destroy them. It was true. If Yoritomo hadn't become the shogun's concubine, they both would have been dead long ago. Yanagisawa loved his son all the more because of the trust Yoritomo placed in him, because Yoritomo wasn't bitter, because Yoritomo loved him despite the humiliation Yoritomo had to endure. Yanagisawa wanted to tell Yoritomo how he felt, but he couldn't. Fathers and sons didn't speak of such things. Fathers used their sons as they thought right. Sons owed their fathers complete obedience.

Yanagisawa settled for saying, "You've done well."

Yoritomo beamed with delight at the praise, then noticed the chart on the desk. "Is something wrong?" he asked, ever sensitive to Yanagisawa's moods.

Yanagisawa rolled up the scroll. "No." He didn't want Yoritomo to worry or lose faith in him. "I was just counting up our allies. We have plenty."

"We should have even more, after today. That was brilliant, what you did to Sano. You threw him right into the middle of the forty-seven *rōnin* business, after he thought he was safe. You also thought of just the right punishment for him in the event that he fails. His wife and children are his weakness. He's sure to lose them, because nobody knows what the right verdict is. However it comes out, it will seem wrong." Yoritomo's eyes shone with admiration.

The praise brought Yanagisawa a warm flush of pleasure. A lot of people praised him, but they were just currying favor. Yoritomo was the only one who was sincere. "With luck, the forty-seven *rōnin* should be the end of Sano. All we need to do is let matters run their course."

Apprehension clouded Yoritomo's face. "Sano is the one who's been lucky in the past. You've been trying to get rid of him for fourteen years, and he's still here." His brow darkened with the memory of the evils that Sano had done to him. "And he usually ends up beating us."

Yanagisawa was painfully aware of that, but he said, "Never fear. If things go too well for Sano, I can change that."

10

THE NEXT MORNING Sano and his troops retraced their path along the southern highway. The weather was even colder than yesterday. The men's faces were muffled up to their eyeballs in scarves; the horses wore quilted caparisons. Clouds lurked around the edges of a blue sky that seemed paled by a scrim of ice between heaven and earth. The sun was a blinding white crystal that gave off no warmth. The thin top layer of the snow that had melted yesterday had refrozen into a crust that the horses' hooves broke with loud, jagged sounds. Sano raised his voice above the noise while he told Hirata and Detectives Marume and Fukida about the *rōnin*'s mistress.

"Do you think Oishi meant that Kira's murder wasn't a simple revenge?" Fukida asked.

"Could he and his comrades have had some other motive?" Marume asked.

"Those questions have been on my mind since Reiko told me Okaru's story," Sano said. "I hope we'll find some answers this morning. The supreme court will convene this afternoon, and I'd like to bring the judges some evidence to review."

He noticed that Hirata wasn't listening to the conversation. Hirata seemed distracted, perhaps because last night Sano had told him about the shogun's threat. Hirata must be worried about what it meant for him. Hirata's eyes darted; he stole glances over his shoulder. Sano knew about the mysterious man who'd been stalking Hirata, and observed that Hirata seemed even more vigilantly on the lookout than usual.

They reached the Hosokawa estate. Dismounting, Sano glanced around the barracks. As he approached the gate, he saw Hirata pause by the bushes outside the wall. Then Hirata joined Sano at the guardhouse.

Two sentries stepped out. Sano said, "We want to see the prisoners."

The sentries summoned a servant, who led Sano, Hirata, and the detectives into the barracks. These had the same form as those in every samurai estate—buildings divided into sparsely furnished rooms where the retainers lived. Sano and his men passed through an entryway crammed with cloaks, shoes, and weapons, just like in the barracks at home. He smelled the same smell of male sweat and tobacco smoke. Talk and laughter issued from a room where a crowd of samurai knelt on the *tatami* floor, eating their morning meal from tray tables. They looked up as Sano and his comrades crossed the threshold. An abrupt silence fell. The samurai set down teacups, chopsticks, and bowls of noodles. Cheerful expressions sobered. Everyone bowed in stiff, formal unison.

"My apologies for interrupting your meal." Sano was puzzled to see many more men than the sixteen prisoners Hirata had brought yesterday. And they bore no resemblance to the scruffy, bloodstained *rōnin* he'd arrested.

They were all clean, dressed in fresh clothes, their faces and the crowns of their heads neatly shaven, their hair oiled and tied in topknots. Then a group of them moved away from their tables to kneel by the walls. Their faces showed guilt, chagrin, and defiance. Sano spotted the crests on their garments: They were Hosokawa clan retainers, fraternizing with the prisoners. It was obvious which side the Hosokawa had taken in the controversy.

Turning his attention to the *rōnin,* Sano caught them staring at him. They dropped their gazes. He counted only fifteen men, most of them in their thirties or forties. Some wore bandages over wounds. He didn't recognize Oishi among them. They seemed confused: With their leader absent, they didn't know what to do. Sano again had the sense that they were parts of a single creature. Their heads swiveled toward the youngest *rōnin,* who leaped to his feet.

"What do you want?" His voice was shaky with fear. Sano recognized him as Oishi's teenaged son, Chikara.

"Just to talk," Sano said.

The seated *rōnin* visibly relaxed. They thought he'd come to deliver them to their death, Sano supposed. They seemed less staunchly resigned to their fate than they had while standing over Kira's head in the graveyard. Sano said, "Where is Oishi?"

"With Lord Hosokawa," Chikara said.

"I'll talk to Oishi," Sano told his detectives. "You and Hirata-*san* will interview these prisoners."

A scraping noise and the sound of quick, departing footsteps startled Sano. He looked at the empty space where Chikara had been standing. A partition that had been closed a moment ago was now open. Sano nodded to Hirata, who went after Chikara while the detectives settled themselves among the *rōnin*. Sano went in search of Lord Hosokawa and Oishi.

He found them in the mansion, in Lord Hosokawa's private office, a grander version of Sano's own. Heat shimmered up through decorative grilles in the *tatami* floor, from braziers underneath. Furniture was spangled with gold crests. Oishi and Lord Hosokawa knelt at the desk, conversing over ledgers. When Sano entered the room, they raised their heads.

Oishi, like the other *rōnin*, had washed, shaved, groomed his hair, and dressed in new clothes. His color had improved; he didn't look as tired or ill. His fierce eyes burned brighter. He gazed at Sano, expectant yet cautious.

Sano exchanged bows and greetings with Lord Hosokawa, whom he knew slightly.

"Oishi-*san* has been giving me ideas for managing my finances." Lord Hosokawa's worried face took on a defensive cast. "They worked very well in Harima Province. I'm eager to try them in my domain."

"I see." Sano saw that Oishi had become friends with Lord Hosokawa overnight. He wasn't surprised, even though Hirata had mentioned that Lord Hosokawa had balked at taking in the prisoners yesterday. Lord Hosokawa probably admired Oishi as an example of samurai loyalty and hoped that if he himself ever needed avenging, his retainers would rise to the occasion as Oishi had for Lord Asano.

"You're not taking him away, are you?" Lord Hosokawa sounded upset by the idea.

"Not yet." Sano explained about the supreme court and his investigation. "I have some questions for Oishi. Is there a place where he and I can talk in private?"

"Here." Lord Hosokawa rose on tottery knees and left.

Sano knelt across the desk from Oishi. The *rōnin* folded his arms. He reminded Sano of a falcon tethered to its perch but not tame. He calmly waited for Sano to speak first.

This interview was different from others Sano had conducted during past investigations. Then, his goal had been to figure out whether someone had committed murder. Now he was on unfamiliar ground, not knowing what he needed to find out and uncertain of what questions to ask. He let himself be guided by experience, which had taught him to learn every detail of a case that might clear up ambiguities and indicate a suspect's guilt or innocence. Thinking back on the events that had led to the murder, he identified one ambiguity that he would like cleared up, even though he knew who the killers were.

"Why was Lord Asano so angry at Kira?" he asked.

Oishi's slanted eyebrows twitched upward before he could hide his surprise: He hadn't expected this question. But he immediately recovered. "Kira made Lord Asano's life miserable." His raspy voice was harsh but controlled. He swelled with portent, a man about to confide a long-kept secret. "I'll tell you exactly how."

1701 April

THE FIRST, FATEFUL meeting between Lord Asano and Kira Yoshinaka took place on a cold spring afternoon at Edo Castle. The old master of ceremonies sat on the dais in his office and peered down his nose at Lord Asano, Oishi, and their attendants, kneeling below him.

"So you're to be the host for the imperial envoys from Miyako?" Dressed in satin court robes, Kira was the picture of haughty elegance.

"Uh, yes." Lord Asano was thirty-four years old but as socially awkward as a youth, and nervous whenever he had to leave his home province and appear in the capital.

"I am to instruct you on how to entertain the envoys," Kira said, eyeing Lord Asano with disgust and condescension. "I'll do my best so that you do not embarrass yourself or the shogun's court."

Oishi took a dislike to Kira. Lord Asano had attained the rank of *daimyo* at age eight, when his father died, and Oishi had taken a major role in raising him. Lord Asano was like a younger brother to Oishi, who hated seeing him disrespected.

Lord Asano cringed. "Many thanks, Kira-*san*."

His fear seemed to disgust Kira all the more. Oishi had often told Lord Asano that he should fight back instead of meekly submitting, but he couldn't. He ruled his domain ably enough under Oishi's guidance, but he wasn't cut out to swim with the sharks in Edo.

Kira preened because he'd cowed a *daimyo* rich enough to buy or sell the likes of him. He waited, an expectant look on his disdainful face. Lord Asano nodded to the attendants. They stepped forward, bearing gifts for Kira.

"Honorable Kira-*san*, please—please allow me to present you with a token of—of my appreciation," Lord Asano said, blushing.

As Kira beheld the finely crafted jade vases and lacquer writing box, his face registered disappointment, then indignation. "Are you forgetting something?"

". . . No," Lord Asano said, puzzled.

Oishi realized that Kira wasn't satisfied with the gifts, even though they were suitable for the occasion.

"Please allow me to mention that your success depends on me," Kira said to Lord Asano. "I will ask you again: Are you forgetting something?"

Now Lord Asano understood that Kira was asking for a bribe. Objection lessened his fear. He was an honest man who deplored bribery. "I haven't forgotten anything."

Kira sat back in surprised confusion. Oishi saw him wonder if Lord Asano was too stupid to take a hint, then realize that Lord Asano had deliberately defied him. "Very well," he said in a voice coated with frost. "Suit yourself."

That night, when Oishi and Lord Asano dined alone together at Lord Asano's estate in Edo, Oishi said, "You must bribe Kira."

"No," Lord Asano said, even though his hands shook so hard with anxiety that he fumbled his chopsticks. "I won't surrender like a coward."

"It's my duty to advise you to bribe him and swallow your pride. If you don't, Kira is bound to retaliate."

"Let him."

The next day, rehearsals for the ceremony began. As Lord Asano practiced marching up to the dais in the reception chamber where the imperial envoys would sit, Kira exclaimed, "You idiot! You're supposed to take eighteen steps, not nineteen!"

Lord Asano faltered. "You told me nineteen steps."

"No, I didn't." Kira grinned like a bully in a group of smaller children. He had the power of his position; he could destroy lives. Rumor said he'd done it often.

"Yes, you did," Oishi said from his place by the door. "I heard you, too."

He and Kira locked gazes. Oishi's scowl told Kira that if he continued to play games with Lord Asano, he would have to reckon with Oishi. Kira responded with a sniff. His lessons continued to be so confusing, and so peppered with insults, that Lord Asano couldn't learn the lines of his speech to the envoys.

"If he slips up during the ceremony, it will reflect badly on you," Oishi told Kira.

"My reputation is unassailable," Kira scoffed. "He will bear the blame for his mistakes."

It was true, as far as Oishi could see. If Lord Asano refused to take Kira's bullying along with the instructions, he must meet the envoys without any idea what to do or say. The audience at the ceremony would witness and scorn his failure. Lord Asano toiled and suffered under Kira's tutelage, while steadfastly refusing to give Kira a bribe.

"Don't let him get to you," Oishi urged as Lord Asano practiced the ritual after the lessons, until late at night.

But the advice was easier given than followed, especially when Kira tormented Lord Asano in public. At a banquet in the palace, Oishi and Lord Asano heard Kira say, "There's the country boor. They apparently don't learn any manners in Harima Province."

The other guests laughed. Lord Asano went pale with rage.

Eventually, he snapped.

"I CAN'T DESCRIBE Lord Asano's attack on Kira," Oishi said. "I wasn't there."

While listening to Oishi's story, Sano had found himself too caught up in it to judge it. Oishi had a talent for bringing characters to vivid life. Sano had experienced outrage at Kira's behavior and sympathy toward Lord Asano. Which was what Oishi had intended, Sano realized now, as they sat together in Lord Hosokawa's office.

"Your story offers a logical explanation for why Lord Asano attacked Kira and puts you in a good light," Sano said. "But is it the true one?"

"It's true," Oishi said, unruffled by Sano's skepticism.

Sano began to understand how Oishi had become the leader of the forty-seven *rōnin*. Oishi was a powerful personality. Sano must take care to avoid falling under his thrall. "After the attack, why didn't Lord Asano say what his quarrel with Kira was?"

"Put yourself in Lord Asano's position. You were picked on by an old man; you were too weak to make him treat you with respect. Would you want everyone to know? Wouldn't you rather take it to your grave?"

"That's a good point."

"Besides, Lord Asano knew that explaining why he attacked Kira wouldn't have saved him. He drew a weapon inside Edo Castle. He was going to die. Telling shameful tales on himself wouldn't have made any difference."

"It might have made one very important difference," Sano said. "Kira might have been punished for starting a feud with Lord Asano."

"Kira was punished." Triumph resounded in Oishi's harsh voice. "Lord Asano knew he could depend on me to see that the bastard got his comeuppance."

"But you took almost two years to do it." This was another issue that Sano wanted to resolve, in case it had any bearing on the truth about the murder and relevance to the supreme court's verdict. "Why did you wait so long?"

"I'm getting to that." Memory coalesced in his eyes, like a flock of ravens gathering around carrion, as Oishi began the next episode in his story.

11

1701 April

LANTERNS GLOWED IN a courtyard, around a square of straw mats covered with a white rug. Lord Asano knelt on the rug, dressed in a white silk robe. A table before him held a short sword on a stand and a scroll bearing the poem he'd written. His youthful face was rigid with terror, misery, and his effort to withhold an unseemly display of emotions. Oishi stood behind Lord Asano, concealing his own anguish behind a grim expression, his sword drawn. Along the courtyard, government officials stood silent under the unearthly radiance of blossoming cherry trees. Petals fell like pink snow, symbols of life's transience.

Lord Asano opened his robe with hands that shook violently. His ragged breathing was the only sound in the cool, quiet night. As Oishi looked down at Lord Asano, he wasn't sure he could perform his part in the ritual. But it would be his last service for his beloved lord, and perform it he must. Hoping that Lord Asano's last words would give him strength, Oishi glanced at the poem.

> *More than the cherry blossoms,*
> *Inviting a wind to blow them away,*
> *I am wondering what to do*
> *With the remaining springtime.*

Tears almost blinded Oishi. That his master wouldn't live to see the rest of the spring! Justice had been meted out with terrible efficiency. This morning Lord Asano had drawn a sword inside Edo Castle. This afternoon the shogun had ruled that Lord Asano must die tonight.

Lord Asano reached for the sword. He grasped the hilt in both hands, the weapon pointed at his abdomen. The blade wavered. Straining to hold it still, he looked up at Oishi.

A memory seized Oishi. In the Asano clan stronghold of Ako Castle, the previous Lord Asano lay dying. His family and top retainers watched him draw his last breath. Oishi looked across the bed at Lord Asano's son, the eight-year-old boy who had just become *daimyo*. The boy turned solemn, frightened, pleading eyes on Oishi, his special friend among his father's men. Oishi nodded, telling the new Lord Asano that he would be there to guide him and protect him for his whole life. *I will do right by you.* And Lord Asano nodded, reassured.

Twenty-two years later, Oishi saw the same pleading in Lord Asano's eyes. Love and heartache flooded Oishi. He nodded. Lord Asano nodded, turned away, and sat straighter. Uttering a loud cry, he thrust the blade into his gut.

Oishi beheaded Lord Asano before he could feel any pain. Blood spattered the poem. The audience gasped. Cherry blossoms fell. Oishi gazed down at the corpse of his master, and rage burned through his grief. He silently vowed, *I will do right by you.*

By the next month, the government had dissolved the house of Asano, officially wiping the clan out of existence. Family members huddled inside Ako Castle while Oishi and the thousands of other retainers massed atop the walls and watched troops marching toward the castle. The men clamored in outrage: "We'll fight!"

"Don't be fools!" Oishi shouted. "There are too many of them! We'll be slaughtered! We must live to avenge Lord Asano!"

Although the men grumbled, they allowed Oishi to herd them from the castle. They stood beside their horses, their possessions in the saddlebags. Oishi led out the Asano family, thankful that Lord Asano's wife needn't see this. She was in Edo, where the law forced *daimyo* wives to reside as hostages to their husbands' good behavior. So were Oishi's own wife and children. Oishi helped the Asano family into oxcarts piled with the few belongings they were allowed to keep. The women and children sobbed.

So did many retainers as they watched the army arrive. This was the worst day of their life, every samurai's worst nightmare. Oishi couldn't believe it was happening to him. He stared in mute shock as troops filed into the castle and filed out carrying furniture, trunks of money, and priceless heirlooms. No one in the Asano group could bear to watch, but everyone stayed until the next day, when the loot was borne off to Edo to be received by the shogun and the army was gone except for a platoon that occupied the castle. Then they faced the terrible moment they'd been dreading.

They were homeless, destitute. The retainers were *rōnin,* stripped of honor, utterly humiliated. They turned to Oishi, even though he was no longer their superior.

"Where are we going to go?" they cried.

"To Edo," Oishi said. "We have work to do there."

But as the procession moved down the highway, it shrank. Some men stayed at teahouses in the villages to find comfort in drink and the arms of prostitutes. Some went off to seek their fortunes alone. Suicides drastically thinned the ranks. The procession left a string of graves in its wake. Oishi arrived in Edo with only a hundred men left. The government seized the Asano estate in Edo. Oishi put Lady Asano in a Buddhist convent and moved his family to lodgings in the Nihonbashi merchant quarter. Then he began a campaign to get the house of Asano reinstated. He wrote letters to government officials. He called in every favor. Nothing worked. His contacts said the shogun couldn't change his mind because that would make him look weak, and he would never reinstate the house of Asano. They told Oishi to make the best of his new life as a commoner.

Instead, Oishi turned his attention to his next duty. One day he walked to Kira's estate. He was so consumed by murderous rage that he could feel his heart burning black. Kira had brought about Lord Asano's destruction. Oishi must make Kira pay.

But Kira evidently expected the Asano *rōnin* to try to kill him. Guards ringed the estate. Oishi saw Kira come out, accompanied by fifty soldiers. Oishi kept surveillance on Kira long enough to know that he never let down his guard. Revenge seemed impossible.

Oishi fell into a state of deep despair. He began drinking because wine eased his pain. He frequented teahouses and stayed out all night. The change in him infuriated his wife.

"You're disgusting! What's the matter with you?" Ukihashi demanded. She'd once been a pretty, sedate woman, but losing her home, her social status, and her servants had made her wretched and shrill. "I know you're upset, but what about us?" She waved her hand at their two little daughters and their fourteen-year-old son. The children sat by a cold hearth, eating millet, the food of poor people. "Have you forgotten that you have a family to support?"

"Shut up!" Oishi couldn't bear her criticism. "Leave me alone."

They quarreled every day until Oishi said, "I've had enough. I'm leaving."

"Good riddance," Ukihashi said bitterly.

Oishi made Chikara go with him. He divorced his wife before he left Edo. It was summer, more than a year after Lord Asano's death. He and Chikara went to Miyako. They earned their rice by working as bodyguards for a merchant, living behind the shop. Oishi continued drinking. At the Ichiriki teahouse he met a beautiful young prostitute named Okaru. With her he found the first pleasure he'd experienced since Lord Asano's death.

After too many drunken binges, his employer threw him out. Oishi couldn't afford to pay Okaru. He couldn't ask his son for the money, because Chikara hated Okaru, hated that Oishi had broken up their family. Father and son became estranged.

Okaru said, "You needn't pay me anymore. I love you. I'll take care of you."

Oishi loved her, too; she made him feel young and hopeful again. He moved into her lodgings. Okaru continued to entertain her customers. Oishi lived on her. She pampered him, but he couldn't make peace with his circumstances. One day he got so drunk that he collapsed on the street. Passersby jeered. A man stood over him and said, "Oishi-*san*? Is that you?"

His square, pugnacious face was vaguely familiar. Oishi couldn't recall his name but recognized him as a merchant from Satsuma.

"Why are you lying in the gutter? What happened?" Catching a whiff of liquor, the Satsuma man recoiled in disgust. "The rumors are true, then. You've become a bum."

He announced, "This is Oishi Kuranosuke, former retainer of Lord

Asano. He doesn't have the courage to avenge his master's death. Faithless beast!" He trampled on Oishi and spat in his face. "You are unworthy of the name of samurai!"

A crowd joined in the taunting, kicking, and spitting. The pain brought Oishi to his senses. Something within him shifted, like fractured ground settling back into place after an earthquake. That day was the last time he ever drank. That day he vowed to fulfill the promise he'd made to Lord Asano. That day he began his journey toward vengeance and redemption.

"YOU KNOW THE rest," Oishi said to Sano.

They gazed at each other across Lord Hosokawa's desk, like two generals across a battlefield. "Not quite," Sano said. "It's a long way from a gutter in Miyako to a slaughter in Edo."

Once more he'd become thoroughly engaged in Oishi's tale, against his will because it had taken him to places he didn't want to go. He'd always wondered how he would handle the most extreme situations a samurai could face. What would it be like to assist in the ritual suicide of someone he loved as much as Oishi had apparently loved Lord Asano?

Sano didn't know whether he could do it.

How would it be to feel such love for his lord that he would give up his family and dedicate his life to revenge?

In his deepest heart Sano admitted that he didn't love the shogun. He didn't know whether he could follow the Way of the Warrior that far. He felt caught between admiration for Oishi, who had proved himself truer to Bushido than most samurai ever did, and antagonism toward Oishi for exposing his own fears and self-doubts.

"Fill in the gaps in your story," Sano ordered.

"In the summer of the year after Lord Asano died, I went looking for his other retainers," Oishi said. "I gathered forty-six of them together, including my son."

Could Sano lead his own son down the same dangerous path that Oishi had led Chikara? That hardly bore imagining. But it was a son's duty to follow his father. Sano and Masahiro came from a long line of fathers and sons who'd marched into battle together. But would Sano bring Masahiro in on an illegal vendetta, a crime? Shouldn't a father protect his child?

"I told my comrades that it was time to avenge Lord Asano," Oishi went on. "We formed a conspiracy. It took almost six months to set our plans. Then we walked to Edo, which took us another two months. When we got here, we rested for a few days. Then we went after Kira."

Sano saw a battle raging during a snowstorm, as if Oishi's memory had brought the scene into the room. He blinked to dispel the vision. He got a firm grip on his objectivity. "You left something out."

An annoyed frown crossed Oishi's face. "What?"

"Your mistress. Okaru. She loved you and cared for you and bedded other men to support you. You left her behind in Miyako. Or so you thought. She's here in town."

Oishi's slanted eyebrows flew up in alarm. "No. She can't be."

"Why aren't you happy to hear that the woman you love is near?" Sano asked.

Oishi massaged his jaw with his fingers. Sano sensed that Oishi wanted time to think about how this development might affect him.

"She followed you to Edo," Sano said.

"How do you know?" Oishi asked.

"She wrote a letter to my wife." Sano explained what the letter had said, then mentioned Reiko's visit with Okaru.

Oishi spat out his breath, shook his head. "She thought she could save me. She's so naïve, and so wrong."

"Maybe not wrong. As you must have guessed by now, there's some confusion about what to do with you and your comrades." Sano told Oishi about the controversy in the government, the formation of the supreme court. He watched Oishi massage his jaw harder. "Whether you live or die depends on whether I find evidence to prove that your actions were justified even though you broke the law."

"What does this have to do with Okaru?" Oishi asked.

"Okaru is a witness in my investigation. She's offered the first evidence in your favor."

Distrust narrowed Oishi's eyes. "What evidence?"

"She told my wife that the vendetta isn't as simple as it appears." Sano had a distinct, puzzling impression that this prospect of a reprieve disturbed Oishi although it should please him. "She said you told her so."

Oishi sat perfectly still and calm, but Sano perceived shock reverberating through him like a gunshot in a tunnel. "What else did Okaru say I said?"

"Nothing else." Was that relief Sano saw in Oishi's hooded eyes? "She claims you refused to explain what you meant. Perhaps you would explain it to me now."

"I can't."

Sano was incredulous because Oishi didn't jump at the chance to put his actions in a better light. "Not even to save yourself and your comrades?"

"I actually don't remember saying that to Okaru." A crestfallen grin flexed Oishi's thick mouth. "I was drunk most of the time I was with her. I did a lot of incoherent rambling. She must be mistaken."

"My wife says Okaru seemed sure of what she'd heard."

Oishi thrust out his jaw; belligerence flared his nostrils wider. "The vendetta is exactly what it seems: Kira destroyed Lord Asano. My comrades and I destroyed Kira. We abided by the samurai code of honor. It's as straightforward as that."

But Sano detected a fissure in Oishi's conviction. "I don't believe you. If you were being so straightforward and honorable, you would have all committed *seppuku* to atone for breaking the shogun's law. Why did you 'await orders' instead?"

"It seemed like the right thing to do," Oishi said stubbornly.

Increasingly mystified, Sano said, "What kind of orders were you expecting?"

Silence descended, like a fog that was invisible but nonetheless hid the truth about the case, a truth that Sano suspected was stranger than he could imagine.

"We had no expectations. But maybe we did right to wait," Oishi said with a glimmer of amusement. "We're still alive, aren't we?"

Sano felt irate because Oishi was playing with him and he had no idea what the game was. Vexed by his own conflicted feelings toward the man, he stood. "Very well. Don't answer my questions if you don't want to. I can ask your comrades."

"Go ahead." Oishi stood, too; he'd regained the composure he'd lost while talking about Okaru. "They'll corroborate my story. The vendetta is exactly what you see."

12

"ARE YOU READY to go?" Masahiro asked Reiko as she sat at her dressing table.

"Not quite." Reiko anchored her hair in place with combs. "We have to get some food to take to Okaru."

Chiyo came into the room with a stack of lacquer lunch boxes that gave off the delicious aroma of miso, fried dumplings, and grilled fish. "Here it is."

"Good," Masahiro said. "Can we go now?"

He jittered with impatience to see Okaru again. She'd been on his mind since yesterday, and he'd been so excited about this second visit that he'd hardly slept last night.

At last he and Reiko and Chiyo emerged into the cold, clear day. The women climbed into the palanquin with the lunch boxes. Masahiro mounted his horse. The guards assembled. The bearers shouldered the palanquin's poles. Masahiro rode ahead of the procession, so deep in thought that he didn't notice the city sights he usually enjoyed.

He'd never been interested in girls. They giggled too much. They talked about boring things like clothes, and they had silly quarrels. He was too busy with important things to pay attention to them. But Okaru was different. She was the most beautiful girl he'd ever seen. She'd stirred up unfamiliar, exciting feelings in him. When he'd told his mother why he wanted to help Okaru, he hadn't been completely honest. Yes, Okaru was poor and helpless and he felt sorry for her; and yes, he did want to pass on the kindness that had been shown to him; but there was more to it than that. He didn't know exactly what.

When he and his companions neared the inn, a crowd was gathered outside. People pressed up against the gate, peering over one another's shoulders. As Masahiro dismounted, and the women climbed out of the palanquin, he heard the crowd shouting, "Let us in! We want to see the *rōnin*'s mistress!"

"Do they mean Okaru?" Masahiro asked.

"It would seem so," Reiko said. "But how did they find out that she's here?"

A panel in the gate opened to reveal the innkeeper's face. "This is private property," he shouted. The crowd booed. "Go away!"

Reiko called to him, "We're friends of Okaru. We visited her yesterday. Don't you remember?" She stood on tiptoe and waved over the crowd. "She'll want to see us."

"Yes, I remember," the innkeeper said, "but I can't open the gate for you, because everyone else will get in, too."

Masahiro began pushing people away from the gate. Reiko's guards held the crowd back while the innkeeper let Masahiro, Reiko, and Chiyo carry the lunch boxes to the guest quarters. Reiko knocked on Okaru's door.

"Who is it?" Okaru called.

The sound of her voice sent a shiver of anticipation through Masahiro. After Reiko identified herself, Okaru flung open the door and exclaimed, "Oh, Lady Reiko! Thank the gods you've come back!" She wore a deep pink kimono; her hair was studded with gold butterfly combs. She looked even more beautiful than she had yesterday. She smiled at Masahiro and said, "Hello."

Too shy and confused to answer, Masahiro could only stare.

"Okaru!" loud voices called. "Okaru!"

Faces cropped up above the fence as men from the crowd pulled themselves onto it. The men pointed and shouted, "There she is!"

Okaru cringed like a fawn cornered by a hunter. Reiko hurried Okaru, Chiyo, and Masahiro into the room and shut the door. Okaru sank to her knees and said, "Those people have been bothering me all morning. I've been so scared."

"Why are you alone?" Reiko asked. "Where's your servant?"

"She went out to get us something to eat. We can't afford the meals here."

"We've brought food," Reiko said. She and Chiyo unpacked the boxes.

"Oh, how wonderful!" Okaru fell upon the food. "You're so kind!"

Her fingers wielded the chopsticks so quickly yet so gracefully. Her perfect little teeth shone as she took each bite of dumpling, pickle, and rice cake. Her soft lips glistened. She licked them with her delicate pink tongue. Masahiro was captivated.

"How did those people find out that you're Oishi's . . . fiancée?" Chiyo asked.

"Yesterday I told the maids who cleaned my room. They brought a friend of theirs—a man who writes news broadsheets. I talked to him. This morning they said he's been selling my story all over town." Chagrined, Okaru said, "I was flattered until those people came and started demanding to see me, as if I were a freak at a peep show."

"You would have been wiser to keep your business private," Chiyo said.

Masahiro sensed that Chiyo didn't like Okaru.

Okaru hung her head. "I realize that now, but they were so interested, and so kind. It was stupid. I'm sorry."

"In the future, don't be so frank with strangers," Reiko said.

Masahiro agreed that Okaru should have kept quiet, but his mother and Chiyo shouldn't blame her; she was too innocent to know that not everyone could be trusted.

Okaru nodded humbly. "Thank you for your advice." She finished eating and said, "I'm so worried about Oishi. Have you any news of him?"

"My husband has put him under house arrest," Reiko said, and explained about the supreme court.

Breathless with relief, Okaru clasped a hand to her bosom. "At least he's still alive."

A pain as sharp as a stab pierced Masahiro's heart. Somehow, it hurt to see how much she loved Oishi. Masahiro was beginning to dislike Oishi, even though yesterday he'd admired the man as an example of samurai honor. Everything had seemed so simple then. The world had turned into a strange, confusing place overnight.

"Is there a chance that Oishi will be pardoned?" Okaru said eagerly.

"Perhaps only a small one," Reiko said. "Many important people are in favor of condemning all of the forty-seven *rōnin* to death. My husband is investigating the case. Everything depends on what he learns. I told him what you said Oishi told you about the vendetta. He promised to take it into account. But it would help if you could remember anything else Oishi said."

Okaru shook her head sadly. "I've tried and tried, but I really don't remember."

The door slid open, pushed so hard that it crashed against its frame. A woman stumbled into the room. She was breathing hard; she brought with her a stale, sour smell. Tall and very thin, she wore a baggy coat and had long, gray-streaked hair twisted carelessly in a knot. Her face was square, her fine features emaciated.

"Which one of you is Okaru?" Her eyes, red and watery from the cold, blazed with anger.

Everyone stared at her in surprise. Reiko said, "Who are you?"

The woman's gaze settled on Okaru. She advanced on the girl, who leaned back, intimidated. She ignored everyone else. Masahiro thought she seemed angry, satisfied, and sad at the same time. "My name is Uki-hashi. I'm Oishi's wife."

Shock parted Okaru's lips. "What—why—?"

As Ukihashi gazed down at Okaru, her expression turned to disgust. "Merciful gods, you're less than half his age." The anger in her eyes flared. "You stole my husband!"

"No," Okaru said in a faint voice. "I didn't—"

"Don't pretend to be so innocent," Ukihashi shouted. "You seduced him. But he's as guilty as you are." Fists clenched, she spat her words into Okaru's face. "Because of him, I've come down in the world. Once I was as pretty as you are, but look at me now!" She flung out her arms. She wore ragged gloves, her fingers bare. Her face had dry, scaly patches of skin; her lips were cracked and raw. Her padded coat was faded, stained, ripped, and leaking feathers.

"I'm sorry." Okaru looked so ashamed that Masahiro felt bad for her. "But, you see, Oishi had already divorced you by the time he met—"

Ukihashi slapped Okaru's face. "You evil little whore!"

Okaru yelped in pain. Ukihashi grabbed the front of her robe, hauled her to her feet, and shook her, spewing curses. "Help!" Okaru cried.

Masahiro rushed to Ukihashi and tried to pull her off Okaru. But Ukihashi was stronger than she looked. Hauling Okaru across the room, she towed Masahiro along.

"Stop!" Reiko ordered.

Ukihashi dragged Okaru out the door and began hitting her. "Thief! You couldn't get a man of your own, so you took mine!"

She shoved Okaru. The girl screamed, fell off the veranda, and landed in the snow. Ukihashi wrenched free of Masahiro, pounced on Okaru, and clawed at her eyes. Okaru struggled, crying, "Leave me alone, you crazy woman!"

Men watching over the fence cheered. The inn's other guests came out of their rooms to see what was happening. The proprietor rushed over and said, "She climbed the fence. I couldn't stop her." He wrung his hands as the two women fought. "Will someone please break it up?"

Masahiro waded into the snow. Ukihashi had Okaru on the ground under her knees. He pulled on Ukihashi while she mashed snow into Okaru's face. Okaru squealed. Ukihashi turned on Masahiro and shrieked, "Stay out of this!"

She punched his face. He yelled as the blow exploded against his nose and propelled him backward. He landed on his buttocks in the snow. Hot, salty-sweet blood trickled down his throat and spilled from his nostrils. He heard his mother call her guards. They rushed in and tore Ukihashi away from Okaru. It took three men to hold Ukihashi while she struggled and screamed and the spectators cheered. Okaru sat up, coughing and spitting out snow. Reiko and Chiyo hurried to Masahiro.

"Are you hurt?" Reiko asked anxiously. "Oh, your nose is bleeding!" Chiyo offered a handkerchief. Reiko pressed it against his nose. "Tilt your head back. Come inside."

As he obeyed, he saw Okaru turn her head in his direction. His face went hot with embarrassment. That he'd tried to protect her and had his nose bloodied by an old woman! And now he was being treated like a baby.

"Leave me alone," he said gruffly. "I'm all right."

Chiyo helped Okaru to her feet and into the room. Masahiro tried to shrug off his mother as she continued fussing over him. Reiko removed the handkerchief long enough to see that blood was still oozing from his nose. "Stay still. Don't be so impatient."

Masahiro couldn't bear to look at Okaru. He couldn't help looking. She smiled at him while she wiped her face and hair with a towel. Embarrassment turned to humiliation.

Lieutenant Tanuma appeared at the door. "Lady Reiko, what do you want us to do with that woman? Should we let her go?"

"No," Reiko said. "I want to talk to her." She turned to Masahiro. "Keep your head back and keep pressing on your nose with the handkerchief."

"Should I come with you or stay with Masahiro?" Chiyo said.

"You can go," Okaru said. "I'll be here."

When his mother and Chiyo left, Masahiro panicked. He'd fought in battles and faced death like a man, but he was terrified to be alone with Okaru. What would he say to her? Masahiro clutched the handkerchief against his nose and stared desperately at the ceiling, as if he could find the answer written there.

Okaru knelt beside him. He glanced sideways at her. She smiled again. Masahiro realized how stupid he must look. He tilted his head down and cautiously sniffed.

"Has the bleeding stopped?" Okaru asked.

"I think so."

"That's good."

Shyness tied Masahiro's tongue. This was the first conversation he'd ever had with Okaru, and he couldn't think of how to keep it going. He took the handkerchief off his nose.

"There's blood on your face." Okaru went to a basin of water, dipped in a cloth, and wrung it out. "Here, let me."

Masahiro sat rigid, afraid to move, while she dabbed his cheeks and lips. Okaru was so close to him that he could hear her soft breathing and smell her sweet, fresh scent. Afraid to stare rudely at her face, he cast his gaze downward. He saw the loose neckline of her kimono and the hollow between her breasts. A thrill swept through him. He felt a rush of pleasure, and a strange, urgent need. His heart began to pound so thunderously, he was afraid Okaru would hear it. He longed to touch her, but he was terrified of what she would think if he did.

"There." Okaru sat back on her heels and studied him. "Your nose is swollen. Does it hurt?" She gently touched his nose.

Masahiro said, "Yes. I mean, no." Her fingertips were as soft and cool as flower petals, but they seemed to burn his skin.

"Thank you for rescuing me," Okaru said.

He frowned, wondering if she was joking; but her expression was serious. "I didn't rescue you," he was forced to admit. "My mother's guards did."

"If not for you, that woman might have killed me before they came." Okaru smiled. "You're my hero."

All Masahiro could do was look at the floor and blush so hotly that he felt as if he were on fire.

13

HIRATA FOLLOWED CHIKARA to a room in the barracks where the Hosokawa clan retainers practiced martial arts. Wooden swords and spears hung from racks. The bare wooden floor was marred by scuffs, nicks, and gouges. Polished steel mirrors were mounted on one wall. Chikara stood in the center of the room, his arms folded, a safe distance from Hirata.

"I've heard of you," Chikara said, his voice unsteady but belligerent. "You're the famous fighter. Well, you don't scare me."

"That's good," Hirata said, "because I'm not here to hurt you."

Chikara looked askance at Hirata. He reached for the swords he usually wore at his waist, but his hand closed around empty air. He glanced at the weapons on the racks, realized that they were wooden and Hirata's blades were steel, and discarded the idea of fighting.

"A good choice," Hirata said. "You're wiser than a lot of men twice your age."

Chikara peered at Hirata, wondering if Hirata was making fun of him. Hirata solemnly returned his gaze. Chikara asked, "What do you want with me?"

"I want you to tell me about the vendetta."

"What about it?" Chikara asked warily.

"Why did you wait so long to go after Kira?" This wasn't a minor issue that Hirata wanted to clear up so that he could set the record straight.

Twenty-two months was a long time. A lot could have happened besides the forty-seven *rōnin* stewing about their master's death and fixating on revenge. Maybe something else had gone on, which could affect the supreme court's decision—and Sano's and Hirata's fate.

Chikara tilted his head. "Isn't it obvious why waiting was a good idea?"

"Suppose you tell me, and I'll decide whether it is," Hirata said.

Chikara hesitated for a moment that was fraught with his reluctance to obey and his fear of the consequences of disobeying. "All right."

1701 May

AFTER THE DISSOLUTION of the Asano estate in Edo, Oishi gathered Lord Asano's remaining men in his shabby little rented house and said, "Let us make our plan to avenge our master."

"Why do we need a plan?" Chikara had always been rash and hotheaded, unlike his prudent, calculating father. "Why can't we just go kill Kira now?"

The other men eagerly seconded Chikara. But Oishi said, "Because Kira is expecting us. He's surrounded by guards. We have to lull him into thinking we're not coming."

"And in the meantime, we do nothing?" Chikara said in dismay.

"Far from it. We have important work to do."

Chikara felt the group's morale rise. His father had given them a mission, a purpose that their lives had lost when they'd become *rōnin*. "What kind of work?"

"I'll try to get the house of Asano reinstated," Oishi said. "I don't expect to succeed, but I owe it to Lord Asano. The rest of you will convince Kira that revenge is the last thing on our minds. You can pretend to accept that you've lost your samurai status and go to work like good little commoners. Or you can pretend to become good-for-nothing bums. Make sure that lots of people see you. We want word to get back to Kira."

One man said, "I'll be a bum. That's easier than working." Laughter arose.

"Remember that it's just an act," Oishi warned. "You have to stay strong and keep your wits. Kira is a careful bastard. Even after he thinks he's safe, he'll still keep troops around him. We'll have to fight. You need to be ready.

"We also need someone to spy on Kira, to determine the best place and time to attack." Oishi chose three of the cleverest men. "Learn his routine. Cultivate some informants. If he's spying on us, we need to be aware. And we'd better split up, so he won't guess that we're conspiring against him." He divided the men into three groups that would stage themselves in Osaka, Kamakura, and Miyako.

"How will we keep in contact?" one of the spies asked.

"Chikara and I will stay in Edo," Oishi said. "Send me messages here unless I give you other instructions. Everyone let me know where you can be reached. I'll let you know when it's time to act." He rose. "Are we understood?"

The men stood and said in unison, "Yes." Chikara felt their spirits and his swell with a sense of destiny.

"Then farewell," Oishi said, "until we meet again."

Time passed. His campaign to reinstate the house of Asano failed. His spies reported that Kira was still vigilant about security. The Asano *rōnin* were scattered across Japan. One night in the early summer of the year after Lord Asano's death, Chikara and his parents were sitting by the hearth, his young sisters asleep in a corner, when there was a knock at the door. Oishi let in Kinemon, one of the spies.

"I've come to warn you," Kinemon said. "Kira is suspicious. He's been making inquiries about you. He thinks you're up to something. I heard that he plans to have you framed for some kind of crime and exiled to Sado Island."

Horror filled Chikara. "What are we going to do?"

"I'll allay Kira's suspicions." Oishi stood, calm and resigned. "I will leave Edo. Tonight."

Chikara's mother stared in shock and grief at his father. She said, "Please don't leave me!"

"My dearest," Oishi said tenderly. "You knew this day would come."

She was the only person outside the group of *rōnin* who knew about the plan. "But not so soon." Tears welled in her eyes.

"You know what I have to do," Oishi said. "You know it's against the law. To save you and our children from sharing my punishment, I must sever my ties with you." He spoke with pain and reluctance. "I will obtain a divorce."

Ukihashi wept, but she didn't protest. She understood her husband's obligations.

Oishi said to Chikara, "You can come with me, or you can stay and take care of your mother and sisters."

Chikara understood that this was the biggest decision he would ever have to make. His mother sobbed. They both knew where his duty lay. Without hesitation he said, "I'll go with you, Father."

As Chikara and his father packed a few belongings, Oishi said, "We won't wake the girls."

"What shall I tell them?" Ukihashi asked.

Oishi held her hands, looked into her eyes. "People will say terrible things about me. They'll probably be true. But I swear that no matter what I do, I love you and our girls. Tell them that. Remember."

Ukihashi whispered, "I will." She embraced him, then Chikara, for the last time.

Oishi and Chikara traveled to Miyako. That summer, at a teahouse named Ichiriki, they secretly met up with nineteen *rōnin* that Oishi had sent there. The men had become laborers, traders, or monks. None sported the trappings of their former class. Oishi and Chikara had left their swords at their lodgings; hats covered their crowns, where stubble had begun to grow. After greetings and toasts, Oishi said, "Let's take an oath." He raised his fist. "I swear, on my ancestors' graves, to deliver Kira to justice and avenge Lord Asano."

Chikara's and everyone else's fists shot into the air. Voices solemnly repeated the oath. A foreboding silence fell. Then one of the men said, "Why have you come, Oishi-*san*? I thought you were going to stay in Edo until it's time for the deed to be done." When Oishi explained, the man said, "Kira has spies in Miyako, too. They're always watching us. They're bound to find out that you're here."

"I'll give them something to report."

The next day Oishi began frequenting the teahouses, where he pretended to drink too much. He became loud and obnoxious; he picked fights. He took a mistress, a young girl named Okaru, who was too stupid to realize that she was just part of his act. One day he poured wine over himself, then collapsed on the street, in a feigned, drunken stupor.

Chikara waited nearby, watching people jeer at Oishi. A man with a cross face stopped and said, "Oishi-*san*? Is that you? Why are you lying in the gutter? What happened?" He recoiled in disgust. "The rumors are true, then. You've become a bum." He announced, "This is Oishi Kuranosuke, former retainer to Lord Asano. He doesn't have the courage to avenge his master's death. Faithless beast!" He trampled on Oishi and spat in his face. "You are unworthy of the name of samurai!"

Oishi signaled Chikara to stand back while a crowd joined in the taunting, kicking, and spitting. His plan to defame himself worked. The winter after he and Chikara left Edo, they learned, from their own spies there, that Kira thought he had nothing to fear from the Asano *rōnin*. His estate was no longer as heavily guarded as a fort. It was time.

Oishi contacted the *rōnin* who'd gone to other cities. Forty-seven men, counting Oishi and Chikara, still remained loyal. They returned to Edo, one by one, anonymously and inconspicuously, and gathered at a cheap inn.

"I've found out Kira is having a banquet at his house tomorrow," Kinemon said. "He and his men are sure to drink so much that they'll be easy targets."

"We'll attack late tomorrow night," Oishi decided.

Kinemon unrolled a large sheet of paper on the table. "Here are the plans for the house."

"How did you get them?"

"I married the daughter of the man who built Kira's estate. I stole the plans from his office."

Reviewing the plans, Oishi discovered the secret exit in Kira's bedchamber. The forty-seven *rōnin* checked the equipment they'd brought; they settled on their strategy. Oishi looked around the table and said, "You can back out if you want."

Chikara and the others were moved to tears. They knew he was giving them a chance to save their lives, and if they took it, he wouldn't think ill of them. He loved them that much. His generosity cemented their loyalty to him and to their dead master.

"We're not backing out," Chikara said. "I swear, on my ancestors' graves, to deliver Kira to justice and avenge Lord Asano." The other men seconded him, renewing their oath.

Oishi's stern expression didn't hide the gratitude in his eyes. "Tomorrow night we go to meet our fate."

WHEN CHIKARA HAD finished his tale, Hirata said, "So you waited almost two years just to put Kira off his guard. That's all there was to it?"

"That's it," Chikara said.

Hirata raised the issue that Chikara's story hadn't clarified. "After Kira was dead, why did you wait for orders?"

"Because my father said we should."

Hirata shook his head.

Chikara frowned, offended. "Are you calling me a liar?"

"You're hiding something. I can tell."

"How?" Chikara backed away from Hirata, suspicious and fearful. "Are you doing some kind of magic on me?"

Hirata had learned to read dishonesty in human energy auras. It made them vibrate at a quick, erratic frequency, as Chikara's aura did now. But he said, "I don't need magic. Look at yourself." He pointed to Chikara's reflection in a mirror on the wall of the martial arts practice room where they stood. "Your eyes are open too wide. That's fake innocence. And if you fold your arms any more tightly around your chest to hold the truth in, your ribs will crack."

Dismayed by his transparency, Chikara let his arms drop and forced his face to relax. "We waited because we had to trick Kira. We waited for orders because my father said to. That's my story. I'm sticking with it even if you torture me."

No one could stand up to the kind of torture Hirata could administer. But Sano was opposed to torture because it often produced false confessions, and Hirata generally agreed with Sano. Besides, Hirata felt a profound respect for Chikara. The young man had gone where few of his elders had the courage to go. Hirata sought a kinder way to make Chikara talk.

"I admire you people. You followed Bushido to its most extreme limits." Hirata wasn't just seeking a way to gain Chikara's trust; he genuinely admired the forty-seven *rōnin*.

Chikara's chest inflated with pride. "Yes, we did."

"Most samurai will never know what that's like."

"No, they won't."

Hirata knew. He'd once taken a blade intended for Sano and suffered the injury that had almost killed him and would have crippled him permanently if not for his mystic martial arts training. But the attack had happened so fast that he hadn't had time to think, whereas the forty-seven *rōnin* had had months to come to grips with the personal risk that their act required. Hirata found himself wanting to save the forty-seven *rōnin,* even though he must maintain his impartiality for the sake of the investigation and he had a duty to uphold the law.

"I think it would be a pity if you were condemned to death," Hirata said. "The world needs good samurai like you."

Chikara smiled at the compliment, caught himself, and resumed his imitation of his father's stern expression. "I did what I had to do. I'm not afraid to die."

Probably he didn't comprehend the finality of death. Hirata remembered his own youth, when he'd felt invincible. He hadn't truly understood that he was mortal until he'd been hurt. And he doubted that any man could imagine the agony of ritual suicide until he did it himself.

"But maybe you don't need to die," Hirata said.

Chikara scowled. "You're trying to trick me. You'll promise to help me, and I'll tell you things, and then you'll break your promise. Well, I'm not that stupid."

"What things?" Hirata asked.

Chikara looked abashed because he'd as good as admitted that he had something to hide. Then he scowled harder.

"The reason we're having this conversation is that the government can't decide whether you're heroes or criminals," Hirata said. "The shogun has formed a supreme court to figure it out. Heroes, you live. Criminals, you die."

Hirata had another, more personal reason—the fact that his master's fate, and therefore his own, hinged on the verdict. He needed to find evidence that would produce a verdict that the shogun, the political factions, and the public would like. If he failed, Sano would be sent away, and Hirata would have to go with him. Because Hirata couldn't take his wife and children along while Sano's were forced to stay behind, he would be separated from his family, too.

"So if you know something that could persuade the judges that you're heroes," Hirata said, "it's in your best interest to tell me what it is."

"I already told you," Chikara said, obstinate. "We avenged our master's death. That's Bushido."

"That's not enough to make the court pardon your gang."

"We're not asking to be pardoned."

Hirata changed tactics again. "You and the other *rōnin* must be pretty close friends."

"Yes. We're like brothers." Chikara spoke with the pride of every young man who'd fought a battle alongside his comrades.

"Then wouldn't you save them if you could?"

"They don't want to be saved. They're as ready to die as I am."

"But you're different from your friends," Hirata said. "You have an obligation to someone else besides Lord Asano."

Confusion wrinkled Chikara's brow.

"To Oishi, your father," Hirata clarified. "It's your filial duty to protect him. If he's condemned to death because you kept your mouth shut, then you're a bad son."

Chikara glared, clenched his fists, and took a step toward Hirata. Then he remembered that attacking the best fighter in Edo wasn't a smart idea, and he halted. "I've honored my father. I'm a good son—anybody who knows us will tell you."

"If you're a good son, then prove it," Hirata challenged. "Tell me what you're hiding. Save his life if you can."

Chikara shifted his weight from one foot to the other. He turned his head from side to side, seeking guidance, escape, or perhaps both. His gaze settled on the mirror that he and Hirata stood facing. Reflected in the polished steel, Chikara looked young and alone and small without his father and friends, but his eyes bravely met Hirata's.

"I've told you the whole truth," Chikara said. "I'm done talking."

He turned and strode out of the room. His shoulder blades were pulled back, as if he expected to be stabbed between them. Hirata was left to wonder why the youth was so bent on evasion. Was it because if he talked, he would make things even worse for the forty-seven *rōnin*? They had one foot in the grave already. As long as the government vacillated about them, they had a chance to live. One piece of adverse evidence—from Chikara or another witness—could sway the supreme court to condemn them to death.

And what would happen to Sano, and Hirata, as a result?

14

AT THE INN, Reiko's guards watched over Ukihashi. The crowd outside chanted, "Okaru, Okaru!" People stood on ladders, to see over the fence. The innkeeper shouted at them, "Go away!"

Ukihashi hunched in her cloak, her hands muffled under it. Her hair hung in wet, lank strands, some stuck to mucus that smeared her face. Her eyes had a vacant, unfocused look.

"I'm going to call the police," the innkeeper told Reiko. "They'll arrest her for attacking my guest."

"Please don't," Reiko said. "Nobody was seriously hurt."

"I don't want her around here."

"We'll take her away."

Reiko and Lieutenant Tanuma walked the woman out the gate, with Chiyo following, while the other guards pushed back the crowd. "We'll go to that teahouse." Reiko pointed down the street, at a building with red lanterns hanging from its eaves.

Soon Reiko and Ukihashi were seated in the private room, a decanter of sake and two cups on a low table between them. Reiko had asked Chiyo and Tanuma to wait in the main room of the teahouse with her other guards. Ukihashi shivered; her teeth chattered. Reiko poured a cup of the heated sake and handed it to her. She gulped the liquor, then let out a tremulous sigh and grew still.

"Do you feel better now?" Reiko asked.

"Yes." Color reddened Ukihashi's cheeks, and lucidity returned to her eyes. "I'm sorry I hit your boy," she said in a quiet, chastened voice. She stole a glance at Reiko. "May I ask who you are?"

"My name is Reiko. I'm the wife of the shogun's *sōsakan-sama*."

Ukihashi's expression combined awe at Reiko's high rank with shamed gratitude. "Thank you for stopping that man from calling the police. I don't know what would have become of my little girls, had I been put in jail. Thank you for your kindness."

Reiko couldn't, in good conscience, call it kindness. "It was nothing." Ukihashi had been married to the leader of the forty-seven *rōnin* and might have information that could benefit Sano's investigation. Yet she did sympathize with Ukihashi and want to help her. This was a woman abandoned by her husband, who'd not only forsaken her for another woman but committed an act that many people considered an atrocious crime, an act that was creating a public uproar. And Ukihashi had young daughters affected by their father's deeds, as well as a son who was one of the forty-seven *rōnin*.

Ukihashi smiled bitterly. "You're the first person who has given me any sort of help since my husband became a *rōnin*. In case you don't know, his name is Oishi. His master was Lord Asano, who was sentenced to death for drawing a weapon inside Edo Castle."

"I know," Reiko said.

"I suppose everyone has heard what Oishi and his friends have done. Tongues are wagging all over town. It's bad enough that the old scandal about Lord Asano has come up again, but since that little whore started blabbing, there's new dirty laundry for the public to smell."

Reiko understood how much Okaru's appearance on the scene had humiliated Oishi's former wife. "Okaru is sorry. She won't talk again."

"That's closing the stable door after the horses have already escaped," Ukihashi said with a humorless laugh. "I didn't intend to attack her. I don't really care if she stole my husband. I just wanted to see her. I lost control. She's so young and beautiful." Envy, like acid, corroded Ukihashi's voice. "Everybody is paying attention to her. Nobody cares about me." She thought a moment, then said, "Maybe I should tell my story."

Here was an opportunity to get Ukihashi talking about her husband and the vendetta. Reiko said, "What would your story be?"

"That my husband served the Asano clan his whole life. So did his family and his ancestors. So did mine. The house of Asano was the reason for our existence." She must have been storing these thoughts inside her, and now they spilled out. "When it was dissolved, we lost our livelihood, our home, and our honor." Whatever polite reserve that her breeding had given her, she'd evidently lost it when she'd been cast out of her station. "And it all happened because of that law against drawing weapons in Edo Castle."

Indignation sparked in her red, watery eyes. "Kira wasn't even seriously wounded! Why should Lord Asano have had to die? The law is ridiculous, and so was the shogun's decision!"

Reiko was startled to hear her criticize the shogun so bluntly. Criticism was tantamount to treason, for which the penalty was death. "Keep your voice down," Reiko warned.

"I'm only saying what many people thought," Ukihashi retorted.

It was true. Reiko recalled the aftermath of Lord Asano's attack on Kira. Sano had told her that after Lord Asano's death there had been much secret discussion, and many government officials thought the law had been applied too harshly. Many said the shogun was so afraid of violence that he wanted to make an example of Lord Asano and prevent similar incidents. Reiko agreed, although she couldn't say so in public.

"No matter what anybody thinks about what Lord Asano did, it wasn't his retainers' fault." Ukihashi clasped a hand to her bony chest. "*We* didn't break the law, yet we paid the price. The government threw us out on the street without a penny to buy rice for our children!"

Reiko knew this was what happened when a samurai became a *ronin*—his whole family suffered. Ukihashi personified Reiko's own worst fears, which arose whenever Sano was threatened with losing his place in the Tokugawa regime and his samurai status. Ukihashi's fate could be Reiko's, someday. Or at least Reiko had thought it was the worst possible fate, until the shogun had threatened to take Sano away from her and the children. It seemed better to be cast out together than divided permanently.

"We became paupers almost overnight," Ukihashi went on. "We could barely afford to rent a hovel in the merchant quarter."

Rapid descent into poverty was typical for *ronin* after they lost their stipends. Reiko wondered uneasily how much money Sano had. Not that she would know how long it would support their family. Ladies of her class didn't deal with finances. The first time Sano had ever talked about money with her was after he'd been demoted and he'd had to tell her to spend less.

"Our relatives and friends cut their ties with us," Ukihashi added.

Custom divided a *rōnin* from the entire samurai class. Friends and kin feared that the taint of disgrace would rub off on them and they might share the outcasts' misfortune. What a blow this must be! Reiko could hardly bear to ask, "How have you survived?"

"By the labor of my own hands." Ashamed yet proud, Ukihashi removed her gloves and displayed her hands to Reiko. The skin on them was red, dry, cracked, and calloused. "I'm a maid in a rich salt merchant's house. Because Oishi refused to work. It was up to me to feed us and keep a roof over our heads. My daughters work, too, even though they're only eleven and eight years old. My son Chikara helped out before he left. He was fourteen at the time."

The children were near the same age as her son, Reiko noted. She hated to think of Masahiro losing all his future prospects—which he might indeed, if Sano went away. How terribly Masahiro would miss Sano! They were so close, and a boy needed his father.

"Chikara did odd jobs around town. He's a good boy." Ukihashi's hard voice softened for a moment. Then her anger revived. "It's bad enough that Oishi took revenge on Kira even though it was illegal, but he had to drag Chikara into it. My son!" She buried her face in her hands and sobbed. "He's as good as dead!"

Reiko felt a pity for Ukihashi that was stronger due to a sense of identification with her. Both their families were at stake. And if Sano were ever duty-bound to carry out an illegal vendetta—the gods forbid— Masahiro would have to go along, and Reiko would have to accept it. Now she sought to offer some comfort to Ukihashi.

"Maybe Chikara won't have to die." Reiko told Ukihashi that the government couldn't settle the controversy about what to do with the forty-seven *rōnin* and so had created a supreme court to decide. "My husband is investigating the case for the court. If you can provide him with evidence that the forty-seven *rōnin* should be pardoned, then maybe they will be."

Ukihashi raised her face. Her eyes streamed with tears but shone with cautious hope. "What sort of evidence?"

"Information that suggests that Kira deserved to be killed, which the shogun didn't have when he forbade action against Kira. Or another kind of clue that Oishi and the other *rōnin* were justified in breaking the law."

Ukihashi's face fell. "Is that what my son's life depends on? Proving that Oishi did the right thing?" Scorn married the despair in her voice. "Well, it isn't going to happen."

"How can you be so certain?" Reiko asked.

"Because I know why Oishi did it. He wasn't justified."

Reiko felt compelled to defend the man. "He was loyal to his master. He did his duty as a samurai. That counts for something. Maybe if there were other factors—"

"Is that what you think this is all about?" Ukihashi interrupted. "Loyalty? Duty? *Bushido?*" She spat the last word as if it revolted her. "Well, nothing could be further from the truth. Listen, and you'll see."

1702 June

ON A WARM, rainy night, Ukihashi trudged up to her house in a row of attached, crowded, ramshackle buildings in a poor district of the merchant quarter. She'd spent a hard day at work. Tired and wet, she lugged a basket of leftovers stolen from her employer's table, pickings to feed her family.

In the house's single room that served as parlor, kitchen, and bedchamber, Chikara and the two girls were building a fire in the hearth with bits of coal and wood they'd scavenged. Oishi lounged on the floor, nursing a jar of cheap wine.

Ukihashi dumped her basket beside him. "Have you been sitting there all day?"

"All day today, all day yesterday." His sarcastic voice was slurred. "And probably all day tomorrow, too."

"How can you just sit around and let your wife and your children support you?" Ukihashi demanded. "Why can't you take care of us as you should?"

Oïshi gulped wine and flapped his hand. "Why don't you just shut up?"

Once, Ukihashi had been a quiet, docile wife, but the hardship of their new life had stripped her of respect for her husband. "Not until you go out and work."

He hurled the jar against the wall. The empty jar shattered. "Didn't I work hard for Lord Asano? Don't you think I would be working now if he was alive?"

The children fled. They hated their parents' quarrels, which often turned ugly.

"Those days are over," Ukihashi retorted. "It's time to accept that."

"I won't lower myself to do menial labor," Oishi said stubbornly. "I won't bring more disgrace on myself." Lurching to his feet, he shouted, "It's not my fault that this happened. It's because of Kira. If not for him, I wouldn't be a *rōnin*. The bastard!" He punched the wall. The tenants next door yelled.

Ukihashi faced him, hands on her hips. "I've had enough of your tantrums and your excuses. Either fulfill your responsibilities as a husband and father or get out."

"I've had enough, too." Oishi staggered around the room, throwing clothes, shoes, and other personal items into a quilt; he tied up its ends. "I'm going."

Ukihashi was shocked; she'd not thought he would call her bluff. "Where? What are you going to do?"

"I'm going to kill that cursed Kira."

Ukihashi had heard him say that many times while he'd ranted about Kira and the suffering the man had caused him. Nothing had come of it. But this time she saw new, fierce determination in Oishi's face. She was suddenly terrified.

"You can't," she said. "The shogun forbade action against Kira. You'll be punished."

"I don't care." Securing his swords at his waist, Oishi headed toward the door.

Ukihashi was appalled that she'd pushed him too far. "Do you realize what will happen to me, and the children, if you do this? We'll be punished, too."

His expression hardened into stone. He was beyond caring how his actions affected his family. She resorted to scorn as her weapon. "What makes you think you can do it? You've said that Kira is surrounded by guards. And look at you—you've become a drunken slob. You're going to kill him?" She laughed, covering her fright with disdain. "You and who else?"

Oishi shouted, "Chikara!"

The boy appeared in the doorway.

"I'm going to avenge Lord Asano," Oishi said. "You're coming with me."

Horror seized Ukihashi's throat. "No! You can't take him!"

"His place is with me," Oishi said. "Chikara, pack your things."

Chikara looked from his father to his mother, torn between them, miserable. But he complied. Oishi told Ukihashi, "I'll get a divorce before we kill Kira. You won't be troubled any further by anything I do."

Too late, Ukihashi remembered how much he meant to her. He was her husband that she loved, her children's father, her life. "No!" she cried, flinging herself at him.

Oishi pushed her away. Their daughters came running; they cried, "Papa, don't go!"

Ukihashi fell to her knees. "Please, forgive me! I'll never scold you again, if you'll just stay!"

She and her daughters wept as Oishi and Chikara walked out into the darkness and rain. She felt her love turn to hatred because Oishi was about to destroy all their lives.

IN THE PRIVATE room of the teahouse, Ukihashi leaned across the table toward Reiko. Her eyes shone with angry triumph as she said, "So you see: The vendetta was Oishi paying Kira back for ruining him. That wasn't loyalty, or duty, or samurai honor. It was pure selfishness."

Reiko sat silent, disturbed by what she'd heard. Was this woman's testimony the critical piece of evidence that would decide the case against the forty-seven *rōnin*? If so, what would it mean for her own family? Reiko also thought of Okaru, who wanted so badly to save her lover.

The expression on Ukihashi's tearstained face combined a cruel smile with pain. "Here's what your husband is going to find out during his investigation. Oishi deserves to die. Chikara and the others deserve to die for going along with him. And then, will the supreme court pardon them?" She uttered a dismal laugh. "I would be fooling myself if I thought so."

15

SANO, HIRATA, AND Detectives Marume and Fukida had spent the morning going from one estate to another, interviewing the forty-seven *rōnin*. Afterward, they began the ride back to Edo Castle. It was late afternoon, and the sun had warmed the air but not enough to melt the snow, which still blanketed the highway. As Sano related Oishi's story, skeptical expressions appeared on his comrades' faces.

"What's the matter?" Sano asked. "Did you hear something different from the men you questioned?"

"As different as night and day," Marume said. Hirata and Fukida nodded.

"I'm not surprised." The ten *rōnin* that Sano had spoken to had their own perspectives on the vendetta, which didn't match their leader's. "Well, we might as well lay out all the statements and see what we've got. Hirata-*san*? What did Oishi's son tell you?"

Hirata summarized Chikara's story.

Sano shook his head, perturbed. "Oishi claims that the vendetta came about because he was humiliated in public. Chikara claims that the vendetta was a conspiracy from the start, and Oishi's bad behavior was a clever act to throw Kira off guard. They certainly aren't seeing eye to eye."

"Certainly not on the matter of why Oishi left his wife," Fukida said. "Oishi says Ukihashi threw him out. Chikara said his father only divorced his mother to protect her."

"And Oishi claims he fell in love with his mistress, while his son claims Okaru was just part of his act," Marume said. "One of them is lying."

"Let's compare their stories with those of their friends," Sano said.

He and Hirata and the detectives took turns relating what the other forty-five *rōnin* had said. By the end, Sano realized that the task of getting to the truth would be even more difficult than he'd first thought. "We have twenty-one *rōnin* who more or less corroborate Chikara's story, but they disagree with him, and each other, on the details. Out of those, eleven claim that the conspiracy started the day Lord Asano died. Ten say it didn't come up until Oishi failed to get the house of Asano reinstated. Fourteen say they put on an act to trick Kira. Nine say it was Oishi's idea; five say it was their own."

"No, it's the other way around," Hirata said. "Nine say theirs; five say Oishi's."

"You're right." Sano threw up his hands in frustration. "Then there are the twenty-four whose stories are closer to Oishi's. They say there was no conspiracy until Oishi gathered some of them together in Miyako, and the things they did after they became *rōnin* weren't an act—they took jobs to support themselves or entered monasteries because they needed someplace to live, or they were so unhappy that they drank too much."

Hirata took up the recitation. "Thirteen of them say they didn't know why Lord Asano attacked Kira and neither did Oishi. Eleven say that Kira had some kind of hold over Lord Asano, but they don't know what it was. Fourteen think Oishi initially accepted the shogun's order against taking action against Kira, then changed his mind because the man from Satsuma humiliated him. Ten think it was because of his wife. When she threw him out, he realized he was a disgrace to the Way of the Warrior and had to reform."

"All these numbers are giving me a headache," Marume said.

"The other *rōnin* didn't witness Kira bullying Lord Asano," Sano reminded Hirata. "Maybe Oishi didn't tell them about it so they assumed he didn't know."

"He apparently didn't tell any of them, not even his son, why he made them wait for orders after Kira was dead," Hirata said. "That's the one thing they all agree on."

"We could decide what's true based on the numbers," Fukida suggested. "Twenty-one *rōnin* corroborate Chikara. Twenty-six, Oishi. If this were a game, Oishi would be the winner."

Sano didn't need to point out that this wasn't a game but a matter of life and death. "I have a feeling that everyone involved is mixing fact and fiction. We're no closer to the truth than we were before our investigation started."

"If anything, it's raised a new question," Hirata said, "which is this: Why are the forty-seven *rōnin* telling so many different stories?"

"You'd think they'd have put their heads together, come up with one story, and made sure everyone told it," Fukida said. "Isn't that what criminals do when they conspire to commit a crime?"

"Often," Sano agreed. "But if they told exactly the same story, it would sound fabricated and rehearsed. Maybe their intention was to confuse us. If so, they've succeeded."

"The forty-seven *rōnin* aren't criminals until the supreme court determines that what they did was indeed a crime and they're pronounced guilty," Hirata said.

Sano heard a defensive note in Hirata's voice. He could tell which way Hirata's opinion was tending. He himself was tending in the same direction, but Fukida seemed to have taken the opposite view.

"It's obvious that we don't have the whole picture," Sano said. "Our investigation has a long way to go. Meanwhile, the supreme court is convening. I'll tell the judges what we've learned so far. It's their job to interpret the evidence."

Yet Sano couldn't deny that this case had engaged him on a deeply personal level, and he couldn't help hoping that he could influence the verdict in the direction that he believed was right. Even though he couldn't quite make up his mind about what the right verdict was, let alone predict its repercussions for him and his family.

WHILE HE WAITED for his mother to return, Masahiro sat with Okaru in her room at the inn.

"Do you have any brothers or sisters?" Okaru asked.

"A sister." Masahiro could barely get the words out. Her nearness filled him with tingling pleasure yet made him uncomfortable.

Okaru smiled. "That's nice. How old is she?"

"Four." He would have to make better conversation than this, Masahiro told himself, or he would bore Okaru. "Do you have any brothers or sisters?" he ventured.

"I had a little brother. He died when he was eight." Okaru spoke with matter-of-fact calmness. "And an older sister. When my parents died, she went away with a man who owned a pleasure house in Osaka. I haven't seen her or heard from her since."

Masahiro was disturbed by the story and the fact that he'd led her to talk about something so painful. "I'm sorry" was all he could think to say.

"That's all right," Okaru said. "It was years ago, so I don't think about my family much. Whenever I do, I remember the happy times."

She was so brave, and so nice despite the bad things that had happened to her, Masahiro thought.

The uproar of an angry mob outside interrupted their conversation. "What in heaven?" Okaru hurried to the door. She and Masahiro peered outside.

The gate was open. A *doshin*—a police patrol officer—and his two assistants were tussling with the crowd that tried to rush into the inn. The *doshin* was a thickset samurai dressed in a short, padded gray kimono, heavy leggings, and leather boots. He waved his *jitte*—an iron rod with a prong at the hilt for catching the blade of an attacker's sword, standard police equipment. The assistants were burly, unshaven commoners; they did the police's dirty work of subduing and capturing criminals and taking them to jail, Masahiro knew. They brandished their spiked clubs against the crowd.

"Oh, good! They're chasing those awful people away!" Okaru said.

Her servant Goza barged through the crowd and in the gate. Goza carried a large hamper as if it weighed nothing. She swatted one police assistant with her arm and jabbed her elbow into the other's eye. Her mustached face wore a look fierce enough to kill. She strode toward Okaru, who called, "Look who's here—it's Masahiro. He and his mother came back."

As Goza tramped onto the veranda, the *doshin* yelled, "Hey, you!

Stop!" He swaggered after Goza. The innkeeper closed the gate on the mob and bustled after the *doshin*. The two men faced Okaru, Masahiro, and Goza, who stood together in the doorway.

"I'm sorry, but you'll have to leave," the innkeeper told Okaru and Goza.

Worry puckered Okaru's brow. Goza said, "We paid for two more nights."

"I'll refund your money," the innkeeper said. "I can't have you here. The commotion is bothering my other guests. Two of them have already left." He gestured toward the fence; beyond it, the uproar continued. "Nobody else will want to stay here with that outside."

Goza folded her arms, planted her legs wide. "We're not leaving."

"I'm sorry," the innkeeper said, genuinely contrite. "You'd better pack your things and go quietly, or I'll have to turn you over to the law."

The *doshin* advanced on Goza and Okaru. Masahiro stepped forward, drew his sword, and said, "I won't let you throw them out."

The *doshin* chuckled and kept coming. "Put that toy away before you cut yourself."

Masahiro was furious at the *doshin* for mocking him in front of Okaru. He could cut the man down dead in an instant, but his father had taught him that a good samurai kills only when absolutely necessary. "My father is Sano, the shogun's investigator," he said. "Let them stay, or he'll have you dismissed."

That stopped the *doshin* in his tracks; he'd obviously heard of Sano, whose name still carried weight even though he'd lost standing at court. The *doshin* said to the innkeeper, "I guess you're stuck with these people," and walked away.

The innkeeper shrugged, resigned. Goza nodded in triumph. Okaru smiled at Masahiro, then sighed unhappily. "I mustn't stay where I'm not wanted."

"Where will you go?" Masahiro asked.

"I don't know." Okaru made a visible effort to boost her courage. She and Goza began packing. "But I'm sure we'll be fine."

Reiko returned with Chiyo. When she learned what had happened, she said, "Okaru, you and Goza must come home with me."

112

Okaru gasped as if she'd just received a splendid, undreamt-of gift. "You mean, to Edo Castle?" She clapped her hands. "How wonderful!"

Chiyo moved close to Reiko. Masahiro's keen ears overheard Chiyo whisper, "Is this wise? What will your husband think?"

"Wise or not, I can't let that poor girl wander the streets," Reiko whispered. "As for my husband, Okaru is a witness in his case, and he would want to keep her safe."

Chiyo nodded reluctantly. Okaru was watching the two women, and her face fell; she understood that her welcome in Reiko's home wasn't certain. "Oh, but I shouldn't impose on you. I can't accept your kind invitation."

"You can and you must," Reiko said. "I insist."

Okaru's smile was so brilliant that it dazzled Masahiro. "A thousand thanks for your hospitality." She bowed deeply to Reiko.

Masahiro's heart beat fast with excitement. Okaru was going to live at his house! He would be able to see her every day!

HIRATA RODE WITH Sano, Detectives Marume and Fukida, and the troops, entering Edo proper along a road lined with food-stalls. They stopped for a quick meal. A vendor lifted the lids on pots of dumplings stuffed with shrimp, ginger, and bamboo shoots. Rich, savory steam billowed. Gulls and crows squabbled over dropped tidbits. After Hirata and his comrades had eaten, they resumed riding and came upon a group of priests walking in the same direction. The priests wore padded hemp cloaks over their saffron robes. Hoods protected their shaved heads from the cold. They carried wooden bowls, which they held out to passersby, soliciting alms. When they heard Sano's procession coming, they moved to the side of the road. They stood motionless, hands clasping their bowls and their heads bowed, as the procession passed. They looked identical, like life-sized dolls crafted by the same artist.

Six crows suddenly took wing. They hovered in a circle above a priest in the middle of the group. Staring in astonishment, Hirata lagged behind his companions. The aura suddenly pulsed; the air scintillated. Sano, the detectives, and the troops rode right past the priest without looking at him or the birds. The other priests didn't move. The vendors, their customers, and the pedestrians in the street went about their business. No one but Hirata seemed to notice the strange phenomenon.

The priest with the halo of birds raised his head and met Hirata's gaze. His hood shadowed one half of his face. The complexion on the other half had a waxen glow, like a candle whose flame has hollowed out its interior. The eye that Hirata could see shone with a strange light. The priest raised his hand, then flicked his wrist.

The birds flew at Hirata and assailed him in a storm of screeches and flapping wings. He shouted as he waved his arms to fend them off. Their claws scratched his face; their sharp beaks pecked at his eyes. He tumbled off his horse and fell into the snow on the road.

"Hey!" Detective Marume called. He and Fukida came running. "Why did you fall off your horse?"

"Didn't you see that?" Hirata stood and brushed snow from his buttocks.

"See what?" Fukida asked. "How come your face is scratched?"

"Those birds—" Hirata glanced around. The birds were gone. So were the priests. "Never mind. Let's go." Sano and the rest of the group turned curious gazes on Hirata as he pulled himself up onto his horse.

"Maybe you could use a few riding lessons," Marume joked, not quite kindly. He and Fukida didn't like Hirata's evasions or inexplicable behavior.

Hirata didn't answer. He resumed his place beside Sano.

"Is there anything wrong?" Sano asked.

"No," Hirata lied.

The priest with the birds might be the man who'd been stalking him. But so might the soldier he'd seen yesterday after he'd found the poem on the bush. Or maybe neither was. But Hirata knew he'd just received another arcane message. And although he couldn't grasp what it meant, he was sure of one thing: His stalker was coming closer.

16

SANO ARRIVED AT the main reception chamber in the palace just as the supreme court convened. The judges ranged in age from late forties to early seventies. Dressed in black ceremonial robes emblazoned with gold family crests, they milled around uncertainly. Sano's father-in-law, Magistrate Ueda, was among them. Their attendants bowed courteously to Sano because he was nominally a high-ranking official, then gave him a wide berth because he was a pariah. Standing alone near the door, Sano heard snatches of conversation.

"So you've been roped into service, too."

"I hardly know whom to thank—heaven or hell."

"Being appointed to this court is an unprecedented honor."

"It's unprecedented, I'll grant you that."

There had never been such a court in Japan, as far as Sano knew. Criminal cases and civil disputes were usually decided by magistrates. But then Japan had never seen a case like the revenge of the forty-seven *rōnin*. This was history in the making.

"What are we supposed to do?" someone asked.

"Why don't we begin by sitting down?" These words, which rose above the chatter, came from Inspector General Nakae. He was in his sixties, broad of figure, and gray-haired. He reminded Sano of an overripe pumpkin—he'd lost most of his teeth, and his face had that caved-in look, with a big patch of dark age spots on his right cheek that looked like mold. Officials quaked when they saw him coming, for he had the authority to reprimand, fine, demote, or oust them for real or trumped-up charges of corruption or incompetence. Diligent rather than clever, he had a humorless, overbearing manner.

The judges knelt on the floor in two rows, seven men facing seven more—Chamberlain Yanagisawa's cronies versus the opposite faction. Inspector General Nakae sat with the cronies. Magistrate Ueda sat with the opposition. He matched the inspector general in age, build, and hair color, but his hooded eyes were bright with intelligence. Smile lines framed his mouth. He glanced at Sano and nodded.

Magistrate Ueda had stood by Sano during his troubles, and not just because Sano's wife was his beloved only child. He believed Sano was innocent of wrongdoing and had received a raw deal because of Yanagi-sawa. A man of integrity, he would not bow to Yanagisawa just to make his own life easy. Sano was thankful for his father-in-law's loyalty, al-though he worried that it would cost Magistrate Ueda.

"What's next?" asked one of the judges, Lord Nabeshima, *daimyo* of Saga and Hizen provinces, who sat beside the inspector general. He was in his seventies, with white hair, his skin and eyes tinged yellow with jaundice.

The other judges spoke simultaneously. A din arose as they tried to outshout one another. Finally Magistrate Ueda clapped his hands. "The first order of the day is to pick a chief judge," he said in a voice that had often silenced a courtroom full of rambunctious citizens. "Who would like to volunteer?"

Everyone quieted while the judges weighed the cachet of being the leader against the risks. Sano watched each man realize that if he were the chief judge, and the shogun didn't like the court's verdict, he could be blamed and punished. Expressions grew cautious. Inspector General Nakae said, "Magistrate Ueda is the only one among us who has experi-ence with trials. He should be the chief judge. All in favor?"

The other judges quickly said, "Yes," in unison. Inspector General Nakae bared his few, decayed teeth in a smile.

Rotten seeds in a rotten pumpkin, Sano thought. Nakae had bad blood with Magistrate Ueda and would love to see him take a fall.

"I am honored by your confidence in me," Magistrate Ueda said. "I gladly accept."

Sano admired his father-in-law, who welcomed a chance to ensure that the court functioned competently and the defendants received a fair trial, even at his own risk. Sano began to hope that the supreme court was a good idea. With Magistrate Ueda as its leader, perhaps the judges' verdict would be fair as well as satisfactory to everyone who mattered.

"My first act as chief judge will be to lay down the rules by which the supreme court will operate," Magistrate Ueda said. "Some of them I'll make up as we go along, since we're venturing into uncharted territory. Others, I'll establish at the outset." His side nodded smugly. The opposition looked leery. "Rule number one: Anybody who wishes to speak must raise his hand first. No one is allowed to speak until I give permission."

The other judges assented, albeit with reluctance. Lord Nabeshima raised his yellowish hand. When Magistrate Ueda nodded at him, he said, "How will we arrive at a verdict? Will each judge get a vote? What if there's a tie?"

"Rule number two: The decision will have to be unanimous," Magistrate Ueda decided. "We'll deliberate until everyone agrees on the verdict."

Sano thought this was the best strategy. He didn't like the idea of the court dispensing liberty or death to the forty-seven *rōnin* based on a scant majority of votes. Nor did he want Yanagisawa's cronies ramming through a verdict that would hurt his family.

"Now we'll determine where we stand as of this moment," Magistrate Ueda said. "Who thinks the forty-seven *rōnin* should be pardoned and set free? Raise your hands."

No one did.

"Who thinks they should be punished for murdering Kira?" Magistrate Ueda asked.

Everyone kept their hands down.

Sano figured that the judges didn't want their opinions spread all over town. Nobody wanted to attract censure from those who disagreed with him.

Magistrate Ueda apparently reached the same conclusion that Sano had, for he said, "Rule number three: The proceedings of the supreme court are to be secret. What happens here, stays here. Everyone who's not on the court and not required to testify before it will leave the room. That means everybody except Sano-*san*."

The people in the audience reacted with frowns and mutters: They didn't want to miss out on the fun. Inspector General Nakae said, "Limiting the number of onlookers is fine, but don't we need someone to write down the proceedings?"

"That's a good idea," Magistrate Ueda said. "I appoint you."

Nakae pulled a disgruntled face. The attendants departed, leaving Sano as the court's lone observer. The chamber seemed cavernous and empty, and cold without their body heat.

Magistrate Ueda said, "Let's try again. Who thinks the forty-seven *rōnin* should go free?"

Four hands rose, including his, then dropped.

"Who thinks they should die?"

Five other hands went up, including the inspector general's.

"It seems that we have a few abstainers who are uncertain," Magistrate Ueda said.

The judges looked at one another in concern. They, and Sano, had noticed that opinions differed within the two factions. The case had the potential to shift alliances and change the political landscape.

Inspector General Nakae raised his hand, was recognized, and said, "Am I going to change my opinion? No." Murmurs of agreement came from the other judges. "How will we even begin to reach a unanimous decision?"

"Our opinions have been shaped by the very little information available to us thus far," Magistrate Ueda said. "We need new evidence to shed light on the case of the forty-seven *rōnin*. Sano-*san* is under orders to investigate the case and bring us that evidence." He nodded to Sano. "Please come forward."

As Sano walked up the length of the chamber, he discerned that except for Magistrate Ueda, he had no friends here, not even among the men he'd nominated to the court. Scorn, pity, repugnance, and fear lurked behind the other judges' neutral expressions. He embodied their worst nightmare, as Oishi embodied Sano's own. Sano represented what could happen to them if their enemies got the better of them. And he still had his reputation as a rogue who would do what he thought was right, in spite of the dangers to himself or anyone else. The judges probably viewed him as a keg of gunpowder dropped in their midst, Sano thought with dour amusement that didn't ease his trepidation. He realized that the supreme court was, from his perspective, a terrible idea, and his situation was even graver than he'd initially thought. Not only would he share the responsibility for the verdict that the judges rendered, but he couldn't control them. None of them except Magistrate Ueda had his interests at heart. The others would do as they pleased with the evidence he provided, his family's welfare be damned.

Sano knelt at the end of the rows of judges, facing them, at Magistrate Ueda's right. He bowed. They bowed. Sano was in a cold, drafty spot, or maybe that was just his imagination.

"What have you to report?" Magistrate Ueda asked.

"I've interviewed the forty-seven *rōnin,* including Oishi Kuranosuke, the leader, and his son Chikara," Sano said. "I also have a statement from a woman named Okaru, who is Oishi's mistress."

While he summarized their stories, he could only hope his work would lead to a just verdict. He wished he were impartial enough to believe that the verdict could be just even if it deemed the forty-seven *rōnin* guilty of unlawful murder and broke up his family.

The instant he finished, hands rose. Magistrate Ueda said, "I'll allow an open discussion."

"Oishi and Chikara have conflicting versions of the events," said Motoori Akihiro, the Minister of Temples and Shrines, a judge on Magistrate Ueda's side. He was almost blind, his eyes cloudy, and almost crippled by stiff, sore joints. "Which is lying?"

"It doesn't matter which," said Lord Nabeshima. "Their stories agree on the most important point, and so do their comrades' stories: The forty-seven *rōnin* banded together to avenge Lord Asano by killing Kira. I don't care whether Oishi planned the vendetta immediately after Lord Asano's death or not until some loudmouth from Satsuma insulted him. Conspiracy is illegal. So, therefore, was the vendetta."

"The forty-seven *rōnin* didn't even show any remorse," said Hitomi Munesuke, a colonel in the Tokugawa army, seated in the inspector general's row. He was vigorous and fit at age sixty, even though he walked with a cane. He had a pleasant, honest face and disposition. Sano had nothing against him, except that he'd had the bad judgment to fall in with Yanagisawa.

"Why should remorse make any difference?" the inspector general asked his friend. "They broke the law. And let us not forget that Kira wasn't their only victim. They also killed his retainers. That was murder of innocent citizens, in cold blood."

"That's a separate issue," Magistrate Ueda said. "Our job is to rule on the vendetta against Kira."

"The vendetta was illegal." The inspector general seemed stuck on this point, like glue. "End of story."

"Not so fast," said a judge from Magistrate Ueda's side. He was Ogiwara Shigehide, a superintendent of finance. Perhaps forty-five years old, he was handsome in a dramatic way, with large, protuberant eyes, red lips and cheeks, and blue-black hair. He would play well on the Kabuki stage, with his booming voice that would carry to the back of a noisy theater. "There are other parties in the case besides the forty-seven *rōnin*. I'm interested in the mistress."

"Why am I not surprised?" Lord Nabeshima muttered, and his friends chuckled. The finance superintendent was a notorious womanizer.

Ogiwara cut his eyes at them. "She could be the key to the whole case. We should bring her in to testify."

"She's just a whore. She would probably say anything to save her lover," Lord Nabeshima said.

"That doesn't mean she's not telling the truth in this instance," Ogiwara said. "The fact that there are discrepancies between the forty-seven *rōnin*'s stories indicates that there are indeed things about the vendetta that haven't come to light."

"Discrepancies such as the different explanations for why Oishi left his wife and took a mistress?" Inspector General Nakae laughed. "We're here to rule on a murder, not wallow in sordid domestic details."

"I thought you liked sordid domestic details," Ogiwara retorted.

Inspector General Nakae had a wife and three concubines who were always at one another's throats, Sano had heard.

"Rule number four," Magistrate Ueda said with the air of a patient father among squabbling children. "No personal attacks."

"I want to know why the forty-seven *rōnin* waited for orders," said Minister Motoori from the magistrate's side. "That information wasn't in their statements."

"Another irrelevant detail," Lord Nabeshima scoffed. "It doesn't have any bearing on what they did to Kira."

"How can you be so sure?" Minister Motoori said.

"Lord Asano's motive for attacking Kira has bearing," said Finance Superintendent Ogiwara. "If Kira really insulted Lord Asano, if he demanded bribes, and if the shogun had known about it, then His Excellency wouldn't have forbidden action against Kira. The vendetta would have been legal."

" 'If, if, if,' " Inspector General Nakae said in a snide imitation of Ogiwara's booming voice. "Has anybody else besides Oishi witnessed what happened between Kira and Lord Asano? No. It's all hearsay from a criminal who's lying to save his skin."

"Even if Kira did demand a bribe and did bully Lord Asano, that's not enough reason to slaughter him," Colonel Hitomi said. "Lord Asano was too sensitive, not to mention stupid to draw his weapon inside Edo Castle. His death was his own fault."

"But it's understandable that Oishi sought revenge on Kira," Finance Superintendent Ogiwara said. "It doesn't matter if Lord Asano was in the wrong."

"The sneak attack on Kira was dirty," Inspector General Nakae said. Other judges who'd remained silent nodded. "That alone makes it a crime, in my opinion."

"Oishi should have challenged Kira to a fair fight, a duel," Colonel Hitomi said.

Finance Superintendent Ogiwara laughed. "What would be fair about a duel between a frail old man like Kira and a tough, expert swordsman like Oishi?"

"We're getting off track," Magistrate Ueda said. "I'm closing the discussion."

Inspector General Nakae raised his hand. "May I make a request?"

"Go ahead."

"I haven't heard anything that I think suggests that the forty-seven *rōnin* should be set free," Nakae said. Sounds of assent and dissent came from judges who hadn't spoken. "And I'd like to see how many people agree with me. Can we take another vote?"

"Very well," Magistrate Ueda said. "All for condemning the defendants?"

This time nine of the fourteen judges raised their hands. Again, the votes were divided between Yanagisawa's allies and enemies. Magistrate Ueda, who hadn't raised his hand, spoke with reluctance. "I must admit that I don't get a sense of any extenuating circumstances, either."

If the most incisive, honest mind in the room didn't see such circumstances, then maybe there weren't any. The judges who still favored the defendants were clearly voting with their hearts instead of their heads. But how long could they hold out against the lack of hard evidence to back up their opinions? Sano's heart sank. All his work had thus far swayed the court further against the men he felt inclined to protect.

Magistrate Ueda asked Sano, "What do you think?"

Sano could say that he commended Oishi and his comrades for their loyalty, but he was reluctant to try to influence the court toward excusing the forty-seven *rōnin*. He remembered the sense of wrongness he'd felt during his first encounter with them, at Lord Asano's grave, and his feeling that Oishi had been hiding something. And then there was the mistress. Her story seemed akin to the tip of an iceberg. Sano wondered whether the part underwater contained evidence that would justify Kira's murder or a reason to condemn the killers.

He told the judges the only thing he could honestly say. "The forty-seven *rōnin* are holding something back. I would like to continue my inquiries, with your permission."

"Permission granted," Magistrate Ueda said. "This court is adjourned for today. Sano-*san*, report to us again when we convene tomorrow at the same hour."

As he left the chamber, Sano was glad he'd bought some time for his family. He wondered if he'd also bought more time for heroes who deserved it or for criminals who didn't.

17

ON THE WAY to Edo Castle, Masahiro rode his horse on one side of the palanquin that carried his mother, Chiyo, and Okaru. The servant Goza plodded on foot on the other side. Hired porters followed behind the mounted guards, lugging Okaru's trunk. Masahiro kept an eye out for danger. He was ready to protect Okaru if necessary.

When she'd left the inn, the crowd had rushed upon her. She'd hidden her head under a shawl while Reiko hurried her into the palanquin. The crowd followed the procession, collecting more people all the way to Edo Castle.

Okaru opened the window, her eyes shining. "I never dreamed I would ever see the inside of the castle. I'm so excited!"

The sentries at the gate ordered her to step out of the palanquin. One ransacked her trunk for hidden weapons, while two others searched her and Goza. The sentry ran his hands over Okaru, ogling her while he peeked up her sleeves and under her skirts. At last she was allowed to ride through the gate. She watched eagerly as the bearers carried her up through the castle's walled passages. When she and the other women alighted inside Sano's estate, she gasped.

"This is your house? Oh, it's so big!"

Chiyo quietly went inside the mansion by herself. As Masahiro dismounted, he saw Taeko, Hirata's daughter, run toward him.

"Masahiro," she called, "will you help me make a snowman?"

He would rather have stayed with Okaru, but Reiko said to him, "We'll have to put Okaru and Goza in your room. You can sleep in Akiko's room. Please move your things."

The house was crowded, because after his demotion Sano had had to vacate the chamberlain's compound and move his family back into his old home, where Hirata's family lived. Ordinarily, Masahiro would have objected to sharing a room with his sister, but he would gladly make the sacrifice for Okaru.

"I can't play with you now," he told Taeko. "I'm busy."

Taeko helped him move his clothes, bedding, toys, martial arts equipment, and school materials while she talked about a cat that had chased a mouse through the kitchen and tripped a cook, who'd dropped a jar of pickles. Masahiro barely listened. When they made the last trip to his room, Okaru was there. A maid was putting fresh bedding in a cabinet.

"I've never slept in such a big, beautiful room," Okaru said. Smiling at Taeko, she asked Masahiro, "Who's your little friend?"

"I'm Taeko." The girl clasped her hands behind her back, regarding Okaru with distrust.

"Well, I'm happy to meet you." Okaru whirled around the room, exuberant. "I'm so happy to be here! Masahiro-*san,* your mother has been so kind to me. I like her so much!"

Masahiro couldn't help hoping that she liked him a little, too.

THE SUN WAS setting when Sano left the palace after his meeting with the judges. A golden glow rimmed the western horizon beyond the city. The snow was a pale, vivid blue beneath an indigo sky that sparkled with stars, the moon a brilliant silver half-coin snared in the branches of cypress trees. Sano strode briskly along a path lined with stone lanterns that spilled flame-light onto the snow. He inhaled cold, smoky air that cleansed his lungs; he blew out the tension from a difficult day.

Two men appeared, walking together toward him. Their identical height, slimness, and imperious carriage told Sano who they were. He bid a regretful good-bye to peace and quiet.

"Good evening, Sano-*san,*" Chamberlain Yanagisawa said.

Sano swallowed repugnance and anger as he civilly greeted Yanagi-sawa and Yoritomo.

"How goes your investigation?" Yanagisawa asked.

"I can't complain," Sano said.

"I don't see why not," Yoritomo said. "You've gotten nowhere with the forty-seven *rōnin*. I hear they have you running in circles, with all the different stories they're telling."

His spite was painful for Sano to bear. Sano could see the hatred cor-roding Yoritomo inside, destroying everything that was decent in him. Sano wished he hadn't had to play that cruel trick on Yoritomo.

"I'll get to the truth eventually," Sano said. "I always do."

"The truth can sometimes hurt," Yanagisawa said. "But I shouldn't need to warn you about that." He paused for a beat. "I had a little talk with Ohgami Kaoru this afternoon."

Ohgami was Sano's only ally on the council of elders. Apprehension tightened Sano's nerves.

Yanagisawa laughed, his breath a malignant white vapor in the cold night. "Some of your other friends joined us. Wouldn't you like to know what we discussed?"

"I'm sure you're going to tell me whether I like it or not," Sano said.

"Your friends feel threatened by the forty-seven *rōnin* business. They'd prefer to distance themselves from it."

"From you, too, since you're caught up in it," Yoritomo said, shrill with gleeful malice.

Sano had foreseen the possibility of this, but he was still shocked to hear that his allies, who'd stood by him during two troubled years, would withdraw their support so abruptly. "You've been quick to capitalize on the situation."

The moonlight shone on Yanagisawa's pale, handsome face; his eyes sparked with amusement. "No one's ever called me slow. By the way, your friends say they won't be happy if the supreme court condemns the forty-seven *rōnin*."

Sano was uncomfortably aware that the court was leaning in that direction. Did Yanagisawa know, too?

"You're going to lose your allies," Yoritomo taunted. "You'll be all alone. We'll crush you."

"It's not just us that you'll have to worry about, if the forty-seven *rōnin* are put to death," Yanagisawa said. "The town is rallying around them." He chuckled. "Commoners love underdogs who defy the powers that be. Imagine how much bad feeling they'll have toward the judges, and toward you, the investigator that brought their heroes down."

"You could become the target of an uprising," Yoritomo said.

"You'd like that, wouldn't you?" Sano said, regretting their lost friendship.

"As much as I'll like it when the shogun gets mad at you and sends you to Kyushu," Yoritomo said. "When you're gone, your family will still be here to bear the brunt of his anger."

"And we won't complain," Yanagisawa mocked. "Now, if you don't mind, we'll be on our way." He gazed pointedly at Sano, who was blocking the path.

Sano waited a moment before he stepped aside. He watched the two tall, slim figures stroll off into the night, shoulders touching, heads tilted toward each other. Sano heard the murmur of their voices and supposed they were cooking up more schemes against him. A wry smile tugged his mouth. The forty-seven *rōnin* affair seemed like a tidal wave that was gathering energy, that would swamp everyone who was trying to ride it. If Yanagisawa and Yoritomo wanted him to take a fall, maybe all they needed to do was wait.

WHEN REIKO WAS showing Okaru and Goza around the mansion, a servant met them and said, "Excuse me, but Lady Wakasa is here."

Reiko told the servant to take Okaru and Goza to her parlor and give them refreshments. Then she hurried to the reception chamber. The old matchmaker sat at the *kosatsu*. The table was littered with cake crumbs, an empty teacup, a tobacco box, and a metal basket of hot coals. Lady Wakasa looked cross as she puffed on her tobacco pipe.

"I've been waiting two hours," she said. "Where have you been?"

"A thousand apologies," Reiko said, bowing and sitting opposite Lady Wakasa. "I had some business to take care of. I didn't know you were coming."

"I just heard that your husband arrested those forty-seven *rōnin*," Lady Wakasa said, "so I rushed over to see if there was any news."

Reiko hesitated to tell Lady Wakasa that she'd just moved the *rōnin* leader's mistress into her house. Lady Wakasa was a big gossip. Reiko knew that the fact of Okaru's presence in her home would eventually become public, but she wanted to delay it until she told Sano. Although she risked angering the matchmaker by keeping her in the dark, Reiko said, "Nothing new yet."

"Oh." Disappointed, Lady Wakasa said, "Well, I have news for you. The Chugo clan has withdrawn their marriage proposal."

Reiko was glad Masahiro wouldn't have that dull girl for his wife, but affronted. "Why?"

"They're leery of the forty-seven *rōnin* business." Lady Wakasa grimaced, showing her blackened teeth. "They think it will finish off your husband."

Reiko was disconcerted, even though she'd known that the case could jeopardize her family's future. She'd not realized until this moment that if the worst happened and Sano was sent away, Masahiro—and Akiko—would need marriage agreements more than ever. Now, the only prospect of that security was lost.

"But it's not my husband that will decide their fate; it's the supreme court," she said.

Lady Wakasa waved her hand, dispersing the smoke from her pipe. "Makes no difference. He'll be painted black with the same ink brush." She seemed to relish delivering this bad news. "Besides, there's another reason why the Chugo aren't eager for a connection with your clan. The leader is sympathetic toward the forty-seven *rōnin*. He thinks they're heroes." She snorted. "Beasts, that's what I say they are. He thinks the supreme court is going to condemn them to death, and he's furious at the judges, and your husband."

Vexed, Reiko said, "I suppose that even if I still wanted my son to marry into his clan—which I don't—there's no use telling him that nobody knows what's actually going to happen to the forty-seven *rōnin*."

"No use at all."

"Are there any new prospects?"

"I'm beating the bushes. We'll see what birds fly out. Dear me, it's late; I'd better go."

Reiko escorted Lady Wakasa to the door. As the old woman rode away in her palanquin, Sano strode toward the house. Reiko met him on the veranda. He said, "Was that the matchmaker?" Reiko nodded; he studied her expression. "Your face says that you don't have good news."

"So does yours," Reiko said. "Let's go inside and we'll talk."

THEY SAT AT the *kosatsu,* warmed their hands on hot bowls of tea, and ate a dinner of buckwheat noodles in fragrant lobster soup and raw sea bream cut in slices and served with soy sauce, pickled ginger, and rice flavored with sugar and vinegar. Through the lattice-and-paper partitions came the sound of their daughter Akiko romping in the corridors with the maids. After Reiko told Sano about the withdrawn marriage proposal, he said, "So it's happening again. The rats are leaving a ship they think is going to sink."

He was used to it. Friends and allies had deserted him in droves during past investigations. But it still hurt. Even though the threat of separation from his family was far worse.

"They'll come back." Reiko sounded as if she was trying to convince herself.

Usually the deserters had returned after Sano had surmounted the difficulties and prevailed over his enemies—but not last time, when the kidnapping case had gone so wrong. "There are two people working hard to make sure they don't," Sano said, then told Reiko about his encounter with Yanagisawa and Yoritomo.

Reiko's expression mixed anger, bitterness, and humor. "I swear that I'll make sure those two get their comeuppance someday."

Sano was amused yet chilled by the determination in her voice. He knew what his wife was capable of, and Yanagisawa and Yoritomo had better pray that they never fell into her hands. "That reminds me of the oath that the forty-seven *rōnin* swore against Kira."

"You spoke with them?" Interest brightened Reiko's mood. "What did they say?"

Sano related the conflicting stories he'd heard from Oishi, Chikara, and their friends. "I told Yoritomo I would get to the truth, but right now I'm utterly at sea."

"Did you report the stories to the supreme court? What do the judges think?"

"I did. But their proceedings are confidential, so I can't tell you which way they're leaning."

Reiko studied his face. "I can guess. Things aren't going well for Oishi."

"I can't deny or confirm that. But I have to admit that I'm biased in his favor."

"Even though you know he's lying to you?" Reiko said, puzzled.

Sano nodded. He described his impressions of Oishi, then said, "He may be the best example of a samurai that I've ever run across."

Reiko frowned. "You've always warned me against being partial toward people who are subjects in our investigations. Now you're losing your objectivity."

"I know, I know." Sano was irritated because women always remembered things a man said and threw them back at him later, and because Reiko was right. "But I can't help hoping that some kind of evidence will turn up, that will absolve Oishi and his friends."

"Neither can I," Reiko confessed.

At least he and his wife saw eye to eye on the case, Sano thought gratefully. The occasions when they'd disagreed had been difficult times in their marriage. But the apprehension on her face sent a jolt of foreboding through him. "What is it?" he asked.

"I heard something about Oishi today." Reiko spoke with halting reluctance. "From Ukihashi, his wife. She found out that her husband's mistress is in town. She showed up at the inn, to get a look at Okaru. I'm afraid you're not going to like her version of events." Reiko told the story of the hardships that Oishi's family had experienced. She described Oishi's bitterness toward Kira, the man he held responsible. "Ukihashi thinks the vendetta was personal."

"You're right," Sano said. "I don't like it." Her evidence made the forty-seven *rōnin* sound like every criminal who'd ever lashed out at somebody who'd crossed him. It added substance to the idea that they'd broken the law and deserved to be punished. "Do you think Ukihashi was telling the truth?"

"She seemed honest," Reiko said, "but we've heard so many

contradictory stories that I don't know whether to believe her or not. Will you tell her story to the supreme court?"

"I'll have to. In the meantime, perhaps I can dig up some facts."

"Where will you start digging?"

"At the place where this whole business started. Lord Asano's attack on Kira."

"Wasn't that investigated at the time?"

"Not by me." Sano felt someone watching him. He looked up at a young, pretty woman hovering in the doorway. "Hello?" he said. "Who are you?"

She smiled, shy and nervous, and bobbed a quick bow. "Please excuse me, I didn't mean to interrupt. My name is Okaru."

Disconcerted, Sano turned a questioning look on Reiko.

Her expression was guilty and defensive. "Okaru-*san,* this is my husband."

The *ronin*'s mistress fell to her knees and touched her forehead to the floor. "I'm very honored to make your acquaintance."

"She had to leave the inn where she was staying." Reiko explained about the mob. "I invited her to stay with us for a while. I hope you don't mind."

Sano wished Reiko had asked him first. Housing under his own roof a witness in a case he was investigating could present serious problems. They'd been down that road before. But Reiko gave him her most trusting look of appeal, and he couldn't have refused her even if he'd been cruel enough to expel Okaru into the cold, dark night.

That would be like putting a kitten out to die.

"Of course I don't mind." Sano beckoned. "Come in, join us."

"Oh! Thank you!" Okaru crept on her knees toward Sano and Reiko.

A closer look at her surprised Sano. She was even younger than he'd initially thought. He'd expected someone harder, more brazen. Okaru seemed an incongruous match for Oishi, the tough *ronin.* Then again, Sano could picture her falling in love with a man old enough to be her father, and Oishi enjoying her charms. She also seemed naïve enough to be fooled by an act that Oishi had put on to convince the world that he'd become a no-good bum.

If indeed it had been an act.

Sano pitied Okaru, unwittingly caught up in violent, scandalous events. He understood Reiko's wish to protect her; he felt it himself. "Is there anything you need?" he asked Okaru.

"Oh, your honorable wife has given me so much already," Okaru said, breathless with gratitude. "Delicious food, new clothes, a beautiful room to sleep in . . ." Pensiveness wrinkled her forehead. "But I wish I could see Oishi. I miss him so much."

"Can I take her to see him?" Reiko asked.

Sano didn't think it would hurt, and maybe it would help his investigation. "That can be arranged."

"Oh, thank you!" Okaru exclaimed.

"There's something I want you to do for me while you're there," Sano said.

"I'll do anything for you, anything at all," Okaru said earnestly.

"Ask Oishi what he meant when he said that the vendetta isn't what it seems," Sano said.

Maybe she could get him to tell the truth that Sano had failed to extract.

IN THE MIDDLE of the night, Yanagisawa awakened suddenly. He heard the noise that interrupted his sound sleep—footsteps in the corridor, on the "nightingale floor," which was designed to squeak when someone walked on it. He jumped out of bed, looked down the dimly lit corridor, and saw Yoritomo tiptoeing like a thief.

"What are you doing home?" Yanagisawa asked. "I thought you were with the shogun."

Yoritomo spun around. His face was stricken, pale. His posture drooped. "The shogun didn't want me. He sent me home." Guilt, shame, and fear played over his features. "He's spending the night with one of his other boys."

Yanagisawa was alarmed, even though the shogun regularly bedded his other concubines. "Has this been happening more often recently?"

Yoritomo looked at the floor. He nodded.

Yanagisawa blew out his breath. He'd known the day would come when Yoritomo grew too old for the shogun's sexual tastes. It had happened to

Yanagisawa when he was about the same age as Yoritomo was now. He'd hoped it wouldn't happen to his son before he'd firmed up his control over the regime.

"Why didn't you tell me?" Yanagisawa asked.

"I was afraid you would be angry," Yoritomo said in a small voice. "I'm sorry."

"It's all right. It's not your fault." Yanagisawa was sad that Yoritomo had borne the burden of his fear alone, yet relieved because Yoritomo wouldn't have to satisfy the shogun's desires for much longer. Then he thought of his chart and the names he would have to cross off his list of allies when it became known that he was about to lose a major source of his influence over the shogun and his son the chance of becoming the heir to the regime.

Yoritomo's gaze lifted to Yanagisawa. His eyes mirrored the consternation that Yanagisawa felt. "What are we going to do?"

Yanagisawa began to pace the corridor. He thought aloud: "I'll have to make sure that Sano doesn't pick up the allies I lose."

"How?"

First Yanagisawa had better find out where the forty-seven *rōnin* business was heading and whether he could count on it to ruin Sano. But he didn't want to admit that his plans were so vague and worry Yoritomo. "It's better for you if you don't know."

18

THE DAWN WAS gray and frigid, the sky like a sheet of steel between the earth and the sun. Frozen piles of snow surrounded the courtyard where Sano, Masahiro, and Hirata practiced martial arts. Although they wore thin white cotton jackets and trousers, they didn't notice the cold. Exertion kept them warm as they engaged in two-against-one combat, Masahiro wielding his sword against Sano and Hirata. Wooden blades clacked. Sano had to admire his son's valiant endeavors. As he and Hirata steadily backed Masahiro toward the wall, Masahiro made the men work to parry and dodge his strikes. Sano began to feel winded. He would soon be too old to keep up with his son.

"You're doing something that will get you killed in real combat with multiple attackers," Hirata told Masahiro.

"What?" Masahiro puffed and grunted as he fought.

"While you strike or defend yourself against one of us, you take your attention off the other," Hirata said. "You have to stay aware of all your opponents at the same time."

Masahiro lunged at Hirata and took a gentle hit on the shoulder from Sano. "How?"

"Have you been practicing the breathing and meditation techniques I taught you?"

"Well . . ."

"I know you think they're boring," Hirata said. "I thought so, too, at first. But they're essential to training your mind, which is your most important weapon."

As Sano ducked wild swings from Masahiro, he reflected that one of the few benefits of his demotion was having Hirata under the same roof, available to practice with Masahiro. Although Masahiro had his own martial arts tutor, Hirata could teach the boy valuable lessons. Sano was thankful, yet sad to realize that he couldn't teach Masahiro everything he needed to know. But it was inevitable that Masahiro would grow up and others besides his parents would shape his world. And Sano feared that it would happen sooner than he'd thought, too soon.

"All right, I'll practice breathing and meditation," Masahiro said, "but in the meantime, what should I do if I'm up against multiple attackers?"

"The experts say . . ." Hirata gracefully parried. "You should run."

Combat dissolved into laughter. Sano watched Masahiro trot into the house. He thought of Oishi, who'd led Chikara into a dangerous vendetta. He thought of Yanagisawa, who'd made Yoritomo into his own image. Sano hoped he could do better by Masahiro than Oishi and Yanagisawa had done by their sons.

"What's the plan for today?" Hirata asked as he and Sano entered the house.

"Before we go over that, there's something I have to ask you," Sano said. "If I have to leave Edo, promise me that you'll take care of Masahiro, Akiko, and Reiko."

"It won't come to that," Hirata protested in dismay.

"If it does, I need you to protect them while I'm gone." Sano hated to think he would fail to steer the forty-seven *ronin* affair to a good outcome, but he felt as if he were trying to drive a cart pulled by runaway horses hurtling toward a cliff's edge. He had to prepare for the worst.

"If you go, I go with you."

"No. You'll stay. Promise." He emphasized, "That's an order."

"All right," Hirata said.

Sano could see Hirata balancing between his relief that he would get to stay with his own family and dread that he might have to honor his promise. They were both sobered by the idea that although their master-retainer bond would continue despite a separation, they might never see each other again.

"Today I'll investigate Lord Asano's attack on Kira," Sano said, glad to return to immediate concerns. "I should be able to get a clearer picture of it than I did of the other events leading up to the vendetta."

"How is that?"

"There was a witness."

"I remember now," Hirata said, walking down the corridor alongside Sano. "A man named Kajikawa Yosobei. A keeper of the castle, isn't he?"

"Yes. A supervisor over the women's quarters. Unlike the other people we've questioned so far, he has no personal stake in the case."

"Better yet—an impartial witness."

"Since the two people involved in the attack are dead and can't speak, I'll see what Kajikawa can tell me about the incident," Sano said.

"What would you like me to do today?"

Sano thought a moment, then said, "We've been treating this murder investigation differently from others we've conducted."

"Because we already know who the culprits are," Hirata agreed.

"But our strategy hasn't led us to the truth about the vendetta. So let's look on the case as a regular murder investigation, in which we don't know who killed the victim or why."

"Good idea," Hirata said.

"With that as the premise," Sano said, "where would you start fresh?"

"With the victim."

"That's right. I want you to look into Kira's background."

REIKO COULDN'T WAIT to embark on the big adventure of the day—taking Okaru to see Oishi. She was eager to meet the famous *rōnin* leader, and she hoped she would learn something that would help Sano's investigation and safeguard her family.

She and Chiyo went to Okaru's room and found Okaru snuggled in bed, fast asleep. The breakfast tray that Reiko had sent her an hour ago sat beside her, untouched.

"I thought she was in a hurry to see Oishi," Chiyo said, her voice crisp with disapproval.

Reiko knew she should be annoyed by Okaru's laziness, for it would delay a crucial part of the investigation, but Okaru looked as sweet as a child. "She's tired after everything that's happened."

"She was up awfully late," Chiyo said. "I heard her chattering with the maids. It sounded as if they were having a party."

Reiko had had to get up and tell them to be quiet, so they wouldn't waken Sano or the children. But she said, "It was her first night here. It's all right that she had a little fun."

"If you don't mind, then I don't," Chiyo said. "But her servant makes me uneasy. I saw her prowling around the house. I think she'd gone out somewhere."

Reiko felt uneasy around Goza, too, but she didn't say so. "We'll let Okaru sleep." Eager for action, she headed down the corridor.

Chiyo followed. "There's no point in visiting Oishi without her. What shall we do instead?"

"I just realized that there's another character in the drama surrounding the forty-seven *rōnin*," Reiko said.

"Who is it?"

"Lord Asano's wife. My husband mentioned that Oishi put her in a convent after the house of Asano was dissolved. I expect she's still there. I'd like to visit her. She may have information that could be helpful."

"That's a good idea." Chiyo hesitated. "If you don't mind, I think I'll stay home."

Reiko suspected that Chiyo wanted to make sure that Okaru didn't cause any trouble. "Very well." Maybe Chiyo would get to know the girl and like her better.

Masahiro met Reiko at the door. Reiko said, "I'm going to visit Lady Asano. Would you like to come?"

"Yes, but I can't," Masahiro said. "I just got a message from the shogun. He wants me."

Reiko felt the usual chill that came over her when the shogun called for her son. "Will you be all right?" she asked anxiously.

"Yes, I can take care of myself."

"Remember what your father told you."

"Try not to attract the shogun's attention, stay in the background, I know," Masahiro said. "Don't worry, Mother."

All Reiko could do was utter a silent prayer for his safekeeping and say, "Be good."

AFTER HE'D BATHED, dressed, and breakfasted, Sano went to the section of the palace that was used for government business. It was like a beehive, honeycombed with crowded offices. He squeezed past clerks who hurried along the narrow corridors with stacks of scrolls in their hands. Although the regime had been built on blood spilled during civil wars, it now ran on those cylinders of wood and paper, like a cart on wheels. Sano wandered around for a while before he found the lair occupied by the keepers of the castle.

The keepers ensured that the buildings and furnishings were maintained, that the servants did their jobs. They knew every corner of the castle's labyrinthine structure. Without them, life at court would grind to a halt. Their office was a warren of desks and cabinets, the walls plastered with schedules, charts, and duty rosters. The keepers smoked pipes, consulted, and argued. Sano said loudly, "Where is Kajikawa Yosobei?"

Someone answered, "In the northern courtyard."

Sano went to the courtyard, which was enclosed by guards' barracks and the castle's outer wall. In through the gate rolled oxcarts piled high with pine branches. Servants unloaded the branches onto the ground. It looked as if an entire forest had been cropped to provide the greenery that would grace the palace during the New Year holiday. Kajikawa, a short man in a fur-lined cloak, bustled around, barking orders.

"Wash the mud off those branches!" In his late thirties, he had a large head that bobbled as if it was too heavy for his slight body. "Cut off the dead parts!"

Servants set to work with clippers and water buckets. Sano approached Kajikawa, introduced himself, and said, "I understand that you witnessed Lord Asano's attack on Kira."

Kajikawa cleared his throat nervously. "That's correct." His features were small in proportion to his body, and delicate like a china doll's.

"I'd like to talk to you about it. Can you show me where it happened?"

"Well, all right." Kajikawa led Sano into the palace and stopped in the main corridor. "Here. In the Corridor of Pines."

This was a passage some two hundred paces long and twenty wide, named for the paintings of pine trees on the sliding doors along it. Sano and Kajikawa stood in the middle of the polished cypress floor while officials and servants strolled past them. Shiny wooden pillars supported the high, coffered ceiling. Footsteps and voices echoed. Sano had walked the Corridor of Pines many times, but now he viewed it through fresh eyes, as a crime scene.

"There's a lot of traffic here every day," he said. "And yet, when Lord Asano attacked Kira, you were the only witness? How is that?"

"There are moments when the corridor is pretty deserted," Kajikawa said. "Lord Asano attacked Kira during one of them."

"Could you tell me what happened?" Sano asked.

Kajikawa's delicate eyebrows drew together; his small mouth pursed. "I've already told the officials who investigated the incident."

Sano sensed that his meekness hid a stronger spine than most people would attribute to him. "Why don't you want to tell me? Are you tired of talking about it, or is something else wrong?"

"No." Kajikawa gave way with the air of a man often defeated. "I'd be glad to tell you."

1701 April

AN ARMY OF officials and servants toiled to entertain the imperial envoys who'd arrived from Miyako. Kajikawa rushed back and forth, busy with a million details. He was on his hands and knees on the floor in the reception chamber, picking up lint, when a messenger told him, "The master of ceremonies says that there's been a change in the schedule. The presentation of the gifts will take place an hour earlier than originally planned."

Kajikawa was in charge of conveying the gifts to the envoys. "Are you sure that's what Kira said?"

"Yes, but you can ask him yourself."

Kajikawa hurried through the palace in search of Kira. He paused in the Corridor of Pines to catch his breath. The corridor was vacant, eerily silent. Then a man appeared at the far end, as if he'd materialized out of thin air. It was Lord Asano. He moved toward Kajikawa.

"Greetings," Kajikawa called. "Have you seen the master of ceremonies?"

Lord Asano didn't answer. As he came nearer, Kajikawa could see that the young *daimyo* was pale and trembling, his face a mass of twitches. His hollow eyes looked straight through Kajikawa. A door opened along the corridor between them. Out stepped Kira, elegant in black formal robes, wearing his usual expression of sour disapproval.

"Kira-*san,* could you please confirm the time of the gift ceremony?" Kajikawa called.

The old man turned toward Kajikawa; he started to answer. Suddenly Lord Asano rushed up behind Kira. Rage distorted his features. He seized the hilt of the long sword at his waist and yanked the blade from the scabbard. Kajikawa gasped, too shocked to move or speak, as Lord Asano gripped the sword in both hands and swung at Kira.

Kira saw the emotion on Kajikawa's face and turned around to see what had caused it. Lord Asano's blade came slashing toward him. Kira yelled and dodged. Lord Asano's sword struck a pillar, cutting into the wood.

"What are you doing?" Kira demanded.

"What do you think?" Lord Asano shouted as he jerked his blade free. "Have you forgotten my grievance?"

"My dear friend, I have no idea what you're talking about." Kira pedaled backward down the corridor, his arms raised in self-defense.

"Oh, yes, you do!" Lord Asano charged after Kira.

As Kajikawa watched with his hands over his mouth, Lord Asano sliced at Kira again. The blade struck Kira on the head. Kira howled, was knocked down, and landed on his back. Kajikawa found his voice and screamed. Kira raised himself on his elbows. His face dripping with blood, he crawled away from Lord Asano, who hacked repeatedly at him and repeatedly missed. Lord Asano shouted, "I know this isn't the appropriate time or place to kill you, but kill you I must, you evil, corrupt old snake!"

"Help! Help!" Kira called.

Kajikawa grabbed Lord Asano and restrained him until the castle guards arrived moments later. As they dragged him away, Lord Asano broke down and sobbed.

NOW, ALMOST TWO years after the attack, Sano stood in the Corridor of Pines and touched the cut on the pillar that Lord Asano had struck, the only evidence left. Sano raised his eyes to Kajikawa, who had put a new, surprising slant on the forty-seven *rōnin* case.

"Did Lord Asano really accuse Kira of corruption?" Sano asked.

"Yes." Kajikawa sounded a bit peeved that Sano would question his veracity. Sano suspected he often felt underrated. "I heard him with my own ears."

"You never reported it during the investigation into the attack," Sano said.

". . . No."

"Why not?"

Kajikawa's head bobbled nervously. "At the time, I didn't know if there was any truth to Lord Asano's accusation. I didn't want to mention it and get myself in trouble with Kira."

"So you withheld the information." Sano eyed the little man with reproach because it was information that related to Lord Asano's grievance against Kira, that pertained to the motive for the attack and the underlying truth about the vendetta.

"I should have spoken up," Kajikawa admitted. "I'm sorry I didn't. But neither did Lord Asano. I thought he would try to justify his attack by casting aspersion on Kira. I was surprised that when he was asked what his quarrel with Kira was, he refused to say."

Sano had been surprised, too. He'd wondered what grievance had driven the man into such drastic action. So had everyone else.

"I decided that if Lord Asano didn't say anything, then it was better that I didn't," Kajikawa said primly.

Sano disliked Kajikawa for his cowardice, which he was passing off as discretion. But the man had given Sano a new direction for his inquiries. "You said you didn't know if there was any truth to Lord Asano's charge of corruption against Kira 'at the time.' Does that mean you've changed your mind since then?"

140

Kajikawa cleared his throat. "I don't like to speak ill of the dead."

"I give you permission," Sano said.

"It's just a rumor I heard about Kira a long time ago. I remembered it months after the attack. I don't know whether it's true."

"I'll determine that. Talk."

Kajikawa sighed, perhaps tired of being coerced, perhaps relieved that he could unburden himself of a weighty secret. "When Kira was young, he had a brother-in-law who was a wealthy *daimyo*, Lord Uesugi of Yonezawa Province. Lord Uesugi didn't have any sons. He named Kira's son as his heir. Soon afterward, Lord Uesugi died. Kira's son inherited his title and estate. The rumor said that Kira poisoned Lord Uesugi."

This was the first evidence a witness not personally involved in the case had given that Kira was other than a blameless man. But even as Sano welcomed the evidence, he remarked on an important point: "Nothing seems to have come of the rumor."

"It was never proven. If the government had thought there was any truth to it, Kira would never have risen so high. So you can understand why I haven't brought it up until now."

Sano unwillingly spotted more weaknesses in the evidence. "Even if it was true that Kira poisoned his brother-in-law, I can't see that Lord Asano would have cared enough to attack Kira." And he was hard-pressed to demonstrate that Lord Asano's motive for attacking Kira had any bearing on the forty-seven *rōnin*'s vendetta.

"Maybe there was a connection between Kira's brother-in-law and Lord Asano. People of their rank are so inbred." Now Kajikawa seemed eager to promote the theory that the supposed murder was the motive behind the attack.

Still, Sano saw a new line of inquiry, the histories of the people involved in the case. It might lead him to proof that Kira hadn't been an innocent victim and the forty-seven *rōnin* had done the world a favor.

He warned himself that he must hold tight to his objectivity despite the evidence that swayed his opinion even further toward pardoning Oishi and his comrades. Even if it meant driving the runaway horse cart off the cliff.

19

RIDING HIS HORSE downhill through the passages inside Edo Castle, Hirata saw auras flare like torches in his mental landscape, given off by the guards stationed in the watchtowers and by people passing him on horseback, in palanquins, and on foot. He didn't detect his stalker's. But the man had access to the castle; once he'd even invaded Hirata's own home. Nowhere was Hirata safe. Hirata thought of the priest and the birds he'd seen yesterday. He felt himself and his stalker moving toward a confrontation.

Would it happen today?

Hirata remembered his conversation with Sano. He hoped he wouldn't be needed to protect Sano's family, because he wasn't sure he would live long enough.

He recognized the aura of the other man for whom he was searching. Its unobtrusive, steady pulse led him to the precinct in the castle that housed the shogun's treasures. Rows of fireproof storehouses with white plaster walls, iron doors, and heavy tile roofs were separated by narrow aisles. They contained furniture, silk robes, antique porcelain, and other priceless artifacts. Some of these were rotated in and out of the palace; others were too old, fragile, or unfashionable, and never saw the light of day. Servants were cleaning snow off the storehouses' roofs with long-handled brushes, so that it wouldn't melt, seep inside, and damage the treasures. The aura Hirata had followed belonged to an older man in a wicker hat, baggy coat, and patched leggings. When Hirata approached him, the man said under his breath, "If you give me away, I'll never give you or your master any more information."

Hirata kept his own voice low as he said, "Your identity is safe with me, Toda Ikkyu. But why is our best spy posing as a servant?"

Toda was an agent with the *metsuke*, the Tokugawa intelligence service, which monitored the citizens and protected the regime from insurrections. His face was so nondescript that people without Hirata's mystical powers had difficulty recognizing him even if they were longtime acquaintances. His forgettable looks served him well in his profession.

"Someone's been filching loot," Toda said. "I'm trying to find out who it is."

"Good luck," Hirata said.

Toda raised his eyebrows at Hirata's unfriendly tone. "You don't like me, do you?"

"That's right. Because you pretend to help Sano-*san* while you help his enemies behind his back."

"Sano-*san* is aware that I play both sides. It's a matter of survival."

That didn't absolve Toda, as far as Hirata was concerned. "The last time he asked you to find out what Yanagisawa was up to, you withheld important information. If you hadn't, the shogun's wife might not have been hurt. Sano-*san* might not have been demoted."

"Speaking of disservice to Sano-*san*, does he know that you ride around town while you're supposed to be working?"

Hirata couldn't hide his chagrin. He'd been aware he was under surveillance by *metsuke* agents but hadn't known they'd thought his actions significant enough to report to Toda.

"What are you looking for?" Toda asked.

"None of your business," Hirata said. "What do you know about Kira Yoshinaka?"

Toda chuckled. "You know I'm not to be trusted, and you ask me anyway?"

"You can give me more dirt on people than anyone else can, even if you hold back half of it."

"All right, as long as you know I might very well hold it back. Here's a story about Kira. He's always enjoyed much more prestige than monetary gain. His annual stipend was low compared to other important officials, and he had financial problems. His banker gambled away a lot of his savings. He overspent on keeping up appearances, throwing lavish banquets and such. He made a little extra money by taking bribes from men he instructed in etiquette."

Hirata had gathered that from Oishi's story. "Go on."

"Kira couldn't keep his head above water. He borrowed money, with his house as collateral. When he fell behind on the payments, the moneylender filed a complaint. The magistrate ruled that either Kira paid off the debt, or the moneylender could seize his house. This was two years ago."

"Kira must have paid," Hirata deduced. "When he died, he still had the house."

"Here's what happened," Toda said. "Lord Asano attacked Kira inside Edo Castle. Lord Asano was put to death. His assets were confiscated. A short time later, Kira paid off his debt and saved his house. Where could he have gotten the money?"

"You're implying that it came from the confiscated assets." Hirata was intrigued by the theory but skeptical. "Are you forgetting that the government received the goods from Ako Castle? They all should have gone straight into these storehouses."

"Should have, but didn't. Several chests of gold went missing."

"So they were stolen along the way. How could Kira have gotten his hands on them?"

"Kira's son-in-law is a captain in the army," Toda said. "He's stationed in Harima Province. He was one of the troops who cleaned out Ako Castle."

"And you suspect that he and Kira took a cut of the loot?"

Toda nodded.

Hirata voiced Toda's unspoken words: "But you have no proof."

"None, unfortunately. The captain and his troops were interrogated. They claimed they hadn't stolen the money. Their quarters were searched; the money wasn't found. But when I investigated their connections, I discovered Kira and his discharged debt. I'm sure he was the brains behind the theft."

Toda smiled and cleaned the snow off another storehouse. "Suppose

144

that Kira had his eye on Lord Asano's fortune. Doesn't that put Lord Asano's death in an entirely new light?"

IN THE SHOGUN'S private chambers, a troupe of young actors, naked except for loincloths and silk capes, sang and danced scenes from popular Kabuki plays. The shogun laughed and applauded, surrounded by his male concubines. Yoritomo, his favorite, sat beside him, keeping a watchful eye on everyone else. Masahiro was careful to sit quietly in a corner, avoiding the shogun's attention and watching Yoritomo.

Yoritomo seemed unhappy because the shogun was ignoring him. Now he noticed Masahiro, and jealousy twisted his face. Masahiro understood that Yoritomo thought Sano meant to gain a hold over the shogun by putting Masahiro in the shogun's bed, where disgusting things supposedly happened. It wasn't true, but Yoritomo didn't want anyone to usurp his place, least of all Sano's son.

Yoritomo called to Masahiro, "It's almost time for lunch. Go to the kitchens and order some food."

Masahiro gladly went, even though he hated being treated like an errand boy by Yoritomo, his father's enemy, who had no right to order him around. At least he would be out of the shogun's sight. As he hurried through the castle, he thought of Okaru and could hardly believe she was living in his house. He'd lain awake most of the night, too excited to sleep. He couldn't stop thinking about Okaru.

REIKO IN HER palanquin, and the guards escorting her, joined a long line of travelers making their New Year pilgrimage to Zōjō Temple, the holy city within the city, home to thousands of priests, nuns, monks, and novices. The going was rough, over trampled snow, but nobody seemed to mind; nor did the cold, gray day diminish the holiday spirit.

Along the approach to the main temple, whose curved roofs and tall pagoda stood out against dark evergreen trees, gongs and bells rang continuously, chasing away the evil spirits of the old year. Market stalls sold a special holiday beverage—*shogazake,* a sweet, milky fermented brew seasoned with ginger root. Lieutenant Tanuma bought a cup for Reiko. She sipped it as her procession wound among the forty-eight subsidiary temples that clustered around Zōjō Temple. Many were prosperous, large, and elegant. The shogun was a devout Buddhist and generous to his favorite religious orders. But Reiko's destination was among the humbler, less favored kind.

Reiko alighted outside a weathered plank fence that enclosed two small buildings. These squatted under a shaggy pine tree. The plaster on their walls was scabby and discolored. Because the Asano clan's fortune had been confiscated, Lady Asano hadn't had a dowry to get her into a better convent. When Reiko rang the bell on the gate, a novice nun dressed in a frayed hemp robe and cloak answered.

Reiko introduced herself. "I'm here to see Lady Asano."

The novice let her inside while her guards waited in the road. The larger of the two buildings was the worship hall. It was deserted, the pine boughs by the door the only sign of the New Year season. Reiko and the novice entered the smaller building, the convent. It was almost as cold as outdoors. Reiko removed her shoes but not her coat. In a small chamber with worn-out *tatami* on the floor, the novice seated Reiko by the alcove, which contained a bonsai in a ceramic planter and a scroll that bore a line from a Buddhist scripture. She fetched a charcoal brazier, placed it before Reiko, and departed. Reiko looked around. Furnishings consisted of a low, scarred table and cabinet. She warmed her hands over the brazier, but her toes were numb with cold by the time a thin, stooped nun arrived.

The nun had sagging features below a stubble of white hair that gleamed like frost on her shaved head. She knelt, bowed, and said, "I am the abbess of the convent. My apologies, but you will not be able to see Lady Asano. She does not receive visitors."

"Perhaps your novice forgot to tell you that my husband is the shogun's chief investigator," Reiko said.

"Certainly I respect your honorable husband's status, but I beg you not to intrude on Lady Asano. She came here believing that she would be safe from the outside world."

"I understand, but this is a matter of life and death."

The abbess blinked at Reiko's strong words. "May I ask, life and death for whom?"

146

"The forty-seven *rōnin*," Reiko said.

"What forty seven *rōnin*?"

Reiko was startled. "Haven't you heard?" She explained, "The forty-seven *rōnin* are Lady Asano's late husband's former retainers. They killed the man they blamed for his death. The man was Kira Yoshinaka, the master of ceremonies at Edo Castle."

The abbess drew back in shock. "I had no idea. We're very secluded here."

A loud clatter came from the doorway. There stood a nun who wore a stained apron over her hemp robe, and a faded blue kerchief knotted around her shaved head. The mop and pail she'd just dropped lay on the floor.

"I prayed that it would happen," she said in an exultant voice. This was Lord Asano's widow, Reiko realized. "Someone has avenged us. At last!" She began to weep.

The abbess gave Reiko a look of reproach. "You've upset her. You should leave."

"No," Lady Asano said, sobbing into her hands. "I must speak to her."

"The affairs of the world are not your concern," the abbess reminded her gently.

"Please!" Lady Asano begged.

"The forty-seven *rōnin* have been arrested," Reiko told the abbess. "They may be condemned to death even though they fulfilled their duty to their master. Lady Asano may be the only person who can save them. Would you want their deaths on your conscience?"

The abbess reconsidered, said, "You may have a few moments with Lady Asano," then withdrew.

Wiping her tears on her sleeve, Lady Asano hurried into the room. She knelt and leaned toward Reiko. "How did the revenge happen? I want to know everything."

Disconcerted by such avid curiosity, Reiko took a closer look at Lady Asano. The woman was at least ten years younger than Oishi's wife, Ukihashi. Her skin was still firm, her body's contours softer. But unlike Oishi's wife, Lord Asano's had never been a beauty. Lady Asano had small, widely spaced eyes and an irregular, full-lipped mouth in a round face. Even in better times she would have been plain.

"The forty-seven *rōnin* broke into Kira's house on the night of the blizzard," Reiko said. "They killed Kira."

"Tell me how." Lady Asano's sallow cheeks turned pink.

Reiko shrank from feeding her bloodlust with gory details, but Lady Asano deserved to know them, and there was apparently no one else to tell her. "They cut off his head."

Lady Asano breathed through her mouth. "Did he feel pain?"

"Probably not much," Reiko said. The disappointment on Lady Asano's face chilled her. Lady Asano clearly bore a grudge against Kira. "It would have happened fast."

"Did Kira have time to be afraid?" Lady Asano seemed to hunger for proof that he'd suffered.

"I expect so. When the forty-seven *rōnin* invaded his house, he escaped through a secret exit and hid in a shed. He'd have listened to them killing his retainers. He'd have heard them coming after him."

"Which one of them did it?"

"It was Oishi."

Gratitude and shame mingled in Lady Asano's expression. "I thought he'd neglected his duty to my husband. But I misjudged him. He's an honorable samurai after all." Apprehension replaced her glee over Kira's fate. "What's going to happen to Oishi? And the others?"

"Nobody knows yet." Reiko told Lady Asano about the scandal, the controversy in the government, and the supreme court.

Lady Asano listened with a bemused air. "To think that all this happened while I've been shut away in here. And I never would have known but for you." Her voice faltered in confusion. "Why did you come?"

Reiko explained that Sano was investigating the vendetta for the supreme court and she was helping him. She forbore to mention that she was trying to save her family; she didn't want to burden Lady Asano with her own problems. "There are questions about what led up to the vendetta. The fate of the forty-seven *rōnin* may depend on the answers. I came because I was hoping you could provide some."

"Me?" Leeriness narrowed Lady Asano's small eyes into slits. "How could I?"

"You were married to Lord Asano. You knew Oishi. And I think that we women often see and hear more than people give us credit for."

Lady Asano clasped her rough hands together, as if protecting something in the space between them.

"Oishi and his men put their lives in jeopardy to avenge your husband," Reiko reminded her. "Shouldn't you help them now that they're in trouble?"

Lady Asano looked down at her hands. "What are they saying about what they did?"

Reiko didn't want to be the one answering questions, but unless she complied, Lady Asano would probably tell her nothing. "Oishi says that Kira bullied your husband because he refused to pay a bribe. He says your husband attacked Kira because he snapped. Oishi's son claims that the forty-seven *rōnin* always intended to avenge Lord Asano, and they waited two years to put Kira off guard."

When Lady Asano remained silent and uncooperative, Reiko said, "But Oishi's wife tells a different story. She says Oishi never cared about avenging your husband's death. She claims he killed Kira because it was Kira's fault that he became a *rōnin*."

"*Ukihashi.*" Lady Asano said the name as if spitting out poison. Her head came up. "I'm not surprised at anything she does anymore."

"It sounds as if the two of you have bad blood," Reiko said, curious. "Why?"

"She was my chief lady-in-waiting. We were friends. Or so I thought." Lady Asano's gaze wouldn't meet Reiko's. "I'd rather not talk about her."

Reiko dropped the matter, for now. "But there are other conflicting stories about the vendetta. My husband doesn't know which to believe, and neither will the supreme court. If you have information that could help the forty-seven *rōnin,* you'd better speak up."

Lady Asano responded with the coy smile of a girl who has secrets she refuses to share. She seemed immature despite the fact that she was in her late twenties. "There are a lot of things that never came out right after my husband attacked Kira and committed ritual suicide."

Frustration beset Reiko. "Then tell me. Or my husband will take you to Edo Castle and make you tell the supreme court."

Faced with this disagreeable alternative, Lady Asano pouted, then said, "I suppose now is a good time for the secrets to start coming out."

20

1701 *March*

LADY ASANO STOOD outside the mansion in her husband's estate in Edo. She waited anxiously for Lord Asano, who was due to arrive today. They'd been apart for eight months because the law required all *daimyo* to spend four months of each year in the capital and the rest in their provinces while their wives lived in Edo all year round. This was one method by which the Tokugawa regime controlled them and prevented insurrections. But even though Lady Asano was eager to see her husband, she fretted. In what condition would he be?

Lord Asano rode in the gate, accompanied by his entourage. He leaped from his horse, as energetic as when he'd left Harima Province two months ago. He laughed with exuberance as he ran up to Lady Asano.

"It's so good to see you, my dearest wife!" His youthful, handsome face shone.

Lady Asano smiled, but her heart dropped. She feared his gay moods because she knew what happened after they passed.

"Let's celebrate!" Lord Asano called to his men, who'd barely gotten off their horses to stretch their stiff muscles.

The homecoming party lasted two days and nights. Lord Asano brought in musicians, singers, and dancers to entertain his household. Wine flowed at a continuous banquet. When it was over, everyone except Lord Asano was exhausted. He said, "I want to go out on the town!"

Lady Asano couldn't stop him; no one could—he was the ruler of his domain. She said to Oishi, his chief retainer, "You'll take care of him, won't you?"

"Never fear." Oishi was used to ensuring that Lord Asano came to no harm.

They were gone for three days. Lord Asano gambled in the Nihonbashi merchant quarter, drank in teahouses, and enjoyed expensive courtesans in the Yoshiwara licensed pleasure quarter. Lady Asano waited at home until Oishi brought Lord Asano back in a palanquin. Lord Asano was worn out, sick, and miserable. As Lady Asano put him to bed, he moaned, "I want to die!"

Early in their marriage Lady Asano had hated him for his wild swings between extravagant behavior that humiliated her and his black despair. But she'd learned that he couldn't help himself; he was possessed by two evil spirits that yanked him up and down like a puppet on a pulley. Now she felt sorry for him. As she tried to nurse him back to health, he said, "Leave me alone." All he wanted to do was sleep.

A few days later, Oishi brought bad news. "Imperial envoys are coming to Edo. The shogun has ordered you to be their host."

Lord Asano's eyes went dark with horror in his sickly, unshaven face. "I can't do it."

"You must," Oishi said.

He got Lord Asano out of bed, washed and groomed and dressed him. They went to Edo Castle, where Kira, the master of ceremonies, would instruct Lord Asano on court ritual. When they returned that night, Lady Asano watched her husband practice the lessons he'd been given.

"I'm going to blunder in front of everyone!" he wailed.

Things went downhill as the lessons continued. Lady Asano sensed that there was more afoot than his usual despair and the strain of the impending visit from the envoys. One night while he lay in bed weeping, she said, "Husband, what's wrong?"

"It's Kira," Lord Asano confessed. "He has it in for me."

"But why? You and he hardly know each other."

"He knows about the things I do. He says I have everything and I'm throwing it away. He calls me a disgrace to the samurai code of honor."

"He's trying to tear you down because he's envious," Lady Asano suggested.

"But he's right." Lord Asano sobbed. "I am a disgrace. He taunts me and goads me to defend myself, and I can't, and he laughs. He says I should put myself out of my misery."

Lady Asano was horrified, and furious at Kira. "The old devil! Don't listen!"

Lord Asano didn't speak of Kira again. He let Oishi drag him to the lessons every day, even though he couldn't eat or sleep. He was a wreck, his eyes red, his face twitching, his body trembling. Every day he came home looking worse.

Until the day he didn't come home.

That was the day Oishi brought Lady Asano the terrible news: Lord Asano had drawn his sword and attacked Kira inside Edo Castle.

Lady Asano was allowed to see her husband one last time before he committed *seppuku* that evening. "Why did you do it?" she cried.

"I couldn't take any more," Lord Asano said. Triumph shone through his misery. "At least I defended my honor."

"INSTEAD OF DESTROYING Kira, my husband destroyed himself," Lady Asano told Reiko. Sitting in the bare, cold chamber of the convent where she'd been consigned to live out her life, she said bitterly, "Kira won."

"Not for good," Reiko pointed out. She now understood why Lady Asano had lusted for Kira's blood. She sympathized with Lady Asano because she herself felt the same toward Chamberlain Yanagisawa, who tormented her own husband. Reiko tasted the fear that Sano would someday crumble as Lord Asano had. "Kira got his just deserts."

"That's some consolation." Lady Asano smiled but quickly sobered. "I've confessed my husband's secret—that he was weak and Kira got the best of him. I've dishonored his memory." She appealed anxiously to Reiko. "Will it save Oishi and the other *rōnin*?"

Reiko had begun to think that Kira was the villain in the case and the forty-seven *rōnin* should be pardoned. "I'll tell my husband about it. He'll tell the supreme court. We'll see."

She would see whether it led to a verdict that the shogun thought was satisfactory, and whether Sano would regain his status or be permanently separated from their family.

SANO CONSULTED THE top expert on samurai clan lineage, an old historian. The historian said, "Lord Asano and Kira's brother-in-law, Lord Uesugi, are related by several marriages, but Lord Uesugi died before Lord Asano was born. I've heard the rumor that Kira poisoned Lord Uesugi, but it faded a few years after Lord Uesugi's death. I would be surprised if Lord Asano cared what had happened to a distant relation he'd never met."

The story that Kajikawa, the keeper of the castle, had told Sano seemed to amount to nothing. If Sano wanted dirt on Kira, he had to dig in other ground.

He located Kira's three former subordinates and two pupils whom Kira had been instructing in etiquette up until the day before his murder. They were in the chamber where the shogun would hold his New Year banquet. The subordinates were samurai in their forties, each the type of conscientious man who kept the government running but would never rise into its upper ranks. They huddled together, arguing about some point of court procedure. The pupils were young officials from the shogun's retinue, who would have some part in conducting the banquet. They stood about looking bored. Sano gathered the five men for a talk about Kira.

"What kind of person was he?" Sano asked.

The onus of answering fell upon a man named Mimura, the new master of ceremonies. Pale, thin, and anxious, he didn't seem happy to be saddled with his role of elected spokesman or his predecessor's duties.

"Kira-san was very dedicated to his job," Mimura said. His companions nodded.

"How was Kira to work with?" Sano probed.

"He was strict about details."

Sano gathered that no one here had liked Kira. "Did he take bribes?"

Mimura paused, torn between his duty to answer honestly and his reluctance to malign his dead superior. "They weren't excessive."

"Is that true of the bribes he took from you?" Sano asked the pupils. They assented, nervously. "Did he treat you well?"

Put on the spot, one of them echoed Mimura: "He was strict."

Sano turned to Kira's subordinates. "What happened between Kira and Lord Asano? Why did Lord Asano attack Kira?"

"We wouldn't know," Mimura said. "We weren't there."

"Had Kira ever done anything that could be considered corrupt?"

"Not as far as I know."

The five men looked everywhere but at Sano or one another.

"This is serious," Sano said. "Forty-seven lives depend on the supreme court, which will base its verdict on the results of my investigation." The thoroughness of his investigation could determine how well the verdict was received, which in turn would determine his own fate. That made Sano impatient toward these tight-lipped witnesses. "If you know anything that could pertain to the vendetta, it's your duty to tell me. Do you understand?"

The men nodded, but no one coughed up any more information.

Sano perceived something big hidden beneath their caution, like a whale swimming just below the surface of the ocean. He sensed that although each man knew it was there, each wasn't sure whether the others did. And none wanted to name it.

AFTER HIRATA FINISHED his talk with Toda the spy, he headed toward Kira's mansion, to get information about Kira from what was left of his household.

Hirata crossed the Ryōgoku Bridge. In the entertainment district on the other side, visitors braved the cold to patronize stalls that sold *shogazake*, red-bean cakes, and barley-sugar candy. Troupes of itinerant actors abounded. They came to town every New Year season; when they left, they would take the evil spirits of the old year with them. Dressed in colorful costumes and masks, they performed plays in exchange for a few coins. Hirata paused to watch a troupe whose leader wore the mask of a lion with snarling mouth and wild yellow mane. He juggled three red balls while his legs pranced beneath his tattered red robe. An audience clapped.

Suddenly Hirata felt his stalker's aura, the mighty, terrifying pulse.

The juggler in the lion mask tossed one of his balls high, high up. As Hirata looked around for the source of the aura, the ball landed in the juggler's hand, ignited with a loud bang, and burst into orange flames. The audience cheered, thinking it was magic, part of the act. The juggler screamed. His other balls dropped. He hurled the fiery orb away from him. It soared above the audience and vanished in a puff of smoke.

Hirata stared, amazed.

The juggler's sleeve had caught fire. His robe went up in flames. Shrieking, he ran and stumbled, a burning lion on a rampage.

Cries erupted from the audience. Hirata jumped from his horse, whipping off his coat as he ran. He beat the coat against the flames while the juggler rolled in the snow. After the fire was out, people flocked around the burned man. He sat up and ripped the mask off his head. He was a young fellow with bushy hair and a good-natured face. He held out his hands, looked at them, then patted his body. Everyone exclaimed, because he wasn't burned at all. The fire had left not one charred patch of skin or fabric.

The juggler jumped up and bowed, happy to take credit for the best performance of his life, even if he didn't know how it had happened. The audience showered him with coins.

The aura thrummed close behind Hirata, so powerfully that it felt like a roll of thunder hitting his back. He turned. A man came striding toward him and stopped within arm's reach. He was a samurai, his shaved crown bare to the winter day. His aura stirred up a wind that keened around him and Hirata. He wore a dark brown coat and flowing black trousers over his tall, muscular physique. He had a square jaw and features so strong and regular that he could pose for a portrait of the ideal samurai. But his perfection was animated by a left eyebrow that was higher than the right. It and a twinkle in his eyes gave him a rakish appearance.

Hirata was rattled by the scene he'd just witnessed, and stunned to find himself face to face with his stalker. "Who are you?" He gestured toward the juggler, who was busy picking up coins. "Did you do that? Why have you been following me around? Who's the priest with the birds? And the soldier I saw when I found the poem?" Hirata ran out of breath. He was shaking with anger and fear.

The samurai's left eyebrow rose higher, in amusement. "My name is

Tahara." His voice had a curious quality that was at once smooth and rough, that brought to mind a stream flowing over jagged rocks. When Hirata started to repeat his questions, Tahara lifted his hand. Hirata felt the words die on his tongue, as if they were flies that Tahara had just swatted.

"We'll talk when the time is right," Tahara said.

His eyes were deep and dark and fathomless behind the twinkle. Hirata's head ached from the pounding of Tahara's aura against his mind. Then Tahara turned to walk away.

Hirata said, "Wait." His voice felt thick and slow in his throat; its pitch sounded strangely low. People around him moved sluggishly, as if through water. Their voices echoed like bells rung under the sea. Tahara walked with an easy gait, but he flashed across space with the speed of lightning. His image flickered along the entertainment district and across the Ryōgoku Bridge. Hirata watched the receding figure grow smaller until he could no longer see Tahara. The aura faded. Hirata blinked, breathed deeply, and looked around. The world had regained its usual noises and bustling motion.

"What's going on?" he said. His voice felt and sounded normal. The ache in his head was gone. But so was the man who could have answered his question. Hirata would have to wait for the right time—whenever that was.

AFTER HE WENT to the palace kitchens to order the food for the shogun's party, Masahiro couldn't resist sneaking home to see Okaru.

He hurried through the castle, afraid that Yoritomo would point out his absence and get him in trouble. His heart beat fast with anticipation as he slipped through a back door of his family's mansion. He didn't want to run into anyone who would ask him why he was home early. He reached the private quarters unnoticed and tiptoed down the corridors.

"Masahiro!"

The sound of his name, called in a high, girlish voice, startled him so much that he jumped and yelped. He turned and saw Taeko.

"Don't ever sneak up on me like that!" he hissed.

Her smile faded. "I'm sorry. I didn't mean to—"

"Never mind," Masahiro whispered.

"Why are you whispering?" Taeko said. "And why were you tiptoeing?"

"It's none of your business. Go away."

Taeko's lip quivered. She turned and fled.

Masahiro felt bad because he'd hurt her, which he hadn't meant to do. Then he heard someone singing quietly. The voice was feminine and off-key but sweet. Masahiro followed the singing to the bath chamber. Steam scented with a floral fragrance seeped from the open door. Okaru sang, missing the high notes. Masahiro heard scrubbing and splashing. He knew it was rude to spy on people while they bathed, but he cautiously peeked.

Okaru crouched naked on the slatted wooden floor, half turned away from him. Her long hair was pinned up in a knot. She scrubbed her arms with a cloth bag of perfumed rice-bran soap. Her skin gleamed wetly. Her bottom was slim but rounded. When she raised her arm to wash under it, Masahiro saw the curve of her small breast, and the nipple like a pink bud.

He'd seen naked women before—the housemaids who opened their robes to fan themselves on hot days, the peasant girls who dived for shellfish at the beach—and he'd never thought anything of it. But the excitement that had been growing inside him ever since he'd met Okaru now surged with a force like thunder. Such a strong, strange desire gripped him that he could hardly breathe.

Oblivious to him, Okaru soaped her chest and stomach; she twisted around to scrub her back. When she washed between her legs, her singing lapsed into a little purr of pleasure. His body's quickening need dizzied Masahiro. Bewildered by what was happening to him, he was terrified that Okaru would catch him spying on her, but he couldn't stop.

Okaru rose, lifting a bucket of water. As she poured the water over herself, she turned. Masahiro stood open-mouthed, watching the water cascade down her breasts. His gaze followed its spill. Her pubis was shaved, the cleft between her legs clearly visible.

Masahiro's excitement soared. Still unaware of his presence, Okaru stepped into the sunken bathtub. Masahiro heard footsteps. Cousin Chiyo came walking around the corner. She saw him, smiled, and started to speak. He sprang away from the bath chamber. Guilty shame flushed his face. Chiyo stopped, puzzled. Her glance moved from him to the bath chamber. She saw Okaru and said sharply, "Okaru-*san*. When you take a bath, please close the door."

Masahiro heard Okaru say "Oh, I'm sorry" and Chiyo slide the door shut. He ran like a burglar caught in the act.

21

WHEN REIKO ARRIVED home from her trip to the convent, Chiyo met her on the veranda and said, "May I speak to you?"

"Of course," Reiko said. "You can come with me to take Okaru to see Oishi. We can talk on the way there."

Chiyo seemed to search for words. "I must talk to you alone. Now, if you don't mind."

"Well, then, let's go inside," Reiko said, "so you don't catch cold."

"Out here is better."

"All right, now I'm curious," Reiko said. "What is it?"

Chiyo said haltingly, "It's about Okaru."

"Has she done something to upset you?" Reiko wasn't pleased to think that her friend's dislike of her guest had worsened. She shouldn't have left them alone together.

"This isn't in regard to me." Chiyo sounded unusually formal, constrained. "I don't think Okaru is good to have around the children."

"Because of her station in life?" Reiko couldn't help being offended by Chiyo's prejudice.

"That's not what I mean," Chiyo hastened to say, then faltered. "It's her manners."

"Even if Okaru's manners aren't perfect, I don't think they'll rub off on Masahiro or Akiko."

"I'm afraid she'll be harmful to them . . . in other ways."

Reiko began to lose her patience. "She wouldn't hurt them. Why, I saw her playing with Akiko yesterday, and she was so gentle and kind."

"It's not Akiko that I'm most worried about."

"You're worried about Masahiro?" Reiko was confused. "He can take care of himself."

"Perhaps not as well as you think," Chiyo murmured.

Before Reiko could ask Chiyo to say exactly what she meant, Okaru came out the door. Her lovely young face was bright with eagerness. "Oh, good, you're back!" she said to Reiko. "Can we go and see Oishi now?"

Hirata walked up to the house, followed by Sano. Sano greeted everyone, then said to Reiko and Hirata, "The supreme court convenes in a few moments, and I have to testify. If you've got any new information for me, tell me now."

Reiko cast a mystified glance at Chiyo, who gazed helplessly back at her. Whatever Chiyo was trying to tell her would have to wait.

SANO ARRIVED IN the palace to find the supreme court already seated. Once again Inspector General Nakae headed the row of Chamberlain Yanagisawa's seven cronies, who included Lord Nabeshima and Colonel Hitomi. Magistrate Ueda headed the row of seven men facing them, with old Minister Motoori and Finance Superintendent Ogiwara. They had already begun to discuss the case, and Sano could see that the acrimony had grown.

"Greetings, Sano-*san*," Magistrate Ueda said. "Have you anything new to report?"

Sano knelt at the end of the rows and bowed. "Quite a bit."

"May it help us settle our differences before something regrettable happens," said Inspector General Nakae, the squattest, surliest pumpkin in his patch.

Chamberlain Yanagisawa sauntered into the room. Sano felt a quick, hot leap of anger. The judges looked surprised. Magistrate Ueda addressed Yanagisawa in a voice that cloaked displeasure and hostility in politeness. "My apologies, but I must ask you to leave, Honorable Chamberlain. The supreme court's proceedings are private and no outsiders can be present unless asked to testify."

Yanagisawa smiled. "You shall make an exception for me." His tone said that he outranked the judges, and anyone who objected to his behavior would pay. He seated himself at the head of the two rows. Magistrate Ueda compressed his mouth in exasperation. Yanagisawa said with mocking courtesy, "Proceed with your report, Sano-*san*. I'm all ears."

Sano thought that Yanagisawa couldn't resist interfering with his work for the supreme court. Or perhaps Yanagisawa wanted to influence the verdict. But he might just be curious about how the court was progressing. At any rate, Sano couldn't disobey an order from the shogun's second-in-command.

Fortified with the information that he and Hirata and Reiko had collected and shared earlier, Sano began his testimony with the story that Kajikawa had told him about Lord Asano's botched attempt to kill Kira.

"I'll allow open discussion," Magistrate Ueda said.

"So Kajikawa changed the statement he gave during the investigation into the attack," Superintendent Ogiwara said in his theatrical voice. "Back then, he said Lord Asano gave no indication of why he attacked Kira. Now he says that Lord Asano called Kira corrupt."

The inspector general grimaced as he scribbled notes. "But did he really? If so, Kajikawa should have said so back then."

Sano could tell that Magistrate Ueda and Superintendent Ogiwara welcomed the news that Lord Asano's attack might have been justified, but Inspector General Nakae and his side didn't. Sano glanced at Yanagisawa. The chamberlain wore his smoothest countenance, but Sano knew he was displeased because Sano had unearthed new evidence.

Lord Nabeshima, seated beside the inspector general, scornfully discredited the castle keeper's evidence. "There's nothing to support the theory that Kira did anything wrong."

"There is." Sano relayed Lady Asano's story, which Reiko had told him, of Kira's campaign to destroy her husband.

"Deplorable," said Minister Motoori from Magistrate Ueda's side. He squinted, half blind but astute, his crippled limbs drawn up like gnarled twigs under his black robes. "Kira preyed on a weak, unstable man. He drove Lord Asano to a mental breakdown."

"I say that constitutes a legitimate quarrel," Superintendent Ogiwara boomed.

"One in which Kira was the aggressor," Minister Motoori clarified. "He goaded Lord Asano into attacking him. If Lord Asano hadn't kept his mouth shut, he would have been excused and Kira would have been the one sentenced to death, for provoking violence in Edo Castle. The forty-seven *rōnin* wouldn't have needed to avenge Lord Asano, and we wouldn't be having this conversation."

"The only information you've brought us about the quarrel comes from Lord Asano, secondhand," Inspector General Nakae said to Sano. "Consider this: What did the first witness hear? Only a snippet of conversation between Kira and Lord Asano. And who is the second witness? She's Lord Asano's wife. She's probably looking for someone to blame for his death and her hard life. She's throwing mud on Kira, now that he's not around to contradict her story."

"Even if her story is true, the quarrel sounds like a personal feud to me," said Colonel Hitomi, the inspector general's ally. The old soldier sat with his cane across his knees. "What Lady Asano described isn't a crime, and I wouldn't call it corruption."

"I agree," Lord Nabeshima said. "Corruption involves crimes against the government."

"I've found evidence that Kira's campaign against Lord Asano was part of a crime against the government." Sano told the story Hirata had heard from Toda the spy, of the goods confiscated from Ako Castle, the missing gold, and Kira's discharged debt.

The judges were shocked wordless. Yanagisawa met Sano's gaze. He slowly brought his hands together, then moved them apart, together and apart, in silent, mocking applause.

Magistrate Ueda recovered his voice. "So it's possible that Kira goaded Lord Asano into drawing a sword in Edo Castle, in order to have his estate confiscated and steal his gold."

"That's what I would call corruption," General Hitomi said reluctantly. "The gold rightfully belonged to the government. Kira cheated the shogun."

Inspector General Nakae narrowed his eyes at his ally who'd switched sides on him. "You're being premature. Has Sano-*san* offered any proof for his theory? No. It sounds to me as if he's fabricated the whole thing out of a few unconnected circumstances."

"These could be the extenuating circumstances we've been looking for." Superintendent Ogiwara's large, protuberant eyes gleamed with satisfaction. "They could justify the shogun voiding his original decision to exempt Kira from punishment for the incident between him and Lord Asano."

Minister Motoori said, "This is the one thing that would allow the shogun to change his mind without losing face: Kira committed a crime against him. Kira deserved to be punished."

"You're building a case out of air and nonsense!" Inspector General Nakae protested. "The theory is incredibly far-fetched!"

"Far-fetched or not, this is the best explanation for Kira's actions that I've heard," Magistrate Ueda said.

Sano watched Chamberlain Yanagisawa, who listened with a calculating look in his eyes. The judges who hadn't spoken yesterday seemed even more inhibited today, by Yanagisawa's presence.

"What do you think?" Sano asked Yanagisawa.

The chamberlain smiled at Sano's attempt to learn where he stood on the issue. "I think the judges should vote."

His opinion had the force of an order from the shogun. Magistrate Ueda looked vexed and said, "We'll take a blind vote." He ordered Inspector General Nakae to tear a sheet of paper into strips, give one to each judge, and pass around his ink brush. Yanagisawa frowned in annoyance because the magistrate had circumvented his ploy to find out the judges' positions. "Write 'condemn' or 'pardon,'" Magistrate Ueda said. "Then pass your votes to me."

Fourteen judges took turns writing while they screened their papers with their hands. They folded the papers into tight little packets. Magistrate Ueda collected the fourteen votes, unfolded them, and divided them face up into two piles. "Six in favor of condemning the forty-seven *rōnin* this time. Eight in favor of pardoning."

Sano felt his spirits rise; yet he wasn't sure he believed in the evidence he'd presented that had swayed the court. Satisfaction showed on Minister Motoori's and Superintendent Ogiwara's faces. Lord Nabeshima looked appalled. Yanagisawa scrutinized the other judges, who kept their expressions carefully blank.

Inspector General Nakae burst out, "All of you who changed your vote to pardoning the forty-seven *rōnin*, you're damned fools!"

"Rule number five," Magistrate Ueda said. "No rude language in the courtroom."

"The hell with your rules!" Nakae retorted.

"Rule number six," Magistrate Ueda said calmly. "Anyone who breaks the rules will—"

"Be thrown off the court?" Inspector General Nakae said, incredulous.

Lord Nabeshima came to the aid of his comrade. "You'd like to get rid of us, wouldn't you? But you can't. The shogun put us on the court. We stay unless he says go."

"—will be escorted to a separate chamber, and will communicate with the other judges via written notes," Magistrate Ueda finished.

Inspector General Nakae rose. An angry blush suffused his face; he looked more like an overripe, moldy pumpkin than ever. "Have you forgotten who you're talking to?"

Lord Nabeshima stood, too. As he and Nakae loomed over Magistrate Ueda, he said, "You're exceeding your authority."

Sano felt the threat behind their words and the hot flare of their tempers. Colonel Hitomi reared up on his knees; Superintendent Ogiwara hopped into a defensive crouch, like a Kabuki actor playing a samurai ready for combat. The other judges recoiled in consternation. Even Yanagisawa looked unsettled. Was the supreme court about to self-destruct in a brawl?

Magistrate Ueda remained seated and unruffled. "Guards!" he called.

Four soldiers appeared, so quickly that Sano figured they'd been stationed nearby, trying to eavesdrop on the court.

"Take them to the east reception room," Magistrate Ueda said.

Inspector General Nakae and Lord Nabeshima spluttered in indignation, but they went. A hostile silence followed their departure. Sano could tell that Magistrate Ueda's high-handed action had offended other judges besides them. His heart sank because the quarrel boded as ill for him as for the court's proceedings.

"The court will take a recess," Magistrate Ueda said. "We'll reconvene in an hour and try again."

As everyone rose and filed out the door, Yanagisawa bumped shoulders with Sano. "It looks as if the judges won't be able to reach a verdict at all, let alone one that pleases everyone." He smiled a smug, vicious smile. "Lady Reiko and the children are sure to miss you when you're gone."

22

CHIYO ASKED TO be excused from the trip to visit Oishi. Reiko didn't press her to go. It was better to keep Chiyo and Okaru apart than increase Chiyo's dislike of Okaru or let it spoil Okaru's pleasure.

Reiko felt bad because Okaru had come between her and Chiyo. She had a dilemma on her hands: She owed her loyalty to her friend and relative, but she couldn't abandon a person in need who was a guest in her house. She must fulfill her promise to help Okaru.

Goza took Chiyo's place inside the palanquin. The servant was dour and silent, but Okaru could hardly contain her ebullience as they rode through the city.

"I can't wait to see Oishi!" Okaru smoothed her hair, which she'd pinned up and studded with paper flowers. "Do I look all right?"

"You look lovely," Reiko said.

"It's been so long since Oishi and I were together. I feel as if we'll be strangers when we meet. Oh, Lady Reiko, what will I do?"

Reiko hardly felt qualified to give advice. "Just act natural, I suppose."

Their procession reached the Hosokawa clan estate, which looked cold and unwelcoming, set amid bare trees, the snow on its roof grayed by soot. Okaru gasped with awe and said, "This is where Oishi is in jail? It looks like a palace!"

A servant escorted Reiko, Okaru, and Goza into an elegant reception chamber in the mansion. "I'm so nervous," Okaru said, fidgeting with her clothes. When they heard footsteps in the corridor, she cried, "It's him!" She leaped to her feet as Oishi entered the chamber.

He wasn't what Reiko had expected. Her imagination had built the leader of the forty-seven *rōnin* into a giant with a face like an iron war mask. But Oishi in the flesh was smaller, older, and clearly not in good health. His strength showed only in his eyes. They had the hard, fiery light of steel heated in a swordsmith's forge. He favored Okaru with a scowl that must have been the last thing Kira had seen before Oishi cut off his head.

Okaru didn't notice. She flung herself at Oishi and threw her arms around him. She wept while murmuring endearments.

His arms shot out, breaking her grasp as if she were a flimsy vine that had twined around him. Okaru stumbled backward.

"My love?" she said, her smile faltering. "What's wrong?"

"What are you doing here?" Oishi demanded.

The jubilance in Okaru's eyes dimmed. "I—I wanted to see you."

She took a step toward him, but Oishi raised his hand to fend her off and said, "You shouldn't have come."

Okaru gazed at him with hurt disbelief, like a child slapped for no reason. "Aren't you glad to see me?"

Reiko couldn't believe Oishi's cruelty, either. She heard a low growl from Goza. The servant's face had taken on the look of a watchdog whose owner is threatened.

"That should be obvious. I never want to see you again." Oishi turned to leave.

With a wail, Okaru lunged after him. She tripped on her skirts, sprawled, and grabbed Oishi's ankle. "My love, why are you treating me like this?"

Oishi kicked savagely at her. "Let go!"

Appalled, Reiko hurried to Okaru and touched her shoulder. "Come away before you get hurt."

Goza stalked toward Oishi with her fists clenched. Okaru hung on, pleading, "Don't you love me anymore?"

"I never loved you." Contempt edged Oishi's voice.

"But—but—" Okaru pulled herself, hand over hand, up his leg.

166

"You promised we would marry someday." Her eyes pleaded with him. "Don't you remember?"

Oishi laughed, a chortle filled with disgust. "I never meant any of those things."

Shock loosened Okaru's grip on him. She sat back on her heels. "You lied?" she said in a tiny voice.

"That's right." Oishi seemed to relish the pain he was causing. Reiko's admiration for him turned to revulsion. "I only told you what you wanted to hear."

"But why?"

"I was using you," Oishi said with brutal honesty. "You were part of my act."

"Act?" Okaru shook her head in confusion. "What act?"

"To make myself seem like a no-good, drunken bum. To make Kira think I'd forgotten about avenging my master. And it worked. I fooled Kira. He's dead. And I don't need you anymore." He averted his gaze from Okaru, as if she were dog excrement.

"No. I don't believe it," Okaru said, even as her eyes widened into dark pools of pain. "You weren't acting, I would have known. You were in love with me. You still are."

"Stop!" Oishi raised his voice over hers. "Face the facts. I wasn't in love with you. I'm not now. My wife is the only woman I love."

His last statement silenced Okaru like a hand closed around her throat. Her mouth opened and closed, emitting strangled gasps before she managed to say, "Your wife? But you divorced her. You said you didn't care about her. You said I was the one . . ."

"I only divorced her to protect her, you silly little fool," Oishi said. "So she couldn't be punished for anything I did. If not for that, we would still be married."

He spoke with conviction, but his words struck a dissonant chord in Reiko. She tilted her head and frowned.

"It's not true," Okaru said, breathless with desperation. "You don't know what you're saying, you're not yourself. You must be ill. Darling, you need me." She stood, lifted her hand, and stroked Oishi's cheek. "Let me make you all better."

Oishi swatted at Okaru. He might have intended only to repel her touch, but his hand struck her face hard enough that she shrieked and fell.

Reiko caught Okaru. Goza assailed Oishi, seized his neck, and began to throttle him. As he tried to pry her hands off him, his eyes bulged. He choked. His complexion turned purple before he drove his knee into Goza's stomach and broke her hold.

She retreated but stood ready to charge again, her face murderous, her fingers curled, and her knees flexed like a wrestler's. Oishi wheezed as he said to Okaru, "Never come near me again."

Okaru collapsed, wailing, in Reiko's arms. As Oishi started to walk out of the room, Reiko realized why his words hadn't sounded right. She called to him, "You say your love for Okaru was just an act, and you only divorced your wife in order to protect her. But that's not what my husband says you told him. Why have you changed your story?"

Oishi left without answering her question.

"I THOUGHT HE loved me!" Okaru wailed as the palanquin carried her and Reiko and Goza through the city. "How could he be so cruel? How could I be so stupid?"

Reiko tried to comfort her, but by the time they arrived at Sano's estate, she was in hysterics. "I can't breathe!" Okaru wheezed and clutched her throat.

"Just calm down," Reiko urged. "You'll be fine."

Okaru fell out of the palanquin, sobbing. Goza picked her up and carried her toward the house. Chiyo and Masahiro appeared at the door and gazed with concern at Okaru flailing and gasping in Goza's arms.

"What's wrong with her?" Masahiro asked.

Reiko explained, then said, "Fetch the doctor. Be quick."

Masahiro ran off. Reiko and Chiyo put Okaru to bed. Okaru writhed under the quilt, mussing her hairdo. Her tears had melted her makeup into a red and gray mess.

"I'm so miserable, I want to die!" A fit of coughing and choking ensued.

Reiko pleaded with her to lie still and try to breathe normally. At last Masahiro arrived with an Edo Castle physician, who made Okaru drink a potion made from dates, sprouted wheat, and licorice to relieve her grief, and a tincture of opium to sedate her. After a while her breathing evened, her struggles ceased, and she drowsed. Reiko, Goza, and Chiyo knelt around her bed. Masahiro hovered anxiously in the doorway.

"Will she be all right?" he asked.

"Yes," Reiko said, although she wondered if it was possible to die of a broken heart.

"We should let her rest." Chiyo spoke to Reiko, but her gaze was on Masahiro.

Reiko saw an uneasy expression appear on his face as he slipped away. She remembered Chiyo's mysterious hints about Okaru. Again she didn't have time to ask what they meant, because when she and Chiyo left the room they met Sano in the corridor. Chiyo greeted him, then excused herself, leaving Reiko and Sano alone.

"I saw the doctor coming out of the house," Sano said. "Is somebody sick?"

"It's Okaru." Reiko described what had happened between Okaru and Oishi.

Sano immediately grasped the significance of Oishi's words. "He changed his story."

"Yes," Reiko said. "I asked him why, but he didn't answer."

Sano massaged his head as if it ached from the barrage of conflicting evidence. "Oishi's new story corroborates his son Chikara's statement that his relationship with Okaru was just a ploy to protect his wife and trick Kira."

Reiko's anger at Oishi resurged. "He may be a hero for avenging Lord Asano, but he was cruel to Okaru, who didn't deserve it. He's lost much of my sympathy."

"A samurai's duty to his master takes priority over obligations to everyone else." Sano clearly didn't like her criticism. "You know that."

Reiko felt the familiar, uncomfortable tension that arose when she and Sano had different opinions about a subject in a case. She started to say that she hoped this case wouldn't come between them, when a manservant appeared and said, "Honorable Master, you have a visitor. It's Ohgami Kaoru, from the Council of Elders."

"I'd better not keep him waiting," Sano said as he headed toward the reception room.

The manservant said to Reiko, "This message came for you today," and offered her a scroll in a lacquer container.

Reiko took the scroll and followed Sano. She stood outside the reception room door, which was open wide enough for her to see Sano kneeling opposite a white-haired samurai with an oddly youthful face. She eavesdropped on their conversation.

ELDER OHGAMI REFUSED Sano's offer of refreshments. "I can't stay long."

That was a bad sign. Sano braced himself for news he didn't want to hear.

"The Council of Elders is concerned that the supreme court is taking too long to announce a verdict," Ohgami said.

"The judges only convened for the first time yesterday," Sano pointed out.

"The Council is aware of that," Ohgami said. "But certain members feel that because the case is so politically sensitive, expediency is of utmost importance."

Sano deduced that "certain members" meant Kato and Ihara, his and Ohgami's opponents. "The judges want to be sure they make the right decision."

"The judges aren't the problem." Ohgami fixed a pointed look on Sano. "Some of us think it's your investigation that's holding things up."

"I'm working as fast as I can." Sano thought, *Here we go again*. His superiors never ceased expecting him to produce instant miracles.

"I have complete confidence that you are. But your detractors wonder if you're being deliberately slow about providing evidence to the court, because you want to delay the verdict and spare the lives of the forty-seven *rōnin* for as long as possible and you're afraid of how the reaction will affect you."

Offense leaped in Sano. "I admit that I'm partial toward letting the forty-seven *rōnin* go free." Even though Reiko's news about Oishi changing his story had reminded Sano that he needed to maintain his objectivity.

"And I can't deny that I have a stake in the verdict. But I would never compromise an investigation on account of my personal feelings."

"I know. But others don't have as much faith in you as I do. They think you're using your investigation to control the court."

"I'm not," Sano said flatly.

"Thank you for the assurance," Ohgami said. "I will relay it to my colleagues. But some of them strongly believe that the forty-seven rōnin should be condemned to death."

"Ihara and Kato made that clear while we were discussing the case with the shogun."

Ohgami winced because Sano had bluntly named names. "And I made it clear that I share your belief that the forty-seven rōnin should be pardoned. But our position is becoming dangerous. Your political opponents are gaining support, and they have much influence with the shogun."

Sano could imagine Yoritomo whispering in the shogun's ear, pouring in poison about Sano. "There are many influential people on my side, too."

"If the forty-seven rōnin are pardoned, you won't have enough allies to protect you. The other side will be out for blood." Ohgami clearly feared for himself as much as for Sano.

This prediction didn't exactly raise Sano's spirits after a difficult day. "Yanagisawa and Yoritomo were kind enough to explain to me what will happen if the verdict goes against the forty-seven rōnin. I'll lose the allies who want them pardoned. I'll also become the target of a popular uprising by commoners protesting the death of their heroes."

"That could come to pass, yes."

"Which means that no matter the verdict, I'm damned," Sano said, as much vexed by the rampant political opportunism around him as troubled by his dilemma. "I'll be run out of the regime as well as lose my family for causing an uproar that displeases the shogun."

Ohgami shrugged and spread his hands.

AFTER OHGAMI LEFT, Sano discovered Reiko standing in the corridor outside the reception chamber. She clutched a scroll container tightly enough to crack it. Her face wore a look of dismay and guilt.

"I suppose you heard my whole talk with Ohgami," Sano said.

Reiko nodded. "I hope you're not angry at me for eavesdropping."

"No," Sano said as they walked toward their private quarters. "You spared me the trouble of telling you the bad news."

"Are things really so bad?" Fear shrank Reiko's voice.

Sano held his breath for a moment, then let it ease out. "I won't lie. But remember, things have often looked bad for us. We've always come out all right." He attempted a joke. "Besides, wouldn't life be dull without a little trouble once in a while?"

Reiko didn't laugh. "It seems worse this time than it ever was."

It did, partly because his position had already been precarious. But Sano suspected that the current situation disturbed Reiko, and himself, more than past difficulties because they'd had their faces rubbed in the consequences of a samurai losing his status. Oishi's story of Lord Asano's suicide and his own hardships had struck too close to home for Sano, and he gathered that Reiko had been deeply affected by the tales of woe she'd heard from Lady Asano and Oishi's wife.

The corridor was cold, as if from the shadow of the cloud that hung over them, the threat of separation. Sano took off his surcoat, wrapped it around Reiko, and said, "We'll get through this."

She managed a smile. He felt her inhale, draw strength from their closeness, and brace herself up. He loved her for her courage and fortitude that had sustained them both during their twelve often tumultuous years together. His love moved him so much that he felt uncomfortable and sought a change of subject.

"What's that you're holding?" he asked.

Reiko opened the bamboo container, unrolled the scroll, and read the written message. Her expression grew more troubled. "It's from Lady Wakasa. She says marriage prospects for Masahiro have completely dried up. Some of the clans she approached are in favor of condemning the forty-seven *rōnin* and they don't want to be associated with us because they think you're trying to influence the verdict the other way. The other clans are in favor of pardoning, but nobody would agree to a *miai*." A *miai* was the ritual first meeting between a prospective bride and groom and their families. "Everybody thinks you're on the way out. So she's giving up searching for a bride for Masahiro until the business is settled."

She lifted her gaze to Sano. A wry smile twisted her mouth. "She's deserting us just when we need her most."

"Who cares about that old busybody?" Sano said, although her letter had added more weight to a heavy pile of worries. "Nobody died and put her in charge."

As he and Reiko enjoyed a laugh at Lady Wakasa's expense, wails drifted through the house. Reiko sighed. "That's Okaru. It's going to be a difficult night."

"Things will look better in the morning," Sano promised.

23

THE JUDGES DEBATED far into the night. They included Inspector General Nakae and Lord Nabeshima, whom Magistrate Ueda had
allowed to rejoin the court. Their chamber was thick with smoke from
their tobacco pipes. They shook their fists and pounded on the floor while
they argued loudly, until Magistrate Ueda said, "Let's take another vote."
His eyes were bleary from the smoke; his head ached. "All in favor of pardoning the forty-seven *rōnin,* raise your hands."

Seven hands went up.

"All in favor of condemning?"

The other seven judges raised their hands.

"This is the third time we've come out divided half and half," Nakae
said.

"We're getting nowhere," Colonel Hitomi said crossly.

"We have to keep at it until we're all on the same side," Superintendent Ogiwara said.

Lord Nabeshima combined a laugh with a snort. "I'm not changing
my mind." He folded his arms and glared at the seven judges who opposed him. "Are you?"

"Not I," they chorused.

Inspector General Nakae's eyes gleamed with cunning. He said to Superintendent Ogiwara, "The next time I audit your department, I might
find a serious discrepancy in the account books."

"What?" Superintendent Ogiwara said, puzzled, fearful, and insulted. "There are no discrepancies."

"I'm sure I can find something." Nakae paused, letting the threat of reprimands, fines, demotion, and dismissal hang in the air. "Unless you change your vote."

Superintendent Ogiwara gasped. "That's blackmail!"

The judges on his side protested. Magistrate Ueda wasn't shocked because Nakae would stoop to such a low tactic, but because Nakae had done it so openly. Nakae was clearly too impatient to wait until he could get each opposing judge alone and negotiate a private deal.

"I can play that game." Minister Motoori said to Lord Nabeshima, "The shogun wants to build new temples. Change your vote, or I'll advise him that you should provide the money."

"You wouldn't!" Lord Nabeshima looked aghast at the thought of the fortune that the new temples would cost him. He glared at his friend Nakae. "See what you've started!"

"Rule number seven," Magistrate Ueda said. "No blackmail and no deals. Anyone who breaks it will spend ten days in Edo Jail."

Inspector General Nakae shook his head in angry disgust. "So you don't like my solution to our problem. What's yours?"

Magistrate Ueda said the only thing he could. "We hope for new evidence, and in the meantime, we continue debating." He looked at the men around him. Their faces were puffy with weariness. "We've all had enough for one day. The court is adjourned until tomorrow."

TEMPLE BELLS TOLLED the hour of the boar as Magistrate Ueda traveled home. His portly figure swayed in the saddle while he rode through the Hibiya administrative district, just south of Edo Castle, where he lived in a mansion attached to the Court of Justice. One bodyguard rode in front of him, one behind. The district was dimly lit by lanterns burning in a few of the houses crouched behind earthen walls. The streets were empty. The horses' hooves crunching on icy snow punctuated the lonely sound of dogs howling.

Magistrate Ueda breathed vigorously, letting the wintry night air cleanse his system of tobacco smoke and bad will. How fed up he was with that stubborn pack of mules! But he must guide the court to a just verdict. He worried about Sano, Reiko, and their children. Whichever way the case turned out, they could suffer.

He was so deep in thought, and his bodyguards so sleepy, that they didn't notice the man who'd followed them from Edo Castle. The man sped along in the shadows along the walls, the noise from the horses muffling his footsteps. Dressed in black, a hood pulled over his head, he moved with sinister stealth.

Magistrate Ueda and his guards rode down a path that bordered a canal. Steep retaining walls descended to the water, which gleamed in the moonlight. Beyond the canal rose mansions; over it arched a wooden bridge. Magistrate Ueda and his guards rode in single file onto the bridge. He was halfway across when the guard behind him uttered a cry filled with surprise and pain. Startled, Magistrate Ueda reined his horse sideways. He saw the guard clutch his neck, then topple off his mount.

"Inaba-*san*!" Magistrate Ueda called. "What——?"

Another cry shrilled. Magistrate Ueda looked at the guard ahead of him. The guard flailed his arms, then slumped. An arrow protruded from his back. His body listed. He dangled from one stirrup as his horse reared and galloped away.

Panic filled Magistrate Ueda: This was an ambush, and he was the next target. But even while he looked around for the archer, while he feared for his own life, he climbed off his horse and hurried to his fallen guard. Inaba was an old friend whom he must try to save. Then he saw the arrow that had pierced Inaba's throat, the great spill of blood on the bridge, and Inaba's eyes blankly reflecting the moonlight.

An arrow whizzed past Magistrate Ueda and struck the bridge's railing. He looked in the direction from which the arrow had come. On the path along the canal, the shadowy figure of the archer took aim to shoot again.

Magistrate Ueda ran. He cleared the bridge and fled into an alley between two estates while footsteps thudded behind him. It was so dark that he had to grope his way, stumbling on snow piles. The archer wouldn't be able to get a good shot, he hoped. He was only a few blocks from his mansion; he would be safe soon. But he was old, fat, and out of shape. He panted and staggered as he neared the end of the alley. The footsteps pounded louder, closer.

A hand grabbed his shoulder. Crying out, he turned and saw his pursuer's black clothed figure. The dim light from the end of the alley gleamed in the man's eyes. The man raised an object. Magistrate Ueda saw the gloved hand and the club studded with shiny iron spikes. He fumbled for the sword at his waist, but before he could draw it, the club came swinging down.

A hard blow landed against his forehead. Pain burst in his skull. His vision fragmented into brilliant shards. He fell through space. An instant later he crashed onto the ground. He tried to call for help, but more blows smote him. His last thought was, *Who wants me dead?*

WHILE SHE SLEPT that night, a part of Reiko remained alert in case her children should cry or danger should threaten her family. The moment she heard Hirata's voice say, "Excuse me, Sano-*san*, Lady Reiko," she was instantly awake.

"What is it?" Reiko threw off the heavy quilts, shivered in her night robe, and squinted in the light from the lantern that Hirata held. Chiyo stood beside him, her expression grave.

"It's your father," Hirata said.

Sano groggily pushed himself upright. "Magistrate Ueda? What's happened?"

"A messenger just came from his house," Hirata said. "He's been attacked."

Reiko's heart began to pound so hard that she felt as if a hammer were striking inside her body. She felt dizzy and faint. "Is he—?" She couldn't bear to utter the word.

"He's alive," Chiyo said quickly.

Reiko felt a flood of relief that dried up as Hirata said, "But he's seriously injured."

"Who did it?" Sano said, as stricken as Reiko was. "How did it happen?"

"The messenger didn't know the details," Hirata answered.

Reiko flung herself out of bed, groping for her clothes. "I must go to him at once!"

Masahiro appeared at the door. "Can I go, too?"

Down the corridor, Akiko let out a wail. Reiko said, "No, Masahiro, I need you to take care of your sister." She didn't want him to see his grandfather hurt and be upset.

"I'll stay with them," Chiyo said.

Reiko managed a smile for Chiyo as she threw her kimono on over her night robe. "Thank you." She spared a thought to hope that Okaru hadn't made a permanent rift in their friendship.

THE PROCESSION STORMED out the gate of Edo Castle. Sano, Hirata, and Detectives Marume and Fukida rode at the front. Troops brought up the rear behind Reiko, who traveled on an oxcart. Reiko couldn't have borne the slow pace of a palanquin. She sat on the edge of the bench behind the driver and the two lumbering oxen. She barely noticed the rattling and swaying of the cart or the cold penetrating the quilt bundled around her. She was frantic to get to her father, terrified that he would take a turn for the worse and she would arrive too late.

When the procession reached the Hibiya administrative district, Reiko unwrapped her quilt, jumped off the oxcart, and ran. The walls outside the mansions and the lights from inside streaked past her. Her breath puffed white vapor into the frigid darkness. She caught up with Sano and his men at her father's mansion. A sentry opened the gate. Reiko rushed in; Sano and Hirata hurried after her. The low, half-timbered mansion where Reiko had grown up was lit with lanterns burning on the veranda and in the windows. Inside, Reiko ran down the corridors. Servants stood back to let her pass. She avoided their gazes for fear of seeing terrible news written there. Reaching her father's chamber, she burst through the door and halted.

Magistrate Ueda lay in bed, covered up to his chin with a brown quilt. His head was wrapped in a white cloth bandage, his face so battered that Reiko barely recognized him. Reddish-purple bruises covered his eyes, which were swollen and shut. His nose and mouth were also swollen, with blood crusted around the nostrils and oozing from a cut on his lip. A doctor sat nearby, an old man dressed in the dark blue coat of the medical profession, with a chest full of medicines and instruments. He measured herbs into a cup of steaming water.

Reiko moaned in horror even while her legs buckled with relief that her father was alive. She fell on her knees at his bedside. "Father!"

Magistrate Ueda didn't speak, open his eyes, or seem to hear her. His breath gurgled in and out of his mouth. Reiko looked anxiously at the doctor.

"He's unconscious," the doctor said. "That's quite a severe injury to his head."

The tears that Reiko had suppressed during the trip now streamed down her face. She reached under the quilt, found her father's hand, and squeezed his fingers. They were cold, inert.

Sano and Hirata came in with the magistrate's longtime chief retainer, an old samurai named Ikeda. He'd taught Reiko to ride a horse when she was young.

"Don't cry yet, little one," he said, kind but brisk. "Your father is too strong and stubborn to be killed so easily."

Reiko felt braced up, the way she had when she'd fallen off her horse and Ikeda had lifted her back into the saddle. She dried her tears.

"Can you tell us what happened?" Sano asked, his face drawn with concern.

"The magistrate and his bodyguards were ambushed on their way home from Edo Castle." Ikeda explained that the guards had been killed by arrows shot at them. "The magistrate must have tried to run away. He was beaten in an alley not far from here."

"How did he get home?" Hirata asked.

"A *doshin* happened to be passing by on his rounds," Ikeda said. "He found the magistrate and brought him home."

"Thank the gods," Reiko murmured, but she was aghast at the thought of the terror and pain her father had suffered. Rage at his attacker began to burn within her. "Who did this?"

"I don't know. The magistrate was unconscious when the *doshin* found him, and he hasn't come to yet." Ikeda told Sano, "The *doshin* is still here. I figured you would want to talk to him, so I told him to stick around."

"Good. I do." Sano's expression darkened with the same anger that enflamed Reiko. "Whoever it was, will pay."

24

SANO AND HIRATA found the *doshin* in an empty chamber, fast asleep. Beside him lay his sword and his *jitte*. When Hirata shook him, he yelled and bolted upright; his hand scrabbled for the weapons.

"It's all right, we're friends," Hirata said, then introduced Sano and himself.

The *doshin* was about Sano's age; he had a weathered, genial face. "I remember you both from when you were in the police department. But I don't suppose you remember me."

"I do," Hirata said. "You're Nomura."

"That's right." Nomura beamed, flattered.

"Thank you for rescuing my father-in-law," Sano said.

"My pleasure," Nomura said. "I'd like to help catch the bastard who did this."

"Good," Sano said. "Tell us what happened."

"Well, I was making my rounds with my two assistants. We heard shouts, and we went to see what was going on. We came out on the path beside the canal, and a horse charged past us. It was dragging the rider. I sent my assistants to help him. Then I saw two other horses on the bridge, and a samurai lying there dead with an arrow in his neck. I figured that there'd been three men riding together and they'd been ambushed by thieves."

That was a common enough crime in Edo, but thieves usually avoided the samurai quarters because of all the armed troops there. Sano had never heard of an ambush in the administrative district.

"But where was the other man?" Nomura asked himself. "Then I heard shouting, from an alley on the other side of the bridge. I ran over there. It was so dark, I could barely see. There was one man on the ground. Another man was beating him. I shouted, 'Stop! Police!' The man doing the beating ran away. The man on the ground was moaning. I figured he'd be all right by himself for a little while, so I chased after the other fellow."

Nomura said regretfully, "I wish I hadn't left him. I didn't know he was Magistrate Ueda, and I didn't know how bad he was hurt. When I came back, he was unconscious. I dragged him out of the alley, and that's when I recognized him. My assistants caught the runaway horse. The rider was dead. We brought Magistrate Ueda home and they took the two dead men to Edo Morgue." Shamefaced, Nomura added, "The attacker got away. I'm sorry."

"I'm glad you were there," Sano said. "If not for you, Magistrate Ueda might not have survived."

"Did you get a good look at the attacker?" Hirata asked.

"No. It was too dark."

Sano tamped down his disappointment and his rage toward the man who'd beaten his father-in-law so savagely. Giving in to emotion wouldn't help him catch the culprit.

"Maybe I can track him," Hirata said. "First, I need to see the crime scene."

"I'll show you." Nomura stood.

"You go," Sano told Hirata. "You're better equipped to find clues at the scene than I am. And I have another line of inquiry that I want to pursue."

DAWN BEGAN TO lighten the sky when Hirata and the *doshin* arrived at the bridge. They found a street-cleaner at work with a bucket and a brush, scrubbing the blood off the bridge's planks. Red-tinted snow and water slopped into the canal below.

"Hey! This is a crime scene!" Nomura said. "Stop!"

The street-cleaner halted, afraid he was in trouble. Hirata said, "It's all right. Keep working." The blood wasn't the evidence he needed. He paced along the path, then the bridge, his eyes scanning the area, his other senses alert.

Nomura trailed him eagerly. "Are you using magic to find the criminal?"

"I'm looking for clues he left behind. It could be a trace of his aura." Hirata explained what auras were and that he could detect them and use them to track people.

They paced together in silence. After a while Nomura said, "Are you getting anything?"

"I'm getting too much. So many people have passed by here. I can't tell which aura belongs to the attacker. It would help if I could find something else he left." Hirata spotted an arrow lying beside the street-cleaner's bucket. "Hey! Did you find that here today?"

"Yes, master," the street-cleaner said. "It was stuck in the railing."

Hirata closed his fingers around the arrow's shaft. He felt the faint aura of the man who had drawn the arrow in the bow and let it fly. The aura evoked a dull red color shot with flinty sparks. Hirata read a distinctive combination of weakness, brutality, and sullen resentment.

"What do you think?" Nomura asked hopefully.

"I'll recognize him if I meet him," Hirata said. "Show me where you chased him."

They traveled through the administrative district, Hirata on horseback, Nomura on foot. Hirata didn't sense the aura in the walled mansions or among the troops and officials emerging as the sky brightened. He and the *doshin* crossed into the Nihonbashi merchant quarter and joined the commoners who streamed through the winding lanes. They stopped at an intersection between three lanes that contained blacksmith shops.

"Here's where I lost him," Nomura said.

Inside the shops, forges roared, warming the air. Smoke billowed. Clanging noises echoed as the blacksmiths pounded red-hot metal into horseshoes, helmets, and armor plates. Hirata tuned out the noise and concentrated.

"Anything yet?" Nomura asked.

"No," Hirata said. "He's gone."

"Maybe he lives around here."

So did too many other people. Hirata prepared for a long search.

Maybe the attacker would cross his path, but in a city of a million people, what were the chances of that happening?

LEAVING REIKO AT her father's bedside, Sano rode back to Edo Castle and went straight to the chamber where the supreme court met. He found the thirteen judges already seated. They looked tired, ill humored. Magistrate Ueda's place was conspicuously vacant.

"What are you doing back this soon?" Inspector General Nakae said. "Isn't it a little early for you to have more news to report?"

"We were going to continue discussing the evidence you brought us yesterday," Superintendent Ogiwara said from the opposite row. "We're just waiting for our chief."

"He's late," Lord Nabeshima said disapprovingly.

"I do have news," Sano said. "Magistrate Ueda was ambushed on his way home last night. His two bodyguards were killed. He was badly beaten, and he's still unconscious." Telling the story whipped up fresh anger inside Sano. He felt a new, visceral sense of identification with the forty-seven rōnin. They had avenged their master. Sano must deliver Magistrate Ueda's attacker to justice. "That's why he's not here."

Stunned silence greeted Sano's words. If the judges had already known about the attack, they did a good job pretending they hadn't. Old Minister Motoori said, "I'm terribly sorry."

The other judges echoed him. "Have you any idea who's responsible?" Superintendent Ogiwara said.

"Not yet," Sano said. "I'm beginning an investigation."

"Maybe it was a robbery," Lord Nabeshima said.

"I believe it was an assassination attempt," Sano said.

"Oh, well, then, doesn't Magistrate Ueda have quite a few enemies?" Inspector General Nakae said. "Thank you for bringing the news, but shouldn't you be investigating them?"

"What makes you think that's not what I'm doing?" Sano swept his gaze over the judges.

Although Inspector General Nakae and Lord Nabeshima retained their places in the row of Chamberlain Yanagisawa's cronies, while Superintendent Ogiwara and Minister Motoori still sat with the opposition in Magistrate Ueda's row, other judges had changed seats. The division now reflected the judges' stances on the case instead of political allegiance, Sano deduced. There would have been seven on each side if Magistrate Ueda was here.

The judges frowned as they absorbed Sano's implication. "You're accusing us of trying to murder Magistrate Ueda?" Superintendent Ogiwara demanded.

"Not the judges who are on the same side as Magistrate Ueda." Sano turned a hard gaze on the inspector general's side. "This case has become a battle. How far would you go to win?"

Nakae sputtered, outraged. "You think we would try to kill a colleague in order to sway the court toward condemning the forty-seven *rōnin*?"

"Did you?" Sano added, "You and Lord Nabeshima weren't too happy with Magistrate Ueda when he had you removed from the court yesterday."

"No, we didn't! That's ridiculous," Nakae said. "Moreover, I'm sure we can provide alibis. My guards and I rode part of the way home with Magistrate Ueda last night. He was fine when we left him. We went straight home, and I stayed there until this morning."

His friends hastened to say they'd been at home all night, too.

"You wouldn't have needed to get your own hands dirty," Sano said. "You have people to carry out your orders."

Inspector General Nakae disdainfully waved away the notion. "Killing Magistrate Ueda would have taken away only one vote from my opponents. There would still be six other judges in favor of pardoning."

"Magistrate Ueda wasn't just one vote," Sano said. "He was the chief judge. He made the rule that the decision had to be unanimous. With him gone, you could change the rule and decide by a majority vote. The verdict would go your way."

"Your reasoning is offensive," Lord Nabeshima snapped. "We don't care enough about the verdict that we would stoop to murdering our colleague."

"Don't you?" Sano stared at Lord Nabeshima.

Lord Nabeshima's gaze shifted first. Inspector General Nakae said, "What if you're correct in thinking that someone was trying to influence the court's verdict by eliminating one of the judges? We aren't the only suspects. Other people have an interest in the outcome, too."

"The whole city is in an uproar over it, in case you haven't heard," Lord Nabeshima said.

"Other people don't know what's going on inside the court and which way each judge is leaning," Sano said. "Your proceedings are confidential."

"Yes, any outsider who wanted to eliminate a judge would run the risk of picking the wrong one." A dirty gleam kindled in Inspector General Nakae's eyes. "But there's one man who does know, even though he's an outsider."

His smile bared his rotten teeth at Sano. The other judges sat back, startled by the turn the conversation had taken.

"You accuse me of trying to manipulate the court's decision by attacking my own father-in-law?" Sano was exasperated. But of course he did bear some blame for Magistrate Ueda's injuries. He had nominated Magistrate Ueda to the court, had put him in harm's way. Guilt spread a nauseous feeling through Sano. He turned his anger at himself on the judges. "That's absurd and insulting!"

They gazed back at him with disapproval, Magistrate Ueda's opponents and allies alike. Sano saw another bad consequence of the attack on the magistrate: He'd lost his only friend on the court, whom he'd counted on to help him protect his family's interests. He said to Nakae, "You're trying to divert suspicion onto—"

A new thought stopped Sano. He realized that Nakae had spoken the truth about one thing: There was an outsider who'd heard the judges' confidential discussions, who'd guessed Magistrate Ueda's position, who surely wanted a hand in the verdict, even though he'd kept quiet about where he stood on the issue of the forty-seven *ronin*. But it wasn't Sano.

"What's the matter?" Inspector General Nakae said. "Choking on your own words?"

"Thank you," Sano said.

Surprise lifted Nakae's sagging brow. "For what?"

"You just provided a new lead for my investigation."

25

REIKO KNELT BY her father's bedside for the rest of the night and all morning. Magistrate Ueda lay so still, his swollen eyes closed, the bruises turning a morbid purple. Not one hint of consciousness did Reiko see in him. His servants brought her food that she couldn't eat. His retainers stopped by to ask about his condition. They spoke kindly to Reiko and she answered, but their sympathy couldn't touch her. She felt imprisoned in some dark place, alone with her terror that her father would die.

Memories glimmered like fireflies through the darkness. She recalled her childhood self running to meet her father. He'd lifted her, tossed her up in the air, and they'd laughed. Her mother had died when she was born, but her father had never held it against her; he'd not been disappointed that she wasn't a boy who could be his heir; he hadn't left her to the care of servants, remarried, and started a new family, as other men would have done. He'd loved her and raised her with such devotion that she'd never missed having a mother. And he'd given her advantages that were usually reserved for sons.

He'd hired tutors to educate her in reading, arithmetic, writing, and history, and a martial arts master to teach her sword-fighting. He'd ignored the relatives who disapproved. He'd said that his daughter was too clever to let her grow up as ignorant as other girls. When she got older, she shared his interest in the law, and spent days in a chamber behind the Court of Justice, listening to the trials he conducted. Often she would whisper advice about questions he should ask the defendants or witnesses, or offer her opinion about whether the defendant was guilty. Her father trusted her intuition; he often took her advice even though she was only twelve, or fourteen, or sixteen years old. Now Reiko mused upon the fact that her upbringing had made possible her unconventional marriage to Sano and the work they did together. She had her father to thank for everything. She adored him for his kindness and his humor. How could she bear to lose him?

Especially if she lost Sano, too?

Reiko fought back tears. Falling apart wouldn't help her father. Neither would letting herself be overpowered by rage at whoever had injured him. She must remain calm, strong. Her father was depending on her now.

She heard a faint groan. The slits of his eyes opened wider.

Reiko's heart leaped. "Father?"

His head slowly turned toward her. "Reiko?" He frowned in confusion. "Where am I?'"

Thank the gods he was conscious! "At home," Reiko said.

"How did I get here?"

"A *doshin* brought you."

Magistrate Ueda made a feeble move to sit up. "My guards are dead. He shot them." Grief appeared on his face as his memory returned. Urgency snapped his eyes fully open. The whites were stained red with broken blood veins. He fumbled to throw off the quilt. "I have to catch him! Before he gets away!"

"He's gone, Father," Reiko said. "It happened last night."

"Last night?" Magistrate Ueda sounded puzzled. "What time is it?"

"It's morning. Around the hour of the snake, I think."

Anger compressed Magistrate Ueda's cut lips. "So he did get away."

"Not for long." Reiko felt the burn of her own anger at the attacker. "My husband is hunting for him. So is Hirata. They'll catch him. Don't worry, Father."

He tried to push himself upright, gasping. "I have to go. I have to help."

Reiko gently restrained him. "You can help us figure out who did this. Do you know?"

"No." Magistrate Ueda spoke with sad regret. "It was dark. I couldn't see his face."

"Did you notice anything about him?"

Magistrate Ueda's eyelids drooped. His body went limp.

"Father?" Reiko could see his consciousness ebbing.

"Two," he whispered.

Puzzled, she said, "Were there two men who attacked you?" A moment ago he'd referred to the attacker as "he." And Sano had stopped in to relay the *doshin*'s story. The *doshin* had said he'd chased only one man he'd seen beating Magistrate Ueda.

"No," Magistrate Ueda said faintly. "Two tattoos. On his arm. I saw."

Comprehension excited Reiko. "He'd been convicted of two other crimes?" Repeat offenders were branded with tattoos on their arms. The tattoos were characters for the crimes they'd committed. If they were arrested again, the police would know they'd been in trouble before. The law would impose a harsher sentence than for a first offense.

"Yes," Magistrate Ueda whispered.

"What were his crimes?" Reiko asked eagerly. "Could you read the tattoos?"

Magistrate Ueda closed his eyes. His breathing slowed.

"Father," Reiko said. He didn't respond. She tried to quell the fear that she'd heard his voice for the last time. She held his limp hand. "I'll find out who he is." The need for revenge consumed Reiko like fire licking dry tinder. It was the same, ancient, bred-in-the-blood impulse that had set forty-seven *rōnin* on the man they held responsible for their master's death. She had joined their brotherhood of avengers even though she was a mere woman. "I promise."

ON HIS WAY out of the house to spend the day with the shogun, Masahiro paused in the corridor, reluctant to leave. His grandfather was hurt, and he wanted to wait for news from his mother. And despite his worry about his grandfather, he couldn't forget Okaru. The memory of watching her bathing yesterday sent waves of excitement, pleasure, and shame through him. Then, after she'd gone to see Oishi, she'd come home crying so hard. Although Masahiro pitied her, he couldn't help being glad that Oishi had rejected her. Masahiro had thoughts that were so wild and improbable that he didn't dare put them into words, even in his mind.

Taeko came down the corridor, walking carefully, carrying a tray laden with a teapot, cup, and covered dishes. When she saw Masahiro, she lowered her gaze. She'd been cool toward him since he'd been mean to her yesterday. He was sorry but too proud to say so.

"Is that food for Okaru?" he said.

"Yes." Taeko edged past him. "I told the maids I would take it to her."

Masahiro sensed that she didn't like Okaru. "I'll take it," he said.

Taeko reluctantly handed over the tray. Filled with excitement and longing, Masahiro carried the tray to Okaru's room. Okaru was in bed, curled up beneath the quilts, only the top of her head visible. Although Masahiro wanted to see her, he thought he probably shouldn't bother her. He tiptoed into the room and bent to set the tray on the table beside the bed.

"Who's there?" Okaru said in a muffled voice thick with tears.

Masahiro dropped the tray on the table with a crash. "It's—it's me. Masahiro."

"What do you want?" Her head emerged from beneath the quilt. Her hair was tangled. Her face was puffy from crying.

"I—I brought your breakfast." Masahiro pointed at the tray.

She ignored the food. "What are you looking at?" she demanded.

Masahiro was dumbstruck by the anger in her red, swollen eyes, embarrassed to see her suffering.

"You must think I'm stupid and pitiful," Okaru said, her voice shaking. "Everybody probably does. I hate you! I hate everybody! Just leave me alone!"

Her words cut Masahiro as if they were knives. He couldn't move or speak.

"Go away!" Okaru shrilled. She sat up, grabbed the teapot, and hurled it.

Masahiro ducked. The pot hit the wall. Tea splashed. The pot and lid landed on the *tatami* floor in a pool of hot liquid. Okaru burst into wild, loud sobbing. Goza hurried into the room, shoved Masahiro aside, and knelt beside Okaru.

Okaru threw herself into Goza's arms and wailed, "I'm so miserable! I want to die!"

Goza scowled at Masahiro. "You'd better go."

HIRATA RODE IN widening arcs away from the blacksmiths' quarter, his senses attuned to the aura of the man who'd attacked Magistrate Ueda. But the man was too long gone; the energy emitted by other people masked the residue of his aura. It was like hunting for one star amid the cosmos. At noon Hirata found himself in the area north of the Nihonbashi Bridge, near Odenmacho—the post-horse quarter, which offered horses for hire and served as the center of the national messenger system. The government employed messengers to carry documents between cities. A messenger dispatched from Edo would run to the next stage along the highway and pass his documents on to the next man. Fast runners could cover the distance to Miyako in sixty hours. Hirata passed the horse stables and the cheap inns, teahouses, and food-stalls where the messengers waited for work. He stopped outside a barbershop.

Its narrow room, behind a dingy plank storefront, was a favorite haunt of mystic martial artists. The barber gave his customers the latest news, gleaned from the messengers, while he cut their hair. Those who lived in Edo came to drink and visit and to meet itinerant comrades who stopped by. The nature of the barbershop was known only to its select community. No one else who peeked in would realize that its few ordinary-looking patrons had enough combat skill to defeat an army. Outsiders would feel a need to leave the premises. The patrons liked their privacy, and they projected energy that repelled the uninitiated.

Hirata hesitated at the door. Seeking Magistrate Ueda's attacker was his top priority, his duty to Sano, and he should be hunting for witnesses. He also had to help Sano bring the forty-seven *rōnin* business to a safe conclusion. But he kept thinking about the samurai named Tahara, who'd said they would meet again. Hirata must prepare.

He entered the barbershop. It was warm from the hearth, the plank walls and ceiling darkened by soot and tobacco smoke. The barber sat alone, sharpening his razors. A seventy-year-old *rōnin* named Iseki, he had a face as lined as a crumpled piece of paper, and he'd been a formidable mys-

190

tic martial artist until, decades ago, an earthquake had brought a house down on him and crushed his sword arm. Hirata watched Iseki deftly handling a razor and sharpening stone. Iseki managed as well with one hand as most men did with two, but his fighting days were long over.

"Greetings, Hirata-*san*," Iseki said. "What can I do for you?"

"I need some information."

"Just ask."

"Do you know a samurai named Tahara?"

Concern gathered the wrinkles on Iseki's face together. "Not personally, but I've heard of him. He's from Iga Province." Iga Province had its own tradition of mystic martial arts. Its samurai had learned from the *ninja,* a cult of peasant warriors adept in stealth. "His kind stick to themselves. They don't come around here. But I can tell you that I wouldn't have wanted to go up against Tahara even when I was in my prime. Do you know him?"

"Not yet." Everything Hirata had just heard increased his apprehension about his next meeting with Tahara.

"I'm surprised," Iseki said. "I thought you would."

"Why?"

"Because he's a disciple of Ozuno."

The news disconcerted Hirata. Ozuno was his teacher and mentor, from whom he'd learned the mystic martial arts. "Ozuno never mentioned Tahara."

But why not? Ozuno had introduced Hirata to his other disciples. The idea that the omission was deliberate bothered Hirata. Had Ozuno wanted to conceal Tahara's existence from him? His dread worsened. That Tahara had Ozuno's training plus a background in the dark arts made him a formidable adversary indeed.

"What else can you tell me about him?" Hirata asked.

"His clan are bodyguards and secret police for the *daimyo* of Iga Province. Tahara came to Edo about two years ago."

For me, Hirata thought.

"Rumor says that the *daimyo* loans Tahara out to other people and Tahara is presently working for the Tokugawa regime," Iseki said.

That would explain how Tahara had access to Edo Castle. "Does he have any friends in town? Specifically, a priest and a soldier?"

"The priest is Deguchi, from Ueno Temple. The soldier is Kitano Shigemasa. They're both great fighters." Iseki gave Hirata a curious glance. "Don't you know them either? They're two more of Ozuno's disciples."

"No," Hirata said, "he never mentioned them." It seemed that Ozuno had deliberately kept him from these three fellow disciples. Now they'd banded together against him.

"My condolences, by the way," Iseki said.

"What for?"

Iseki looked grave, sympathetic, and puzzled all at once. "Ozuno's death. Is that something else you didn't know about?"

Hirata felt as if he'd been punched in the stomach. "I didn't."

"Sorry to deliver the bad news."

"How did Ozuno die? And where?" Hirata had known that Ozuno was ancient, but he'd seemed immortal.

"At a temple in Nara where he was staying. He went peacefully in his sleep."

"When was this?" Hirata said.

"About two years ago."

That was around the same time that Tahara had come after Hirata. It couldn't be a coincidence. But what did Tahara and his friends want?

"If you hear anything about Tahara or his friends, will you let me know?" Hirata said.

"I will." Iseki warned, "If I were you, I would avoid them at all cost."

192

26

SANO WENT TO the secluded compound inside Edo Castle where Chamberlain Yanagisawa lived. It had become Sano's home when Yanagisawa was exiled, when Sano had been promoted to chamberlain. Sano had continued living there after Yanagisawa's return, while he and Yanagisawa had served as co-chamberlains. But after Sano's demotion, Yanagisawa had reclaimed his compound. Now Sano looked over the stone wall at the rooftops of the barracks where he'd once housed his retainers and the mansion in which his daughter had been born. It didn't matter that the compound had originally belonged to Yanagisawa. The reminder of what Sano had lost enflamed his rage toward Yanagisawa.

The gate opened from inside, to let out a group of officials. Sano strode in without waiting for permission.

"Hey, you can't go in there!" The sentries ran after Sano.

Sano marched into the mansion. By the time he reached the anteroom outside Yanagisawa's office he had some twenty guards trailing him. They ordered him to stop, but they were obviously afraid to lay a hand on him. Perhaps they thought he'd gone mad. Sano swept past the crowd waiting to see the chamberlain. He threw open the door of the office he'd once called his own. There Yanagisawa sat on the dais in the study niche at a black lacquer desk. With him were Kato and Ihara, his cronies from the Council of Elders.

"Sano-*san*," Yanagisawa said. Irritation failed to conceal his dismay that his foe had breached his security. "How did you get in here?"

"Never mind," Sano said. "I want to talk to you."

"Should we throw him out?" asked one of the guards crowded together in the doorway.

"No. I'll hear what he has to say." Yanagisawa raised his eyebrow at Sano's expression. "You seem upset. But of course, your father-in-law was attacked last night. My condolences."

His sympathy was so patently false that Sano wanted to throttle Yanagisawa. "How do you know about the attack?"

"Word has filtered up to Edo Castle," Ihara said. He and Kato looked uncertain as to whether they wanted to watch the scene between Sano and Yanagisawa or leave before they got burned by the fireworks.

"My intelligence system is very efficient, as you're aware," Yanagisawa said smoothly.

Hatred threatened to overcome Sano's self-control. "You didn't need spies this time. I think you knew about the attack before it happened."

Yanagisawa chuckled. "How? I've many talents, but I'm not a fortune-teller."

"Drop the innocent act," Sano said. "The answer is obvious."

Both of Yanagisawa's eyebrows rose, in mock astonishment. "Do you mean that you think I was behind the attack?"

"Were you?"

"That's absurd." Yanagisawa laughed, flashing his sharp, perfect teeth. "Why would I want to attack Magistrate Ueda?"

"Just answer the question."

"If you insist." Yanagisawa spoke with emphasis: "I am not responsible for the attack on Magistrate Ueda." He looked Sano straight in the eye.

Sano couldn't tell if he was lying. Yanagisawa was a consummate actor.

The sardonic humor vanished from Yanagisawa's expression. The room turned cold with his hostility toward Sano. "Now you can answer my question: Why would I have wanted to attack Magistrate Ueda? That's the very least you owe me after barging into my house."

"If you insist," Sano said. "You want the supreme court to condemn the forty-seven *rōnin*. You knew that Magistrate Ueda is leading the faction that wants to pardon them, because you barged in on the court yesterday. You figured that if you killed him, you would shift the balance toward the verdict you want." Sano felt the fever of his craving for battle. "My father-in-law was nothing to you but an inconvenience to eliminate!"

"I repeat, that's absurd," Yanagisawa said flatly. "In the first place, why do you think I want the forty-seven *rōnin* condemned? I've never said so. I have no opinion on the issue."

"Because you think it's the verdict that would cause the most negative reaction and bring the shogun's wrath down on me," Sano hazarded.

"Rubbish. In the second place, I was at home last night. My retainers will confirm that."

"Of course they will. They're beholden to you. And you could have sent one of them."

"In the third place," Yanagisawa said, "if I want to influence the verdict, I can do it without resorting to murder. A little coercion from me, and the judges will rush to cooperate."

Although Sano knew it was true, he still had reason to think Yanagisawa was guilty. "Even if you really don't care which way the verdict goes, you see this case as a chance to get rid of me at last."

Amusement colored Yanagisawa's hostility. "You think everything is about you and me. You're obsessed."

"The obsession is yours, not mine," Sano said coldly. "You're the one who's been fixated on destroying me. You've attacked me again and again, even though I did nothing to deserve it. So excuse me for thinking that the attack on Magistrate Ueda is more of the same."

"Your mind is stuck in the past. I don't need to attack you anymore. I've already beaten you."

"Not quite. I'm still here."

Yanagisawa smiled a thin, cruel smile. "Just barely. And not for long. The forty-seven *rōnin* case will be the end of you, no matter which way the verdict goes."

Sano was all too aware of that probability, but he said, "That's what you've hoped about every other case I've investigated. And you're forgetting that this case could take down other people besides me. You're not immune to the consequences of a verdict that's sure to be unpopular."

He saw a flicker of apprehension on Yanagisawa's face. But Yanagisawa retorted, "You're forgetting something, too: Other people are far more incensed about the forty-seven *rōnin* than I am. And I'm not the only one who knew where the judges stood as of yesterday."

"Confidentiality is a joke," Kato interjected.

"Fourteen judges equal fourteen holes in the court," Ihara said. "Too many to plug."

It had occurred to Sano that judges might have leaked the content of their discussion to persons outside the court. He would worry about that possibility later. "Don't bother trying to deflect my suspicions. You knew, and I think you used what you heard to your own advantage."

Yanagisawa's eyes gleamed maliciously. "You knew, too. You were there."

"Your friend Inspector General Nakae was nice enough to point that out to me already," Sano said. "I suppose you're going to follow his example and say I attacked my own father-in-law, then accuse me of trying to frame you."

"That is a good theory," Yanagisawa said. The elders nodded. "But I'll grant you this: I don't believe you tried to assassinate Magistrate Ueda. You're not that ruthless."

"Thank you." Sarcasm edged Sano's voice.

"However, one could argue that what happened to Magistrate Ueda is indeed your fault," Yanagisawa said.

"What kind of smoke are you fanning up now?" Sano demanded.

"You've had numerous opportunities to kill me," Yanagisawa said. "During your first investigation for the shogun, for example, when you got me and that mad killer out on a boat on the Sumida River. You could have drowned me, with nobody the wiser."

Sano wondered where the conversation was going. "I couldn't," he said with regret. "You were my superior. I owed you the same loyalty as I owed the shogun."

"That wasn't the only time you could have eliminated me with no witnesses," Yanagisawa said. "Twelve years ago, while we were in Miyako, you trapped me at swordpoint. Why didn't you just cut my throat?"

"The same reason. Honor. Duty." The principles of Bushido that governed Sano's actions, that frequently opposed his desires. Sano often thought that Bushido was like an iron weight around the neck of a man swimming in a shark-infested sea.

"After I was exiled, you realized that I'd sneaked back to Edo," Yanagisawa went on. "You could have found me and secretly killed me while everyone else thought I was still on Hachijo Island. It would have seemed as if I'd vanished into thin air."

Had that idea occurred to him? Sano recalled that he'd concentrated on exposing Yanagisawa's machinations while solving a murder case in which his mother was the primary suspect.

"It's what I would have done," Yanagisawa said.

"I'm not you," Sano said, proud that he'd never stooped to such a tactic.

"Indeed you're not." Yanagisawa matched Sano's pride. "You don't have my imagination or foresight."

"The gods be praised," Sano said.

"But suppose—just suppose—that I was responsible for the attack on Magistrate Ueda. You could have prevented it if you'd seized one of your chances to kill me. I couldn't have attacked him if I were dead, could I?" Yanagisawa pointed a finger at Sano. "If your theory that the attack was my doing is correct, then you're ultimately to blame. Because you could have protected Magistrate Ueda by killing me a long time ago and you didn't."

"That's the most convoluted logic I've ever heard," Sano exclaimed.

"Your justifications for your actions are the most feeble excuses I've ever heard." Yanagisawa moved out from behind his desk, stepped off the dais, and faced Sano. "You say it was loyalty and duty. I say you're hiding behind Bushido. You're afraid to do what a real samurai would, to seize the upper hand. You're afraid of the consequences. You"—his finger jabbed Sano's chest—"are nothing but a coward."

Coward. Coward. Coward. The worst insult that a samurai could receive echoed through Sano like the tolling of a bell. Rage exploded inside him with such force that at first he couldn't speak. Caught in a firestorm of howling winds, leaping flames, and smoke laden with hot ash and stinging cinders, he choked while his heart thudded furiously. He saw Yanagisawa's sneering face as if through the orange haze of the fire.

"How dare you?" was all he could manage to say.

"How dare I tell you the truth about yourself? How dare I humiliate you in front of our colleagues?" Yanagisawa laughed. "Oh, I dare. Because I'm not afraid. No matter what people think of me, no one would ever call me a coward." He mimicked Sano's words: "I'm not you."

The firestorm of rage burned hotter, fueled by a voice that whispered in Sano's mind, *Maybe Yanagisawa is right. Maybe I am a coward because I've endured insults and injuries for all these years instead of putting an end to it once and for all.*

"Well, look at that, everyone!" Yanagisawa pointed at Sano's hip. "Maybe he has some samurai courage after all."

Sano looked down. He saw that his hand had moved involuntarily to his sword. His fingers gripped the hilt. The hot cyclone of his rage swirled around him, but a deadly quiet settled over his body, as if he stood in the eye of the firestorm.

"Here I am," Yanagisawa said. "Do what you've been wanting to do all these years." He flung his arms wide, offered himself as a target.

The temptation was so strong that Sano forgot the prohibition against drawing a sword inside Edo Castle. He forgot Bushido. His muscles tensed to draw the weapon.

"Go ahead," Yanagisawa said with a tantalizing smile. "Prove that you're a real samurai."

Even as Sano felt the impulse to kill rise like a monster inside him, Yanagisawa, the room, and the other men in it faded from his vision. He was walking down the Corridor of Pines. Kajikawa, the keeper of the castle, appeared and spoke words that Sano didn't hear. A door opened along the corridor between them. Out stepped Kira. Sano charged at Kira, drew his sword, gripped it in both hands, and swung.

Everything went black.

Then Sano was back in the office with Yanagisawa and the elders, who were eagerly waiting to see what he would do. Sano stood thunderstruck by his vision in which he'd been Lord Asano. The shock restored his wits. He realized that Yanagisawa was goading him into emulating Lord Asano. If he took the bait, he would be sentenced to death.

He would be one obstacle cleared from Yanagisawa's path toward taking over Japan.

Reason dashed cold water onto the firestorm of rage. Sano let his hand drop from his sword. The elders' faces sagged with disappointment and relief. Yanagisawa smirked; he opened his mouth to make another cutting remark.

Sano hauled back his fist and punched Yanagisawa on the nose. Yanagisawa yelped as the blow slammed his head backward. He lost his balance, fell, and lay on the floor. Blood gushed from his nostrils. He and everyone else regarded Sano with complete, stupid astonishment.

"You think you have so much foresight, but you didn't see that coming, did you?" Sano's fury gave way to humor.

Yanagisawa began to sputter.

"How dare I?" Sano mocked. "Oh, I dare. Now if you'll excuse me, I'm going to find out who's behind the attack on Magistrate Ueda. If it's you, I won't let you off with a bloody nose." Sano strolled out of the room.

27

REIKO LEFT HER father in the doctor's care and went to the part of the mansion that housed the Court of Justice. Today it was empty; all court business had been postponed. Ikeda, the magistrate's chief retainer, stood at the open door, facing out toward the courtyard which was usually crowded with police officers guarding criminals scheduled for trial. Today it contained only two men, who had the fashionable, well-fed look of prosperous merchants.

"The magistrate won't be hearing any disputes for a while," Ikeda told them.

"Why not?" asked one of the merchants.

"Because he's on the supreme court for the forty-seven *rōnin* case. And because he was seriously injured last night."

"Well, I'm sorry he's hurt," the other merchant said, "but it's not fair that everything should grind to a halt because of those criminals."

"They're not criminals, they're heroes," the first merchant said angrily. "They avenged their master's death."

"Go ask the other magistrate to settle your dispute." Ikeda closed the door, turned, and saw Reiko. "How is your father?"

"He regained consciousness long enough to tell me something about the man who beat him." Reiko described the tattoos on the man's arm.

"Maybe he's someone that your father convicted," Ikeda said. "Maybe he had a grudge."

"That's what I'm thinking. I want to search the court records for names of repeat offenders. Will you help me?"

"Certainly." Ikeda accompanied Reiko to the magistrate's office.

The office was dear to Reiko. When very young, she'd played with her toys and kept her father company while he worked. When she was older, she'd helped him copy his notes into the official records that filled ledgers and scrolls in fireproof iron trunks stacked to the ceiling. The unoccupied desk brought tears to Reiko's eyes. She and Ikeda lifted down trunks and began sorting through the records. It was no quick task; her father had been magistrate for almost three decades, and he conducted hundreds of trials every year.

"I wish there were a faster way to weed out cases that involve defendants who obviously didn't attack my father, like these female thieves and prostitutes," Reiko said, as she and Ikeda skimmed pages of court proceedings.

"Your father's clerks did make a note when a defendant had been previously convicted," Ikeda said. "Here's one—but this trial was for his third offense. That's too many."

After two hours, Reiko had made a list of the names of twelve male criminals who each had two convictions and were young enough and presumably able-bodied enough to have managed the attack on Magistrate Ueda. She'd also written down their places of residence.

"What are the chances that they're still living there?" she said.

"Not very good," Ikeda said. "Perpetual criminals move around a lot. And some of these may not be living at all. Their kind tends to die early."

"At least we have some possible suspects." Reiko tucked the list under her sash. "I'll give this to my husband. Maybe it will help him catch the assassin."

HIRATA RETURNED TO Edo Castle at dusk. He'd spent the afternoon hunting for Tahara, Deguchi the priest, and the soldier named Kitano Shigemasa. His sources had told him that Tahara had a house in the Kanda district. Hirata had gone there and spoken to a servant, who'd said that Tahara was out. Next, Hirata had ridden to Ueno Temple. Deguchi wasn't there; he was ostensibly begging alms in the city. But a monk told

Hirata that Deguchi's friend Kitano was a retainer to Lord Satake. Hirata went to Lord Satake's estate, where no one would tell him anything about Kitano. By then Hirata was thoroughly frustrated. As he rode up through the walled passages inside the castle, he felt guilty because he should have spent more time investigating the attack on Magistrate Ueda.

"I hear you've been looking for us," someone behind him said.

The voice was a blend of smoothness and roughness, instantly familiar. At the same time, Hirata felt the aura strike him like a series of thunderbolts. Hirata froze in his saddle. He clamped his will down on the terror that leaped in him because Tahara had said "us," not "me."

All three of them were here.

Hirata forced himself to turn nonchalantly. He saw, bracketed by the high stone walls, Tahara and another samurai on horseback and a priest in a hemp cloak and saffron robes standing between them. The cold, drafty passage was empty of other people. Lanterns in the corridors atop the walls cast a dim, flickering glow on the men. Tahara smiled; his eyes twinkled in his handsome, rakish face. Hirata took his first good look at his other stalkers.

"Kitano-*san*," Hirata said.

The soldier bowed; he removed his iron helmet. He was older than his robust figure had led Hirata to believe—in his fifties. The hair in his topknot was streaked with gray. His skin was a mesh of scars. His eyes crinkled, but the rest of his face remained immobile. The cuts that had made the scars must have damaged his facial nerves.

"Deguchi-*san*," Hirata said.

At first the priest seemed a mere youth. His long, oval face and shaved head had a smooth complexion untouched by life. He wasn't handsome— his eyes were too heavily lidded, his nose too flat, and his mouth too pursed—but he had a strange, radiant beauty. Then Hirata noticed the whisker stubble on Deguchi's cheeks and the tough sinews in his neck. Deguchi could be any age between twenty and forty. He didn't speak; he only bowed.

"How does it feel to be the hunted instead of the hunter for a change?" Hirata asked.

"Don't be so sure our positions are reversed," Tahara said with pleasant humor.

Anger made Hirata belligerent. "I know who the three of you are and where you live."

"All that from the one clue that Tahara gave you, his name." Kitano's genial voice had a coarse provincial accent. "You've lived up to your reputation as a good detective."

Deguchi the priest said nothing. He just watched.

"Apparently you've decided that the right time to talk has finally come," Hirata said.

"Yes." Tahara looked behind him. Patrol guards approached. "Let's go somewhere more private."

All his instincts told Hirata not to go with the men. Two years' worth of curiosity wouldn't let him refuse. He accompanied Tahara, Deguchi, and Kitano to the castle's herb garden, where the shogun's apothecaries grew medicinal plants. The garden was deserted, its plots covered with snow tinted mauve by the setting sun. Beyond it loomed the forest preserve. As he jumped off his horse, Hirata tried to quell the hum of anxiety that sped along his nerves. He tried not to show his terror as he faced his adversaries.

Was this the showdown he'd been dreading?

Would he die here, tonight?

He hadn't said good-bye to his wife, his children, or Sano.

Would he fail to honor his promise to take care of Sano's family?

Tahara and Kitano dismounted. The soldier and priest flanked Tahara, who was clearly their leader. But Hirata knew that the other two men had powers nearly as great as Tahara's—and greater than his own. He gave in to his urge to delay the battle for as long as possible.

"Whose aura is it that I've been feeling?" he asked.

"It's a triad made up of all of ours," Tahara said.

Hirata was disturbed to learn that all three men had been present whenever he'd seen or thought it was only one. All of them had been stalking him, as a team. Even worse, Hirata sensed that the sum of their power was not greater than its parts. Each third was still many times greater than his own.

"Ozuno is dead," Hirata said. "Did you know?"

The men's gazes intensified, their only acknowledgment of the fact that he'd discovered that they were all disciples of the same teacher.

"Yes," Tahara said. Emotion veiled the twinkle in his eye.

"Why didn't you tell me?"

"I didn't want us to be the messengers of bad news," Tahara said. "I thought it wouldn't make you feel very friendly toward us."

"You want me to feel friendly toward you?" Hirata laughed in disbelief. "What do you want with me? To fight?"

"Oh, good heavens, no," Tahara said. Deguchi and Kitano shook their heads in disdain. "We're not like those fools who want to beat you and call themselves the top fighter in Japan." He spread his arms, as if to embrace his two friends and Hirata. "Here we have the greatest collection of martial artists the world ever saw. If we fought, some or all of us would be killed. What a stupid, boring waste of talent!"

For two years Hirata had been bracing himself for the fight of his life, and now it wasn't going to happen. His shameful relief quickly gave way to suspicion. "Then what do you want?"

"We want you to join us," Tahara said.

Confused, Hirata said, "Join you, in what?"

"In our secret society," Tahara said.

Never had Hirata imagined that this was the purpose behind the stalking, the poem on the bush, the birds, or the fire at the street show. "What kind of secret society? Who's in it?"

"Just us," Kitano said, "and you, if you decide to join."

"We four are Ozuno's most accomplished disciples," Tahara said. "We've gone further with the mystic martial arts than anyone else ever has. My friends and I aren't concerned with fighting anymore. It's time to put our training to better use."

Hirata had thought that fighting was a samurai's ultimate purpose in life, the reason for their training. "What better use is there?"

"We want to influence the course of fate," Tahara said, making the proclamation sound at once grand and simple.

That didn't enlighten Hirata. "You mean, start a war and make sure your side wins?"

Tahara shook his head impatiently. "I told you this isn't about fighting."

"Then how do you think you're going to influence the course of fate?"

"We'll work behind the scenes," Tahara said. "We'll manipulate things, people, and events. Our actions will be small and unobtrusive, but they will transform the world."

Hirata had heard many tales about the feats performed by mystic martial artists. They could defeat armies without striking a single blow; they could cause earthquakes. Most of the tales were exaggerations, but some were true; some of the feats Hirata could perform himself. But he'd never heard anything like this.

"I can see that you don't believe me," Tahara said.

"You're right, I don't," Hirata said. "How are you supposed to know what actions to take or what they'll accomplish?"

"By conducting magic rituals," Tahara said.

The society was sounding more preposterous by the moment. "Ozuno never taught me any magic rituals of that kind."

"But he knew them," Kitano said.

Hirata was dismayed by the idea that his teacher had withheld important information from him but not these other disciples. "And he taught the three of you?"

A glance passed between them. "After he died, we found an ancient, secret martial arts text among his things," Tahara said. "It contains instructions for the magic rituals. It was his legacy to us."

They were hiding something, Hirata knew. But he began to believe that they were telling the truth about the magic rituals, that they could indeed influence fate. They didn't seem foolish or deluded or crazy. And Hirata knew that the cosmos encompassed more and greater things than humans could imagine. He felt a thrill of excitement. Every serious martial artist wanted to expand his skills, to go beyond what seemed possible. Could this be Hirata's chance to attain powers normally reserved for gods? But he held on to his skepticism and distrust.

"Show me a magic ritual," he said.

"You have to agree to join our society first," Tahara said.

"How do I join?"

"You have to take an oath of loyalty to the society," Kitano said. "You swear that it is your top priority, that you will never reveal its business to anyone outside, and that you will abide by all its decisions."

That was an obvious conflict with Hirata's other loyalties. "Sorry."

Although Hirata felt a twinge of regret, he spoke without hesitation. He started to back away.

"Wait," Tahara said.

Hirata heard an urgent note in the man's voice. He paused, surprised that Tahara had dropped his air of mocking superiority. It was obvious how badly Tahara and the others wanted Hirata to join them. Hirata could smell their fear that he would slip from their grasp.

"I can't reveal our secrets," Tahara said, "but I can demonstrate what we do." He held up his finger, looked around, then walked toward the wall that separated the herb garden from the forest preserve.

Hirata and the other men followed. Tahara picked up a branch that had fallen from a tree. It was as long as his arm, almost as thick, covered with black bark, and straight except for a kink near one end. A thinner branch studded with twigs protruded from the kink. Tahara broke off the thinner branch. He held up the stick for Hirata to examine. "Memorize this."

Hirata did, but he was puzzled; the branch seemed so ordinary.

Tahara drew back his arm and threw the branch. The branch flew high and fast into the sky. It made a whizzing sound as it soared over the castle's rooftops and disappeared into the darkness. Hirata had to strain his ears to hear it land, with a harmless plop, somewhere near the palace.

He turned to look at the three men. "Is that all?"

Tahara nodded.

"Now what?"

"Now you wait and see what happens."

28

THE GATE OF Edo Castle discharged a horde of officials on horseback and in palanquins, escorted by troops and servants. Among the horde were the supreme court judges. Inspector General Nakae, riding on a brown mare, led his colleagues, who were also mounted, except for old Minister Motoori in his palanquin.

Someone called, "There goes the supreme court! Hey, when are you going to condemn those forty-seven *ronin* criminals to death?"

Nakae saw traffic slow down as people turned to look at the judges and hear his response. Cries went up along the promenade, from the itinerant peddlers, beggars, and other commoners who always loitered outside the castle. "The supreme court? Where?" "They're not criminals, they're heroes! They ought to be pardoned!"

The commoners stampeded toward the officials, squeezed them together, and brought traffic to a halt. Eager, frantic faces bobbed below Nakae and the other mounted samurai. Voices shouted, "Pardon!" "Condemn!" Nakae felt Minister Motoori's palanquin slam his left shoulder as the pressure increased. On his right side, someone else's horse was jammed against his. Nakae felt a stab of panic.

"Chase those people away before we get hurt!" he called to his troops.

The troops urged their horses toward the crowd, shouting, "Move back!"

The crowd pushed harder even though people within it screamed in fright. Nakae saw a beggar go down, trampled. A woman frantically lifted her baby above the packed bodies that surged toward the judges.

"Stop!" Nakae yelled.

Minister Motoori screamed as his palanquin swayed and its bearers struggled to hold it up. Troops and crowd began fighting. The supreme court was caught in the middle of the riot.

IN THE EARLY evening, Sano returned to Magistrate Ueda's house. He found Reiko sitting at her father's bedside. The doctor was checking the pulses at various points on Magistrate Ueda, who was still unconscious.

"Has there been any improvement?" Sano asked.

"He came to for a few moments this morning," Reiko said, her face drawn, her eyes underscored by dark shadows.

"What are his prospects?" Sano asked the doctor.

"It's hard to say. There may be bleeding inside his skull. His brain may be permanently damaged. If he doesn't revive within the next day or so . . ."

Reiko's eyes welled. Sano patted her hand, wishing he could offer more comfort.

"You should go home to your children and rest," the doctor told Reiko.

Sano agreed. "You'll notify us if there's any change?"

"Of course," the doctor said.

Reiko touched Magistrate Ueda's arm, said, "I'll be back tomorrow, Father," and let Sano lead her out of the room.

On the way back to Edo Castle, Sano rode alongside her palanquin through the cold streets where lights burned at gates and smoke veiled the moon. Detectives Marume and Fukida and his troops followed. Sano asked, "Has there been any progress toward finding the attacker?"

"I don't know," Reiko said. "Hirata-*san* never came back."

Sano was surprised because he hadn't heard from Hirata, either.

"Have you learned anything?" Reiko asked.

Sano told her his theory that the attack on her father was connected to the forty-seven *rōnin* case. "The supreme court judges claim they're innocent. Yanagisawa says he is, too." Yanagisawa's accusations had left a festering cut inside Sano. He was ashamed to tell Reiko what Yanagisawa had said, afraid that it was true. "I checked with my spies. There's no sign that Yanagisawa ordered the attack on your father, although he's still my favorite suspect."

"If he did, I'll kill him." Reiko's face, visible through the window of her palanquin, was fierce.

Yanagisawa had better pray he never fell into her hands, Sano thought. "I asked around the castle to see if any information has leaked from the supreme court. But even the biggest know-it-alls don't seem to have heard anything about the judges' opinions. The confidentiality of the court hasn't been breached, as far as I can tell. Then I went to the scene of the attack and looked for witnesses." Sano and the detectives had knocked on every door, questioned every resident. "Some people heard shouting last night, but nobody saw anything."

None of the people he'd interviewed had mentioned being interviewed before, and many had been surprised to hear about the attack. Shouldn't Hirata have interviewed them when he'd gone to the crime scene earlier? And where was Hirata?

"I have some information." Reiko said that her father had told her about a tattoo he'd seen on his attacker's arm. She showed Sano a list she'd written. "I got these names of repeat offenders from the Court of Justice records."

"That's the best news I've heard all day." Sano was glad for Reiko's initiative. "But I can't believe the attack was about a small-time criminal with a grudge against your father."

"Neither can I, now that I've heard your theory. Maybe the repeat offender was hired by someone else."

As they neared Edo Castle, Sano heard shouting and saw a crowd massed outside the gate. The shouting sounded angry, interspersed with cries of pain. Palanquins bobbed above troops who were fighting a horde of peasants.

"Wait here," Sano said.

Leaving Reiko with her guards, he and his men rode toward the riot. The troops outside the castle lashed their swords at the peasants. A young man fell, his head cleaved open. People on the ground screamed as the crowd trampled them.

"Get back! Everybody, go home!" Sano herded peasants away from the riot. His men dispersed them with threats and waving swords.

"Help!" Minister Motoori cried from his palanquin.

Beside him were Inspector General Nakae and Lord Nabeshima, on horseback. Lord Nabeshima flailed his sword. Nakae yelled as he dodged his friend's blows. Nearby, Superintendent Ogiwara struggled to stay on his bucking, whinnying mount. As Sano fought through the mob to rescue the supreme court, Minister Motoori's bearers went down. The palanquin sank below the riot and crashed.

Someone shouted over the hubbub, "Open the gate!"

It was Hirata. Standing on the roof above the gate, he yelled to the sentries to let the officials inside the castle. The sentries ignored him. They stood with their backs against the gate, keeping the mob out. Hirata jumped down inside the gate and opened it. As officials swarmed in, Sano and his troops scattered the rest of the crowd. The last officials and their entourages fled inside the castle. Sano looked around.

Corpses littered the promenade. Groans came from people who lay injured. Minister Motoori's palanquin had broken into pieces. Sano jumped off his horse and uncovered the old man. Minister Motoori was curled up on the ground, keening in pain. Attendants carried him into the castle. Sano ordered the sentries to fetch doctors for the wounded, then escorted Reiko's palanquin through the gate.

"What was that all about?" Reiko asked.

"I'm going to find out," Sano said.

When she was safely on her way home, Sano and Hirata joined the remaining supreme court judges. The twelve men huddled together inside a guardhouse, unharmed but shaken.

"What happened?" Sano asked.

"We were leaving the castle, and those ruffians got wind of it. They wanted to tell us what they thought our verdict should be. They started a riot." Inspector General Nakae was furious. "We might have been killed."

Superintendent Ogiwara looked around, counting heads. "Where's Minister Motoori?"

Sano explained that Motoori had been hurt. Colonel Hitomi said in dismay, "That's two of us down now."

"We'd better not leave the castle until the forty-seven *rōnin* business is settled," Lord Nabeshima said. "But we'll have to postpone our verdict until Minister Motoori and Magistrate Ueda can rejoin us."

The other judges agreed, although they complained about the inconvenience of going into hiding. Sano realized that if Minister Motoori was seriously injured, two judges who favored pardoning the forty-seven *rōnin* would be off the court. That might make it easier to agree on a verdict. But in view of the riot, a verdict that condemned the forty-seven *rōnin* seemed unlikely to settle the controversy. Sano pitied the judges: They were as much in jeopardy as he was. An unpopular verdict could bring doom for them, too. But the future remained to be seen. For now, Sano saw a chance to clear up one matter.

"Have you told anyone about the court's proceedings?" he asked the judges.

"Certainly not," Superintendent Ogiwara said. The other men shook their heads.

They all looked offended because Sano had suggested that they'd broken their rule of confidentiality. If they hadn't, and if his theory that someone was trying to influence the verdict by murdering Magistrate Ueda was correct, then the pool of suspects was limited to himself, Yanagisawa, and the judges themselves. And Sano knew which suspect he still favored.

A messenger entered the guardhouse and said to Sano, "Excuse me, but the shogun wants to see you. Immediately."

SANO AND HIRATA found the shogun in his bedchamber. He reclined on cushions, bundled in fur-lined silk robes, his bare feet in a bucket of hot water. A towel swathed his head. His teeth chattered violently; his complexion was ashen. Yoritomo hovered anxiously near him while a physician mixed a pungent medicinal tea.

"What's wrong, Your Excellency?" Sano asked.

"I've just had the, ah, most terrible fright of my life!" The shogun panted. "I went for a walk along the wall, and——" The doctor held the cup of tea to his lips. He coughed as he drank.

Sano was surprised, because the shogun rarely went outside on cold days. "What was His Excellency doing out there?" he asked Yoritomo.

Yoritomo favored Sano with a hate-filled stare. "His Excellency has been wanting to know more about what goes on outside the castle. We were up in the guard tower near the main gate, looking out at the city, when we heard a commotion. We looked down and saw—"

"A mob trying to force its way into my castle!" the shogun exclaimed, sputtering tea. "I was so terrified that I almost fainted!"

"I saw you there." Yoritomo spoke accusingly to Sano.

"It's a civil war! I'm under invasion!" The shogun moaned. "My worst nightmare!"

"I advised His Excellency to send for you," Yoritomo told Sano. "Make him understand that it isn't a war and he's not in any danger." His hostility toward Sano equaled his concern for his lord's health and his own welfare. "And while you're at it, explain what that scene outside *was* about."

"Sano-*san* doesn't take orders from you," Hirata said.

Sano gave Hirata a look that warned him not to start an argument with Yoritomo. He didn't need any more problems from that quarter. He gave an edited version of what had happened: "There's a lot of public interest in the forty-seven *rōnin* case. People heard that the supreme court was leaving the castle, and they wanted a look at the judges. They got too eager and started pushing."

"Not a war, then," the shogun said, relieved.

"Weren't a lot of people hurt?" Yoritomo asked. "I saw what looked like a stampede."

"Some." Sano admitted, "Minister Motoori fell."

The shogun trembled with fresh anxiety. "Ah, my poor old friend. And what's going to happen to me? Are those ruffians still out there?"

"No, Your Excellency," Hirata said. "It's over. You're safe."

"Well, then." The shogun sighed and relaxed on his cushions. He waved the doctor away. "You can go. I feel so much better."

"This happened because of the forty-seven *rōnin* affair," Yoritomo said. "There's bound to be more trouble unless the affair is settled. And do you know why it's not settled yet, Your Excellency?" He smiled a cruel, dazzling smile at Sano. He looked like a young incarnation of his father.

"Why not?" the shogun said cautiously.

"Because Sano-*san* is supposed to investigate the case for the supreme

212

court, and he's not making any progress," Yoritomo said. "Therefore, the riot was his fault."

Sano thought that Yanagisawa couldn't have done a better job of casting blame on him. "The riot was nobody's fault. It was an accident."

"Sano-*san* chased the mob away," Hirata said. "He protected Your Excellency."

"If he'd done his duty, the riot wouldn't have happened," Yoritomo persisted. "While he drags his feet, there could be another riot. Next time the mob might break into the castle!"

"Merciful gods, no!" The shogun clutched Yoritomo's sleeve. "What should I do?"

"You should get rid of Sano-*san*," Yoritomo said promptly. "Don't wait for a verdict on the forty-seven *rōnin*. Send him away now."

"Maybe I should." The shogun spoke with unaccustomed firmness.

A peal of doom resonated through Sano. Had the day finally come when he couldn't escape punishment? Was he soon never to see his family again? At the same time Sano was outraged. Fourteen years of loyal service to the shogun had brought him to this! Bushido had rarely been harder to stomach than it was now. Anger gave Sano the nerve to take a gamble instead of hurrying to placate the shogun.

"If you want me gone, it's my duty to go," Sano said. "I'll leave before the day is done. Then you can find someone else to clean up the mess that the forty-seven *rōnin* made and solve all the other problems that I usually solve for you." He spoke slowly, giving the shogun time to visualize the consequences of banishing him. "And everyone will know that you punished me for something that Yoritomo-*san* says is my fault even though it isn't."

"Ahh. Well, ahh." The shogun shrank into his robes, like a quail hiding in the grass from a hunter. Losing a man he'd always depended on was too much for the shogun, who didn't like to think that he was being manipulated. "I guess that's not, ahh, quite what I want." He turned a baleful look on Yoritomo.

Sano breathed. Hirata hid a smile. Lacking his father's talent for the quick comeback, Yoritomo spluttered. His face red with rage, he huffed out of the room.

"What's wrong with him?" the shogun said.

"I don't know." Sano thought it best to beat a retreat before the shogun changed his mind about sparing him. "If Your Excellency doesn't mind, we'll be getting back to the investigation."

"Very well," the shogun said. As Sano and Hirata departed, he called, "If this, ahh, forty-seven *rōnin* business isn't resolved soon . . ."

They didn't need to hear him complete his threat.

29

YORITOMO WAS WAITING for Sano in the corridor, his hands on his hips, his legs spread wide, his chin out-thrust. Sano said to Hirata, "Meet me at home. We need to talk."

He faced Yoritomo. The corridor was empty but for them. "You think you're so smart." Yoritomo's voice trembled with rage. "I bet you're laughing at me inside. Well, just wait until next time." He jabbed his finger at Sano. "You won't ever laugh at me again."

Despite the fact that Yoritomo had worked hard to destroy him, Sano felt a compassion for the young man that was tinged by guilt. Yanagisawa had made Yoritomo a political pawn, and on him lay the blame for Yoritomo's unhappy life. But it was Sano's trick that had changed Yoritomo into a bitter, hate-consumed, obsessive man like his father.

"I'm not laughing," Sano said. He fervently wished he could take back his trick, no matter that Yoritomo had deserved it, and not only because he was paying the price now. He deplored himself for killing what was good in a youth he'd liked and hadn't wanted to hurt. He would also hate for anyone to treat Masahiro the way he'd treated Yoritomo. "And I don't want there to be a next time. Can't we call a truce?"

"After what you did to me? Never!"

"I've apologized," Sano said. "I miss the friendship we once had. Don't you remember how we used to talk and practice martial arts together?"

"Yes, when my father was exiled." Rancor pervaded Yoritomo's voice. "After he came back, he told me that you'd been pretending to like me, because you wanted to use me to get back at him." Yoritomo chuckled at his own innocence. "My father was right. You were never my friend."

"Your father was wrong. He sees everything through his own warped vision. Don't always trust his judgment. Don't be like him."

As Sano spoke, it occurred to him that Masahiro had inherited many of Sano's own traits—his individuality, his willingness to take dangerous risks—and maybe Yoritomo wasn't the only son who would be better off for not imitating his father.

"Don't you criticize my father!" Yoritomo was so angry that spittle frothed out of his mouth. "He's the only person who cares about me. You're the one who's untrustworthy! You betrayed me! And now you're trying to turn me against my father!"

"That would be the best thing that could happen, for your sake, not mine. If you continue to follow your father's example, you're heading for serious trouble."

"I won't listen to any more of this! I don't care what you think!" Yoritomo thrust his face close to Sano's, shook his fist, and spoke through gritted teeth. "You are my enemy. The fight between us won't end until one of us is dead!"

HIRATA MET DETECTIVES Marume and Fukida outside Sano's office. "Well, hello," Marume said. "I haven't seen you in such a long time, I almost didn't recognize you."

"Where have you been?" Fukida asked.

Hirata didn't answer. He felt their antagonism and fear as they brushed past him. Waiting in the cold, dim passage, he dreaded his talk with Sano. His nerves were still on edge from his encounter with Tahara, Deguchi, and Kitano. Could they really influence fate through magic rituals? Hirata had begun to doubt it, even though he wanted to believe it. Were they the most accomplished martial artists in history, or were they mad? And what did they expect to happen as a result of a thrown branch?

Sano arrived. His face was somber; his aura glinted with strain and frustration beneath a haze of fatigue. Sometimes when two people had an exchange that produced strong emotions, each transferred energy to the other. Hirata sensed a tinge of Yoritomo's malevolent energy on Sano. Whatever had occurred between Sano and Yoritomo hadn't been good.

"Come in," Sano said, and walked past Hirata into his office.

His brusqueness told Hirata that nothing good was going to happen during this exchange, either. They knelt, Sano behind his desk on the dais and Hirata opposite on the floor.

"Have you identified Magistrate Ueda's attacker?" Sano asked.

"Not yet, but I found a clue at the scene." Hirata explained about the arrow. "I followed the man's trail, but I haven't been able to pick up his aura."

"Did you look for witnesses?"

Hirata could see that Sano knew he hadn't. "I'll do it tomorrow."

"Never mind. I saved you the trouble. There aren't any witnesses." Sano leaned his elbows on his desk and studied Hirata. "What have you been doing all day?"

Hirata owed Sano the truth. "I found out who's been stalking me." But he didn't want to reveal the details until he'd had time to think them over. He merely named Tahara, Deguchi, and Kitano. "I went looking for them."

"Did you find them?"

Hirata especially didn't want to tell Sano about the secret society. Sano wouldn't believe its claims. And despite the fact that Hirata was skeptical himself, he felt strangely protective toward the three men.

"No," Hirata said. It was technically the truth: They'd found him. "But before I knew it, the day was gone." The disappointment in Sano's eyes hurt Hirata more than anger would have. "I'm sorry."

"I'm sorry that you're having this trouble. I know it's serious, and I've tried to be patient, but—" Sano's breath gusted out. He said with a mixture of concern and vexation, "This isn't a good time for you to be going off on personal business. If I can't count on you, then tell me. I can have Detectives Marume and Fukida take over your duties."

They would like that, Hirata thought. "That won't be necessary," he said, although he appreciated Sano's offer. Most masters expected unstinting service, no excuses or exceptions; but Sano wasn't that sort of master. He never forgot that Hirata had saved his life, at great cost to himself, and he was always ready to repay the debt. That made Hirata reluctant to take advantage of Sano's generosity. "I won't take off again."

"Good." Sano seemed glad to consider the air cleared and the issue settled. "Because I have a new task for you." He took a folded paper from beneath his sash. "These are suspects in the attack on Magistrate Ueda." He explained how Reiko had identified them from the tattoo her father had described and a search through the Court of Justice records. "Track them down."

Hirata took the list. "I'll start first thing in the morning." As he walked down the passage toward his quarters, he vowed to atone for neglecting his duty. He wouldn't let the secret society override his loyalty to Sano.

BY MUTUAL AGREEMENT Sano and Reiko didn't talk about Magistrate Ueda, the forty-seven *rōnin,* or anything else disturbing while they ate dinner with Chiyo and the children. Later, when they went to bed, Reiko fell asleep at once, but Sano lay awake beside her in the gray glow of moonlight on snow. Troubling thoughts made his body restless despite a long, difficult day and the previous night with little sleep. He couldn't find a comfortable position.

Reiko stirred. "Can't you sleep?"

"No." Sano flopped onto his back.

Reiko curled against him, warm and drowsy. "What are you thinking about?"

"The attack on your father. Maybe I've been approaching the investigation in the wrong way."

"What do you mean?" Reiko was fully awake now.

"I assumed that the judges or Yanagisawa were behind the attack, because they were the only ones besides myself who knew what was going on in the supreme court. But maybe the person who's responsible is someone who doesn't know where the judges stand. Someone who has a personal stake in the outcome of the case nonetheless."

He felt a jolt of surprise run through Reiko. "Are you talking about Oishi?"

"All the forty-seven *rōnin*," Sano said.

Reiko propped herself on her elbow to look at him. "Do you think they're behind the attack on my father? But they're locked up."

"There are ways to get around that. And who else would care as much about the court's verdict?"

Reiko turned over on her back. Gazing at the ceiling, she said, "The verdict will mean life or death for them. That's more serious than politics or principles, which are the reasons that other people are interested in the case."

"Killing judges would certainly delay the verdict."

"Every day it's delayed is another day that the forty-seven *rōnin* get to stay alive."

"They wouldn't have known that your father is leading the faction that wants to save them." Sano added, "I shouldn't have told you that."

They pondered in silence. Then Sano said, "There are other people besides the forty-seven *rōnin* who have a personal interest in the verdict. Oishi's wife. And Lord Asano's."

Reiko protested, "I can't believe it's one of them! They're just . . ."

"Just women?" Sano chuckled. "There are other women besides you who are capable of killing or sending someone else to do it." During past investigations he'd met several.

"I don't believe Ukihashi and Lady Asano are capable," Reiko said.

"If we want to get to the truth about this, we should keep our minds open."

"You're right. I'll go and see them tomorrow."

"I'll question Oishi and his men." A thought struck Sano. "There's somebody we're forgetting."

"Who?"

The sound of weeping drifted down the corridor. Their guest was having a sleepless night, too. Reiko said, "Okaru?" in a tone of disbelief.

"Okaru also has a stake in the case. And remember, we're keeping our minds open."

Reiko sighed. "Very well. I'll talk to her, too."

Exhaustion overcame her and Sano. They slept.

IN THE ROOM next to theirs, Masahiro lay awake. He'd heard his parents' conversation, and he was troubled by the part about Okaru. Could she really be responsible for the attack on his grandfather? What should he do?

30

WHEN MORNING CAME, Reiko was reluctant to speak to Okaru. She didn't want to disturb the poor girl, especially since Okaru was a guest. Reiko lingered over breakfast with the children. Finally, unable to avoid the difficult task, she went to Okaru's room.

The room was empty, the exterior door open. Reiko stepped out onto the veranda, blinking in the pale sunlight, folding her arms against the cold. Okaru was crouched near the foot of the steps, digging with her hands in ground she'd cleared of snow.

"What are you doing?" Reiko asked.

Okaru looked up and brushed a strand of hair off her tear-swollen face. Her fingers smeared mud on her cheek. She gave Reiko a wan smile. "Digging a hole. To bury this." She pointed to a small red lacquer box on the step.

"What's in it?" Reiko said.

Okaru opened the box's hinged lid to reveal a pink paper flower, a writing brush with frayed bristles, and a lock of black and gray hair tied with a green thread. "Oishi bought me this flower. He threw this old brush away, and I picked it out of the trash. He let me clip some of his hair to keep." She gently touched each item. "They're all I have left of him."

Pity for Okaru made Reiko's task even harder. "Why do you need to bury them?"

"Because after what happened with Oishi the other day, I can't bear to look at them." Okaru's eyes welled. "The memories hurt too much. I hope it's all right to bury the box here. I don't have any place else."

"It's all right."

Okaru sniffled, said, "Thank you," and finished digging. She set the box in the hole.

"I need to talk to you," Reiko said.

"About what?" Okaru's hands trickled dirt onto the box.

"My father. He was attacked the night before last. He was badly beaten." Reiko swallowed. "He may die."

"I'm sorry." Okaru looked up. "I didn't know."

Studying her closely, Reiko saw sympathy in her eyes but no sign of falsehood. "Did you know that my father is Magistrate Ueda? And that he's a judge on the supreme court that will decide what should happen to the forty-seven *rōnin*?"

"Yes. I heard the servants talking about it."

The suspicions that Sano had raised about Okaru last night seemed ridiculous now. Reiko could hardly envision a person less capable of an assassination attempt. Furthermore, Okaru hadn't been out of the estate—except for the trip to see Oishi—since Reiko had brought her here. Yet Reiko knew that unlikely people did commit crimes.

"Are you angry at Oishi?" Reiko said.

Okaru patted down the dirt that covered the box. Her hands were black with soil. "I guess I am, a little."

"Did you want to hurt him because he hurt you?"

"No." Okaru sounded as if the thought hadn't occurred to her. "I would never."

"Have you changed your mind about wanting to save him?" Reiko asked. "Do you want him to be put to death?"

Okaru gaped. "Of course not. I still love him. Even though he doesn't love me."

"Did you ask someone to make the supreme court condemn him and his friends?"

"I don't understand. How would someone make the supreme court do anything?"

"By killing my father, the judge who was leading the faction that wants to pardon the forty-seven *rōnin*," Reiko said.

222

"I didn't even know that your father wants to pardon them." Okaru stood up and regarded Reiko with bewilderment. "And even if I had wanted to kill him, who would I have asked to do it? I don't know anyone in Edo except the people in your house."

"You do know someone else in Edo," Reiko said. "Your servant. Goza."

Okaru's mouth and eyes opened into perfect circles. "She wouldn't—"

"She's devoted to you. She tried to strangle Oishi. Why stop at that? Why not have him put to death?"

"Goza was only protecting me!" Okaru cried. "Now that I'm safe, why should she want to hurt Oishi anymore?"

"To pay him back for breaking your heart," Reiko suggested.

"If you knew Goza, you wouldn't think that." Okaru hastened to explain, "Goza is an orphan, like me. She grew up cleaning teahouses in Miyako. People used to make fun of her. They threw stones at her and called her ugly names. But Goza never lifted a hand to them. She's really a gentle person. She doesn't care about revenge."

"Maybe not for herself, but what about for you?" Reiko said, warming to her own theory. Her fondness for Okaru gave way before a new onslaught of suspicion. "I think she would do whatever you asked. That includes hiring an assassin to kill my father and turn the supreme court against Oishi."

"I didn't ask!" Indignation filled Okaru's eyes. "We would never do anything to hurt your family."

"Where is Goza?" Reiko asked. "Let's hear what she has to say."

Suddenly frightened, Okaru said, "I—I don't know."

Reiko recalled Chiyo saying she'd seen Goza sneak in and out of the house. Horror trickled through Reiko. Was she harboring the people responsible for her father's injuries? Had she ruined her friendship with Chiyo for someone who'd repaid her kindness with evil?

"Tell me the truth. You owe me that much," Reiko said, her sympathy toward Okaru cooling fast. "Did you plot with Goza to kill my father?"

Although her face was a picture of terror and misery, Okaru spoke bravely: "No, I didn't. But I can see that you don't trust me. I think Goza and I should leave."

"You're not going anywhere. Until I find out the truth, I want you where I can watch you." Reiko marched Okaru into the mansion, called

Lieutenant Tanuma, and told him, "Find a place to lock her up, and her servant when she comes back. Guard them and don't let them out of your sight."

WHEN SANO ARRIVED at the Hosokawa clan estate, the guards directed him to the martial arts practice room in the barracks. There, a crowd of samurai cheered the two men engaged in combat.

Naked to the waist, dressed in white trousers, Oishi and his son Chikara brandished swords, circled, lunged toward, and struck at each other. Their reflections in the mirrors on the wall followed their moves. The room echoed with their grunts, the clang of their blades, the stomp of their bare feet, and the audiences' cheers. Sano watched Oishi and Chikara. The son was quicker, but the father moved with the skill that comes only from long experience. Sano noticed that their swords weren't wooden practice weapons; the blades were steel.

Cupping his hands around his mouth, Sano yelled, "That's enough!"

The audiences' shouts dwindled into silence. Oishi and Chikara retreated.

"What is this?" Sano asked the Hosokawa men in the audience. "You're supposed to be guarding them." He pointed at Oishi and Chikara. "And you put real weapons in their hands?" He ordered, "Drop those swords."

Oishi obeyed, his face impassive. Chikara waited a moment, in defiance, then followed suit. They took their white coats from a rack and draped them over their shoulders. One of the Hosokawa men said sheepishly, "They weren't going to hurt anybody."

"That's what Kira thought until they cut off his head." Sano turned to Oishi and Chikara. "I want to talk to you."

"We can go to my quarters," Oishi said.

He and Chikara led Sano into the mansion, to a guest chamber with gold-inlaid teak cabinets, a matching desk in a raised study niche, embroidered screens, and a wall mural that depicted water birds by a river. Heat shimmered up from sunken braziers. The lavish accommodations were further evidence of the Hosokawa clan's goodwill toward the *rōnin*.

Oishi put a silk cushion in front of the alcove, which contained a calligraphy scroll hanging above a branch of winter berries in a black ceramic vase. Sano knelt on the cushion, in the place of honor. Oishi crouched opposite; Chikara hovered near the door. The atmosphere was as charged with the heat of combat as the martial arts practice room. Father and son waited expectantly, identical scowls on their faces.

"There's been a problem with the supreme court," Sano said. "One of the judges was ambushed and beaten the night before last. He's unconscious. Another judge was hurt in a riot." Sano had checked on Minister Motoori and learned he'd broken his leg. "The court has postponed deciding on a verdict. You're safe for a while."

Chikara betrayed his relief with a sigh. Oishi said blandly, "So we've heard."

"How?" Sano asked.

"Our hosts have been kind enough to fetch us news from town," Oishi said.

"Did they also tell you that the judge who was beaten is my father-in-law?"

"They mentioned it."

"Did they mention that the supreme court is divided on the issue of whether you should live or die?"

"No." Puzzlement crept into Oishi's scowl. "How could they know? The supreme court proceedings are secret."

"Why are you asking us these questions?" Chikara demanded.

"Mind your manners," Oishi warned.

"Why should I?" Chikara grinned at Sano despite the fear that showed in his eyes. "The Hosokawa men brought us some news about you, too—you're out of favor with the shogun. Nobody cares what you think."

His insolence stung. Sano controlled his temper. "You should care. What I think will affect my investigation, which could influence the supreme court one way or the other."

"My son's question was a good one," Oishi said. "So your father-in-law was beaten: What has that to do with us?"

"I want to know if you or your men are responsible," Sano said.

"How could we be? We've been under house arrest for the past five days."

"What else have the Hosokawa men been kind enough to do for you besides bring you news?"

Caution settled over Oishi; he exuded a stillness the way a tree does when the wind dies down and its branches cease to toss. "I don't get your meaning."

"Did you ask them to prolong your life by attacking the supreme court?" Sano asked. "Did they hire an assassin to kill my father-in-law? Or let you out so that you could?"

Oishi turned away, massaging his jaw with his fingers. It was the same reaction as when Sano had told him that his mistress was in town. Oishi seemed even more discomfited now, by Sano's accusation. Maybe he was innocent and the idea that anyone would think him responsible for the attack had never occurred to him. Or maybe he was guilty but he'd counted on nobody connecting him with the crime because it had happened while he was imprisoned.

"I didn't ask them." Oishi spoke slowly, as if buying himself time to think. "Even if I had, they wouldn't have done it. And they haven't let me or any of my men outside."

A Hosokawa retainer who was fanatical about Bushido and idolized the prisoners might have thought them worth risking the consequences of murdering an important official like Magistrate Ueda. Sano wasn't ready to give up his theory, especially since he sensed that Oishi had something new to hide.

"My father didn't arrange the attack." Chikara moved to stand beside Oishi.

"Then maybe you did," Sano said.

"Me?" Chikara drew back in surprise and fright. He looked to Oishi.

"He didn't do it." Oishi flung out his arm, a barrier between Sano and his son.

Sano remembered making the same gesture himself, when Masahiro had tried to run into the street as a group of samurai on horseback raced by. "If you're guilty, then you'd better admit it," he said, "or I'll take Chikara to Edo Jail and torture him until he confesses."

Although clearly dismayed by the threat, Oishi declared, "We're both innocent." He stood. "And we're through with this conversation."

Sano rose, too, his bluff called. "You haven't seen the last of me. If I discover that you or your comrades were responsible for the attack on my father-in-law, I'll execute the whole pack of you even if the supreme court pardons you for the vendetta."

As he stalked from the room, he was astonished to recall that not long ago he'd respected the forty-seven *rōnin* as exemplars of Bushido. Now he suspected them of trying to murder his kinsman. Even if they were innocent, he believed that their vendetta had led to the attack on Magistrate Ueda, and they were therefore indirectly responsible. If they were truly guilty, he would have their blood and his own revenge.

AFTER THINKING OVER the conversation he'd overheard between his parents last night, Masahiro had decided what to do.

He would conduct his own investigation into the attack on his grandfather.

The first step was to interview the suspect.

His heart pounded as he went to Okaru's room. He wanted to see Okaru as much as he wanted to find out if she was involved in the attack. Peering through the open door, he discovered that she wasn't there. Bedding lay in a heap on the floor. A maid stood at the cabinet, taking out clothes.

"Where's Okaru?" Masahiro asked.

"Your mother moved her into the servants' quarters. She doesn't want her so close to your family."

Masahiro felt a stab of apprehension. "Why not?"

"She thinks Okaru might have had something to do with the attack on Magistrate Ueda."

If his mother thought Okaru was guilty, then perhaps she was. Masahiro's heart sank.

"Lieutenant Tanuma is guarding Okaru," the maid added.

So much for Masahiro's plan to interview her. He couldn't do it in front of Lieutenant Tanuma, who would tell his mother, who probably wouldn't approve. It was time for the second step in his investigation.

"You can leave," he told the maid.

"Your mother told me to move these things to Okaru's new room."

"Come back later," Masahiro said.

He was the master's son. The maid went. Masahiro hesitated, feeling guilty about snooping and afraid of what he might find. He gingerly sorted through the kimonos on the floor. Okaru's sweet scent wafted up from them. He caught up a robe and buried his face in the soft, bright floral fabric. Embarrassed, he dropped the robe as if it were on fire. He didn't find anything suspicious among Okaru's clothes, shoes, and few other personal items in the right side of the cabinet. He examined a doll that had a chipped porcelain head. A girl who still liked dolls couldn't be a criminal, could she?

Masahiro moved to the left side of the cabinet. Here robes and trousers were neatly folded, their material sturdy, their colors drab. They must belong to the servant named Goza. All were masculine in style. Masahiro searched the cabinet until he came upon a bundle on the floor. The bundle was a brown kimono wrapped around a pair of gray trousers with rope drawstrings. Both garments were blotched with stiff, reddish-brown stains.

A bad feeling came over Masahiro.

The stains were dried blood.

A high, feminine, angry voice behind him demanded, "What are you doing?"

Taken by surprise, Masahiro yelled. He dropped the clothes and banged his elbow painfully on the cabinet as he turned.

Goza stood there, her fists clenched, a savage look on her mustached face. Masahiro stammered, "I was just looking——"

"For what?" Goza towered over him, trapping him against the cabinet.

Masahiro remembered that this was his house, he was a detective, and he was the one supposed to ask the questions. He snatched up the clothes he'd dropped and thrust them at Goza. She stepped back. Moving away from the cabinet, he said, "Where did this blood come from?"

Goza's eyes were like a pig's, small and mean, sunken into the thick flesh of her broad face. "None of your business," she said, and grabbed the clothes.

"You have to answer," Masahiro said. "Or I'll get my father, and you can tell him."

The piggy eyes glinted with fear and antagonism. "It's from a bloody nose."

"Whose nose? My grandfather's? Did you beat him up?"

228

"Stupid boy," Goza said. "You don't know anything."

"Where were you the night before last?" Masahiro persisted.

"Here. In the house."

"No, you weren't," Masahiro said disdainfully. "I already asked the guards. They said you left and didn't come back until the next morning. Where were you really?"

Goza muttered a curse. "I was out."

"Out, where? What were you doing?"

A dirty, sly gleam crept into Goza's eyes. "Do you like Okaru?"

Masahiro was taken aback by the change of topic. His first impulse was to lie rather than tell Goza to mind her own business. "No."

"Yes, you do." Goza regarded him with amused contempt. "I've seen the way you look at her. You want her, just like all the other men."

His face aflame with embarrassment, Masahiro could only shake his head. If Goza knew how he felt about Okaru, who else did?

Goza grabbed him by the front of his kimono and yanked him close to her. Masahiro was so startled that he forgot to resist. She said, "Listen, stupid boy. Better not tell anybody what you found." Masahiro recoiled from her hot, sour breath. "If you do, it won't just be me that gets in trouble. It'll be Okaru, too. Because I'm her servant. Whatever I've done, it was because she told me to. She'll be arrested and killed. And it will be your fault."

As Masahiro gaped in horror, the floor in the corridor creaked under footsteps. He heard the maid say, "I just saw Goza, she went in there."

Goza released Masahiro, stepping back from him just before the maid and a guard entered the room. "You're not allowed in here anymore," the guard told Goza. "Come with me."

Goza bent a warning look on Masahiro. "Remember what I said."

Before she and the guard left the room, Masahiro caught a fleeting glimpse of two crude black tattoos on her wrist.

OKARU'S NEW ROOM was a cubbyhole in the servants' quarters, an outbuilding near the kitchens. Lieutenant Tanuma leaned against the wall in the corridor outside, guarding Okaru. Before Reiko left the estate, she looked in on her prisoner. Okaru knelt on the mattress on the wooden pallet, her sad face lifted to the sunlight that came through the paper panes of the barred window. When she saw Reiko, her eyes filled with hope and entreaty. Reiko shut the door, pulled her cloak tighter around herself, and left the servants' quarters. Walking up the path to the mansion, she met Chiyo.

Chiyo fell into step beside Reiko and voiced the thought that was on both of their minds. "Did she do it?"

"I don't know," Reiko said. "But I don't think so."

"I must say that neither do I," Chiyo said. "When we first met Okaru, I was distrustful of her, but I can't believe she has it in her to deliberately harm anyone."

Guilt distressed Reiko. "If she didn't have anything to do with the attack on my father, then I'm being cruel to treat her like this." Suspicion provoked a burn of anger. "If she did, then I'll never forgive myself for bringing her into my family."

Chiyo didn't say she'd warned Reiko not to get involved with Okaru. She said soothingly, "You couldn't have known what would happen to your father. It isn't your fault, even if it is Okaru's. You were trying to help someone in need. And maybe Okaru is innocent."

Even if she was, she'd certainly opened the door to a lot of trouble. Without her story about Oishi and the vendetta, Sano's investigation might not have taken the course that it had. Magistrate Ueda might not have been attacked.

But Reiko said, "You're right. The assassin could be someone who has a personal grudge against my father. And if he was hired by someone, there are other people besides Okaru who could have done it. I'm going to see Oishi's wife and Lady Asano."

She and Chiyo reached the front courtyard, where her palanquin, bearers, and guards stood waiting. Chiyo said, "Shall I come with you?"

"I'd better go alone." Reiko needed time to think.

The two women bid each other a stilted good-bye. Reiko climbed inside her palanquin, unhappily aware that she'd hurt Chiyo's feelings. Even if Okaru was innocent, she had come between Reiko and Chiyo.

RIDING AWAY FROM Edo Castle, Hirata studied the list of repeat offenders. Their residences were scattered all over town. He

230

wouldn't have time to look for Tahara, Kitano, and Deguchi. Now that he'd slept on his encounter with them, it seemed unreal, the aim of their society a joke. Magic rituals to influence the course of fate, indeed!

He glanced backward at the palace, where Tahara had thrown the branch, and snorted. What did those men think was going to happen? The hill under Edo Castle would erupt like a volcano?

One repeat offender, named Genzo, lived near the blacksmiths' district, where the *doshin* had chased Magistrate Ueda's attacker. Hirata rode along a narrow lane. Between the gates at the ends were tenements— ramshackle, two-story, connected buildings. A woman came out of a room on a lower floor and dumped a pail of dirty water onto muddy snow. Balconies fronted the upper stories. Smoke from the blacksmiths' shops fouled the air with soot.

A man emerged onto a balcony. He had shaggy black hair; his gray kimono strained across his thick shoulders. He looked out onto the street, yawned, and scratched his head. Hirata saw two black tattoos on the man's arm, at the same instant he sensed the sullen red aura with glinting sparks, the energy that bespoke weakness and brutality. A combination of Reiko's detective work and Hirata's supernatural powers had led to the culprit.

The man turned his head toward Hirata. Recognition flashed in his puffy eyes, even though he and Hirata weren't acquainted: A perpetual criminal knows the law when he sees it coming after him. He rushed into the room behind the balcony. Hirata galloped his horse toward the house, stood in the saddle, and jumped.

He caught the wooden railing of the balcony and pulled himself up. He charged into a room cluttered with an unmade bed, heaps of clothes, and a bow and a quiver of arrows. The man was nowhere in sight. Hirata heard footsteps pounding down stairs. He sped through a curtained door, into a dim, narrow stairwell. Clearing the stairs in one leap, he saw the man run across a courtyard. Hirata caught the man by the shoulder just before he reached the gate. The man turned, his eyes wide with shock: He couldn't believe Hirata had caught up with him so fast. Hirata squeezed a nerve in his shoulder. The man crumpled, howling with pain.

"Who are you?" He clutched his arm, which jerked in spasms. "What did you do to me?"

Hirata said, "Don't worry—the damage isn't permanent. My name is Hirata."

The man gasped. He obviously knew Hirata's reputation. "What do you want?"

"Are you Genzo, convicted twice for assault?" Hirata asked.

"Yes. But I haven't done anything wrong since then."

"You ambushed three men the other night," Hirata said. "You killed two of them and beat the third so badly that he may die, too."

"How did you know I did?" Genzo was so flabbergasted that he didn't think to deny the accusation. Confusion, terror, and pain had caused him to blurt out his guilt.

"Never mind." Hirata seized Genzo by his uninjured arm and hauled him to his feet. "You're under arrest."

As he marched Genzo out of the courtyard to the street, Hirata looked up at Edo Castle. It looked the same as ever, with a smoke haze around its hill and its white walls and tile roofs shining in the sun. Nothing had happened yet, as far as Hirata could tell.

31

REIKO REMEMBERED THAT Oishi's former wife had said she worked as a maid for a salt merchant. Accompanied by her guards, Reiko rode in her palanquin past the salt warehouses along a canal near the reeking fish market in Nihonbashi. Peasants hefted crocks of salt out of boats moored at the quays. In the district where the merchants lived, Reiko's guard captain asked a watchman at a neighborhood gate, "Where can we find a woman named Ukihashi?"

"Oh, the samurai lady. She works for Madam Yasue," the watchman said, and gave directions to the house.

Ukihashi had said that her employer enjoyed having a samurai lady for a servant, Reiko recalled. Evidently, Madam Yasue was so proud of it that she'd spread the word.

The procession stopped in a street of houses that were big but plain. Sumptuary laws prevented commoners from flaunting their wealth; the penalty was confiscation of their assets. Any expensive things were hidden behind those bamboo fences and half-timbered walls. Reiko climbed out of her palanquin, went up to the gate, and rang the bell.

A girl answered. She was about ten years old and wore the indigo kimono and white headscarf of a maid. Reiko said, "I'm looking for Ukihashi. Is she here?"

Before the girl could reply, the door of the house behind her opened. A stout, middle-aged woman emerged. Her upswept hair was dyed a fake, bronzy shade of black. She wore thick makeup and a garish floral kimono. "Who's there?" she barked at the girl.

"A lady," the girl mumbled. "She wants to see my mother."

Reiko noticed that the girl had Ukihashi's square face and delicate features. The woman, presumably Madam Yasue, raked her gaze over Reiko. "Who are you?"

Reiko introduced herself.

"Ukihashi is a servant who has work to do," Madam Yasue said, "but I'll let you see her for a few minutes." She jerked her chin at the girl.

The girl trudged toward the rear of the house. Reiko followed. She pitied Ukihashi and her daughter, employed by that mean, vulgar woman. She tried not to think that their fate could be hers someday. If Sano left, there was no telling what depths she and the children might sink to, even if he wasn't made a *rōnin*.

The kitchen occupied a building attached to the house by a covered corridor. Its yard contained buckets, a storage shed, and slop barrels. Steam that smelled of fermented soybeans billowed from the open door. Reiko heard rattling, sizzling, and hissing noises. She entered, peered through the steam, and saw two women at a table surrounded by pots boiling on the hearth, dishware on shelves, utensils hung from the ceiling, bales of rice, and ceramic jars of food. Ukihashi was cleaning fish, slitting their bellies with a sharp knife and scraping out the entrails. The other woman knelt with her back to Reiko. All Reiko could see of her was her head drape and her cloak.

Ukihashi glanced up and noticed Reiko. Her raw, chapped lips parted. The other woman turned. It was Lady Asano. The drape covered her shaved head. Her plain, round face revealed shock and dismay. Reiko had never seen two people less glad to see her.

Ukihashi said, "What are you doing here?"

"I need to talk to you again," Reiko said.

Lady Asano rose hastily. "I'll be going, then."

"Stay," Reiko said. "I need to talk to you, too."

Lady Asano reluctantly knelt. "About what?"

"First, I want to know why you're here," Reiko said.

"We're friends." Lady Asano's small, wide-set eyes skittered. "I'm just visiting."

."I thought you'd had a quarrel," Reiko said.

"We've made up," Ukihashi said in a flat tone meant to discourage more questions.

Reiko sensed the strain in the air that accompanies a serious, intimate discussion. The women's eyes were red and swollen. "Why have you been crying?"

"It's none of your affair." Ukihashi gutted another fish. "Either say what you came to say or go. I'm busy."

"A judge on the supreme court was attacked the night before last," Reiko said. "He's my father." She watched the women; their expressions were blank. "He was badly beaten."

"I'm sorry," Lady Asano said with the indifference of a person so beleaguered by her own problems that she didn't care about anyone else's. "But what has that to do with us?"

"My husband and I think it was arranged by somebody who wants to sabotage the supreme court." Reiko sprang her accusation on both women. "Was it you?"

Lady Asano laughed, an involuntary outburst, behind her hand. Ukihashi said, "No." Her tone was incredulous. "Why would you think it was us?"

"Because you have an interest in the verdict." Although their reaction suggested that her suspicions were baseless, Reiko said, "Ukihashi-*san,* you would seem to want your husband punished. Lady Asano, you would surely rather have the forty-seven *rōnin* pardoned."

"I didn't beat your father," Ukihashi said, indignant. "I've never wanted to hurt anybody."

Her bloody hand gripped the knife. Reiko remembered the ferocity with which she'd attacked Okaru.

"Me, either," Lady Asano said.

"My husband and I think this attack was done by a criminal for hire," Reiko said.

"How could I have hired a criminal, even if I knew how, which I don't? I've been cooped up in this house, working," Ukihashi retorted. "You can ask my employer."

"I've been stuck in a convent for two years, remember," Lady Asano said. "This is the first time I've been out."

"Besides, where would I have gotten the money?" Ukihashi demanded. "I earn barely enough for me and my daughters to live on."

"My fortune was confiscated by the government," Lady Asano said.

Reiko had forgotten how circumscribed their lives were, how limited their means. Their logic, and their sincerity, and the problem of how they would have learned which judge on the supreme court to attack, convinced her that they were innocent of the crime against her father. But she could smell secrets in the air, like a whiff of the fish entrails on the table.

"Somebody will pay for my father's injuries," Reiko said. "When my husband finds out that you wouldn't cooperate with me, he may decide that it should be . . . you." Reiko settled her gaze on Lady Asano.

Lady Asano jerked back as if Reiko had thrown mud on her. "That's not fair! None of this is! I've never done anything wrong, and I've been punished anyway. Isn't it someone else's turn?"

"Fine. I'll tell my husband to pick you." Reiko turned on Ukihashi.

"No. Please." Alarmed, Ukihashi raised her hands. "I don't care about myself, but if I'm put to death, who will take care of my daughters?"

"If it has to be one of us, then let it be me," Lady Asano said, moved to sacrifice herself for the sake of friendship. "I'm all alone in the world."

"It doesn't have to be one of you." Reiko was merciless, even though she hated tormenting these helpless women. She was fed up with people lying to her and Sano and withholding information. Determined to learn the truth about the vendetta, keep her family together, and find out who'd hurt her father, she said to Ukihashi, "Your son would be a good scapegoat."

"Not Chikara!" Vicious anger transformed Ukihashi's face. She lunged toward Reiko, her slimy hands outstretched to maim. "Leave him alone!"

Lady Asano grabbed Ukihashi and cried, "Don't! You'll only make things worse!"

As Ukihashi struggled and shouted protests, Reiko said, "If Chikara is convicted of hiring the assassin that hurt my father, then it won't matter if the supreme court pardons the forty-seven *rōnin*. He'll be sentenced to death."

Lady Asano looked around, in desperate hope of escape or salvation. Finding neither, she said to Ukihashi, "We have to tell her."

"Tell me what?" Reiko said, elated that her tactic had worked, yet ashamed of her cruelty.

Ukihashi's face was a mess of tears and panic. "We promised it would be our secret!"

"We must," Lady Asano said, "if you want your son to have a chance to live."

Resignation settled over Ukihashi like an invisible net that pulled tight and squeezed the defiance out of her. "All right. But it won't be what you expected to hear."

1701 April

INSIDE LORD ASANO'S estate in Edo, Ukihashi dressed her two daughters in new, matching pale green kimonos. She smiled at the girls and said, "Don't you look pretty!"

A servant interrupted. "Kira Yoshinaka is here to see you."

Ukihashi was surprised. What could the shogun's master of ceremonies want with her? She hurried to the reception room and found the old man kneeling by the alcove. His head tilted upward at a haughty angle, and his eyebrows had an arrogant arch, but he smiled warmly.

"Hello, my dear," Kira said. "You're every bit as beautiful as I've heard."

Flattered, confused, and timid, Ukihashi blushed as she knelt and bowed. "You're too kind . . . I don't deserve . . . May I offer you some refreshments?"

While they drank tea and nibbled cakes, Kira chatted about the weather. His bright-eyed, intense scrutiny made Ukihashi uncomfortable. Finally he said, "My dear, I wonder if you would do an old man a favor."

"If I can," Ukihashi said, mystified.

"I would like to set up a romantic liaison between you and Lord Asano. So that the two of you can bed each other, to put it bluntly."

The request was too shocking and offensive for Ukihashi to even consider. "Why . . . ?"

Sly pleasure crept into Kira's smile. "Arranging tableaus is my specialty. I do it in my work at court, but this one would be strictly for my own private entertainment. Are you willing?"

"Certainly not!" Ukihashi was so outraged that she forgot her shyness and courtesy. "Lord Asano's wife is my friend. I would never do that to her or to my husband. I'm a good, faithful wife, and I have no desire to commit adultery for your selfish pleasure. You are a cad for suggesting such a thing!"

Unruffled, Kira said, "Allow me to explain why you should cooperate, my dear. Unless you do, I will tell the shogun that your husband has been speaking ill of him. That's treason."

"Oishi hasn't!" Ukihashi protested. "I'll swear to it!"

Kira regarded her with pity. "Who is the shogun going to believe? A silly woman or me, his master of ceremonies?" His smile turned cruel. "May I remind you that the family of a traitor shares his punishment? Either you do as I ask, or you and Oishi and your children will be put to death by tomorrow."

Although the very idea of betraying her friend's trust and her husband's love made her ill, Ukihashi had to protect her family. "Promise me that Oishi and Lady Asano will never know."

"Thank you, my dear." Kira chortled. "You can trust me to be discreet."

The next day Ukihashi went to a squalid inn by the river, where Kira had set up the liaison. Nauseated and shaking, she waited in the dingy room. She began to be furious at Lord Asano. How could he go along with Kira's scheme? Lady Asano had told her about his affairs with other women, but couldn't he leave the wife of his loyal chief retainer alone?

When Lord Asano arrived, he was so upset that his face twitched and he shook with dry sobs. "I don't want to do this any more than you do. I respect your husband, and I hate to betray him. But Kira said that if I don't, he won't instruct me on court etiquette. I'll flub the ceremony for the imperial envoys and disgrace myself."

Ukihashi realized that he was as much an innocent victim as herself. She was appalled at how Kira had manipulated both of them, but it made the situation more bearable. "Let's get it over with, shall we?"

They turned their backs to each other and undressed. They lay down on the bed and fumbled through the motions of lovemaking. Ukihashi felt dirty being touched by a man not her husband and mortified because she could see Kira's shadow on the paper windows. Through a hole in one pane, his bright, evil eye gleamed.

In the room next door, Lady Asano watched the couple through a crack in the wall. She pressed her hand over her mouth. She hadn't heard their whispered conversation. All she knew was that her husband and her friend were lovers. When Kira had told her yesterday, she hadn't believed him. He'd said she should rent this room and see for herself. And now here was the terrible proof! She didn't mind so much about her husband— she was used to his affairs. But how could Ukihashi do this to her? Lady Asano would hate her for as long as they lived.

"THAT'S WHY WE stopped being friends," Ukihashi said to Reiko.

"I didn't tell her I'd seen," Lady Asano said. "I was too angry and hurt."

Reiko sat in the steamy kitchen, astounded by what she'd heard. The women's story of the events that had led up to the vendetta was stranger than she'd ever imagined.

"But I knew she'd found out," Ukihashi said. "I could tell by the way she acted. I thought Lord Asano had told her. I didn't know it was Kira. Until now. That's what we were talking about when you came." Anger sparked in her tear-swollen eyes. "Kira told us both to keep quiet." She added regretfully, "And I was too ashamed to tell anyone."

"Now that Kira is dead, he can't hurt us," Lady Asano said. "So I came here to confront Ukihashi."

"She scolded me until I told her what Kira had done," Ukihashi said.

It must have been quite an emotional conversation, Reiko thought.

"I realized I'd misjudged her," Lady Asano said. "We made up." She and Ukihashi exchanged affectionate smiles.

"When I talked to you before, everything I told you was the truth," Ukihashi said to Reiko. "I just left out the part about Kira and Lord Asano and me."

"Me, too," Lady Asano said.

The implications of their tale stunned Reiko. "Is that why Lord Asano attacked Kira? Because Kira forced him to take part in the tableau?"

"Yes. On top of insulting him and humiliating him." Lady Asano's voice was harsh with the rancor she still felt toward Kira. "It must have been the thing that finally made my husband snap. Because he attacked Kira the very next day after the liaison at the inn."

Reiko was exhilarated. She had discovered the secret that many had speculated upon for almost two years and none had guessed—the motive behind the attack. But the cruelty of the truth lessened her pride in her accomplishment. Kira had turned Lord Asano into a sexual puppet. Lord Asano must have declined to say why he'd attacked Kira because he'd been too ashamed and he'd wanted to protect the women from disgrace. And Kira hadn't confined himself to tormenting Lord Asano. He'd made Ukihashi and Lady Asano part of his game. Kira had been a monster who'd enjoyed shaming other people and watching them suffer. Reiko could believe he'd deserved to die.

"What will you do, now that you know?" Ukihashi said. She and Lady Asano regarded Reiko with fear that their candor had averted one threat but brought on another that was worse.

"I'll have to tell my husband," Reiko said.

Ukihashi leaned her elbows on the table piled with fish and hid her face in her hands, heedless of the viscera on them. "I can't bear for it to become public! I don't want Oishi to know what I did!"

Reiko recalled her first talk with Ukihashi, when the woman had expressed such hatred toward her husband. Why should Ukihashi mind what Oishi thought of her now? She must care more for him than she would admit.

"I think that since we gave you what you wanted, you should do something for us," Lady Asano said. "Can't you and your husband keep our secret to yourselves?"

Reiko felt that she did owe the women a favor. "We'll try."

Ukihashi dropped her hands. Her face was smeared with slime from the fish. "Will it make any difference for the forty-seven *rōnin*?"

"I don't know," Reiko said, honestly at a loss. She hadn't had time to think of all its ramifications. "Maybe." Eager to bring Sano her new evidence, she rose.

The women rose, too, as if they didn't want Reiko to leave without giving them more reassurances. Lady Asano said, "Now do you believe that we had nothing to do with the attack on your father? We won't get in trouble?"

"Yes." Reiko truly did. The air around the women seemed clearer than when she'd arrived; her sense that they were hiding something was gone.

"What about my son?" Ukihashi said. "And Oishi?"

"If they're innocent, they won't get in trouble, either," Reiko said.

But someone would pay. The need for vengeance still burned in Reiko.

She thanked the women for their help, then departed, still stunned by the turn of events. She'd solved one mystery but was no closer to discovering who had attacked her father. Nor had she ensured that her family would be safe.

32

SANO SQUINTED UP at the sky as he and his troops gathered outside the Hosokawa estate. The sunlight had changed color from morning's thin silver to the brass of afternoon. Sano tightened his mouth in frustration because half the day was gone and he had little to show for it. They'd just finished interrogating the forty-seven *rōnin*. All the men claimed they had nothing to do with the attack on Magistrate Ueda.

"We're up against a conspiracy of silence," he said to Marume and Fukida.

"Who's in on it?" Fukida asked.

Sano looked toward the Hosokawa estate; the guards stationed outside gazed stonily back at him. "Oishi, Chikara, and the other fourteen *rōnin* in there." The men at the other estates had appeared honestly mystified by the attack on Magistrate Ueda, although some had seemed glad that it would delay the supreme court's verdict. "Also Lord Hosokawa and all his people."

"What do you think they're covering up?" Fukida asked.

"Maybe the fact that one of them set up the ambush," Sano said. "Or maybe something entirely different."

A samurai on horseback came galloping up to Sano. It was one of Hirata's retainers. "Hirata-*san* asks you to come to Edo Jail at once. He's arrested the criminal who attacked Magistrate Ueda."

"Well, well," Marume said to Fukida. "It looks like Hirata has made up for going missing in action."

EDO JAIL WAS a cold portal to hell. The canal that formed a moat in front of it was partially frozen, with dirty ice chunked up against its banks. A thick pall of smoke from the surrounding slum hung over the high stone walls, the dilapidated buildings inside them, and the guard turrets. The sentries warmed themselves at a bonfire while police officers escorted prisoners with shackled wrists and ankles through the gates. Inside the dungeon, Sano and Hirata stood in a dank, frigid corridor that echoed with the inmates' groans. They peered through a small barred window set at eye level in an ironclad door. A man crouched inside the cell, his arms hugging his knees, the sleeves of his gray coat pulled over his hands to keep them warm. The toes of sandaled feet in dirty white socks protruded from beneath his gray trousers. His hair was disheveled, his blunt profile sullen.

"So that's Genzo," Sano said, filled with anger, revulsion, and disbelief.

The man seemed so ordinary, like thousands of petty criminals who roved Edo. Scratch their surfaces and you would find the reasons why they'd gone wrong—poverty, ignorance, misfortune. But no sad tale could excuse this man who had injured Magistrate Ueda so severely and murdered his guards. Sano thought of his father-in-law's wisdom, compassion toward the defendants that appeared in the Court of Justice, and integrity. Genzo, in comparison, was too worthless to live.

Hirata unbolted the cell door. He and Sano entered. Genzo shot to his feet. His hairline receded even though he was only in his twenties. His evasive eyes glinted dimly from between flat lids. He had a thin, mean mouth.

"Why did you do it?" Sano asked.

"I didn't." Genzo's voice was a toneless mutter. Slouching, he rocked his weight from one foot to the other. He said to Hirata, "You got the wrong man."

Now that he'd had time to think, he'd decided to try to weasel out of his confession, Sano observed with disgust.

"That won't work," Hirata snapped. "We know it was you."

"Speaking of getting the wrong man, that's exactly what *you* did." Already Sano had to struggle to control his temper. "You beat up Magistrate Ueda, who happens to be my father-in-law. You killed his two guards. You won't be let off with a few months in jail and another tattoo this time. You may as well say good-bye to your head now."

"This is the shogun's chief investigator," Hirata told Genzo. "It really wasn't a smart choice of people to ambush. But then you're stupid, aren't you?"

Surprise registered in Genzo's eyes, then sank into their sullen murk. "That was Magistrate Ueda?"

"Who did you think it was?" Sano asked.

"Uh."

Hirata touched his sword. Genzo saw and seemed to understand that lying was pointless. He said, "A man named Nakae. A big judge on some court at Edo Castle."

Astonishment hit Sano like a club to his chest. Inspector General Nakae, not Magistrate Ueda, had been the assassin's target. "Why did you want to attack Nakae?"

Genzo shrugged. He reminded Sano of a reptile, whose few basic, primitive emotions didn't show much on the outside.

"Fine," Hirata said. "We'll skip the interrogation, and the trial, too. I'll call the executioner." He turned, as if to leave.

"Wait," Genzo said in that same flat mutter. "If I tell you, will you spare me?"

He wasn't the brightest criminal Sano had ever seen, but he realized that Sano and Hirata wanted the information he had and he could use it to bargain for his life.

"Forget it," Hirata said. "This is your third offense. You're finished."

"Let's listen to what he has to say first." Sano told Genzo, "If it's good enough, I can save you."

Sano and Hirata had often played this game, one badgering and threatening their subject, the other acting kind and conciliatory, working as a team to extract his cooperation. But never had Sano enjoyed the latter role less. Still, in a case as personal to him as this, it was best that Hirata took the former role. Sano wasn't sure he could play it and resist the urge to kill Genzo before they got the information they needed.

Hirata pretended to be put out by Sano's leniency. "All right," he said to Genzo. "Talk."

A brief smile flexed Genzo's mean mouth. "I was hired to kill Nakae."

"Who hired you?" Sano asked.

"I don't know."

"You'll have to do better than that," Hirata jeered. "Or I'll kill you and put you out of your stupidity."

"I never saw him." Genzo explained, "I was coming out of a teahouse in Nihonbashi. He was sitting in a palanquin, with the windows closed. He hissed at me and asked, did I want to make some money. I said, what do I have to do? He said, kill Nakae."

"That's ridiculous," Hirata said. "People don't ask strangers on the street to kill people for them."

Genzo seemed as indifferent to Hirata's disbelief as he'd been unsurprised by the offer from the man in the palanquin. "This fellow did."

Odder things had been known to happen. Sano said, "Did he say why he wanted you to kill Nakae?"

"No," Genzo said, "and I didn't ask."

Sano wondered if hired assassins thought they were better off not knowing their employers' motives. Or maybe curiosity had been left out of Genzo's personality. "Go on."

"I told him a thousand koban. He said five hundred. I said——"

"So you haggled over the price," Hirata said. "Then what?"

"He described Nakae. Big older man, big dark spot on his face. He said to wait for Nakae outside Edo Castle, follow him, and do it. He warned me that Nakae would have bodyguards and I would probably have to kill them, too."

"All that went on and you never saw who hired you?" Sano said skeptically.

"He stayed inside the palanquin. He opened the window just enough to pass me half the money. We agreed he would leave the rest behind my house after Nakae was dead." Genzo added with dull rancor, "He never did, the bastard."

"Because you ambushed the wrong man, you idiot," Hirata said. "How did that happen?"

Genzo glowered at the insult. "Nakae came out of the castle with another samurai who looked like him. I followed them. They split up."

Sano recalled the inspector general saying that he and Magistrate Ueda had ridden part of the way home together.

"It was dark," Genzo said. "I couldn't see which was Nakae. So I went after the one I thought was him." He shrugged. "I guessed wrong."

Sano was so infuriated by Genzo's mistake, and Genzo's indifferent attitude, that he couldn't restrain himself much longer. He had to force himself to speak calmly. "The man who hired you—can you describe his voice?"

"High-class," Genzo said.

"What about his palanquin?"

"It was black."

That narrowed the field down to the entire upper samurai society. "Were there any identifying crests on it?"

"Not that I saw."

Sano marveled that anyone would agree to commit a murder for a person unknown, unseen, and of dubious trustworthiness. But of course the money had been a big incentive. "What did his bearers look like?"

"I don't remember," Genzo said, bored. "Who notices bearers?"

"Can you think of anything you did notice that might help us identify the man in the palanquin?"

"No."

Not even to save his life, Sano thought. In addition to his other sins, Genzo was a deplorably bad witness. Sano turned to Hirata. "We're finished here."

"I agree." Hirata looked as fed up with Genzo as Sano was. He opened the door of the cell. He and Sano started to walk out.

"Hey," Genzo called in a voice louder than his usual mutter. "Do I get to stay alive?"

"No," Sano said.

Disbelief pricked up Genzo's flat eyelids. "But you promised."

"No, I didn't," Sano said. "Next time, you should be more careful about who you do business with. Except there isn't going to be a next time."

"That's not fair!" It was as if the reptile had basked in the sun long enough to bring its cold blood to a boil. Temper animated his eyes, clenched his fists, and revealed the brute who'd savaged Magistrate Ueda for a few pieces of gold.

"You may not think it's fair," Sano said, "but it's justice."

"DO YOU THINK Genzo was telling the truth?" Hirata asked Sano as they rode across the bridge that spanned the canal outside Edo Jail.

"Yes," Sano said. "He hasn't the imagination to make up that story."

"So do I. How should we go about identifying the man in the palanquin?"

"We could start at the teahouse where Genzo met him. Maybe someone there saw him even though Genzo didn't. Or saw where he went after he and Genzo made their deal."

"Or can give us a better description of the palanquin and the bearers." Hirata glanced around at the shacks that lined the road through the slums as he said, "If the Hosokawa people wanted to kill Inspector General Nakae, wouldn't they handle it themselves? Why take a chance on hiring a stranger who could and did botch the job?"

"Whoever hired Genzo didn't want the blood on their own hands. But you're right, the whole assassination attempt smacks of incompetence."

"That would exonerate Yanagisawa," Hirata pointed out.

"That and the fact that he wouldn't have wanted Nakae killed. Nakae is his crony."

"There's still the question of how anyone besides Yanagisawa and the judges and you could have known Nakae's position on the vendetta," Hirata said. "But maybe Nakae let his opinion be known before he was appointed to the court. Or maybe it was a personal enemy of his who wanted him dead, and the attack had nothing to do with the case."

The inspector general had plenty of enemies, but Sano still believed that the attack and the case were connected. Sano followed Hirata's gaze to a group of men huddled around a bonfire. Hirata was looking for his stalkers, Sano thought.

"Well, there are still other suspects besides the forty-seven *rōnin* and the Hosokawa clan," Sano said. "Before we try to pick up the palanquin man's trail, let's hear what my wife has to say about Ukihashi, Lady Asano, and Okaru. She was supposed to talk to them today."

WHEN SANO AND Hirata arrived at home, Reiko hurried to meet them while they were hanging their swords in the entryway. "I'm so glad you're back!" She sparkled with excitement. "I must tell you what I've learned!"

While she helped Sano remove his coat, while she served him and Hirata hot tea in the private quarters, Reiko related the story she'd heard from Ukihashi and Lady Asano. She was breathless by the time she finished. Sano and Hirata were thunderstruck.

"So that's why Lord Asano attacked Kira," Sano said. The story revealed what Kira's subordinates must have known about Kira but had kept hidden, the whale Sano had sensed beneath the water.

"I knew it had to be more than just because Kira harassed him," Hirata said, "but I never imagined this."

Sano shook his head in disgust as he envisioned the scene that Reiko had described—the forced sex between Lord Asano and Ukihashi, with Kira watching in ugly, perverted pleasure and Lady Asano in agony. "Kira made victims of them all."

"Do you think this will save the forty-seven *rōnin*?" Reiko asked, her voice colored by doubt as to whether they should be saved.

"I think Lord Asano had a valid reason for attacking Kira," Sano said. "I also think Kira should have been punished for his role in their feud and that since the government didn't punish him, it's good that someone else did. But it's not up to me. The supreme court will decide whether Kira's behavior justified forty-seven *rōnin* breaking the law and murdering Kira."

Reiko's sparkle dimmed. "Then even though we know the truth behind the incident in the Corridor of Pines, it might not change anything."

"It might. It's an extenuating circumstance," Sano pointed out. "And there may be others we haven't discovered yet."

"Such as the real reason why the forty-seven *rōnin* took so long to take revenge on Kira," Hirata said, "and why they 'waited for orders' afterward."

"But we've made progress on one front," Sano said. "Hirata-*san* caught the man who attacked your father."

Reiko exclaimed, "Who is it? Why did he do it? I want to see him!"

If he let her at Genzo, they wouldn't need an executioner, Sano thought. "Maybe later." He told Reiko about his and Hirata's interview with Genzo.

"But who was the man in the palanquin?" Reiko asked, so agitated she couldn't sit still. "Why did he want to kill Inspector General Nakae?"

"I have a hunch that once we have the answers to those questions, they'll help us bring your father's attacker to justice," Sano said, "and they'll put the vendetta in a different light."

"But how do we find them?" Reiko asked.

"You've discovered a new lead," Sano said. "Let's follow it and see where it goes."

33

REIKO AND UKIHASHI rode in a palanquin up the highway toward the Hosokawa estate, escorted by Sano, Hirata, and troops. Ukihashi wore a rich burgundy padded silk coat over a moss-green silk kimono with pine boughs embroidered around the hem, and high-soled black lacquer sandals. Her hair was brushed into a sleek roll anchored with lacquer combs. Finished off with white powder and red rouge, she was the beautiful samurai lady she'd once been.

The new clothes and accessories were gifts from Reiko, brought when she'd returned to Ukihashi and told her they were going on this trip. Ukihashi had balked at first, even though she was overjoyed by the thought of seeing her son.

"How can I face my husband?" she'd cried. "After what I did?"

"You must," Reiko said. Sano had decided that bringing Ukihashi and Oishi together was crucial to the investigation.

Given no choice, Ukihashi had let Reiko help her fix herself up. She wanted to look good for the husband she still loved in spite of her anger at him for dragging their son into an illegal vendetta. Now Ukihashi grew nervous as she and Reiko drew closer to their destination.

"Don't bite your lips," Reiko said gently. "You're chewing off the rouge."

Ukihashi gnawed her fingernails instead. "What if Oishi won't see me?"

Reiko recalled the disastrous trip with Okaru, but she said, "He

250

will." Sano wouldn't give Oishi the option of refusing. "He loves you. He said so."

"What will I say to him?"

"Just tell him what you told me about Kira."

"Will it help Oishi and Chikara?"

"My husband thinks it's the only thing that can," Reiko said, although when Sano had broached his plan, he'd said he couldn't predict the results.

The procession arrived at the Hosokawa estate. Reiko's own anxiety mounted as she and Ukihashi climbed out of the palanquin. Sano escorted them through the gate. Hirata went ahead to fetch Oishi and Chikara. Reiko walked beside Ukihashi. The woman ignored the Hosokawa troops staring at her while she moved up the steps to the mansion. She looked straight ahead, as if her world had narrowed to the path that led to her husband and son. Emotions worked her face, pulling it into a joyous smile one moment, a mask of fear the next.

Sano brought Reiko and Ukihashi to a reception chamber. Ukihashi stood rigid, her clasped hands twisting inside her sleeves, all her attention focused on the door. Hirata brought in Oishi and Chikara, who was a younger, softer version of Oishi. When father and son caught sight of Ukihashi, their faces went blank with surprise.

Ukihashi uttered a sob wrenched from her depths. "Chikara!"

"Mother?" the young man said.

He rushed to her as she rushed to him, as if an invisible cord that had joined them since his birth had snapped them together. Ukihashi clung fiercely to Chikara. Tears streamed down her face while she murmured, "How tall you are! You're a man now."

Chikara sobbed against her shoulder like a child. Reiko felt her own eyes sting. She looked at Oishi. His ferocity had dropped away like armor discarded after a battle. While he watched his wife, his face was a naked display of anguish and yearning. The thunder deity had become human.

Chikara stepped out of Ukihashi's embrace. Ukihashi trailed her fingers down his arms, reluctant to let him go. Turning to Oishi, she looked blinded, dazzled, like a woman who has been living in a dark cave and sees the sun for the first time. The emotion on Oishi's face deepened. Chikara backed away from his parents. Reiko envisioned their past as a

251

river running between them, full of turbulent rapids, shoals, and whirl-pools.

Ukihashi fell to her knees. "Husband, I've done a terrible thing. I dishonored our marriage. I was unfaithful to you." She was sobbing so hard she could barely gasp out the words. "It was with Lord Asano."

"Mother," Chikara said, horror-stricken.

Reiko remembered how Oishi had violently spurned his mistress. Would he spurn Ukihashi now, because of her confession?

Oishi gazed tenderly down at his wife. He knelt before her and spoke in a gruff, abashed voice. "I know."

Reiko and Sano looked at each other, amazed. They'd thought the story about Ukihashi and Lord Asano would be news to Oishi, but it wasn't.

"You do?" Ukihashi raised streaming, bewildered eyes to her hus-band. "But how?"

Oishi exhaled; he spoke with resignation. "You've made a clean breast. I owe it to you to do the same."

1701 April

DURING ANOTHER ETIQUETTE lesson, Kira mocked Lord Asano so cruelly that Lord Asano broke down. Oishi took Lord Asano home, put him to bed, then returned to Edo Castle and accosted Kira. "Start behaving respectfully toward my master, or I will destroy you!"

"Before you take action against me, listen to a bit of advice: Don't waste your loyalty on Lord Asano." Kira smiled maliciously. "He's hav-ing an affair with your wife."

Oishi was furious. "You're lying, you evil old crow."

Kira shrugged daintily. "They're meeting tomorrow afternoon, at the River Inn in Nihonbashi. Rent the room on the western end. There's a crack in the wall. See for yourself."

Oishi didn't believe Kira. Lord Asano had never taken a woman who belonged to a friend. But Kira had planted a seed of suspicion in Oishi's mind. The next day Oishi went to the inn, rented the room, and waited, peering out the window.

Ukihashi and Lord Asano arrived separately. Each sneaked into the room next door. Oishi's heart dropped. Kira was right: His master and his wife were deceiving him. He spied on them through the crack while they made love. Consumed by jealousy, rage, and hurt, he didn't think to wonder how Kira knew about the tryst and the crack in the wall. And the next day, Lord Asano attacked Kira in the Corridor of Pines.

"THAT'S WHY I treated you so badly," Oishi said to Uki-hashi as they sat in the reception room of the Hosokawa estate. Intent on each other, they'd forgotten that Sano, Reiko, and Hirata were present. They seemed unaware of their son, who stared at them in dismay. "I thought the two people I loved the most had betrayed me. That's why I got drunk and quarreled with you, for all those months before I decided I could never forgive you and I had to leave you. That's why I divorced you and took a mistress. That's why I didn't bother avenging Lord Asano at first. I hated him. I was glad he died."

"Father, please don't say any more!" Chikara exclaimed.

Oishi regarded him with sorrowful affection. "There have been too many secrets. They've caused too much suffering. I mustn't keep them any longer."

"But I tried to protect you!" Chikara was aghast. "That story I told Sano-*san*, it was to make you look good."

"You lied for me," Oishi said. "So did our comrades, when they took it upon themselves to tell contradicting stories and confuse Sano-*san*. They guessed that I had something to hide, and they helped me hide it even though they didn't know what it was. I appreciate their loyalty, and yours, my son. But the time for lying is past."

Sano was amazed that his scheme had worked, the question of what was true and false in the stories had been answered, and the mystery of why the revenge had taken so long was solved. But what had finally triggered the vendetta?

"I was mean to you because I felt so guilty about Lord Asano. I'm sorry." Ukihashi wept. "Can you forgive me?"

Oishi held her hands. "I already have."

Sano glanced at Reiko. She dabbed her eyes, moved by the tender scene. Sano himself was relieved that Oishi didn't hold the adultery against Ukihashi anymore. He pitied Oishi, who was about to learn that he never should have blamed or punished his wife.

"I didn't want to do it," Ukihashi said. "Kira forced me. He set up the meeting between me and Lord Asano. He made us go through with it. He threatened us."

"I know," Oishi said. "It wasn't your fault. Kira was to blame."

Another surprise stunned Sano. Ukihashi wept with relief. Oishi said, "I'm the one who should apologize. I'm sorry I misjudged you. I'm sorry about taking a mistress. She was nothing to me except revenge on you."

Reiko looked queasy. Sano could see that she was glad for Ukihashi's sake but unhappy for Okaru's, and she still didn't think well of Oishi.

"Can you forgive me?" Oishi said.

"With all my heart!" Ukihashi wept and pressed her face to Oishi's hands.

"You are my wife," Oishi whispered. "You always will be."

Sano interrupted: "How did you find out that Kira had set up your wife and your master? Who told you?"

Oishi turned toward Sano. His expression was dazed, as if he were awakening from a dream. He looked surprised to see Sano and everyone else. "It was Kajikawa Yosobei."

"Who is he?" Ukihashi said, puzzled.

"A keeper of the castle," Sano said. "He witnessed Lord Asano's attack on Kira."

Kajikawa had seemed to have a minor role in the forty-seven *rōnin* case. Sano was startled to learn that his assumption about Kajikawa was wrong.

"When did Kajikawa tell you about Kira?" Sano asked.

"After I moved to Miyako," Oishi answered. "As I said, I had no intention of avenging Lord Asano. Then one day I ran into Kajikawa. He said he was in town on business. He invited me to a teahouse. I didn't know him well, but he was the only person from my former class who'd bothered to notice me since I'd become a *rōnin,* and I couldn't pass up a free handout. So I accepted. After a few drinks, he told me about Kira, Lord Asano, and my wife."

"How did Kajikawa know what Kira had done to them?" Sano asked.

"Kajikawa said that keepers of the castle are part of the scenery, nobody notices them. He sees and hears a lot."

Here was another big piece that had been missing from Oishi's story the first time, Sano thought. Kajikawa had kept it secret, too.

"I wanted to rush out and confront Kira and kill him right then," Oishi said. "But Kajikawa said he was heavily guarded. If I went after him, I would only get myself killed. Kajikawa told me to wait. It was his idea that I should act like a drunken bum and let word get back to Kira so that he would think he was safe from me."

Kajikawa, the invisible man, had had a hand in the vendetta from the start.

"Why did Kajikawa go to any trouble for you?" Sano asked, his mind reeling from so many surprises. "What he did was conspire to commit an illegal vendetta. Why put himself in danger, when the two of you hardly knew each other?"

"I asked him. He said he felt sorry for me. I wondered if it was more than that, but I really didn't care." Oishi explained, "He promised that if I killed Kira, he would get me pardoned. He said he would use his influence with the shogun."

"I didn't know he had any," Hirata said.

"The shogun probably doesn't even know that Kajikawa is alive," Sano said.

"I'm not very familiar with who has influence at court and who doesn't," Oishi said. "I wanted to believe him, so I did. After you arrested us, I realized my mistake." He smiled wryly. "I expected us to be set free. It didn't happen."

Enlightenment washed over Sano like a sunrise. "Those were the orders you were awaiting? To be told that the shogun had pardoned you and you could go on your way?"

"Yes," Oishi admitted.

"You must have been furious at Kajikawa for misleading you," Sano said.

"I was," Oishi said. "When he came to see me—it was on the night of the day after we were arrested—I wanted to kill him."

Another mystery was solved. "So that's what your comrades and the Hosokawa clan were keeping quiet about," Sano said. "The fact that you had a visitor and it was Kajikawa."

"If I'd told you, the whole story would have come out. I didn't want that. Now I wish I had told." Guilt tinged Oishi's manner. "But I didn't know what was going to happen."

"He let part of it slip out," Reiko murmured to Sano. "When I brought Okaru to see him. When he said his wife was the only woman he loved."

Oishi resumed his story. "I raged at Kajikawa for breaking his promise to save us. But he was furious at me, too. He said that if he'd known I would bring forty-six other men in on the vendetta, he never would have made that promise. He said that because we'd caused such an uproar, there was nothing he could do. Our fate depended on the supreme court, and he had no influence with it. He also said there were too many judges in favor of condemning us. Our chances didn't look good."

"How did Kajikawa know that?" Sano asked.

"There's a secret chamber built into a wall of the room where the supreme court meets. Kajikawa has been hiding in there, eavesdropping."

So that was how the proceedings had leaked. The keeper had put his special knowledge of the castle to use.

"Kajikawa broke down," Oishi said. "He cried and begged me to forgive him. He promised he would make things right."

Premonition seeped into Sano like cold needles infusing his blood. He saw astonishment dawn on Reiko's face. "How was Kajikawa going to make things right?"

"I didn't bother to ask him," Oishi said. "I didn't believe him; I'd lost all faith in him. Then I heard that one of the judges had been attacked. And I realized that Kajikawa had tried to keep his promise."

Reiko exclaimed, "Kajikawa hired that criminal who beat my father!"

"The man in the palanquin," Hirata said. "It was Kajikawa."

Sano was elated to learn the culprit's identity. Contempt mixed with his anger at the little keeper of the castle. "It sounds just like him. Too cowardly and weak to do the job himself. Timid, hiding his face. Foolish and desperate enough to hire a stranger off the street."

"A stranger that attacked the wrong judge," Hirata added.

"My father, who wants to pardon the forty-seven *rōnin*." Reiko was shaking with rage.

Sano thought, *We can handle our enemies, but the gods save us from incompetence!* He said to Oishi, "The last time I spoke with you and your son, you were upset about something. Now I know what."

Oishi nodded somberly. "Three innocent men were attacked on our behalf. Two of them are dead and the other is severely injured because of us."

Chikara blurted out, "We never meant for anybody except Kira to be harmed!"

"We apologize to you and your wife, for what it's worth," Oishi said with humble contrition.

Ukihashi turned to Reiko. "Please forgive them! They didn't even know what Kajikawa was going to do!"

"There's no need for them to apologize or for me to forgive them," Reiko said, although visibly struggling to control her temper. "It wasn't their fault."

"Kajikawa is responsible for the attack on Magistrate Ueda, not them," Hirata said.

The apology seemed to Sano like a gift of spoiled fish. Kajikawa's culpability didn't negate the fact that much damage had stemmed from Oishi's actions. In Sano's eyes, the shine of honor had worn off the vendetta. Nonetheless, Sano could forgive the forty-seven *rōnin,* who had been unwitting servants for Kajikawa.

"Kajikawa is responsible for more than the attack on Magistrate Ueda," Sano said. "He set the vendetta in motion."

Reiko gazed at Sano, astounded. "Okaru was right. There was more to the vendetta than met the eye."

"I lied when I said I didn't remember telling her that," Oishi said sheepishly. "When I drink, it's hard to keep my mouth shut." He said to Sano, "When you told me that she was in Edo, I was upset because I might have told her more than that, and I was afraid she would remember and tell you."

Guilt changed Reiko's expression. "I've done Okaru an injustice."

"So have I." Oishi said with remorse, "I shouldn't have used her."

"But why did Kajikawa set the vendetta in motion?" Reiko asked.

"I suspect he had his own grudge against Kira." Sano recalled his talk with Kajikawa. "He tried to cast aspersion on Kira twice. First he said that Lord Asano had called Kira a corrupt snake. Then he brought up the rumor about Kira poisoning his brother-in-law the *daimyo*. It's time for another talk with Kajikawa. We're going back to Edo Castle."

"Do I have to leave, too?" Ukihashi clung to her husband. She held out a hand to her son. Chikara took it, although he was obviously disturbed by the revelations he'd heard. She appealed to Reiko. "May I stay?"

"My hosts will find a room for her," Oishi said, "and for our daughters."

"Is that all right?" Reiko asked Sano.

"Yes." Sano didn't want to separate the reunited family any more than Reiko did. The fate of the forty-seven *rōnin* was still up in the air, and whatever time they had left, Oishi and his wife and children should spend together. On the verge of being torn from his own family, Sano couldn't wish the same on anyone else.

34

BACK AT EDO Castle, Sano, Hirata, Marume, and Fukida went to the office of the keepers of the castle. It was late in the evening; only a few men were still present, tidying their papers, extinguishing lamps. Sano said, "Where is Kajikawa?"

An old assistant with a humped back led Sano to an empty desk enclosed by lattice partitions. "That's odd. He was here a moment ago."

"The lamp on the desk is still lit," Hirata pointed out. "He must have just left."

Sano felt a chilly draft, which he followed down a passage. He and Hirata and the detectives gazed out an open door onto a courtyard. Barely visible in the twilight were footprints gouged into the snow, left by a man running.

"He heard me asking for him," Sano deduced. "He guessed that we found out he hired the man who attacked Magistrate Ueda, and he panicked."

"Shouldn't you be able to track him down?" Marume asked Hirata in a challenging tone.

"He has a weak aura," Hirata said. "It'll be hard to detect, but I'll try." He moved swiftly, following the footsteps.

"Organize search parties," Sano told the detectives. "Comb the castle. I'll tell the captain of the guard to have all the gates closed. But just in case Kajikawa slips out, send a search party to his home." Sano turned to the assistant. "Where does he live?"

The assistant gave directions to a house in the district near Edo Castle occupied by the hereditary Tokugawa vassals. As Sano, Marume, and Fukida hurried off, the assistant tagged after them. "Did Kajikawa really hire someone to kill the magistrate?"

"It's looking that way," Sano said.

"I can't believe he would do such a thing. He seems so harmless. Although he hasn't been quite himself recently. But then it's understandable."

"What's understandable?" Sano slowed down, his curiosity piqued.

"That he would be depressed. His son committed suicide three years ago."

Was this the event that had turned Kajikawa from a good man into a criminal? "Tell me how it happened," Sano said.

"Kajikawa's son was named Tsunamori. He was twelve years old," the assistant said. "He hanged himself."

Sano was shocked and grieved that a boy only a little older than Masahiro had taken his own life. He became aware of a recurring pattern in the events that had followed the vendetta: Sano and Masahiro; Oishi and Chikara; Yanagisawa and Yoritomo; fathers and sons. Here was another father-and-son pair, at the heart of the pattern.

"Why did he do it?"

"I don't know. Kajikawa doesn't talk about it. But one night soon after it happened, I came upon him crying at his desk. He was cursing and muttering. He didn't notice me, and I thought it best to leave him alone. But I heard him say something to the effect that he blamed his son's death on Kira Yoshinaka."

Sano felt a mounting excitement. Even if he didn't yet know how Kira was involved in the boy's suicide, he had Kajikawa's motive for wanting Kira dead, for setting the vendetta in motion. The forty-seven *rōnin* had been Kajikawa's tool for his own revenge.

"I WANT A game of *go*," the shogun announced to the boys gathered in his chamber. Some were playing music on samisens and flutes or singing, some joking among themselves. His gaze settled on Masahiro, who was trying to be unobtrusive. "Bring me my set."

Carrying the lacquer case, Masahiro mounted the dais. As he passed Yoritomo, who sat beside the shogun, Yoritomo stuck out his foot. Masahiro tripped, went sprawling, and dropped the *go* set. Black and white marbles flew everywhere. Everyone laughed. Masahiro flushed with embarrassment and seethed with anger as he picked himself up.

"What a clumsy oaf Masahiro is," Yoritomo said to the shogun. "Shall we send him away before he hurts somebody besides himself, Your Excellency?"

Masahiro knew he should have been paying closer attention to Yoritomo, but he'd been too busy thinking about Goza, the bloody clothes, and the tattoos. He felt a pang of fear. Was Yoritomo finally about to succeed in putting him out of the shogun's good graces? What would his parents say?

"No, it was just a, ahh, harmless mistake." The shogun smiled kindly at Masahiro and patted the floor on his other side. "Come sit by me."

Almost as dismayed as he was relieved, Masahiro sat. The shogun told Yoritomo, "Pick up those marbles. Set up the board. Masahiro and I will play."

Yoritomo obeyed, looking so furious that Masahiro imagined smoke coming out of his ears. The shogun smiled too fondly at Masahiro as they took turns placing marbles on the gridded board. Masahiro squirmed. He heard the other boys whispering. They were probably betting on whether he would become the shogun's next favorite. But not even that threat could distract Masahiro from his present dilemma.

He had to tell his parents about Goza. There was no question in his mind. He owed his first loyalty to them. But he hated to get Okaru in trouble, especially since he couldn't help thinking she was innocent in spite of the evidence against her servant. He was so preoccupied that he almost forgot to lose the game.

"I win!" the shogun exclaimed. Everyone clapped. "Now it's time for my massage."

He left with Yoritomo, who gave Masahiro a baleful parting glance. Masahiro went home, dreading what he had to do. At the gate, he asked the sentry, "Are my parents here?"

"No, young master."

But Masahiro couldn't put off telling them forever. If Okaru and Goza were responsible for beating his grandfather and killing the two bodyguards, they must be punished. "Did anything happen while I was gone?"

"Hirata-*san* caught the man who attacked your grandfather." The sentry told Masahiro about the hired assassin.

It wasn't Goza! Masahiro felt a huge relief. He wouldn't have to tell his parents. He wouldn't have to see their disappointment that he'd kept a bad secret from them. But his relief quickly faded as suspicion reared its head again. "Who hired him?"

"Your parents are trying to find out."

It could have been Goza, Masahiro thought unhappily. "Where's Okaru?"

"Still under house arrest."

That meant his mother still didn't trust her. Masahiro decided to talk to Okaru. Maybe he could help her prove she was innocent. He ran so fast that he was out of breath when he arrived at her room. Outside it, Lieutenant Tanuma sat against the wall. He saw Masahiro, jumped up, and said, "Young master, can you guard Okaru for a moment? I have to go to the Place of Relief." He rushed off without waiting for an answer.

Masahiro went into the room. Excitement mounted in him; his heart thudded. Okaru knelt on the bed, plaiting her hair into thin braids, then combing them out with her fingers. She turned to him. Her beautiful face was sad, scrubbed clean of makeup, and puffy around her eyes. She looked as if she'd stopped expecting anything good.

"I—is there anything you need?" Masahiro said.

Okaru forced a smile. Her lips looked soft, bruised. "No, but thank you for asking." She added, "I'm sorry I was mean to you yesterday."

"That's all right." Masahiro was embarrassed and unhappy to see her so sad. "They caught the man who attacked my grandfather," he blurted out.

"I know," Okaru said. "I heard one of the guards tell Lieutenant Tanuma." Sighing, she twisted her hair around her hand. "I feel so bad that your mother thinks I had something to do with the attack. She thinks I'm a dog who bites the hand that feeds me. But I can understand why she does. Girls like me . . . well, we're famous for causing trouble and taking advantage of people. But your mother has been so good to me." Her eyes briefly glowed with her affection for Reiko, then filled with anguish. "I would never do anything to hurt her family. *Never!*"

She wasn't angry, Masahiro saw. He would have been furious at anyone who wrongfully accused him. But Okaru made excuses for his mother and blamed herself. "I believe you," he said, carried away by the conviction in her voice and his admiration for her.

"You do?" Delight bloomed on Okaru's face. "Oh, thank you!" She sprang up and threw her arms around Masahiro.

Masahiro was so surprised that his eyes popped and he choked on his breath. He lost his balance and fell onto the bed, dragging Okaru with him. Exhilaration and rapture filled him as she hugged him and pressed her cheek against his. He felt the softness of her skin, the warmth of her body, and her breasts touching his chest. He wanted to hold Okaru. He strained away from her because he was afraid that if she knew how he felt, she would be upset.

Now her face was wet with tears. Masahiro awkwardly stroked her hair as she cried, trying to comfort her. Its silky strands tangled in his fingers. He couldn't bear to take pleasure from her that she hadn't offered, but his desire and excitement leaped even higher than when he'd watched her in the bath chamber.

Her arms loosened their embrace; she drew back. "You remind me of my little brother who died." She cupped his cheek in her soft hand and smiled mistily.

Desire vanished. Her little brother! That was how Okaru thought of him. Not as a man she could like, or even a friend, but as a child.

Masahiro didn't have time to feel the worst of his mortification, because he heard his mother's voice say sharply, "Masahiro! Okaru!"

ALARMED, REIKO STARED at her son and Okaru sprawled on the bed. The girl had her arm around Masahiro and her hand cradling his cheek. Masahiro's hand was in Okaru's hair. They turned at the sound of her voice.

"What are you doing?" Reiko asked.

They sprang apart and stood up. Reiko saw Masahiro's face turn red, and fear in Okaru's eyes. Suddenly she recalled her conversation with Chiyo. Now she understood: Chiyo had been trying to warn her about what could happen when a boy on the verge of manhood and a beautiful young girl lived under the same roof. Chiyo must have noticed an attraction between Masahiro and Okaru. Reiko belatedly realized what had happened. Okaru had a broken heart and needed comfort; Masahiro was experiencing the sexual desires that boys did. It was natural that they should come together.

Reiko turned on Okaru. "Were you seducing my son?"

"No," Okaru said in a small, chagrined tone. "It's not what you think."

Reiko was shocked, even though she knew that samurai boys began having sex at an early age and it was considered acceptable as long as they confined themselves to women from the lower classes and didn't ruin girls from good families who were reserved for marriage. Reiko had caught Sano's young retainers coupling with the maids and politely looked the other way. But Masahiro wasn't grown up enough for sex!

"Mother," Masahiro said. The word was half protest, half plea. He looked miserable.

The idea of him with Okaru filled Reiko with aversion, even though she'd prided herself on overlooking class distinctions. She'd taken the girl into her house, and Okaru had blithely helped herself to Reiko's son! No matter that Okaru was innocent of the attack on Magistrate Ueda, she was dangerous. Inexperienced boys like Masahiro often fell in love with girls like Okaru. The affairs begat jealousies, quarrels, duels between men vying for the same girl, and often babies. Custom forbade such couples to marry, and too often they committed *shinjū,* double love suicide. Reiko saw a new, perilous world opening up for Masahiro. She'd tried so hard to protect him from his father's political enemies, but she'd not thought to shield his heart.

"Go to your room," Reiko told him, angry at her own obliviousness, wanting to separate Masahiro from Okaru and shut the door on his new world even though it was too late.

He started to protest, to defend Okaru. Lieutenant Tanuma rushed into the room.

"Where have you been?" Reiko asked Tanuma. "Didn't I tell you to watch Okaru?" Before he could answer, she said, "Take Masahiro to his room."

Tanuma and Masahiro slunk out like whipped puppies. Reiko turned to Okaru. The girl knelt on the bed, hands clasped behind her back, like a child caught stealing candy.

"Now," Reiko said in as level a tone as she could manage. "Explain what you were doing with my son."

"Nothing," Okaru said. "I hugged him because he was kind to me. That's all."

But Reiko had seen the look on Masahiro's face while he and Okaru were touching. A hug could easily lead to other things—perhaps things that had already happened when she wasn't there to see. For the first time she experienced the jealousy of a mother who realized that someday she would no longer be the woman her son loved best.

"You'll stay away from Masahiro from now on," Reiko said. "Do you understand?"

Okaru nodded, her complexion gray, lips pressed together as if she feared that if she spoke she would be sick. Her eyes were huge and solemn.

"Good." Reiko felt a pang of shame for treating the girl so harshly. She remembered why she'd come to see Okaru. "I have news. My husband and I have found out who's responsible for the attack on my father. It's not you. You're exonerated."

Tears of relief spilled from Okaru's eyes. She murmured, "Thank the gods. I prayed that I would be proved innocent." She gazed up at Reiko in sudden apprehension. "Does that mean you're letting me go?"

Reiko knew she was thinking of the cold night and her lack of a place to stay. "You don't have to go now." Reiko wasn't heartless enough to put the girl out. "Tomorrow I'll have my husband's troops escort you and Goza home to Miyako."

"A thousand thanks. You're so kind even though you think badly of me. I'm sorry I've displeased you." Okaru smiled nervously. "But . . . I wish I could stay in Edo and see what happens to Oishi. I can't help hoping . . ."

"That he'll be pardoned and he'll take you back? I'm afraid I have more news," Reiko said, unable to resist a little spite. "Oishi has reunited with his wife. If he lives, he'll be going to her, not you."

The smile vanished from Okaru's face, which turned white. Her eyes rolled up, and she fell onto the bed in a dead faint.

REIKO SUMMONED A doctor to care for Okaru, then went after Masahiro. He was in his room, kneeling at a table on which toy soldiers were set in battle formation. His hands fidgeted atop his knees. He wore an expression she'd never seen before—a mixture of anger, pride, and shame. As Reiko sat beside him, he glanced up at her, then down at the soldiers again. She felt uncomfortable and shy, as if he were a stranger, not her little boy.

"I didn't know you liked Okaru," she ventured.

Masahiro scowled. An almost visible barrier loomed between them. Although he'd never had secrets from her, he did now. Reiko was surprised at how much it hurt.

"It's understandable that you would like her," Reiko said. "Boys do become interested in girls. And Okaru is very pretty."

Masahiro picked up a toy soldier and examined it with studied concentration.

"There are some things I must talk to you about," Reiko said. "When a boy and a girl . . . get close . . . well, the girl might have a baby."

A blush reddened Masahiro's face. Reiko's own face felt hot. She'd never talked to him about sex. She'd thought his father would do it later, but it couldn't be put off. How much did Masahiro already know? He'd seen animals mating and the young born, but Reiko wasn't sure he was aware that the same process happened with humans.

"When a baby is born and the boy and girl aren't married, there can be trouble. Especially if they come from different classes, which means they can't marry. The girl's family will probably disown her. She'll have to raise the child herself."

Men weren't usually held responsible for their illegitimate children, and their reputations didn't suffer, but Reiko didn't want Masahiro casually fathering babies as other samurai youths did. If he did, she would feel bad about the ruined women and abandoned children, even though other ladies of her class pretended not to notice the situation.

"So it's best not to . . . well . . ." Reiko couldn't tell Masahiro not to have sex until he was married. That went against custom; men behaved as they pleased. "You shouldn't be with too many girls or do it too often."

Masahiro set the toy soldier carefully on the table. The blush had crept down his neck. Reiko wished she'd never brought Okaru into their home.

"There's something else I have to tell you," Reiko said. "Sometimes a girl will take advantage of a boy. She may pretend to like him, and—and do things with him, so he'll give her money or presents." That was how prostitutes hooked patrons, Reiko had heard. "But she doesn't really care about him; she's just using him. You must be careful, because your family is rich, and a girl might think she can get—"

"Stop! Be quiet!" Masahiro turned on Reiko, his eyes hot with temper.

"Masahiro!" She was shocked because he'd never spoken to her so rudely.

"It wasn't like that!" he yelled.

"Then what—?"

He flung out his hand, swept the toy soldiers off the table, and jumped to his feet. "I don't want to talk about it. Leave me alone!" He ran from the room.

Reiko sat for a moment, incredulous and bewildered. Then, hearing men's voices, she drew a deep breath, rose, and went to greet Sano in the corridor.

"I just met a messenger from your father's house," Sano said. "He says your father is still unconscious; there's no change in his condition."

Reiko's fear for her father worsened. "What if he doesn't recover?"

"Don't worry. He will." Sano said, "Are the children all right?"

"I'm afraid Masahiro is upset with me." Reiko explained.

Sano smiled ruefully. "I suppose we should have been prepared for this sort of thing. Shall I talk to him?"

"Let's give him some time to calm down," Reiko said. "Have you arrested Kajikawa?"

"Not yet." Sano explained that the castle keeper had gone on the run. "I've got search parties looking for him. He won't get far."

35

THE SEARCH WENT on through the night. Sano stopped to visit the supreme court judges, who had temporary quarters in the palace. He relayed the new testimony from Oishi, Ukihashi, and Lady Asano. The judges were gratified to know the true story behind the vendetta but were more at a loss for a verdict than ever.

"Why does the truth have to be so complicated?" Inspector General Nakae said.

"We'll probably still be deliberating in a month," Superintendent Ogiwara said.

They began to argue about the new evidence. Sano resumed the search for Kajikawa. As he and Detectives Marume and Fukida rode through Edo Castle, a hard, driving rain began to fall. The air grew so cold that the rain froze. Passages turned slick and treacherous. The horses' hooves skidded. Patrol guards clung to the walls for support. Brass lanterns at checkpoints dripped icicles. Near midnight, in the courtyard just inside the main gate, Sano and his detectives met up with the party he'd sent to Kajikawa's house.

"He's not there," the leader said. "He left for work as usual this morning, and his wife and servants haven't seen him since."

The Edo Castle guard captain came riding up through the rain that streamed down in liquid silver lines. "I've checked with all the sentries. Kajikawa hasn't gone out through any of the gates. He's still inside the castle."

"How can he have evaded the search parties for so long?" Marume asked.

"There are many hiding places here," the guard captain said, "and a keeper of the castle knows them all."

"Fetch the other keepers," Sano ordered. "Have them show you their secret spots."

When dawn came, Kajikawa was still missing. The rain stopped. Sano, Marume, and Fukida climbed to the top of a guard tower and looked out at an unearthly sight. Every wall, pavement, roof, and tree inside the castle was glazed with a translucent coat of ice. Snow had frozen solid. The passages and grounds were deserted except for the search parties; everyone else stayed indoors rather than risk breaking their necks. Below the gray sky, the buildings in the city gleamed. Nothing moved there. The scene was spectrally, frighteningly beautiful.

"I think this is the end of the world," Marume said.

Sano heard his name called. He looked up. Hirata was leaning out the window of a tower higher on the hill, waving. He called, "Kajikawa has been sighted!"

BREAKFAST AT SANO'S estate was a tense affair. Akiko chattered gaily to Chiyo, but Masahiro glowered as he shoveled noodles into his mouth. Reiko toyed with her food and listened to the frozen trees rattle outside. As soon as Masahiro finished eating, he rose, said, "I have to wait on the shogun," and stomped out the door.

Reiko sighed. Chiyo gave Reiko a questioning look.

"He's cross because of what happened yesterday," Reiko said. "I caught him with Okaru. Now I understand what you were trying to tell me. I'm sorry I was so dense."

"I'm sorry I didn't speak more plainly," Chiyo said with sad regret. "Did they . . . ?"

"I was afraid to ask. And Masahiro won't talk to me. I handled the situation badly."

"He won't stay angry." Chiyo soothed her. "Everything will be fine."

But Reiko's concern for Masahiro persisted. The thought of Okaru, locked in the servants' quarters, made her conscience uneasy. The trees rattling sounded like fingernails tapping on a door, someone trying to get out. Reiko worried about her father, whom she couldn't visit today. The cold air sank into her spirit, along with a sense of foreboding.

"KAJIKAWA WAS SEEN near the palace and at the Momiji-yama within the past hour," Hirata said.

"You take the Momijiyama," Sano said.

He and Marume and Fukida sped to the palace. Icicles hung from the eaves like jagged teeth. Pines wore heavy, grotesque swags of ice. Dismounting outside the main door, Sano called to the sentry, "Where is Kajikawa?"

The sentry gestured. "In the back garden."

Sliding on the hard, smooth snow, Sano and his men hurried around the palace. The bridge over the frozen pond and the pavilion in the middle seemed sculpted from ice. Trees clattered in the wind. Ice shards tinkled on the ground. A guard pointed at the latticework that enclosed the space beneath the palace's foundation and said, "We chased Kajikawa under there." A panel of lattice had been removed and thrown aside. A dark hole gaped. From it came scuffling and yelling.

"Some of the troops went in after Kajikawa," the guard said. "Some ran around the building to try to catch him when he comes out."

"He could come out inside the palace," Sano said. Its floor was riddled with openings. "Is anybody watching for him there?"

The guard's chagrined expression said nobody had thought of that. Sano and his men stampeded through the door. They ran off in separate directions along the corridors. Sano flung open doors, surprising a few officials who'd shown up for work. None had seen the fugitive. Sano heard thumps as the searchers groped their way through the palace's underbelly. He sped along a covered corridor that joined two wings of the building. At the end was a door, decorated with gold Tokugawa crests, that led to the shogun's chambers.

Premonition made Sano's heart drop.

He tried the door, which was locked from the inside. He kicked the wooden panels until the door caved in. Stale, overheated air that smelled of smoke and medicines wafted out. As Sano raced down passages lined with movable wall panels, he heard shouts and whimpering. He halted at the threshold of the shogun's private sitting room.

Inside, amid clouds of smoke, servants exclaimed and coughed as they beat brooms at flames that spread across the *tatami*. An overturned brazier had spewed hot charcoal around a large, square hole in the floor. People shrank against the walls. Sano pushed past the servants, treading over cinders and ash. He stopped near a low platform backed by a mural of white cranes and a red sun. Four men occupied the platform, like actors onstage who were so intent on their drama that they didn't notice that the theater was on fire.

The shogun held a cushion in front of his chest like a shield. His cylindrical black cap was askew. He cringed away from Kajikawa, who knelt at the left edge of the platform.

"A thousand apologies, Your Excellency." Gasping, Kajikawa staggered on his knees toward the shogun. "Please excuse me for intruding on you like this."

The other two men on the platform were Yanagisawa and Yoritomo. Yoritomo put his arm around the shogun. "Don't come any closer!" he yelled at Kajikawa.

Standing behind his son and the shogun, Yanagisawa ordered, "Get out this instant!"

His face, and Yoritomo's, showed shock as well as anger. Sano pictured the scene he'd just missed—the brazier erupting out of the floor, the burning coals flying, and Kajikawa surfacing like a demon from the underworld.

Kajikawa ignored Yanagisawa and Yoritomo. "I can explain everything, Your Excellency. I beg you to listen!"

The shogun whimpered in fright. Yanagisawa called to the men hovering by the walls. "Don't just stand there. Take him away!"

Three palace guards stumbled forward. The other men were the shogun's boy concubines and Yanagisawa's two cronies from the Council of Elders.

"In all my years, I've never seen such a thing!" Kato said.

"It's an outrage!" Ihara said.

Dismayed by the way his search for the fugitive had ended, Sano shouted, "Kajikawa!"

The servants put out the fire. The guards paused. Everyone turned toward Sano.

"Ahh, Sano-*san*. Good." The shogun smiled weakly; he'd forgotten he was displeased with Sano. He looked hopeful that Sano could restore order.

Yanagisawa's and Yoritomo's expressions hardened into hostility. Surprise marked Kato's mask-like features and Ihara's simian face. Kajikawa turned to Sano. The little man's clothes were streaked with grime, drenched from the rain. His topknot had unraveled; soot smeared his delicate features. His eyes were wild, his mouth a downturned grimace.

"I'm sorry. I didn't mean to hurt your father-in-law." Kajikawa seemed horrified by his predicament, by the forces he'd unleashed that had spun out of his control. "I didn't mean for anyone to be hurt except for Kira."

"I know. You wanted to punish Kira, and you weren't able to do it yourself." Although Sano pitied Kajikawa, his tone was hard. "So you set Oishi on Kira. It was revenge by proxy."

Kajikawa's grimace gaped with surprise. "How did you know?"

Yanagisawa recovered his voice. "If you want a little chat, have it someplace else." He obviously realized that revelations about the vendetta were forthcoming.

"Oishi told me," Sano said to Kajikawa.

"He promised not to tell, but I knew it would come out," Kajikawa lamented.

The shogun flung aside his cushion. "What is he talking about?"

"Nothing," Yoritomo said, eager to prevent Sano from getting credit for discovering the truth about the vendetta.

"You should have thought before you told Oishi about his wife and Lord Asano and Kira," Sano said.

"I couldn't have known what would happen!" Kajikawa cried. "I made a mistake!"

"You should have thought before you started a manhunt for Kajikawa and chased him into the palace," Yoritomo shrilled at Sano. "You're the one who made a mistake."

Sano belatedly noticed Masahiro among the shogun's boys. He was astonished because he hadn't known Masahiro was serving the shogun today. Masahiro looked just as astonished to see his father. Sano decided he'd better break up this scene before something worse happened.

"I apologize for the inconvenience, Your Excellency," Sano said, then beckoned to Kajikawa. "Come with me. You're under arrest."

"No!" Kajikawa raised palms that were burned red from pushing up the hot brazier. He began to weep. "I'm sorry! I didn't mean for any of this to happen. Forgive me for hurting Magistrate Ueda! That fool I hired went after the wrong man!"

Yanagisawa said to the guards, "Remove him! Now!"

The guards advanced. Sano cut ahead of them. Kajikawa scrambled to the back of the platform and cried, "Don't—don't touch me!" He fumbled the sword at his waist out of its scabbard. His shaking hand held the gleaming steel blade aloft.

Everyone was stunned speechless. Sano and the guards stopped. Yanagisawa and Yoritomo froze, mouths dropped, angry words stuck in their throats, while the elders, the servants, and the boys stared. The shogun had never looked stupider.

Drawing a weapon inside Edo Castle was a bad enough crime. Doing it in the shogun's presence was unthinkable. Sano thought of Lord Asano's attack on Kira while Kajikawa watched. This time it was Kajikawa, the witness, who'd snapped.

Sano started to climb the three steps to the platform to seize Kajikawa before he could do any harm. Kajikawa shrieked, "Leave me alone, or—or—"

He swung the sword down at the shogun. The room gasped. Sano's breath caught; his steps faltered. The shogun squealed, dodged sideways, and fell on his back. He lay with his knees bent, his toes in their white socks curled on the floor, his arms outstretched and fingers stiff. Fright wrenched his face into a pop-eyed, slack-jawed expression while Kajikawa stood over him, the blade against his throat.

"I WANT TO go outside," Akiko said.

She and Reiko had been playing together in the parlor all morning.

Dolls littered the floor around them. Although Reiko was worried about her father, and impatient for news about Kajikawa, she enjoyed spending time with her daughter. But Akiko had grown restless.

"No, it's too cold and icy." Reiko heard the wind keening and ice shards shattering on the roof. "We have to stay inside."

Akiko marched to the exterior door and pushed it open. Reiko sighed. Her daughter was so much like herself—determined to do what she wanted.

The crystalline trees and the jagged icicles that hung from the eaves, the veranda railings, and the pavilion in the center of the frozen pond gave the garden a dreamlike quality. Hirata's children, dressed in bright, puffy coats, ran across the frozen snow and slid.

"Me, too." Akiko ran into the garden.

"Wait," Reiko called, following her daughter. "Not without your coat and shoes!"

She minced over the slippery snow. Akiko joined Taeko and Tatsuo. She ran and slid, laughing gleefully. Reiko chased and caught Akiko and carried her toward the house.

"Naughty girl," she scolded. "Can't you ever listen to me?"

Akiko was brave about physical danger and pain, but she couldn't bear censure from her mother. She began to cry.

Chiyo met them at the door, her face worried. "I've just heard that there's trouble in the palace. Something terrible has happened. No one seems to know what. Your husband is there. So is Masahiro."

THE ATMOSPHERE IN the chamber reminded Sano of the moment after an earthquake has toppled buildings across the city. As Kajikawa held the sword to the shogun's throat, there was a hush except for the shogun's whimpers and Kajikawa's panting breaths. Sano halted with one foot on the platform and one on the step below, hands flung up. Everybody else was perfectly still, as if afraid that the slightest movement would trigger an aftershock.

Kajikawa's face was deathly white beneath the soot. He gazed at the sword in his hand, as though he couldn't believe that his actions had brought him to this. Neither could anyone else, Sano thought.

"Don't come any closer, or I'll—" Kajikawa gagged, his next words stuck in his craw. His mind wasn't so completely unhinged that he could openly threaten the shogun.

"We won't," Sano hastened to say.

He didn't dare try to wrest the sword from Kajikawa. In a tussle, the blade could go anywhere, including through the shogun. Sano backed down the steps with slow, exaggerated care, his pulse and mind racing.

"Help!" the shogun cried in a voice squeezed thin and high by terror.

Yoritomo turned to Yanagisawa. "Father, do something!"

Yanagisawa ordered, "Put that sword down!" His voice was sharp with indignation.

They were scared of what would happen to them if anything happened to the shogun, Sano knew. They weren't the only ones.

Kajikawa looked at Yanagisawa and Yoritomo as if they'd spoken a language he didn't understand. He panted and moaned. He didn't move.

Ihara spoke up. "Are you a complete idiot, man? Haven't you learned anything from Lord Asano's example?" His croaky voice was filled with contempt.

"That was an order," Yanagisawa rapped out. "Put it down!"

"My father is the chamberlain. You have to obey him," Yoritomo said.

Sano saw offense flare in Kajikawa's eyes. He had to pacify the man, fast. "Let's all just calm down," Sano said in as soothing a tone as he could muster.

"In case you've forgotten, the penalty for drawing a sword inside Edo Castle is death," Kato informed Kajikawa. "For threatening the shogun, it's death, too."

"We'll have to execute you twice." Ihara uttered nervous laughter that sounded like a monkey hooting.

"Don't you mock me!" Kajikawa said through gritted teeth. "I'll kill him, and then we'll see who laughs!"

The shogun wailed.

"Never mind them, Kajikawa-*san*," Sano said, appalled that the elders were making the situation worse, their judgment impaired by panic. "You wanted to explain. Let His Excellency go, and you'll have your chance."

"Shut up!" Yanagisawa told Sano. "You've already caused enough trouble. I'll handle this." Turning to Kajikawa, he spoke with kindly concern. "It's true that you've committed two capital offenses. But I can bend the rules. If you drop the sword and step away from His Excellency, I'll grant you an official pardon. I'll also pardon you for your role in the forty-seven *rōnin*'s vendetta and the attack on Magistrate Ueda. You'll walk away from this as if nothing had happened. I promise." He smiled, focusing all his charm on Kajikawa. "Have we a deal?"

It was the best performance Sano had ever seen from Yanagisawa. But Kajikawa reacted with a disdainful snort. "You'll never pardon me. You're just saying what you think I want to hear, so I'll do what you want."

"My word is good." Yanagisawa's voice fairly dripped with sincerity. "I swear."

Kajikawa laughed, a bitter bark. "You're forgetting, I've been in this court for a long time. I know what you are. How stupid do you think I am?"

Sano winced.

"Listen to the chamberlain," Kato urged. "You need his help. Take the deal."

"It's the best you'll get," Ihara said.

Holding the shogun pinned to the platform with his sword, Kajikawa poked his finger at Yanagisawa. "If you expect me to believe you, then you're not only a corrupt, lying cheat, you're the one who's stupid!"

"Don't talk to my father like that!" Yoritomo said.

"I know you, too," Kajikawa said with the relish of a man who has kept his opinions pent up for ages and finally lets them spill. "You bedded your way to the top of the regime, just like your father did. If I kill His Excellency, you're both as good as dead, too. Just watch!"

He moved his blade in a sawing motion a hair's breadth above the shogun's throat. The shogun flinched, moaning. Kajikawa let loose a hysterical giggle.

"Your entire family will pay for this," Ihara blustered.

"They'll all die with you," Kato said.

"Be quiet!" Kajikawa yelled. "I've had enough of you two!"

"What are you going to do? Kill us?" mocked Kato.

The elders were trying to divert Kajikawa's ire toward themselves, Sano realized. They hoped he would charge at them, the guards would seize him, and the shogun would be saved.

"I don't have to kill you," Kajikawa said with cunning born of desperation. "You're going to do it for me." He pointed at a guard.

The guard looked startled to find himself singled out, then chuckled as if he thought Kajikawa was joking.

"Kill the old monkey," Kajikawa ordered. "Or I'll kill the shogun."

Dismay crinkled Ihara's simian features. "You're not serious."

"Go ahead!" cried the shogun.

Reluctant, yet unable to disobey the shogun's order, the guard drew his sword. Yanagisawa, Yoritomo, and Kato looked on in horror. Sano said, "Think about this for a moment, Kajikawa-*san*," but the shogun shrieked, "Do it!"

As Ihara backed away, too dumbfounded to plead for his life, the guard slashed his paunchy middle. A huge, bleeding gash doubled him over. He gurgled blood from his mouth. His knees knocked and he collapsed dead.

Cries of horror blared. The shogun retched and choked, vomiting. Horrified by the sudden carnage, Sano looked at Masahiro. The boy was as gray and rigid as a stone statue. He'd seen death before, but not a murder in Japan's most secure, civilized place.

"There!" Kajikawa laughed, triumphant. "I showed the monkey!"

Kato shouted, "Ihara!" Yanagisawa was too stunned, and too appalled by the death of his ally, to speak. The guard let his bloody sword dangle. The gaze he cast around the room pleaded for absolution. Nobody offered any.

"Masahiro! Leave the room!" Sano said, anticipating more violence.

Masahiro hesitated, loath to abandon his father, then started toward the door. Servants and boys hurried after him. "Stay where you are, or the shogun is next!" Kajikawa said.

The rush stopped. Detectives Marume and Fukida peered in the door. Kajikawa yelled at them, "Go away! Clear everybody out of the palace, or the shogun dies!"

"Do as he says!" the shogun cried.

The detectives went. The atmosphere turned even more lethal now that the hope of rescue was gone. Everyone who remained seemed shrunken in size, diminished, except Kajikawa. The little man swelled with exhilaration and power over his superiors. The sword in his hand was steady over the shogun, who wept and cringed.

"Guards," Kajikawa said. "Take everybody's weapons. Then get out. You go, too," he told Kato. Sano realized that although Kajikawa had been acting on impulse, he now had some sort of plan. When the guards hesitated, he said, "Or shall I make you kill somebody else?"

"Do as he says," Yanagisawa told the guards, his voice tight with fury.

The guards collected the swords from Yanagisawa, Yoritomo, and Sano. They even took Masahiro's junior-sized weapons. They carried the swords out of the room. Kato beat a fast, cowardly retreat. Sano stood beside Masahiro while he thought as fast as he could.

One wrong word could provoke another disaster.

Kajikawa bobbled his head at Yanagisawa. "You thought I was weak. You thought you could beat me down. Well, you were wrong. I have the upper hand." He tittered exultantly. "Fancy that!"

"Please, please," the shogun gasped out. "Have mercy!"

"You're a fool who's lost the brains he was born with," Yanagisawa said, too incensed to control his sharp tongue. "You should have been content to see that the privies are cleaned. But no—you meddled in business that wasn't yours. You've gone too far. Not even I can save you now."

"Oh? Is that what the great chamberlain says?" Kajikawa's glee turned to rage. "Then what have I got to lose by killing the shogun?"

Sano realized that Yanagisawa was the one who'd gone too far. Aghast, Sano said, "Wait, Kajikawa-*san*—"

Kajikawa pressed down on his blade. The edge sank into the shogun's neck.

36

REIKO COULDN'T BEAR to sit at home and wait for news.
Leaving Akiko with the nurse, she strapped her dagger to her arm under
her sleeve, threw on her cloak, and hurried to the palace. The passages
were full of guards and officials rushing in the same direction. Everyone
had heard about the trouble; everyone wanted to find out what it was.
Reiko's sandals slipped on the icy paving stones as she ran. People slid, col-
lided, fell. She kicked off her sandals and forged onward. She barely felt
the cold through her thin cotton socks. Reaching the palace, she found a
huge, noisy crowd. The Tokugawa army milled through groups of officials
and servants. Guards blocked the doors. People craned their necks, buzzed
with speculation.

Reiko looked around for Masahiro and Sano, in vain. Hearing her
name called, she saw Detectives Marume and Fukida weave through the
mob toward her. She greeted them eagerly. "What's happened?"

"Kajikawa is trapped in the shogun's private chambers," Fukida said.

Marume's usually cheerful face was grave. "He's threatening to kill
the shogun."

Reiko clutched her throat. "He wouldn't, would he?"

"He's already killed Ihara from the Council of Elders," Fukida said.

"Or rather, he forced one of the guards to kill Ihara while he held the
shogun at swordpoint," Marume said. "He ordered us to clear the palace
or the shogun dies."

The news was so disastrous that Reiko could hardly take it in. Fukida said, "There's been no communication from Kajikawa since. So we don't know what else has happened."

"Where's my husband?" Reiko asked anxiously. "Where's Masahiro?"

"With Kajikawa and the shogun," Marume said. "And Yanagisawa, Yoritomo, and a bunch of boys and servants."

Reiko's blood went as cold as the ice that filmed the castle. She began to shake with terror. She trusted Sano to take care of himself, but her child was trapped in a volatile situation where at least one person had already been murdered. And they'd parted on bad terms, barely speaking to each other. "Can't you do something?"

Marume gestured toward the guards. "They won't let anybody in."

Reiko gazed at the army, powerless against one fugitive.

"You should go home, Lady Reiko," Fukida said. "It's cold out here, and there's nothing you can do."

But something might happen, and Reiko wanted to be among the first to know. When Marume and Fukida turned to speak with some other men, she edged around the crowd, circling the palace. Nothing was visible except shuttered windows and blank walls. Reiko mingled with a crowd of women and girls, the shogun's relatives and concubines and their attendants. They chattered and fretted. They didn't notice Reiko sidling toward the building. Neither did the guards. As she swept her gaze over the palace, desperate for a hint of what was going on inside, she saw a gap in the latticework that covered the space under the palace. She hesitated, fighting temptation. Maternal instinct outweighed the risk. Reiko dropped to her knees and scuttled through the gap.

BLOOD WELLED FROM the thin line that Kajikawa's blade cut on the shogun's neck. The shogun squealed like the pigs butchered at the wild game market. His eyes bulged so wide that the white rims showed all the way around his pupils. His mouth opened so far that Sano could see down his pinkish-gray gullet. His arms and legs shot out in an involuntary spasm. Sano was astounded as well as horrified.

The shogun's blood was red like everyone else's! Sano had been conditioned to think of the shogun as a sort of god, even though he knew the shogun's human failings all too well. The shogun, although weak and sickly, had been such a constant, dominating force in Sano's life that Sano was shocked to realize he was mortal.

The shogun touched his neck. He lifted his trembling hand in front of his face and saw the blood on his fingers. His breath sucked inward so fast that he choked. His complexion turned ghastly white. Groans poured from the other people in the room.

Kajikawa posed by the shogun, his sword still holding the shogun captive. His features wavered between a grin like a skull's rictus and an upside-down smile of tragic woe. He resembled an actor who'd thought he was the hero in the play and has just discovered he's the villain.

The shogun began to shake violently. He pressed himself against the platform as if he could sink through it and escape the blade that verged on slicing through his windpipe. He screamed, "Help!"

"This is blasphemy!" Yanagisawa exclaimed.

Kajikawa pointed at Yanagisawa and said, "That's enough from you!" His head bobbled at Yoritomo. "Gag him!"

Yoritomo stared in fresh shock. "What?"

"Take off your sash," Kajikawa ordered Yanagisawa. When Yanagisawa and Yoritomo started to protest, he said, "Or I'll finish off the shogun!"

The shogun began shrieking hysterically. He drummed his heels on the platform. Infuriated but cowed, Yanagisawa stripped off his sash, threw it to Yoritomo, and knelt.

"I'm sorry, Father." Yoritomo's voice quavered as if he were about to cry. He tied the sash around Yanagisawa's mouth.

Yanagisawa glared above the red and black cloth that muffled his tongue, that separated his lips and teeth. Sano didn't dare say a word, lest he be gagged and lose his speech, too. The other people in the room were silent while the shogun shrieked.

"Tie his hands and feet, too," Kajikawa said. "With your own sash."

His breath puffed and sweat glistened on his forehead, but he was calmer now. Sano wondered what on earth he thought could possibly save him. Yanagisawa extended his legs and hands. Yoritomo bound Yanagisawa's ankles.

"Tie his hands behind his back," Kajikawa instructed.

Until he knew what Kajikawa had planned, Sano couldn't formulate a counterstrategy. Yanagisawa lay on his side on the platform while Yoritomo tied his hands. The sash connected them to his trussed ankles. Sano waited despite a fever of suspense that was almost as unbearable as the shogun's screams. He braced himself with the thought that when the moment came for him to act, this was one time when Yanagisawa wouldn't be able to interfere.

"While you're at it, tie everybody else up," Kajikawa said.

As Yoritomo trussed the servants and boys, he looked furious as well as despondent without his father to guide him. When he reached Sano, he tied the knots with vicious yanks, cruelly tight.

"Loosen them," Sano whispered. "So I can save the shogun."

Yoritomo uttered a breathy, scornful laugh. "Big talk."

He pulled the sash so tight between Sano's ankles and wrists that Sano's spine curved backward. Sano stifled a cry. He watched in helpless fury while Yoritomo tied up Masahiro, who bravely endured his pain. When Yoritomo was done, the scene resembled a tuna auction. Bodies lay scattered on the floor, as immobile as dead fish for sale. Mouths were open as if gasping last breaths. Sano couldn't bear to look at Masahiro and see his son's gaze begging him to do something. The time wasn't right.

Maybe it never would be.

Kajikawa withdrew his sword from the shogun and said, "Get up."

The shogun's screams dwindled into a whimper. He tried to rise, but he shook so hard that he fell back on the platform. "I can't," he wailed.

"Get up." Kajikawa jabbed the point of his sword at the shogun's nose.

Cross-eyed as he gazed at the blade, the shogun levered himself up on his elbows and got his feet under him. Knees wobbling and arms windmilling, soiled with vomit, he looked like a drunk thrown out of a teahouse. Kajikawa caught him from behind, locking his left arm across the shogun's chest.

"We're going to walk out of the palace." He held his blade against the shogun's blood-smeared throat.

Kajikawa planned to use the shogun as a hostage and ensure his passage to freedom. Sano thought of everything that could go wrong and end up with the shogun killed. But he saw a glimmer of light, the opportunity he'd been waiting for.

Kajikawa propelled the shogun off the platform. The shogun whimpered and stumbled, his legs as limp as noodles. Kajikawa held him up and urged him toward Yoritomo, who stood beside his trussed, gagged, and fuming father. Yoritomo wrung his hands. His chin trembled.

"Walk ahead of us," Kajikawa said, "Whoever we meet, tell them to get out of the way, or I'll kill the shogun."

With an agonized glance at his father, Yoritomo fell into step. Sano called, "Kajikawa-*san*." He squeezed his voice through the pain growing in his bent spine. He tried not to strain against his bonds and make it worse. "You won't get away with this."

"Why not?" Kajikawa kept moving. "I've already gotten away with plenty that you never thought I would." But his steps slowed as he neared the door.

Sano hoped it meant he wanted to be stopped. "By now everybody knows what's happened. The palace will be surrounded by troops."

"They won't touch me as long as I've got His Excellency."

The shogun moaned. "Somebody help me!"

Sano wriggled across the floor and blocked Kajikawa's path. Agony shot through his spine. His muscles contracted. The sash pulled tighter. He gasped.

"You can't stop me." Kajikawa edged around Sano.

"Where do you think you're going?" Sano asked.

"Someplace. Anyplace away from Edo." Kajikawa sounded forlorn.

"You obviously haven't thought it through. Let me tell you what will happen when you get outside." The sash cut into Sano's flesh. His fingers and toes were going numb. "The army will surround you and follow you wherever you go."

"I don't want to die!" the shogun blubbered. "Please!"

The other people in the room lay silent, listening. Sano felt them depending on him. The air stank with their fear of what would happen if he failed to save the shogun. Everyone present would surely be punished. And then a war for control of the regime would begin. Yanagisawa's gaze shot daggers of hatred, rage, and hope at Sano.

"The army won't touch me." Kajikawa grunted with exertion as he pushed the shogun ahead. "As long as I've got His Excellency, I'm safe."

"You can't hang on to him forever," Sano pointed out. "You'll have to rest sooner or later. And then it'll be over. You should surrender now, while you can."

Kajikawa abruptly stopped a few paces from the door. Sarcasm, terror, and desperation played with his face like wicked ghosts. His eyes watered. "You're such a know-it-all! So tell me: I'm doomed if I go through with this, but what good will it do me not to?"

Even though Sano saw how badly Kajikawa wanted to be persuaded to surrender, he had nothing to offer Kajikawa in return. Kajikawa wouldn't believe false promises; Yanagisawa had proved that. Sano ransacked his imagination.

"You wanted to explain why you did what you did," Sano said. "If you go out there, you'll be too busy trying to fend off the army." Muscle spasms tortured him. His back was breaking. "This might be your last chance. Why not take it? You have a captive audience."

Kajikawa hesitated. Sano heard the people on the floor draw their breath. He said, "When you die, it will be too late."

Kajikawa's eyes revealed the inner battle between his urge to flee and his desire to justify himself.

"Wouldn't you rather talk while you can?" Sano coaxed. There was no feeling left in his hands or feet, and he knew Masahiro wasn't any better off. A tremendous guilt crushed him. He was responsible for Masahiro being here. He'd done no better by his son than Yanagisawa had by Yoritomo or Oishi by Chikara. "Wouldn't you like everybody to know what happened to your son?"

Kajikawa's rage flared. "Don't drag Tsunamori into this."

"Tsunamori is already in the middle of it," Sano said. "He's the reason you manipulated Oishi into a vendetta against Kira."

"How do you know?"

"Your assistant told me that you blamed Kira for Tsunamori's suicide."

Kajikawa shook his head, and tears flew from his eyes. "I don't want to talk about it." He clasped the shogun as tightly as a drowning man would his rescuer.

"Expose Kira for what he was, a monster who fed on the pain he caused other people," Sano urged. "It's the only way for you to get justice for your son."

284

"Justice was done when Oishi killed Kira!"

"Not quite," Sano said. "The forty-seven *rōnin's* score is settled, but yours won't be until your story is out in the open."

The battle in Kajikawa's eyes waged, shame versus his need for retaliation. Then Kajikawa said, "You're right." His voice broke. "I need the world to know."

THE UNDERSIDE OF the palace was a cold, dark maze that smelled of earth. Guided by diamond-shaped patterns of light from the openings in the lattice, Reiko crawled past stone piers that supported the building, over rough ground that scraped her knees, gouged her hands, and snagged her robes. Cobwebs dangling from the floor joists brushed her face. Reiko had never been in the shogun's private chambers, but she knew they were at the center of the palace. She inched along, trying not to make a sound. She ducked to avoid bumping her head on braziers suspended under the floor. Stinking basins set on the ground marked the locations of privies. No sound came from the rooms above her until she saw a square patch of light on the ground ahead. The light came from an opening in the floor, as did voices. Reiko looked up the hole, through the room above her, to a ceiling crisscrossed with carved beams. The hole was a space where a brazier had been removed. Reiko felt a draft as the room's heated atmosphere sucked cold air up through the hole. A man stammered and ranted. Was it Kajikawa?

Were Sano and Masahiro there?

The urge to raise her head through the hole and peek was almost irresistible. But if Kajikawa should see her, there was no telling what would happen. Reiko crept toward the side of the building. She pushed and pulled the lattice until it loosened. Crawling from beneath the palace, she emerged in a courtyard garden that resembled a frozen sea studded with boulders like black icebergs. She climbed the steps to a veranda, moved sideways between curtains of icicles, and slipped through the door.

Inside, she tiptoed along dim corridors. The voice led her around a corner. Here the passage was suffused with lantern light that shone through a paper-and-lattice wall. Reiko saw indistinct shadows on the other side. The voice that she took to be Kajikawa's broke into sobs. Desperate to know what had become of her husband and son, Reiko pulled her dagger out of its sheath under her sleeve and poked it through the paper pane. She winced at the faint noise of the blade slicing the stiff, brittle rice paper. Ages seemed to pass before she'd cut the top and sides of a square no wider than her eye. She peeled down the flap and peeked through the hole.

On the other side was a room, a vacant platform to her right. Yoritomo stood by the opposite wall. His shoulders were slumped; his beautiful face wore a look of misery. Reiko's eye darted left, toward the voice that spoke words too low for her to understand. It came from a short, dumpy samurai who stood with his back toward her. He must be Kajikawa. With his left arm he held someone pressed against him. His body partially hid the other man. But she could see the cylindrical black cap that the other man wore. It was the shogun. Kajikawa's right elbow was cocked upward; he held a sword against the shogun's throat.

Alarm flashed through Reiko. What had become of Sano and Masahiro?

Her gaze dropped to the floor. Human bodies lay, in contorted positions, strewn across it. Blood gleamed in a shocking red puddle around one body. Reiko's heart gave a sickening thump. Were all those men dead? Had Kajikawa murdered everyone?

She heard whimpering and thought it came from her, but it was the shogun's. She peered more closely at the bodies and noticed that their feet and hands were bound with cloth strips. Their eyes blinked. Their faces twisted in expressions of woe. Everyone was alive but the gray-haired old man lying in the blood.

It was Ihara. Not Sano or Masahiro.

Relief cheered Reiko. She scrutinized the other men. Some had the cropped hair and cotton garb of servants. Some were youths—the shogun's boys. Reiko couldn't find Sano, but she recognized the brown-and-orange-striped kimono that Masahiro had been wearing this morning.

Masahiro lay on his side, turned away from Reiko, about fifteen paces distant. His bound wrists and ankles were drawn so tightly together that his spine arched. He trembled with pain. Horrified by the sight of her child suffering, Reiko wanted to tear through the wall and rescue him, but if she did, Kajikawa might panic and kill the shogun. Reiko thought of the forty-seven *rōnin*. They'd had to choose between their duty to the shogun and their loyalty to Lord Asano, the person who mattered more to them. Reiko could stand idle for the shogun's sake, or she could help her son.

She carefully cut the hole bigger, enough to speak through and look through at the same time. "Masahiro," she whispered.

He didn't react. He couldn't hear her. Other people lay between them. One, a boy who was facing Reiko, met her gaze. Reiko shushed him, then whispered Masahiro's name louder. He jerked as he recognized her voice.

"Don't look at me," Reiko whispered urgently.

Masahiro froze. Kajikawa rambled on. Reiko whispered, "Move this way. Slowly. Don't make a sound."

Masahiro wriggled backward. The others shifted out of his way. Reiko held her breath, afraid Kajikawa would notice, but he didn't turn. Yoritomo seemed oblivious. When Kajikawa paused, a voice uttered quiet prompts. It was Sano's voice. Kajikawa was talking to Sano. Reiko almost fainted with gladness that her husband was there, alive. He must have convinced Kajikawa to talk, in order to buy himself time to save the shogun.

Masahiro moved beneath her vantage point. Reiko heard his muffled, pained grunts and the soft scrape of his body against the straw matting. At last he stopped, panting, at the wall. She knelt and cut another hole that framed Masahiro's hands and feet.

"Don't move." She sliced the red and orange sash that tethered Masahiro's wrists to his ankles. His spine relaxed; he sighed. When she cut the bonds, there was no time to be careful. Her blade made bloody nicks in his skin. Her heart broke while he endured the pain. At last he was free, but he remained in the same, contorted position, as if still tied up.

"Wait until I tell you to move," Reiko whispered. She thrust the dagger into Masahiro's hands. "Then do exactly as I say." She hoped she would know what to tell him, and when.

37

1700 Autumn

ON A GLORIOUS, sunny day, Kajikawa and his son Tsunamori walked up the white gravel path to the palace. Kajikawa looked at Tsunamori with pride. Tsunamori was a fine boy, even though he was small for his twelve years. He was also an only son, a precious thing. In him resided all Kajikawa's hopes for the future.

Kajikawa stopped, turned Tsunamori to face him, and said, "This is a very special day."

"Yes, Father." Tsunamori's eyes were bright with anticipation. He could hardly wait to start his first job in Edo Castle.

"You'll be working for a very important man." Kajikawa glanced toward the palace and saw Kira Yoshinaka strolling toward them. "Here he comes now."

Dressed in his black court robes, Kira was a tall, dark silhouette cut out of the bright day. He joined Kajikawa and Tsunamori and looked down at them. His face was in the shadow that he cast over Tsunamori.

Father and son bowed. Kajikawa said, "Greetings, Honorable Master of Ceremonies. This is my son. A thousand thanks for allowing him to be your page."

"I'm sure he'll make my favor worthwhile." The smile Kira gave Tsunamori was tinged with something ugly. "Are you ready to learn your duties?"

Shy and nervous, eyes cast politely downward, Tsunamori said, "Yes, master."

"Work hard," Kajikawa told his son. "Do everything Kira-*san* says. The honor of our family depends on you." As he watched Tsunamori follow Kira into the palace, Kajikawa had no idea that he'd just given his son over to a monster.

He ignored the signs at first. Every day, after work, Tsunamori was unusually quiet. When Kajikawa asked him what he'd been doing, he made brief, vague replies. Kajikawa thought it was because he was growing up and wanted privacy. Then one night Tsunamori came home with his face bruised, his clothes torn.

"What happened?" Kajikawa said, alarmed.

Tsunamori mumbled something about a fight. Kajikawa knew that the boys at the castle always picked on newcomers. Tsunamori would learn to defend himself, like everybody else, and then he would be fine. Or so Kajikawa thought, until the day he visited Kira and asked for a report on Tsunamori's progress.

"He's doing an excellent job," Kira said. "See for yourself, if you like. He's at the Momijiyama, helping to prepare it for a ceremony."

Kajikawa went to the Tokugawa ancestral worship shrine inside the castle. He walked under the *torii* gate, along the flagstone path flanked by temple dogs, through a forest where maple trees sported brilliant red leaves amid the evergreens. Kajikawa was puzzled because the shrine was so quiet, apparently deserted. Then he heard grunts, whimpers, and rustling noises from the forest. Curious, he followed them, through the trees to a clearing.

There he saw three figures joined together. In the center was Tsunamori, naked, on his hands and knees. A castle guard knelt behind Tsunamori. His kimono was hiked up around his waist, his loincloth hanging. He grunted as he rammed himself against Tsunamori's buttocks. Another guard, similarly undressed, held Tsunamori's face against his crotch. Tsunamori whimpered as the men took their pleasure.

Kajikawa was so sick with horror that he almost vomited. Sex between men was rampant in Edo Castle; he'd happened onto similar scenes before. He knew that the shogun's older retainers often used the younger ones. It was the custom. It had happened to Kajikawa when he was young, and he'd almost forgotten it. But this was his son!

"Stop!" Kajikawa rushed into the clearing. He shoved the guards. "Leave him alone!"

They slunk away, straightening their clothes. Kajikawa knelt beside Tsunamori, who lay sobbing on the ground. "Has this been happening since you started working in the castle?" Kajikawa asked.

Tsunamori nodded. He picked up his clothes and slowly dressed.

"Well, it's the last time," Kajikawa said. "I'll have those guards thrown out of the regime. They'll never touch you again."

"No!" Tsunamori cried with a vehemence that startled Kajikawa. "You mustn't!"

"Why not?"

"Kira told them they could have me. He told me that if I didn't let them do whatever they wanted, I would lose my post."

Kajikawa was thunderstruck. He couldn't believe Kira would do such a thing! But he could see that Tsunamori was telling the truth. "Go home," he said grimly. "I'll handle Kira."

By the time he found Kira, in the Corridor of Pines, he was shaking with rage. "You forced my son to service those animals! You're nothing but a dirty pimp!"

Kira smiled, the same ugly smile he'd given Tsunamori at that first meeting. "Oh, you saw the little scene at the shrine. Good."

Fresh shock left Kajikawa breathless. "You meant for me to see? That's why you sent me there!"

"Of course. What good is a performance without an audience?"

The gall, the heartlessness, the sheer perversion of the man! "You won't get away with this! I'll—I'll—"

"Report me to the shogun?" Kira snickered. "His Excellency isn't likely to frown on pursuits that he himself enjoys."

Kajikawa was disheartened; he knew it was true. "I'll tell everybody what you are!"

The smile dropped off Kira's face. "If you utter one complaint or accusation, I'll have you and your son both thrown out of the regime." He raised a finger at Kajikawa, a warning that it wielded more power than Kajikawa had in the world. Then Kira turned and glided away.

Kajikawa spent a sleepless night. His fear of Kira argued with his need to protect his son and his thirst for revenge. He'd never been a brave man, and fear won out. It would be best, for him and Tsunamori both, if he did nothing rather than risk the disgrace and hardship of their becoming *rōnin*.

"You'll just have to put up with it until the guards get tired of you or Kira finds someone else to pick on," Kajikawa told Tsunamori the next day.

"Yes, Father," Tsunamori said meekly.

As months passed, Kajikawa couldn't meet Tsunamori's eyes and think of what his son suffered while he looked the other way. He couldn't bear to admit he'd let Tsunamori down.

One winter night, Tsunamori didn't come home. The next morning, Kajikawa ran all over the castle, searching for him. He found Tsunamori at the shrine, dangling from a noose tied to a branch of a tree in the clearing where the guards had raped him. Kajikawa had come too late. Tsunamori was dead.

In his anguish, Kajikawa blamed Kira. Kira had brought about the degradation that had caused Tsunamori to take his own life. Kira should be punished. But Kajikawa was still afraid of Kira. Instead of registering a vendetta and killing his enemy, Kajikawa sought another way to settle the score. He began spying on Kira. He secretly watched and listened to Kira torment Lord Asano. He witnessed sharp exchanges between Kira and Oishi. Eventually, he followed Kira to the squalid little inn by the river.

He hid in a bamboo grove and watched Kira peek through a hole in the window of a room. After a short while, Kira left, smiling his ugly smile. Then Kajikawa saw Oishi exit the room next to the one Kira had spied on. Oishi's expression was grim enough to turn wine into vinegar. A few moments afterward, a woman ran weeping from the room on the other side. Interested to see what had upset her and Oishi so much, Kajikawa tiptoed to the window and looked through Kira's peephole.

In the room, Lord Asano slumped naked on the bed. A woman stood with her back to him, dressing. Her head was bowed as if in shame. Lord Asano said, "Your husband is my loyal chief retainer and best friend. I wish I could take back what I did."

"I wish I could take it back, too," the woman said. "Your wife is my best friend."

They both sounded remorseful about their illicit love affair. Kajikawa deduced the women's identities: This one was Oishi's wife. The weeping woman from the next room must be Lord Asano's.

"I'm sorry," Lord Asano said.

"It's not your fault," Oishi's wife said bitterly. "It's Kira's."

Kajikawa realized that he and his son weren't the only people that Kira had manipulated into a sordid scene for his own pleasure. Kira had forced Lord Asano to bed Oishi's wife, and arranged for Oishi and Lady Asano to see it. Kajikawa was disgusted by the enormity of Kira's perversion. He was elated when Lord Asano attacked Kira, and disappointed because Kira didn't die.

After months of ruminating on past events, he realized that Lord Asano had presented him with an opportunity for revenge. He concocted a plan and worked up the nerve to set it in motion.

Kajikawa went looking for Oishi and discovered that the man had gone to Miyako. He traveled there, found the house where Oishi was living, and waited outside. When Oishi emerged, Kajikawa said, "Oishi-*san*, what a surprise. How about a drink?"

When they were seated in the teahouse and had drunk a few cups, Kajikawa described what he'd seen at the inn. He told Oishi that Kira had organized the tryst between Oishi's wife and Lord Asano.

Oishi pounded on the table and cursed. "Kira is a dead man!"

Kajikawa felt a searing satisfaction in his heart. What he couldn't do, Oishi would. He felt guilty as he egged Oishi into plotting an illegal vendetta, but he told Oishi, and himself, that he could protect Oishi from the consequences. They would both get their revenge, and neither would be punished.

HIRATA RACED THROUGH the *torii* gate that led to the Momijiyama. Temple dogs glared at him through a coating of ice. A forest of crystallized trees shivered around him as he skidded along the slippery flagstone path. He perceived a faint trace of Kajikawa's aura and stopped. He lifted his head. The aura emanated from the forest, which was silent except for the tinkle of falling ice crystals. Hirata followed the aura, crunching on brittle snow. He arrived at a clearing where rays of pale daylight shone through the ice-draped canopy of tree branches.

The clearing was empty. The aura came from a strip of white paper that lay atop frozen leaves. Hirata picked up the paper. Written on it in shaky calligraphy were the words, *Tsunamori. Your father is sorry.*

Hirata laid down the paper and left the forest. On the path he met a Shinto priest, who said, "You're too late. He left almost an hour ago."

Hirata remembered where else Kajikawa had been sighted. He ran for the palace.

IN THE SHOGUN's chamber, Sano realized that he had finally uncovered the truth behind the forty-seven *rōnin*'s vendetta. The story of the vendetta was like a tapestry, thickly woven with details. Sano had picked apart the many threads—the conflicting versions of events—before discovering that the forty-seven *rōnin* hadn't been the only men bent on destroying Kira.

There was a forty-eighth avenger.

But even while Kajikawa held his blade to the shogun's throat, he seemed the unlikeliest avenger in the world.

"I thought Oishi would kill Kira and I could feel that I'd paid Kira back for my son's death," Kajikawa lamented, his tiny features dripping tears. "I can't believe how wrong everything went. All I wanted was justice for my son!"

"And you got it," Sano said, thinking fast, searching for the words to turn the situation around. "Even though I don't approve of the way you went about it, I think you did right by your son." One's son deserved vengeance even more than one's lord did. If Sano had discovered that Kira had made a prostitute of Masahiro, he would have killed Kira on the spot instead of bringing in another injured party to do it. Still, Kajikawa had done the best he could. "Kira was a monster."

"Yes!" Kajikawa gasped in his relief that Sano understood. "Kira deserved to die!" He spoke into the shogun's ear. "Your Excellency thought Kira shouldn't be punished for his quarrel with Lord Asano because Kira fooled you. He fooled everybody into thinking he was good, but he was an evil, corrupt old snake. Lord Asano never said so, but I put the words in his mouth because they're true!"

The shogun was beyond hearing. His mouth gaped like that of a fish thrown ashore, fighting for its last breath. The other people in the room listened, silent, immobile, and helpless.

Kajikawa's eyes shone with triumph. "We put an end to him, Oishi and I!" Then he relapsed into misery. "I'm sorry for getting Oishi and his men in trouble. They wouldn't have gone after Kira if not for me. The supreme court is going to sentence them to death, and it's my fault. I'm sorry about Magistrate Ueda, too." Sobs choked him. "I'm sorry for everything except that Kira is dead."

Sano seized on the words. "Yes, you did put an end to Kira. And now it's time to put an end to this, before any other innocent person is hurt. Let go of His Excellency. Walk out of the palace by yourself and surrender."

A yearning expression came over Kajikawa's face. Sano could tell how much he was tempted to give up, how eager for the relief. Kajikawa said, "But if I were to surrender, I would be a coward. I was a coward when Kira abused my son and I looked the other way. But I'll never be a coward again." He sniffled, blinked away tears, firmed up his mouth, and said to Yoritomo, "Let's go."

With a desperate glance at his father, Yoritomo trudged forward. He walked through the door, his shoulders slumped and head bowed.

"Not yet," Sano said urgently. "We're not finished talking."

"I am." Kajikawa edged around Sano. The shogun was so senseless with hysteria, his body so limp, that Kajikawa was almost carrying him. "I've had my say. I'm going to meet my fate like the brave samurai I should have been when my son needed me." He and the shogun followed Yoritomo out the door.

"Kajikawa!" Sano shouted.

OUTSIDE THE CHAMBER, Reiko whispered urgently through the hole in the wall to Masahiro: "Free your father! Quickly!"

Masahiro jumped up, her dagger in his hand. Voices inside the room exclaimed. Reiko heard Sano say, "How did you get loose? Where did you get that dagger?"

294

"From Mother," Masahiro said as Reiko ran down the passage and around the corner.

"She's here?" Sano sounded almost as much vexed as pleased.

"Yes," Reiko called. She reached the doorway to see that Sano's hands were free; Masahiro was cutting the bonds from his ankles. "Hurry!"

The blood flow to his feet had been stopped for so long that Sano could barely stand. He winced in pain. Yanagisawa writhed, grunting through his gag. The other men begged Masahiro to free them, but there was no time. Supporting Sano between them, Reiko and Masahiro toiled through the palace. Sano limped and cursed. They heard the shogun wail, but he and Kajikawa were far ahead. Sano stumbled and went down on his knee on the polished floor of the corridor whose walls were decorated with paintings of pine trees. The Corridor of Pines, Reiko thought. This was where Lord Asano had attacked Kira, where everything had started.

Reiko and Masahiro helped Sano rise. They caught up with Yoritomo and Kajikawa near the main entrance. Kajikawa lumped the shogun along the hall like a sack of radishes. The shogun screamed every time his knees hit the floor. Kajikawa panted, straining to lift the shogun and urge him ahead while holding the sword to his throat.

"Wait!" Sano called.

Yoritomo reached the door and opened it. Daylight shone in. Reiko heard a roar of voices rise as Yoritomo led Kajikawa and the shogun outside. Another roar came from behind her and Sano and Masahiro. Reiko turned and saw Yanagisawa hobbling down the corridor. Somehow he'd gotten free. While she and Sano and Masahiro labored toward the door, Yanagisawa was in hot pursuit.

38

BREATHLESS AND SWEATING, Hirata arrived at the palace to find a noisy, agitated mob outside and hear the words that passed from one person to another: "Kajikawa is holding the shogun hostage!" He pushed through the mob and came up against a ring of troops stationed some twenty paces from the palace. They spread their arms to prevent people from moving closer.

"Stand aside!" Hirata shouted at the nearest guard.

The guard recognized him but didn't budge. "My orders are to keep everybody away from the palace. If you go in there, you could get the shogun killed."

A cry went up from the crowd: "Somebody's coming out!"

The palace door opened. Guards drew their bows, aimed arrows at it. Yoritomo stepped onto the veranda. His face blanched with terror. His hands flew up.

"Don't shoot!" he cried. "His Excellency is coming!"

The shogun stumbled out the door. The crowd gasped. His knees buckled; his feet dragged; his eyes rolled. His hands clawed at an arm clamped across his chest. The arm belonged to Kajikawa, who walked behind him. They looked like a Bunraku puppeteer and puppet—a puppeteer who held a sword against his living puppet's throat. Kajikawa's expression was defiant as he pushed the shogun forward. The guards lowered their bows. Apprehension chased through Hirata.

Kajikawa was insane. He would never survive this. Neither might the shogun. And what had become of Sano?

Yoritomo descended the stairs, his hands raised in supplication. "Kajikawa wants to leave the castle. You have to let him go, or he'll kill His Excellency!"

People moaned, exclaimed, and passed the news to others behind them. Guards frantically conferred among themselves, trying to figure out what to do. Hirata seized control.

Shouting, "Clear a path!" he plowed through the mob, pushing people right and left. Troops hurried to help. A path opened from the palace to the gate. Troops held back the mob while Hirata stood at the edge of the path, ready to grab Kajikawa when he passed. With Yoritomo leading the way, Kajikawa lugged the shogun down the stairs. Anxious murmurs swept the audience. Yoritomo drifted sideways and lagged behind Kajikawa. Kajikawa dragged the shogun across the empty space around the palace.

They'd traversed half the distance, when four figures burst out the door.

The first figure was Sano, followed by Masahiro and Reiko. The last was Yanagisawa. The crowd roared.

"Kajikawa!" Sano ran down the stairs.

Kajikawa half turned but kept walking.

"Don't do this. Let His Excellency go." Sano gestured toward the troops, the mob. "Wherever you go, this is what you'll meet. You won't get away."

Kajikawa seemed to notice the pandemonium for the first time. Fear cracked the shell of his defiance. He paused. Reiko descended the stairs with Masahiro; they stopped at the bottom, her arm around him. Yanagisawa clutched the railing and panted, out of breath.

Suddenly Hirata felt the familiar aura. He looked across the cleared path. Tahara, Deguchi, and Kitano stood in the crowd on the other side. They returned his gaze, impassive. A movement on the periphery of his vision turned Hirata's head. He saw Yoritomo stoop to pick up something from the ground. It was a branch. Yoritomo raised it in both hands as he sneaked up behind Kajikawa. His expression wavered between terror and determination. Hirata's gaze homed in on the branch like a falcon sighting a sparrow aloft in a vast sky. The branch was black, as long and almost as thick as a man's arm. It was coated with ice from the storm. Hirata recognized the kink near the end where Yoritomo gripped it. A broken-off stub protruded above Yoritomo's hands.

The branch was the one Tahara had thrown.

Flabbergasted, Hirata looked at Tahara, Deguchi, and Kitano. They were intently watching Yoritomo.

Cheers blared as the crowd noticed Yoritomo preparing to attack Kajikawa. Kajikawa frowned, puzzled and suspicious. Yoritomo was within striking distance when Kajikawa turned, slewing the shogun around with him. Kajikawa saw Yoritomo ready to bring the branch down on his head. Surprise and dismay appeared on both men's faces. Kajikawa flailed his sword at Yoritomo. It seemed more reflex than deliberate. Yoritomo had no time to dodge or strike back. The blade swiped the left side of his throat.

The crowd's cheers deepened into groans. Shock altered Hirata's perception. Time seemed to slow down, as if cosmic forces had stayed its flight.

Sano's expression filled with horror. His lips parted. He uttered words that were drawn out like the sonorous notes from a war trumpet, unintelligible.

The cut on Yoritomo's throat was a thin red line that broadened like a river during the rainy season. Blood spurted, gushed, and stained his clothes. His eyes and mouth opened wide. Pain twisted his features. He let go of the branch. It drifted downward through the air, like a feather, while his arms fell to his sides and his legs gave way. A dull sheen spread over his gaze. He crumpled to the ground. The branch landed, bouncing twice before it came to rest.

Reiko pressed her hand to her mouth. Beside her, holding a dagger, Masahiro gaped. Kajikawa's mouth flexed, forming a smile, then a downturned grimace, smile, then grimace, childlike glee, then ghastly horror. His arm around the shogun loosened. The shogun collapsed like bamboo blinds folding.

A loud bellow, as if from a wounded animal, drowned out the exclamations from the crowd. Yanagisawa staggered down the steps and dropped beside his son. He hauled Yoritomo into his lap. He shouted into Yoritomo's lifeless face.

Hirata was dumbstruck by the consequences of a trivial action, a branch selected at random and casually tossed. The crowd heaved around him, buffeting him, squeezing him, in a wave of mass shock. He turned to the secret society.

Tahara smiled, as if to say, *I told you so.*

"YORITOMO!" YANAGISAWA SHOUTED, cradling his son in his arms. "Yoritomo!"

Dread was a cold iron cage crushing his ribs, his heart. Nobody else spoke. A hush fell over the crowd. The only sound was water dripping. The ice on the trees and palace roofs had begun to melt.

Yanagisawa patted Yoritomo's cheeks, which had turned pale. Horror sickened him. He pressed against Yoritomo's neck in a futile attempt to stop the bleeding. "Speak to me!"

Yoritomo didn't speak or move. Yanagisawa saw nothing but the reflection of his own terrified face in his son's opaque eyes. Yoritomo was dead.

"No!" Yanagisawa cried.

Disbelief and denial passed in an instant.

All meaning, hope, and happiness in his life vanished.

Grief assaulted Yanagisawa like a storm that exploded up from the depths of his spirit. Past concerns suddenly seemed trivial. He didn't care that he'd lost his advantage over his enemies, his potential heir to the Tokugawa regime, his chance to rule Japan. All he wanted was his son back, his beautiful, beloved Yoritomo alive again. But all his power, all his clever scheming, couldn't resurrect the dead. Yanagisawa threw back his head and howled.

Through the storm of his grief screamed a primitive desire for revenge, for someone other than himself to blame.

SANO STARED, OPEN-MOUTHED with shock, at Yanagisawa and Yoritomo.

He'd never expected Yoritomo to try a sneak attack on Kajikawa. He'd thought Yoritomo was too timid. That the young man had found the courage! That it had been so foolhardy! Pity and regret pained Sano. He wondered what he could have done differently, and he cursed himself for letting this happen.

All the evil in Yoritomo had been laid to rest, but so had all the good.

Yoritomo and Yanagisawa formed a tableau as poignant as it was terrible. Yoritomo's blood colored the ice around them a bright red, strangely beautiful. Grief reduced Yanagisawa from a ruthless politician to a tragic figure, a father mourning his dead son. Ashamed to witness his enemy's naked emotion, Sano turned his attention to Kajikawa.

Kajikawa lowered his bloody sword. He looked as if he couldn't believe what he'd done. He didn't seem to notice that he'd let go of the shogun, who lay at his feet. Sano himself, and Reiko and Masahiro, were too stunned to move.

The shogun crawled away from Kajikawa, toward the crowd. Now Kajikawa realized his hostage was escaping. "Come back here!" he shouted.

Racing after the shogun, he bent and caught the hem of the shogun's robe. The shogun strained like a dog on a leash. The silk fabric slipped from Kajikawa's hand. The shogun scuttled frantically. Sano rushed to help him. Kajikawa hacked at the shogun with his sword. Yells blasted from the crowd. Kajikawa lost his balance, slipped on the melting ice, and missed.

"That's enough!" Sano said as troops hurried to his aid. "Drop that sword!"

"Stay away! Leave me alone!" Kajikawa whipped the sword at Sano.

Sano dodged. He reached for his sword, but his hand closed on empty air. He and Kajikawa wheeled around the shogun, who screamed while Kajikawa slashed at Sano. Sano ducked and feinted. He tried to lead Kajikawa away from the shogun, but troops surrounded them. As Sano made a grab for Kajikawa's wrist, the shogun caught hold of Sano's trousers. Sano stumbled and went down.

Kajikawa shrieked and chopped wildly at Sano. His blade whistled close to the shogun. Sano rolled to avoid the slashes, lunged in an attempt to shield the shogun from them with his own body. Some of the troops attacked Kajikawa while others grabbed for the shogun. Kajikawa whirled and struck at them. Scrambling to his feet, Sano saw Yanagisawa raise his head. Yanagisawa gazed over his dead son, straight at Sano. His eyes streamed. The rage and hatred in them was so intense that Sano felt as if he'd been charred by flames. Yanagisawa eased Yoritomo's body onto the ground and rose. He ran to one of the soldiers who were holding back the mob. He shouted a command. The soldier gave his sword to Yanagisawa.

The troops lashed their swords at Kajikawa. He parried, evading injury by sheer dumb luck, treading on the shogun. Sano was about to rejoin the fight, when he heard Reiko cry, "Look out!"

Sano saw Yanagisawa charging toward him, yelling words garbled by sobs. Yanagisawa's face was ugly with rage. He gripped the borrowed sword in both hands over his head. Sano was facing the showdown with Yanagisawa that had been fourteen years in the making, and he was unarmed.

Even as Sano looked around for a weapon he could use, Yanagisawa barreled past him, shouting, "My son is dead. I'm going to kill yours!" He ran at Masahiro.

Through his horror, Sano saw alarm on his wife's and son's faces. A moment flashed by, during which the plight of the forty-seven *rōnin* became drastically personal for Sano. Duty required that he go to the shogun, defend his master. Fatherhood demanded that he protect his son. Could he choose the person who mattered most to him over the lord to whom he owed his highest loyalty?

Sano recognized his dilemma, but he didn't have time to think about what to do. Hirata broke free of the crowd, ran at Kajikawa, and roared. Mystical power radiated from him like a halo of shimmering heat. Kajikawa saw him, froze, then backed away from the shogun. The shogun crawled toward the soldiers and threw himself into their arms.

The moment passed. The shogun was safe. Sano raced to rescue his son.

SHRIEKING CURSES, YANAGISAWA sliced at Masahiro. Masahiro parried with his dagger, but although he was a good fighter for his age, he was no match for a crazed, murderous adult. The force of Yanagisawa's blows drove him backward. His short blade put him at a further disadvantage.

Reiko screamed and threw herself between Masahiro and Yanagisawa. She didn't care about her own safety. Her son's was all that mattered. Masahiro pushed her away, to protect her. Reiko fell. Her left elbow hit the ice so hard that pain shot up the bone to her neck and skull. Her vision shuddered.

Yanagisawa delivered a blow that sent Masahiro's dagger flying and knocked Masahiro to the ground. His teeth were clenched, his lips pulled back in an unholy grin. He was covered with Yoritomo's blood. Masahiro rolled from side to side as Yanagisawa hacked at him repeatedly.

"Stop him!" Reiko called to Sano.

Sano came running with all his might. He assaulted Yanagisawa from behind. He seized the wrist of Yanagisawa's sword hand while he grabbed Yanagisawa's left arm and bent it backward. Yanagisawa cursed as he struggled. Sano twisted his wrist. Yanagisawa shrieked in pain, but he held on to the weapon. Sano fought to subdue Yanagisawa. Kajikawa fended off troops. More troops held back the crowd that surged chaotically.

Reiko hurried to Masahiro. "Are you all right?"

Masahiro was already on his feet. "Yes, Mother. What about you?"

Reiko's arm ached as if something was broken, but she had to help Sano. He was struggling with Yanagisawa, who jerked, contorted, and tried to kick Sano's legs.

"I'm all right." Reiko saw her dagger, the one that Yanagisawa had knocked out of Masahiro's hand, lying near the palace. She rushed to it, snatched it up, and pointed it at Yanagisawa's middle. "Drop the sword, or I'll stab you!"

Yanagisawa froze, his eyes widening. His stomach contracted as the tip of the dagger touched it. His fingers uncurled. The sword clattered onto the ground.

Reiko stared at him, fascinated. This was the closest she'd ever been to Yanagisawa. Although she knew him from everything that Sano had told her about him, they'd never met, never exchanged a word. She was shocked because he was just a man. He breathed. His eyes were red from weeping over his son. The skin on his face had blemishes and lines. She could smell his sweat. This demon, her husband's worst enemy, who had menaced her family for years and had just tried to kill her son, was as mortal as herself.

"I'm going to kill you," she said in a voice so jagged with fury that she barely recognized it as her own. "I'm going to make you pay for everything you've done to us."

Sano's face, behind Yanagisawa's, filled with dismay. "Don't," he said. "You've disarmed him. That's enough."

"No, it's not!" Every muscle in Reiko tensed, ready to drive the dagger home.

"Kill him!" Masahiro jumped up and down with excitement.

Yanagisawa smiled, oddly satisfied. "Go ahead, Lady Reiko. You'll never have another chance like this."

"Don't listen to him," Sano pleaded.

"He's a danger to us as long as he lives," Reiko said, confused because Sano wanted to prevent her from doing what needed to be done. "I have to get rid of him once and for all."

"Good for you, Lady Reiko." Yanagisawa breathed hard, his smile fixed. "Your husband hasn't the courage. You have."

"He wants you to do it," Sano warned. "Because you'll be put to death as punishment. So will I. So will Masahiro."

"That's right, Lady Reiko," Yanagisawa said, laughing although terror clutched his voice.

"You won't be around to enjoy seeing us punished." Reiko was furious at his mockery. "You'll be dead."

Fresh tears streamed down Yanagisawa's face. His smile brimmed with pain. "I don't care. Now that Yoritomo is dead, nothing matters. I'll gladly die so we can be together."

Was he playing on her sympathy, trying to get her to spare his life? Or did he truly want her to put him out of his misery? In spite of herself, Reiko pitied Yanagisawa. He had lost his child. His grief was genuine. It transformed him from a villain into a man who deserved compassion. Reiko hesitated.

Yanagisawa's eyes entreated her. The noise from the crowd rose louder. A horde of troops faced down Kajikawa. The shogun, safe with his guards, pointed at Kajikawa and yelled orders. Kajikawa wailed as he realized that he had nothing left with which to bargain for his escape. As the troops charged at him, he turned and ran for the palace, toward Reiko.

Here came the man responsible for the attack on her father.

With an effort that wrenched her whole spirit, Reiko tore herself away from Yanagisawa. She stood in front of the stairs that led to the door. She watched Kajikawa running toward her, out of breath, his heavy head bobbing, legs pumping, sleeves flapping, his eyes wild with panic. He'd looked bigger when she'd seen him holding the shogun hostage inside a room full of people tied up on the floor. Now, as he desperately fled his pursuers, Reiko noted his smallness, his insignificance. He was nothing but a puny coward!

As he neared Reiko, he waved his sword at her. "Get out of my way!"

But smallness didn't negate the crime he'd committed. That his evils paled in comparison to Yanagisawa's didn't excuse Kajikawa. Reiko felt centuries of samurai heritage rise up like a flaming tidal wave in her blood.

Kajikawa was almost upon her. The troops stampeding after him blurred into the background. The roars from the crowd faded. The world contained only herself and Kajikawa. She didn't need to think before she acted. A lifetime of martial arts training had prepared her for this moment. Instinct took command of her body.

Reiko flicked out her dagger.

39

SANO TOOK CHARGE after the debacle. Everyone else was too shocked. Although he himself was still reeling from the day's events, he ordered the army to disperse the crowd and court physicians to attend to the shogun. He sent servants to clean up the shogun's chamber and arranged for the dead to be removed. Everyone obeyed Sano for want of any other authority. Officials returned to their duties, troops to their posts. A sad parade moved out the gate—porters carrying three litters bearing the corpses of Kajikawa, Ihara, and Yoritomo. Yanagisawa accompanied his son. Tears streaming down his face, he stumbled like a blind man. Sano walked home with Reiko, Masahiro, Hirata, and Detectives Marume and Fukida, through the strangely deserted, quiet castle.

A pale sun and patches of blue showed through the clouds in the sky. Sheets of ice slid from roofs. Water dripped from trees and eaves and cascaded down the walled passages along which Sano and his companions trudged. The crystalline world was thawing into puddles, slush, and mud.

"That was some show," Marume said.

"People will be talking about it for a hundred years," Fukida said.

Sano heard a hollow note beneath their humor. They were as shaken as he was. Reiko asked the question that was on everyone's mind: "What's going to happen to me?"

Her face was drawn, frightened. Masahiro held her hand. All present understood the gravity of the situation: She'd drawn a weapon inside

Edo Castle, killed a man, and threatened the chamberlain. That would surely have repercussions.

As would Yoritomo's death.

Marume and Fukida looked at the wet pavement instead of answering Reiko's question. Hirata brooded in some private, dark study of his own. Sano said, "I doubt you'll be punished. Nobody will take against you on Kajikawa's behalf. And I'll protect you."

Reiko forced a smile, pretending she was reassured. "At least the mystery of the vendetta is solved. The supreme court can decide the fate of the forty-seven *rōnin*."

40

1703 March

MORE THAN TWO months after the forty-seven *rōnin* killed Kira, their trial finally took place, in the reception room at the Hoso-kawa estate. Sano knelt at one side of the dais upon which the supreme court judges sat in a row. Magistrate Ueda occupied the place at center stage.

The bruises on his face had faded, although the wound on his head had left an ugly scar. His voice was strong as he said, "We are gathered to render a verdict in the case of the vendetta perpetuated against Kira Yoshinaka by the former retainers of Lord Asano."

The forty-seven *rōnin* knelt in four rows below the dais, on a sheet of cloth covered with white sand: a makeshift *shirasu*—white sand of truth, a feature of courtrooms, where the defendants sat. It was the largest *shirasu* in Japan, for the largest trial in history. Oishi knelt in the front row, his son Chikara beside him. All the men were dressed in formal black silk robes. Their faces wore identical, stoic expressions. Again Sano had the sense that they were one being. He could almost hear their pulses beating in unison. They looked straight ahead at the court, ignoring the spectators who overflowed out the door. These included officials from every govern-ment department. They wanted to be among the first to hear the verdict. They were as hushed and still as the forty-seven *rōnin*.

"This is an unprecedented situation," Magistrate Ueda went on. "Not only was the vendetta particularly violent and not sanctioned by the law, but it had many facets, which raised many questions. Because we the judges of this court have had such difficulty in determining what really happened, we have been unable to agree on a just decision. Until now."

Sano felt suspense build, a rumbling sensation, as if an underground volcano were about to erupt. He had to force himself to breathe. Every investigation he'd undertaken had brought troubling consequences, but never had the fate of so many people hinged on his actions. This time he'd wielded more influence over fate than in previous cases, because he'd shaped the law to fit his own notion of justice.

It was too late to wonder whether he'd done the right thing.

"At last we know the truth," Magistrate Ueda declared.

The forty-seven *rōnin* didn't react, but the spectators' heads turned toward Sano. He'd told the court the story of the vendetta. The judges had kept it confidential from everyone else except the shogun, although many other people knew some or all the details—those present during Kajikawa's confession; Hosokawa clan members; the Council of Elders. Accurate and false versions of the story had spread through Edo. And many people knew that Sano was responsible for dragging the truth into the light.

"An unprecedented situation calls for an unprecedented response," Magistrate Ueda said. "Therefore, we have decided not to render the usual sort of verdict."

Sano was also responsible for this decision. He'd proposed it to the judges, and after debating it strenuously for two months, they'd agreed that it was the best course of action.

Murmurs of surprise swept through the audience. The forty-seven *rōnin* remained unperturbed: Sano had told them about the decision three days ago, as soon as it had been made.

"We will allow you, the defendants, to decide your own fate," Magistrate Ueda said. The audience clamored so loudly that he had to raise his voice. "I have ordered each of you to look into your spirit, to let your honor and your conscience be your guide in determining whether you should be punished by death or pardoned and set free."

Inspector General Nakae and Lord Nabeshima tightened their mouths. Superintendent Ogiwara and Minister Motoori, his broken leg propped on cushions, nodded. Magistrate Ueda had had quite a time convincing all the Judges that Sano's plan was the best way to calm the controversy and prevent the forty-seven *rōnin*'s supporters from going to war with their detractors. He and his allies had finally prevailed over the Yanagisawa faction, which was in chaos.

After his son's funeral, Yanagisawa had secluded himself inside his compound; no one had seen or heard from him since.

"Have you decided?" Magistrate Ueda asked the forty-seven *rōnin*. They'd been given the three days to discuss the matter among themselves.

"Yes, Honorable Magistrate, we have," Oishi said in a loud, clear voice.

The noise subsided into an expectant hush. "Tell us, then," Magistrate Ueda ordered.

Oishi spoke in an even tone devoid of melodrama. "We take pride in the fact that by killing Kira, we have discharged our duty to our master. We are certain that it was righteous."

Sano wholeheartedly agreed. He'd been unable to prove that Kira had connived to destroy Lord Asano and steal his gold, but people had come forward with tales of how Kira had hurt and humiliated them and enjoyed their suffering. Oishi and Kajikawa were among legions.

"But after having examined our consciences, we realized that our reasons were never as straightforward as we purported," Oishi said. "I myself had a personal grudge against Kira. It played a big part in my decision to carry out the vendetta. And I'm not the only one who confused personal issues with duty. Some of us blamed Kira for their hardships and their disgrace. Others were angry at the world and eager to strike out at any target. Many thought they had nothing to live for, and they wanted to go out in a blaze of glory."

Oishi paused, swallowed, and struggled to contain his emotions. Sano felt a lump in his own throat. The other forty-six *rōnin* listened, their somber gazes trained on Oishi. He seemed to draw from them the strength to continue.

"Our motives were never as pure as Bushido requires. We did not truly follow the Way of the Warrior; we followed our own selfish hearts. Even though we performed the highest act of loyalty, we are criminals at the bottom of it, a disgrace to the title of samurai. Our vendetta led to a situation in which the shogun's life was endangered. Therefore—" He drew a deep breath and spoke in a rush: "We have decided to commit *seppuku*."

Muted exclamations rippled through the audience. Magistrate Ueda looked saddened but gratified. "So be it," he said. "Your decision is the court's verdict."

The other judges shook their heads in amazement: They'd expected the forty-seven *rōnin* to seize their freedom. Sano hadn't known what to expect. He felt a mixture of awe and distress. No matter their human failings, Oishi and the other men were sacrificing their lives for the sake of honor. It occurred to Sano that their decision had taken into account other considerations besides those Oishi had mentioned. The unavoidable fact was that they had disobeyed the shogun. The shogun would have had to put them to death—even if it had meant overruling the supreme court—or lose face and authority. Now he didn't have to make the hard decision that he'd created the supreme court in order to avoid. The forty-seven *rōnin* had made it for him. They'd done their duty to him after all.

They were true heroes, paragons of samurai loyalty, exemplars of Bushido, even though they called themselves criminals. What a tragedy that they must die!

"We thank the honorable judges," Oishi said, his voice firm. "We apologize for the trouble we have caused."

"Accepted." His voice heavy with resignation, Magistrate Ueda said, "Your ritual suicide will take place tomorrow morning."

The assembly bowed. Sano gazed at the bent backs of the forty-seven *rōnin*. He looked hardest at Oishi and Chikara. Father and son would die together. Sano pictured himself and Masahiro in the same position. He blinked to dispel the vision, but its darkness lingered.

"The supreme court is dissolved," Magistrate Ueda said.

41

THE SUMMONS CAME a month after the forty-seven *ronin* died. The shogun had taken that long to recover from his ordeal. He'd spent the time in his chambers, attended by physicians and priests, seeing no one else. Edo Castle was rife with rumors. Some said the shogun was dying; some said he was going to abdicate; others said a major purge and reorganization of the government was imminent. Sano didn't know which, if any, to believe.

When Sano arrived in the palace reception room, the dais was vacant. The mural on the wall behind it depicted cherry trees in pink bloom, appropriate for the season, too cheerful. Yanagisawa was kneeling below the dais. This was the first time Sano had seen him since the day of Yoritomo's death. Yanagisawa had completely withdrawn from politics.

Sano knelt a cautious distance from Yanagisawa. Yanagisawa turned. Sano was shocked by the change in him. He'd lost so much weight that his body was like a skeleton under his dark green silk robe. Sharp bones protruded through the waxen skin of his face. His eyes were underlined by shadows, his lips raw. Sano thought of Oishi and Chikara. He wondered if Yanagisawa would trade places with them if he could. If Masahiro died, could Sano bear to live?

The shogun minced onto the dais, accompanied by two adolescent boys. When he sat, they knelt on either side of him. Their rosy, sweet faces and bland smiles were identical. One of the rumors was true, Sano noted.

The shogun had twins as his new favorites. Sano glanced at Yanagisawa. How terrible for him to see that Yoritomo had been replaced so quickly!

As Yanagisawa bowed to the shogun, he appeared indifferent to everything except his own pain. Sano bowed, too, observing that another of the rumors was false: The shogun wasn't dying; rather, he looked healthier than usual. The cut on his neck had healed. His holiday from court responsibilities had done him good.

"Forgive me for, ahh, making you wait such a long time to see me." The shogun's perfunctory smile conveyed how little he cared about anyone's feelings except his own.

"Yes, Your Excellency," Sano replied politely, even though the suspense was killing him. Yanagisawa didn't answer.

"I suppose you, ahh, think I've forgotten what happened the last time we were together." The shogun's expression turned peevish. "Well, I haven't."

Yanagisawa gazed through the shogun as if he weren't there. Sano braced himself.

"You," the shogun said, pointing at Sano, "protected me from Kajikawa. And your wife killed him." He beamed. "She saved me the trouble. You both served me very well indeed."

Sano was relieved that apparently Reiko wasn't going to be punished and their family could stay together. The shogun hadn't drawn a connection between Sano's investigation and Kajikawa's desperate act.

"Whereas you—" The shogun bent a pouty glare on Yanagisawa. "You completely, ahh, lost your wits! You made Kajikawa angry. You got yourself gagged so you couldn't even speak on my behalf. You were worthless!"

Yanagisawa didn't protest as the shogun said, "I am relieving you of your post as chamberlain. You've been, ahh, neglecting your duties lately, anyway."

Sano had taken them over because the government needed a chamberlain at the helm.

"I am demoting you to the, ahh, position of my third-in-command. You will vacate your residence immediately." The shogun added spitefully, "Consider yourself fortunate. If not for our long friendship, I would throw you out of my regime altogether."

The shogun's callousness had reached an extreme that Sano could hardly believe. Yanagisawa had lost his son, and the shogun hadn't offered a single word of condolence! Did he not recall that Yoritomo had died trying to save his life? He seemed to have forgotten that Yoritomo had ever existed. His turning against Yanagisawa was insult piled upon injury.

"Yes, Your Excellency." Yanagisawa's voice was cracked, bereft of strength, an old man's.

"Sano-*san*, you will take over as chamberlain," the shogun said. "You can move back into your compound. Hirata-*san* will be chief investigator again."

As Sano bowed and thanked the shogun, his triumph in his and Hirata's redemption was spoiled because he pitied Yanagisawa so much.

"That's all," the shogun said, stroking the sleek heads of the twins. "You're dismissed."

Yanagisawa walked from the room as if in a trance. Sano followed. Outside, Sano started to say how sorry he was about Yoritomo. But the look in Yanagisawa's eyes silenced him. It was fury, hatred, and bitterness transformed into something deadlier than Sano had ever seen.

Someday you'll wish your wife had killed me.

Yanagisawa turned and walked away, his message delivered without a word.

"I HAVE GOOD news," Lady Wakasa told Reiko. "The Todo *daimyo* clan is very interested in your proposal. They asked me to arrange a *miai*. Shall I go ahead?"

"Yes. That's wonderful! Thank you." Reiko poured tea and handed Lady Wakasa a cup. Outside her chamber, the garden was radiant with pink cherry blossoms. Masahiro, Akiko, and Hirata's children ran about, catching falling petals. "What's the bad news?"

"There isn't any," Lady Wakasa said. "Your husband's fortunes are about to rise, I've heard. People are glad he settled the forty-seven *rōnin* business."

But Reiko couldn't be happy about the outcome. Forty-seven men were dead, and mourned by those they'd left behind.

The day after their ritual suicide, Reiko had gone to visit Lady Asano and Ukihashi. She'd found the women together at Lady Asano's convent.

When Reiko offered her condolences, Lady Asano said, "I don't think they should have had to die. But it was their choice, so I can't complain. I'll always be grateful to them for avenging my husband."

"I'm grateful to you, Lady Reiko, for reuniting Oishi and me," Ukihashi said. "At least we parted in love instead of anger."

Reiko bowed. "I thank you for your help. Without it, my husband couldn't have guided the affair to a peaceful ending." Before she left, she asked, "Will you be all right?"

"Yes," Ukihashi said, even though tears filled her eyes and Reiko knew she was grieving for her son and husband. "The priests at Sengaku Temple have been very kind. They send me a portion of the alms they collect. My daughters and I don't need to work anymore."

Lady Wakasa's voice drew Reiko back to the present. "What a lucky break for your husband—Yanagisawa lying down and playing dead. Never thought I'd see the day."

But Reiko couldn't feel any better about Yanagisawa than she did about the forty-seven *rōnin*. They at least had decided their own fate. Yanagisawa had been struck by the worst catastrophe a parent could imagine, his child's death. Reiko wouldn't wish that on anyone.

"I'll consult my astrologer about an auspicious date for the *miai*." Lady Wakasa departed.

The *miai* was just a formality. The families were already acquainted, and Reiko liked the Todo daughter, a pretty, sweet, intelligent girl. Masahiro was as good as betrothed. At least Reiko could be glad about that. But unfinished business hung over her like a cloud.

When she'd come home after the incident at the palace, she'd found that Okaru had left. Reiko hadn't seen Okaru since. She wondered what had become of the girl and felt guilty about the way she'd treated her. And although the tension between Reiko and Masahiro had eased, she knew he missed Okaru.

Lieutenant Tanuma entered the room. "There's a visitor asking to see you. It's Okaru. She's down at the castle gate."

Reiko was surprised; it seemed as if her thoughts had summoned the girl. "Bring her in."

Soon Okaru arrived. "Lady Reiko!" Arms flung wide, she smiled as if they'd parted on the friendliest terms. "I'm so happy to see you again." She knelt and bowed.

"I'm happy to see you looking so well," Reiko said, relieved because Okaru had apparently not suffered since she'd left. In fact, Okaru was lovelier than ever. Her cheeks were as rosy as the cherry blossoms printed on her new kimono. "Where have you been?"

"Goza and I went back to the inn. The proprietor let us stay because nobody knows we're there." Okaru smiled ruefully. "I've learned my lesson about talking to news-sellers."

"But how . . . ?"

"How can we afford it? Oh, Goza has a job at a teahouse that has women's sumo wrestling matches." Okaru added, "She was wrestling the night your father was attacked."

That was one more mystery solved. Here was Goza's alibi, and the reason for the blood on her clothes, which Masahiro had told Reiko about.

"We couldn't tell you because women's sumo was against the law then, and we were afraid she would get in trouble," Okaru explained. The government periodically issued edicts against sumo, which were later rescinded.

"Why does Goza have tattoos on her wrist?" Reiko asked. Masahiro had told her about that, too.

"She was arrested for stealing food when she was a child. But soon she won't need to steal or work to support herself and me anymore. Because—" Okaru paused, sparkling with glee. "I'm getting married!"

Reiko was astonished. A short time ago Okaru had been in love with Oishi and heartbroken because he'd jilted her. Now she'd found someone else. "Who is he?"

"His name is Jihei. He has his own furniture shop. He's rich, and handsome, and not too old." Okaru bubbled, "He's so good to me! We're so much in love! I'm so happy!"

"How did you meet him?" Reiko asked, impressed by Okaru's fast work.

"His shop is near the inn, and he saw me that day when the crowd was hounding me. He thought I was so beautiful, he fell in love at first sight. He couldn't forget me. After I went back to the inn, I peeked inside his shop one day, and he saw me, and he rushed out and introduced himself, and I fell in love with him, too." Okaru blushed and giggled.

Reiko wondered if a love match made in such haste could bring lasting happiness. Then again, many arranged marriages didn't. "Well. I'm glad you'll be settled comfortably." But she couldn't help thinking of Oishi, forgotten so soon.

Tears misted Okaru's eyes. "I'll never forget Oishi, though." She smiled sadly. "If not for him, I wouldn't have come to Edo, and I wouldn't have met Jihei. In a way, he brought us together. I visited his grave at Sengaku Temple, and I thanked him and prayed for his spirit. Have you been there?"

"Not yet," Reiko said. "My husband is taking me today."

"Before I say good-bye, I want to thank you for your kindness," Okaru said. "You helped me when I had no one else to turn to."

"It was nothing," Reiko said, glad that Okaru didn't bear her any grudge.

"There's something I'd like to ask . . . ?"

"What is it?"

"Masahiro was kind to me. May I say good-bye to him?"

"Of course." Reiko didn't think it could hurt. "He's outside."

As soon as Okaru had left, Chiyo arrived for a visit. "Did you hear that?" Reiko asked.

Chiyo nodded. "I couldn't resist eavesdropping."

"What do you think?"

"I think that although many people have suffered because of the forty-seven *rōnin* business, Okaru has managed to land on her feet." Chiyo spoke with annoyance and admiration.

"She certainly has." Reiko added ruefully, "You were right about her being trouble."

"But you were right to act on Okaru's information about the vendetta," Chiyo hastened to say. "Discovering the truth is important, no matter the cost."

They smiled at each other. Reiko was glad that Okaru hadn't permanently come between them. Their friendship had weathered a difference of opinion and emerged stronger because each could appreciate the other's viewpoint.

MASAHIRO HEARD OKARU call his name and saw her tripping toward him beneath the cherry trees. His heart soared. Ever since she'd left, he'd felt a hollow ache inside. He'd thought of looking for her, but his shame about what had happened while she was here had stopped him. He wasn't only bothered by his mother catching them together; he felt guilty because of Goza, the tattoos, the bloody clothes, and the fact that he'd delayed telling his parents about them because he'd wanted to protect Okaru. It was his first, upsetting taste of divided loyalty. Now he was glad he hadn't gone after Okaru, because although she smiled and held out her arms, he could tell that she didn't feel the same way about him as he did about her.

She wasn't in love with him, and she never would be.

"Hello! Do you remember me?" Okaru said gaily.

Masahiro was so downcast that all he could do was nod. She thought he was a child, like Akiko and Taeko and Tatsuo, who were running and playing nearby.

"I felt bad because I left without saying good-bye to you," Okaru said.

She'd come to say good-bye now, Masahiro realized. The ache inside him grew. "Where are you going?" he managed to say.

"Not far. I'll be staying in Nihonbashi." Dimples wreathed Okaru's face. "I'm getting married."

The news was like a stab to his heart. All his vague dreams about Okaru died for good. While she rambled on about her fiancé, the house she would live in, and the children she hoped to have, Masahiro was struck by how far apart the few years' difference in their ages put them. Okaru was a grown woman, while he was still a boy. Sadness filled him, but he also felt relief. He wasn't ready for marriage, or housekeeping, or even love. He had too many other things to do first. And although he still desired Okaru, they weren't meant for each other. He could accept that they belonged to different worlds.

"It would be nice if you would come and visit me," Okaru said.

"Yes." But Masahiro knew he would never see her again. That was as it should be.

After a pause, Okaru said, "I wanted to tell you I'm sorry about . . . what happened."

Masahiro felt his cheeks flame.

"I didn't mean anything by it. I was so unhappy, I needed somebody, and you were there." Okaru seemed ashamed, too. "I'm sorry I upset your mother."

To her, the embrace that had caused him so much excitement and pleasure had been nothing but a mistake. But Masahiro could accept that, too. "It's all right," he said.

"I'm glad you're not mad at me. I'll never forget how you protected me from Oishi's wife." Okaru smiled fondly. "You're my hero." Then she took a closer look at him, and surprise raised her eyebrows. She frowned as her gaze held his.

Masahiro heard a thought, as clear as if she'd spoken it: *If things were different* . . . His heart was suddenly lighter.

Okaru's smile turned wistful. "I guess I should be going." She bowed. "Good-bye."

"Good-bye," Masahiro said.

Okaru hesitated, then held out her hand. Masahiro hesitated, then reached for it. Their fingers clasped, then let go. The soft warmth of her skin lingered on his as Okaru walked away through the rain of falling cherry blossoms.

"Masahiro!" Taeko called. "Try and catch me!"

And now he was running, laughing as he chased Taeko. It felt good to be so carefree. Masahiro spared a moment to wonder if he would fall in love again someday. Would he be lucky enough that the girl he fell in love with would fall in love with him, too?

He thought he probably would.

"SHH, DON'T CRY," Hirata crooned to his baby daughter. He rocked her in his arms. "Papa's here."

The baby squalled, her little fists waving, her feet kicking inside the blanket wrapped around her. Hirata smiled. It was amazing how much one could love such a tiny, new person.

Midori bustled into the room. "She's hungry. Give her to me."

Hirata handed the baby over. "She's also wet," he said, holding out the damp sleeve of his kimono. "It's amazing how much water such a tiny person can make."

"Oh, I almost forgot to tell you," Midori said. "You have visitors."

When Hirata went into the reception room, there were Tahara, Deguchi, and Kitano. They bowed politely. "Hello," Tahara said with his rakish smile.

Chilling fear and fuming anger beset Hirata. "What are you doing here?"

"Now, now, is that any way to greet your guests?" Kitano's eyes crinkled in his scarred, paralyzed face.

"We haven't seen you in a while," Tahara said, "so we decided to stop by." Deguchi watched Hirata through heavy-lidded eyes, inscrutable. "Have you been avoiding us?"

Hirata had. Whenever he'd felt their aura, he'd walked in the opposite direction. Whenever he'd seen them around town, he'd pretended not to notice them. He hadn't wanted to talk to them until he'd made sense of the incident at the palace. But no matter how much he mulled it over, he ended up with the same questions that only they could answer.

"We thought it was time for another talk," Kitano said.

"I agree," Hirata said, "but not here." He didn't want them in his house.

They went to the castle's herb garden. The plots were green with new spring plants, the air scented with mint, coriander, and honeysuckle. Bees hummed; butterflies flitted.

"Did you know that Yoritomo would pick up the branch?" Hirata demanded. "That if it hadn't been there, he wouldn't have tried to attack Kajikawa and he would still be alive? Or that if he hadn't, the shogun might have died?"

Tahara, Deguchi, and Kitano exchanged unreadable glances. "Not exactly," Tahara said.

"What's that supposed to mean?" Hirata said, vexed by their obtuseness.

"The rituals tell us what to do," Kitano said. "Not always the specifics or the results."

"Did you want Yoritomo to die?" Hirata pressed. "Why? What are you up to?"

"It was meant to be," Tahara said. "Our mission is to see that destiny is fulfilled."

"Without knowing how? Or who'll get hurt?" Hirata was incredulous. "Shouldn't you figure out what's going to happen first, and then decide what's best to do?"

Tahara shrugged. Deguchi shook his head, calm and radiant. Kitano said, "That's not how it works."

Hirata folded his arms. "Well, I won't even consider joining your society until you tell me more about these rituals and what your plans are."

"When you join us, you'll be told," Tahara said.

"I'm supposed to take an oath of loyalty to the society, swear that it's my top priority, that I'll keep its business a secret, and that I'll abide by all its decisions, based on nothing?"

"Based on what you've witnessed," Tahara said.

Hirata laughed. "That's insane!"

"That's how it works," Kitano said.

"This is your last chance," Tahara said. "Are you in or out?"

Hirata had known the answer to that question when Tahara had previously invited him to join the secret society. He owed his complete loyalty to Sano and the shogun. Bushido forbade him to put anything else ahead of them. If he tried to juggle his duty to them with commitment to the secret society, his interests would conflict sooner or later. Yet he couldn't quite turn Tahara down flat.

"What if I'm out?" Hirata said.

Tahara nodded, acknowledging his implicit threat—that Hirata would decline to join the secret society and oppose its actions. Tahara's expression became a degree less genial. "Let's just say that you don't want to make enemies of us."

They would destroy anyone who opposed them, Hirata understood; and they had the power to stand against all outsiders. But if Hirata were inside their society, he would learn how they divined what actions to take. He would have a say in what they did. Somebody had to control them, and who better than he? Furthermore, he must protect Sano, the shogun, the regime, his family, and all of Japan from these dangerous men.

These noble goals fit with a motive that was more personal. If Hirata joined the society, he would gain access to the rituals, spells, and secrets that would raise his mystical martial arts expertise to a new level. He wanted this with a fierce longing that overpowered his reservations.

"Well, then," Hirata said. His excitement and his eagerness to be initiated into the secrets of the cosmos warred with his dread that this was a decision he would live to regret. "I'm in."

NOISY CROWDS STREAMED in and out through the arched gate of Sengaku Temple. Sano and his troops escorted Reiko in her palanquin through a new marketplace where booths sold noodles, dumplings, rice cakes, dried fruit, sake, and dishware. Peddlers hawked candles, prayers written on wooden stakes and paper strips, and incense. When Sano dismounted, a tout from a theater pressed a playbill into his hand. Such heavy clouds of incense smoke hung over the temple buildings that it looked as if they were on fire.

"I didn't know there was a festival today," Reiko said, climbing out of her palanquin. She was bright-eyed and gay, relieved because Sano had told her the good news that she'd won the shogun's favor by killing Kajikawa, and that the shogun had demoted Yanagisawa and promoted Sano.

"There isn't a festival," Sano said. He was happy because Reiko had told him the news about Masahiro's betrothal. "This is in honor of the forty-seven *rōnin*."

Inside the temple precincts, Sano and Reiko squeezed past peasants, merchants, beggars, and squadrons of samurai. Pilgrims, who carried walking sticks and banners from their home villages, besieged the worship hall. Around the well where Oishi and his men had washed Kira's head, prayer stakes were stuck in the earth amid layers of coins. Sano and Reiko joined a long line outside the cemetery. When they finally got through the gate, the small graveyard was so jammed that they could hardly move. Smoke from incense vats formed a sweet, pungent, suffocating atmosphere. Where Oishi and his men had once stood, bloodstained and awaiting orders, now there were stone tablets that marked their graves.

Lord Asano, in his tomb, was no longer alone. His loyal retainers had come to join him. His disgrace had been obliterated by acclaim for them. Visitors bowed to the grave tablets; they stroked the stone lantern at which the forty-seven *rōnin* had laid Kira's head; they tied paper prayer strips to the stone fences, where thousands of strips already fluttered. They left offerings on the bases of the tablets, which were already covered with rice cakes, cups of sake, and cherry blossoms. Adulation swelled the voices that murmured in awe, chanted prayers. Samurai wept.

Reiko was crying, too. "They're heroes," she said.

"Yes," Sano said. The public had settled the issue. "Even though they broke the law." Or perhaps because they'd broken the law. The public loved renegades. "Even though they had to die." Had they not died, opinion would have still been divided about them. They would have been excoriated, persecuted; and as *rōnin,* they would have worn the mantle of disgrace even though they'd avenged their master. Death shielded them from censure. But in spite of his cynical thoughts, Sano felt tears sting his own eyes. It was impossible not to be moved by the spectacle of such reverence for the highest acts of loyalty and atonement that a samurai could perform. Even though he was uneasy about his own role in the business.

He looked at the playbill in his hand. Its heading read, *The Forty-Seven Loyal Retainers*; it was illustrated by a crude drawing of samurai in battle and listed a cast of famous actors. Oishi and his men had caught the fancy of the theater world. They were famous, on their way to becoming immortalized.

"Where is Oishi's grave?" Reiko asked.

They found it in a corner of the cemetery. It was a stone tablet flanked by vases of flowers and enclosed on three sides by a wooden cage. As Sano and Reiko paid their silent respects to Oishi, a fashionably dressed man elbowed through the crowd.

"Forgive me, Oishi-*san,*" he cried, prostrating himself before the grave. He had a square face with an aggressive jaw. "When I saw you lying in the gutter in Miyako, I thought you'd become a worthless bum. But now I know I misjudged you. You were a true samurai."

Sano stared, amazed. "That's the man from Satsuma," he told Reiko. "The one Oishi mentioned in his story."

They took the long route back to their escorts, around the temple, skirting the woods. It was quiet and peaceful here, and lush with spring, but Sano's thoughts were dark, troubled.

"What's wrong?" Reiko asked.

"I feel as if I don't deserve the promotion," Sano said.

"Why on earth not?"

Sano hadn't told Reiko about the moment when he'd been presented with the choice between rescuing the shogun or Masahiro. In all the confusion no one but himself had noticed it. He told Reiko now.

"If Hirata and the soldiers hadn't helped the shogun, you'd have done it and let Yanagisawa kill Masahiro?" Reiko's voice was filled with horrified indignation. Then she looked stunned as the opposite scenario occurred to her. "You would have saved Masahiro and abandoned the shogun?" She sucked in her breath, then released it in a whisper. "Oh."

It was clear that she recognized the dilemma that Sano had experienced and saw that whichever his choice, the consequences would have been disastrous. She waved her hand, as if to fend off the very idea of them. "But you didn't choose. You didn't have to, thank the gods. So let's not even think about it."

"I can't help thinking about it," Sano said. "I keep wondering whom I'd have chosen. Could I put Bushido and loyalty to my lord ahead of Masahiro's life? Or would I have made the same choice as Kajikawa, who put his feelings for his son above all other concerns?" Sano glanced toward the temple. "When I looked at Oishi's grave, I felt inferior."

Reiko was silent for a long moment. Sano could tell that she thought he should have saved their son and the shogun be damned. She was Masahiro's mother. Her maternal instinct outweighed Bushido.

When she spoke, she picked her words carefully, as if trying to assuage Sano's doubt about his worth as a samurai while stifling her urge to impose her own opinion on him. "In the end, I think actions matter more than motives. The forty-seven *rōnin* avenged their master's death. History will remember them for their loyalty, not everything else. The same applies to you." She gently touched Sano's arm. "The shogun thinks you protected him from Kajikawa. It's true. But he's forgotten that you've risked your life for him many times." She smiled, tender and proud. "You're every bit as much a samurai hero as the forty-seven *rōnin*."

Her praise lifted Sano's spirits. "I suppose I have to believe you, because you're always right," he said.

It felt good to be out of disgrace and officially back at the helm of the regime. Sano decided to stop dwelling on what he might have done under different circumstances. Instead, he would renew his commitment to Bushido and do his loyal best to serve the shogun. He would turn his attention to the future.

The war between him and Yanagisawa wasn't over. Yanagisawa blamed him for Yoritomo's death. It was the one offense that Yanagisawa would never forgive. When Yanagisawa emerged from mourning, there would be hell for Sano to pay.

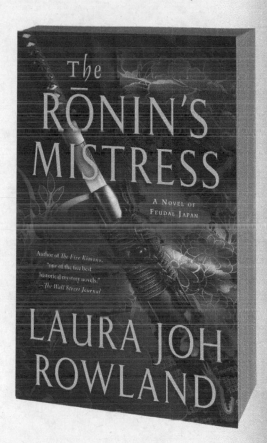